Praise for Felicity Niven

Felicity Niven's writing is sharp and exquisite.

— Julia Quinn, author of *Bridgerton*

With her complicated and lovable characters, achingly tender love stories, and scorching steam, Felicity Niven has quickly become one of my all-time favorite authors.

— Alexandra Vasti, author of *Ne'er Duke Well* and *Earl Crush*

Anything Felicity Niven writes is a joy to read.

— Elizabeth Everett, author of *A Lady's Formula for Love*

Niven is a masterful storyteller, deftly weaving beautifully drawn characters with taut, witty prose. A sensational new voice in historical romance.

— Erin Langston, author of *Forever Your Rogue* and *The Finest Print*

A Perilous Flirtation

Her prospects ruined by scandal.
His hopes crushed by cowardice.
A journey. A twist of fate. A reckoning.

Her desire betrayed her. Arabella Lovelock, seduced and disgraced at age eighteen by a tall, dark stranger, flees to Scotland and builds a new life for herself in a remote village.

Her wealth and beauty convinced him she was beyond his reach. Dr. Alasdair Andrews, lonely and longing for Arabella, must bring her home to her family.

A brutal snowstorm blocks their way. Forced to take shelter at a manor house in the north of England, Arabella must face the man who stole her innocence and convince the man of her dreams that she hungers for him and only him.

Sometimes your second chance is your destiny.

Detailed content notes available on the author's website:
www.felicityniven.com

A Perilous Flirtation

A Perilous Flirtation

The Lovelocks of London

Book Three

Felicity Niven

Bletherskite Books

Edited by Grace Bradley, gracebradleyediting.com
Cover by James, GoOnWrite.com

Dedicated to Dr. James Barry, c. 1789–1865.
(born Margaret Anne Bulkley)

CONTENTS

Prologue	1
Chapter 1	7
Chapter 2	13
Chapter 3	20
Chapter 4	30
Chapter 5	37
Chapter 6	44
Chapter 7	47
Chapter 8	52
Chapter 9	62
Chapter 10	68
Chapter 11	79
Chapter 12	83
Chapter 13	94
Chapter 14	98
Chapter 15	106
Chapter 16	123
Chapter 17	139
Chapter 18	147
Chapter 19	155
Chapter 20	165
Chapter 21	176
Chapter 22	181
Chapter 23	189
Chapter 24	198
Chapter 25	216
Chapter 26	221
Chapter 27	228
Chapter 28	245
Chapter 29	255
Chapter 30	258

Chapter 31   269
Chapter 32   275
Chapter 33   284
Chapter 34   302
Epilogue   313

More   317
Author's Afterword   319
When Ardor Blooms   323
Acknowledgments   339
Also by Felicity Niven   341
About the Author   343

Prologue

CORNWALL. MAY, 1819.

Twenty-five-year-old Mary Lovelock Vaughan, the Viscountess Tregaron, leaned over and picked up a flat stone from the shingle.

"You may have seen something shocking today at the inn," she said and tried to skip the stone across the water, but the waves were too rough.

Arabella said nothing.

"You know men and women lie down together, don't you?" Mary's voice was light, and her tone was almost playful, but her face was serious. She continued walking down the beach, and Arabella followed her.

"Yes."

"Do you know why they do that?"

"To have children?"

"Not entirely. In fact, that is just a very small part of it. David and I haven't had any children yet, and still we lie together."

"You weren't lying down today!" Arabella burst out.

"No, he was standing. And I was kneeling, wasn't I? You weren't meant to see that, of course."

Arabella stayed silent.

"As your sister, I'd like to talk to you about what you saw, but I also don't want to force you to talk about it."

"I want…I want to talk about it." Arabella stooped and picked up a pink shell.

"You're seventeen, aren't you? I am trying to remember what I wanted then. I remember thinking kissing would be very enjoyable. And guess what, Arabella?"

"What?"

"It is." Mary smiled just a little. "And I thought I would like to press my body up to a man's body and have him hold me. And that turns out to be very enjoyable, as well. And I thought I might like to do the same thing but without clothes. And that is…"

"Enjoyable too?" Arabella felt rather like squirming while talking to her half sister about this, but she also wanted to understand.

"Not enjoyable. Ecstasy."

Arabella looked up at Mary's face. Calm, willowy Mary, married to the very controlled and elegant David Vaughan, the Viscount Tregaron. Mary's dark eyes were far away now, pointed towards the sea, her mouth open slightly, her skin flushed, her dark-brown curls pushed off her face by the wind.

Then she came back from wherever she had been. "With certain things, it is true there is some pain the first time, but it goes away quickly. And most things have no pain, only pleasure."

"Why do the things that cause pain, at all?"

Mary laughed. "Well, as luck would have it, the painful thing is the one that produces children, and it's nothing to be frightened of, even the first time, if you are with a good man. And it is the thing that makes me feel the closest to David."

"So David is a good man?" Arabella pushed her own

windswept golden tendrils off her face and looked up at the much taller Mary.

"David is the best man. For me. You will find your own best man."

They walked along the shore, Arabella holding her shell in her hand, running her thumb over the ridges.

"I didn't think much of the men I met last Season in London."

"No," Mary said.

"And here with you…I mean I am enjoying the trip, but I don't think I am going to have any Season at all this year. Do you know why Mama sent me away from London?"

"No, but I am sure it has nothing to do with you, only with her. And you will have other Seasons. I hope you will be patient."

"Yes. I know that not everyone is lucky enough to meet their husband at their first ball in their first Season," Arabella teased.

Mary's lips curved into the smallest of smiles, her dimples barely showing. Mary had done exactly that, of course, five years ago.

The two women walked a bit farther and then turned around to walk back.

"Do you touch yourself, Arabella?"

Arabella was glad they were walking side by side so Mary would not see her blush. Mary was wholly unembarrassed about all of this. Perhaps that was what being married did.

"Yes," Arabella finally answered.

"Good. You should. When you are married, you will know what you like, what you want. No one's feelings get hurt by acts of self-love as it is the most private of actions. It is your concern and yours alone. And you cannot get with child from it."

"What is the exact thing that gets one with child?"

"You don't know?" Mary turned to look at Arabella.

Arabella shook her head.

"You're old enough to know. You should know. I'm surprised Mama Katie hasn't talked with you. Perhaps she has some difficulty since you are the youngest of us. She wants to keep you a girl. But you are a woman, and women your age are getting married every day and having children. After all, Queen Charlotte married at seventeen. You should know about making babies, about coupling."

Arabella suddenly felt very aware of the breeze on her chest and arms, how the tops of her legs rubbed together as she walked.

Mary went on, her voice clear and calm, "You have seen the phallus on the statues of Greek gods in museums, haven't you? A husband puts his phallus inside the place from which the wife's monthly courses issue. He will rub himself there and put his seed in the woman."

"That's the thing that hurts?"

"Just the first time or the first few times. When you are married to the right man, you will want it. More than that, you will hunger for it. And the man is always hungering for it."

"And only married people couple?"

"No."

"Oh."

"But it's better to be married. And not just because it avoids scandal and bastards, but because everything is better if you are having this kind of pleasure and intimacy with someone you love. I wouldn't want to do it with someone I didn't love."

"Then why do men go to brothels?"

Mary stopped walking, so Arabella stopped, too.

"It is troubling, and I can't speak for men," Mary said slowly. "They have very peculiar notions about it all. They have difficulty with delaying their gratification. And they can be rather stupid."

"I see," Arabella said, not seeing at all.

They walked on, with Mary explaining why she had been kneeling and David had been standing and other variations on the pleasures a man and woman can provide to each other.

That night, in her own bed, Arabella made a vow to herself.

I am not *going to marry a stupid man.*

ONE

Two months after her return to London and her mother's subsequent marriage, Arabella Lovelock had finally solved the problem of what to call her stepfather when amongst members of the family.

"Middlewich." She lifted her chin and dabbed at the beads of perspiration on her neck with her mother's handkerchief, her own having been lost on the lawn of the castle. She had just come in from playing shuttlecock with her new aunt Lady Marianne Cavendish, one year older than she.

"I'm not calling him Papa or Father or Uncle," Arabella said. "He's none of those things. And he's only twelve years older than I am. I'm not calling him James or Jamie. That would be disrespectful. No, not because he is a duke. Harry's husband is an earl, and he wants me to call him Thomas, and I already call Mary's husband David. But I am not going to call the man married to my mother, the father of my future brother or sister, by his first name. I asked the duke what the men at his club call him. They call him Middlewich. So that's what I am going to call him."

"It's a mouthful," said her mother Catherine, the very pregnant and very new Duchess of Middlewich.

Arabella shrugged. "Arabella has more syllables."

The stepfather in question, James Cavendish, the Duke of Middlewich, was just coming into the room, and he was delighted by the news. "Shall I call you Lovelock then, like we had gone to school together?"

Arabella laughed. "No, Middlewich, you must call me what Mama does. Arabella. Besides, I won't be a Lovelock forever."

She saw her mother and her stepfather exchange looks.

Really, they had to get used to seeing her not as a child but as a woman. She would be eighteen next year, plenty old enough to get married and to change her name.

And certainly old enough to know she wanted to change it to Mrs. Alasdair Andrews.

She had waited all summer for an invitation from her sister Harry or her brother-in-law Thomas to come to Sommerleigh, their country estate. She had written letters to both, hinting at her desire to visit.

Once she was at Sommerleigh, she thought she might feign an illness. And then Dr. Alasdair Andrews, the local physician, would have to be sent for. She would wear her prettiest nightdress. She would have her golden hair down, around her shoulders and flowing down her back, because what lady wore hair pins to bed?

He would come and lay his head on her chest to listen to her heart. Oh, the thrill she would feel to see the shiny waves of his auburn hair when he bent his head down, putting his ear and maybe even his cheek against her bosom. Would he know, from listening to her heart, how she felt about him?

Next, his hands would touch her while he looked at her

with his green eyes, the left eye perhaps hidden by that single lock of dark-red hair that she had seen droop down when she had met him. That lock he had pushed back while speaking to her. And oh, those beautiful, long, strong fingers pressing against her.

Where would her ailment be? Her stomach, she thought, some pain. And he would touch her stomach through her thin nightdress. A firm but gentle touch, she thought.

And then the thought of his devastating hands, perhaps under the nightdress, made her throb in a place that was quite a bit lower than her stomach.

But the invitation to summer at Sommerleigh never came.

Her mother, newly married herself, said of Harry and Thomas, "They are on their honeymoon. I should think they will not want visitors now."

Honeymoon? What was her mother on about? Harry and Thomas had been married for over a year! Really, these married people—Mary and David, her mother and Middlewich included—were so tiresome.

She had met Alasdair only once. In June. In the study of the bishop of London in St. Paul's Cathedral. This was just after her time in Cornwall and Bath with Mary and David. Her mother had called Arabella back to London to tell her she was marrying the Duke of Middlewich. And there was a baby on the way. In fact, the baby was coming very soon.

Arabella had accompanied her mother and Middlewich to the cathedral to discuss their nuptial banns with the bishop. Of course, the required three weeks of banns had turned out to be much too long for the groom-to-be, and he had applied to the Archbishop of Canterbury and paid for a special license since he was, after all, a duke. Her mother and Middlewich were then able to have a lovely garden wedding a few days later, and Arabella wore her new rose-pink dress.

She had hoped the doctor might be invited to the

wedding. Yes, in part so he could see how pretty she was, but mostly so she could see *him*, talk to *him*, flirt with *him*. But he was not invited. After all, he was Thomas and Harry's friend, not her mother's, not Middlewich's. She tried very hard not to sulk on the wedding day and instead be happy for her mother and Middlewich.

But how would she ever see Alasdair again? The meeting at the cathedral had been entirely accidental. The doctor had accompanied her sister Harry to help clear up a misunderstanding between Harry and Harry's husband Thomas that somehow involved the bishop. That was all Arabella was told. She didn't really understand, and her mother had declined to explain further, saying she thought it was likely a private matter. Later, after the wedding, Arabella had applied to Middlewich on the question, and he had said she surely better ask Harry about it herself.

But one didn't really ask Harry personal questions like that. The answer would be confusing and not at all accurate. Perhaps she might ask Thomas?

And, anyway, the ostensible reason why they—Arabella, Alasdair, her mother, Middlewich, Harry, Thomas—were gathered at the cathedral was hardly the point.

The point was, of course, that it had been how she had come to meet Alasdair. It was meant to be.

To think she had almost not come with her mother and Middlewich, imagining it would be rather boring. And, in truth, because she was a little envious of her mother and her mother's obvious infatuation with Middlewich. Not that Arabella harbored feelings for Middlewich. Actually, he seemed too young for Arabella but just right for her mother. How funny was that?

No, she just was jealous of love. In general. Mary, Harry, her mother. As always, she was last in everything. When was she going to meet him? The not-stupid man of her dreams?

And then she did.

She and Alasdair spoke together for ten minutes in total. Oh, how she cherished every single one of those minutes. She would lie in bed at night and carefully extract from her memory each exchange that had passed between them, turning them over in her mind like an old miser polishing his gold coins.

The discussion of the weather. His answers to her questions about his burr. His lovely Scottish burr. And he mentioned his home village of Bailebrae, far in the north, in Caithness County. "The lowest and flattest of the Highlands," he said. Then he asked if she liked mathematics like her sister Harry, the Countess Drake, and when she said she did not, he seemed relieved. He wanted to know more about her interests. She wanted to confess that, at the moment, she was chiefly interested in *him*. But she did not. Instead, she mentioned her love for the works of Mr. Walter Scott. Oh, the doctor had not read any of his novels or poems? But he must. Arabella could give him many recommendations.

And before they spoke together, he took her hand and bowed low over it. He was not wearing gloves, and, oh, how she wished she had not been wearing gloves herself. But how glad she was that she had taken extra care with her dress and hair that day. Her mother was always saying one never knew whom one might meet on an errand.

Yes, Arabella thought gleefully, one never knew. One might even meet one's future husband. And when she saw Alasdair's dimples for the first time, she knew, for certain, she had.

But the weeks of summer went by with no opportunity to travel to Sommerleigh, and she could think of no other way to meet Alasdair again. Arabella fretted and embroidered another tablecloth for her trousseau trunk as well as a christening dress and two baby bonnets for her future baby brother or sister.

Her mother's confinement was to be in September. Yes, her mother and Middlewich had only been married for three months. And, yes, she understood what that meant even before her mother spoke to her about it. She was not a child. After all, Mary had schooled Arabella on that beach in Cornwall. She understood what the baby meant about her mother. Her mother had lain down with Middlewich before the wedding. In fact—Arabella made a swift calculation—her mother had lain with Middlewich during Christmastide when they had all been together with Harry and Thomas at Sommerleigh.

There would be no problem with the baby's legitimacy; what was important to the law of primogeniture and to the Church was that her mother and Middlewich married before the birth. Arabella knew of an astounding number of plump nine-pound infants who had come into the world only six months after a wedding. However, in her mother's case, it was only three months, which seemed to Arabella rather shameful. Her mother should have known better.

Arabella was sent away in September. Middlewich's seven sisters scattered to various aunts and uncles. Arabella hoped to be sent to Sommerleigh where she might see Dr. Alasdair Andrews. But, no. She was sent to Derbyshire, to Lord and Lady Dalrymple and their daughters.

Two

At eighteen, raven-haired Lady Juliana Dalrymple was the eldest of the five Dalrymple daughters. Arabella always said she loved the Dalrymples equally, but when she was honest with herself, in her heart of hearts, she loved the light brown-haired Lady Rebecca Dalrymple more than Juliana. Rebecca was six months younger than Arabella and far more impressed with her than Juliana was. Indeed, Juliana had a smugness about her and was always intimating she knew far more than Arabella since she was older.

One evening after dinner, Juliana and Rebecca and Arabella were all together in Rebecca's bedchamber. Juliana was sitting at the dressing table, trying on every piece of Rebecca's jewelry. Arabella and Rebecca were lying on their stomachs on the bed and looking at the dresses in a copy of *Ackermann's Repository*.

"That's an old one," Juliana said.

"From this spring!" Rebecca protested.

Juliana sniffed. "When I am married, I will have new gowns made every winter, spring, summer, autumn."

Arabella looked up from the illustrated plate that featured

a pink dress with a large white band near the hem and a white hat that looked almost military in its shape.

"Are you to be married, Juliana? Are you engaged? To Sir Timothy?"

Juliana held up a pearl necklace in front of her throat. "We are engaged to be engaged."

"I have never heard of such a thing," Arabella said.

"He has not asked me, but he has asked me if he can ask me." Juliana lifted her rather fierce eyebrows.

Arabella swung herself around so she now sat on the edge of the bed, her legs dangling off.

"And has he kissed you?"

Rebecca raised her head from the periodical to hear her sister's answer.

"I told him," Juliana said primly, "we could not kiss until we were properly engaged."

Rebecca went back to the *Ackermann's* and flipped the page.

"B-but," Arabella faltered, "what if you don't like his kisses? What if his breath is bad? Or he is not passionate enough?"

Juliana's dark brows knitted together, and she glared at Arabella in the reflection of the mirror. "There are more reasons to get married than kissing, Miss Lovelock."

The *Miss Lovelock* was to remind Arabella she was not a member of the peerage and had no courtesy title even though her stepfather was a duke and her mother was now a duchess. Her late father had, after all, only been a very rich banker.

"Yes, Lady Juliana," Arabella said. "But if the kissing is not good, how could the coupling be any better?"

Arabella had shared her sister Mary's lessons regarding coupling with Juliana and Rebecca a week ago. Juliana had asserted she knew everything already, but Arabella noted she had drawn near and paid as close attention to Arabella as her sister Rebecca had.

Now, Arabella felt the bed begin to shake. It was Rebecca, who rolled onto her back, laughing. An insulted Juliana turned around on the stool and faced a serious Arabella and a howling Rebecca.

"There are—" Juliana started in an imperious fashion, but she could not be heard over Rebecca's laughter. And, as the seconds passed, Arabella's lips could not help quirking into a smile. Juliana lost her scowl, and she began to titter. Soon, all three girls were roaring, holding their stomachs and kicking up their feet.

A knock came, followed by the countess putting her head around the door. She was greeted by the sight of three young women, weak with laughter, tears streaming down their faces.

"Girls," she said. "Henrietta, Emma, and Frederica are preparing for bed. You must hush." But she smiled and used a kind voice.

"Yes, Mama," gasped Juliana and Rebecca, and Arabella said, "Yes, Lady Dalrymple."

The girls quieted themselves, but as soon as the countess had closed the door behind her, there was an outburst of suppressed giggles.

"What I was going to say," Juliana wiped her eyes, "is there are other reasons to get married besides coupling."

"Yes," Arabella said. "Love. Which has to do with coupling."

"Children," Rebecca said. "Which also has to do with coupling."

"Money," said Juliana. "Land. Titles. Dresses. Jewels."

"Are you marrying Sir Timothy for those things?" Arabella was shocked.

"I am not marrying him yet! We are merely engaged to be

engaged. But perhaps I am drawn to him for those reasons." Juliana shrugged. "We are not all heiresses like you."

The Earl Dalrymple had a lovely estate, but the lands were not extensive, and Arabella knew the Dalrymple girls might not have every luxury they wanted. Also, with five daughters to be married, the funds for dowries would be stretched thin, and the girls would need to marry rich men who had no need of generous marriage settlements.

"But don't you want love?" Arabella asked.

"I do," Rebecca said and slipped her hand into Arabella's and gave a quick squeeze.

Juliana bit her lip. "I don't know. It seems like love might give someone a desperate power over you."

"Yes," said Arabella and smiled. "And you over him."

Juliana narrowed her eyes. "Are you in love, Arabella?"

"I don't know." Arabella looked down at the toes of her slippers.

Juliana leaned forward, intently. "You have some secret, I can tell."

Arabella had held her thoughts of Alasdair close for months now. She had never kept a secret so long. She had never had a secret so important. She yearned to tell Juliana and Rebecca of her feelings.

She spoke slowly at the start. "I have met him only once. But I think," she felt herself blush, "no, I know I could be in love with him. Very easily. I want to…oh, so many things."

Now Rebecca and Juliana both joined Arabella in sitting on the edge of the bed, each sister flanking her.

"You must tell us," Juliana said.

"Oh, please do, Arabella," Rebecca breathed.

"His name is Alasdair."

The Dalrymple girls were silent for several seconds.

"I know of no Alasdair among our acquaintance in London," Juliana finally said. "Is he in *Debrett's*?"

"No, he is a physician and lives near Sommerleigh, my brother-in-law's estate."

"A physician?" Juliana frowned. "But your two sisters? I mean to say, one married a viscount, the other an earl, and now your mother is married to a duke. I would have thought you wouldn't settle for anything less than a baron. Won't your mother oppose your marriage to a mere physician?"

"No," said Arabella stoutly, but she did tremble a bit inwardly since her mother had permitted her to have Seasons, starting when she was sixteen. What other purpose was there for a Season with the *ton* of London but to attract a lord as a husband? Her mother must want that for her.

"No, she won't think it important," Arabella went on. She must believe that. "My father was a cit and my mother loved him, and he loved her. And she came from farmers, you know."

The Dalrymple girls did know, of course. They also knew Catherine had been an actress before she married the banker Edward Lovelock. And she had now married a duke, seventeen years younger than she, and she was about to have his baby. The *ton* had talked of nothing else for the last two months of the Season.

"Tell us more about Alasdair, Arabella," Rebecca said.

"He is from Scotland—"

The Dalrymple girls hooted at this. Arabella had gone to Scotland the August of the previous year, long before she had met Alasdair, and had come back enraptured. She had become fascinated by all things Scottish and had had several dresses made up in tartan and, in fact, was wearing a blue-and-green one tonight. She had even tried a nip of her stepfather Middlewich's illegal Scottish whisky last month, and, although it was not to her taste, she had vowed she would try it again.

"He is tall and has dark-red hair and green eyes and dimples."

The description seemed inadequate to Arabella. How could she put into words the feelings that had swept over her when she had spoken with him? How she had instantly known he was all that was good and kind. How he was devastatingly handsome. And for the first time, how she had really understood why men and women wanted to lie down together, naked.

And how he was the not-stupid man of her dreams.

"And his hands…" Arabella was lost, thinking about those hands.

"Have you kissed him?" Juliana asked.

Juliana's question brought Arabella's mind back to the here-and-now. "I have met him only once, and our meeting was only ten minutes, a quarter of an hour at most. In June. At St. Paul's Cathedral. So, no, I have not kissed him."

She thought of Alasdair's mouth and the dimples that bookended his smile. *But I want to kiss him so badly.*

"Does he write to you?" Rebecca asked.

"No."

"Do you write to him?"

"How can I?" Arabella fell backwards onto the bed. "It would be so forward. I have to find some other way to meet him again."

Juliana scoffed and got off the bed. "You have met a man for ten minutes, and you think you love him. And you want to advise me on my engagement."

"On your engagement to be engaged," Rebecca said and fell back so she was lying next to Arabella. She held Arabella's hand.

"You will see him again, Arabella, I am sure of it," Rebecca whispered.

Arabella stared up at the canopy of the bed.

She was not so sure.

Every day her memories—of what he looked like, what

they had said, how she had felt—waned and became dimmer and dimmer. And he had not pursued her, had not asked her mother if he could write to her, had not come to London or to the duchy of Middlewich to pay a call. Surely, if he felt for her what she had felt for him, he would do something. He had the freedom of action she did not.

Oh, to be a man.

Arabella blinked several times and set her jaw.

No, not to be a man. To have the liberty of a man.

Three

A year and some months had passed since their one and only meeting. Since her mother's remarriage. And a year since her brother Sebastian's birth.

Alasdair had not come for her. He had not written her. He had not wanted her.

The ten minutes in the bishop's study in the cathedral were enshrined forever in her memory, but, at times, it was as if those minutes had happened to someone else and she had merely read about it.

But then she would spot a head of auburn hair on a baby and suffer a wrenching pain deep in her womb.

She first saw Giles at the theater. At the Theatre-Royal, Drury Lane, to be precise, as she sat in her stepfather's box. Historically, the Cavendish family had always had a very good box, but after James Cavendish, the Duke of Middlewich, married her mother, they had been given an even better box—one right next to the Prince Regent's. The improvement in the family's seats was owing entirely to her mother, a leading actress at this very theater, years ago. The management was nothing if not sentimental. One of their own was a duchess!

They would acknowledge and celebrate that with the third-best box in the theater.

Yes, the Prince Regent was no longer the Prince Regent; he was King George IV and sat in the King's Box. Still, the Middlewich box was excellent. And Arabella loved the theater, especially when the story was about separated lovers who were reunited in the last act through some bit of fate or wonderful *deus ex machina*.

She was in the box with four of her young aunts, all chaperoned by her sister Mary and her husband, David Vaughan, the Viscount Tregaron. Mary was finally pregnant but was not to have her baby until next year and had told Arabella she was "determined to enjoy the best of London until I become tied to a nursery in Wales."

Halfway through the first act, Arabella noticed a glimmer of light out of the corner of her eye. She turned her head to the left and saw a man in one of the boxes that faced the stage. He had a spyglass to his eye, and the lens at the end was the source of the reflected light that had caught Arabella's attention because the spyglass was not directed towards the stage but at an angle towards the Duke of Middlewich's box.

As she gazed at him, he took the spyglass down and inclined his head, acknowledging her. He was a big man. Tall. Broad shoulders. A powerful chest. His hair was dark and wavy and long enough to come down over his cravat. His eyes were dark. His jaw was square.

As he straightened back up from his small bow and gazed at her, she felt a shiver run up and down her spine.

She turned her head to look at him twice more in the course of the play, and, each time, he was looking back at her, once with the spyglass, once without.

In the crush of leaving the theater and making her way to one of the two waiting Middlewich carriages, he was suddenly there, behind her. She felt something being pushed into her hand. It was a folded piece of paper, and she turned to look for him, but he was walking away, a head above everyone else in the crowd. She put the paper inside her glove, where it sat, nestled between her glove and palm during the interminable carriage ride back to Mayfair.

When she got to her bedchamber at the Middlewich town house, she slid the paper into the book of poetry she had at bedside. Only after her lady's maid Green had taken her hair down and helped her into a nightdress and left her alone, did she allow herself to take the piece of paper out and read it.

You are quite simply the most beautiful girl I have ever seen. I must meet you. Tomorrow. Two o'clock in the afternoon. The Cake-House in Hyde Park.

Trembling in adoration,
Giles Fortescue.

She did not know how she would sleep, her excitement was so extreme. But, eventually, she did.

Arabella felt herself fortunate in the timing of her rendezvous. First, her thirteen-month-old baby brother Sebastian was teething, and his fuss definitely distracted her mother. Second, all seven of her stepfather's sisters were due to leave that same morning to go back to the duchy of Middlewich. Arabella's mother was completely taken up with making sure the packing was complete and the sisters were in agreement on who was sitting with whom and in which carriage.

At breakfast, Arabella told her mother that her sister Mary was coming to take her to look at a bonnet on Bond Street. Catherine smiled in a distracted manner and turned and asked Lady Grace Cavendish if she remembered that one of her bonnets was still at the milliner's for a new trimming. Yes, she,

Catherine, would make sure it was collected when it was ready and would bring it to Middlewich in November.

By luncheon, the Cavendish ladies were *en route*, Sebastian was in his nursemaid's arms, happily chewing on an ivory teething ring, and the duchess had declared herself exhausted and in need of a nap.

Arabella knew all about these naps. Her stepfather seemed to join her mother quite frequently in needing an afternoon rest, and, although both seemed refreshed afterwards, neither seemed exactly rested, and, if anything, they would retire even earlier in the evening. However, she didn't want to think too closely on the subject.

Not about her mother.

At half past one, even though her mother was safely closeted in her own bedchamber with Middlewich, Arabella completed the fiction by pushing open the heavy door of the house and standing on the threshold and saying loudly, "Mary, how lovely you look! Yes, I'm ready." Arabella then stepped out and closed the door and went into the empty street and walked as quickly as she could to Hyde Park.

She could not approach the Cake-House too closely; some person of her or her family's acquaintance might see her waiting there and think it odd she was out by herself. So she set herself behind a cluster of trees that shielded her from direct view of those who might come near the Cake-House as well as those who might look across the banks of the Serpentine River, which cut through Hyde Park. And she waited.

Finally, she saw him. That height, those big shoulders. A powerful swagger. But he was surprisingly light on his feet for being such a brawny gentleman. He was probably a divine dancer. Oh, to dance the waltz with him and be encased in those big arms.

She did not like to call out and attract too much attention, so she stepped from behind the trees, hoping he would see her.

His head swung over to her almost immediately. As he left the gravel path and crossed the grass.he stepped back behind the trees, her heart beating rapidly.

Then he was there. He bowed. She curtsied.

She looked up at him. What beautiful dark eyes.

"Mr. Fortescue," she said.

He smiled. "You have the advantage of me."

Oh, yes. "I am Miss Arabella Lovelock."

Was that a look of disappointment? Had he thought she was a Lady Someone, one of the Cavendish sisters, since she was sitting in the box with them?

She felt she should explain. "My stepfather is the Duke of Middlewich."

Now his eyes were warm again. And passionate. "Miss Lovelock." He took a step towards her and seized her gloved hand.

She began to feel hot all over and knew she was blushing. The way he took her hand was so demanding. As if he owned it and had a right to touch it, with or without her say. None of the young men of her acquaintance had ever touched her outside of a brief clasp of her hand when greeting her and bowing over it. Or during the set movements of a dance. And certainly none had ever laid hold of her in that way. Even those who had asked to marry her and whom she had refused.

Now it was clear why she had refused them.

Giles was meant for her.

He was turning her little hand over and over in his large ones. And now…she inhaled sharply. He was worrying at the two little pearl buttons at the wrist of the glove. He had unbuttoned her glove!

He turned his dark eyes to hers. "Arabella," he murmured as he slowly, finger by finger, drew off her glove. He crumpled it in one of his own hands as he used the other to guide her hand to his mouth.

The softest of kisses on the back of her hand. She had not known her skin was so sensitive there.

She felt she must say something. "Mr. Fortescue."

He raised his head from her knuckles for a moment.

"Giles," he corrected her.

Giles. She thrilled even more at his first name than at the kissing of her hand. Such intimacy. And now he was nibbling on her fingers. Kissing and biting lightly at the pads of each of her fingertips.

"Giles," she said and tried to withdraw her hand. He held her wrist for a moment as she tugged. Then he let go.

He looked at her. His eyes now revealed some hurt, some pain. He was wounded in some way.

"I..." She did not know what to say. "I am delighted to make your acquaintance."

The hurt look in his eyes melted away, and he suddenly laughed.

"I see," he said. "Yes, and I yours, Miss Lovelock. I am overwhelmed with pleasure that you accepted my invitation. Shall we stroll around the park?" He offered her his arm.

Arabella bit her lip.

"Oh," he said, nodding. "Yes, I understand. Others will see you have no chaperone. Well," he leaned against a tree next to her, "shall we stay then in this grove of trees, where no one can see us?"

"Yes," Arabella breathed.

He crossed his arms. She felt his gaze rake over her, from the top of her head down to where her slippers peeped out from under her dress. Perhaps that was why some young men were called rakes? She grew warmer still and felt a peculiar tightness in her breasts, near the tips.

"Yes," he said, and he paused, his mouth open slightly. "Yes, I'm right."

"What are you right about, Mr. Fortes—Giles?"

"You *are* the most beautiful girl I've ever seen."

She tried to laugh, but it came out strangled. "I am too short," she said, shaking her head.

"No, in fact, you may be a bit too tall," he said. "But otherwise, you are everything that is alluring. To me."

She could feel herself blushing again.

"We have not met before. I mean, I have not seen you before," she said and gulped. "Giles."

He smiled. "I do not go to the theater much. Even last night, I scarcely counted that I was there since I paid so little attention to the stage. There were far greater delights to be had by observing the contents of the box on my right."

He *had* been looking at her all night.

"But, during the Season, I saw you at no balls?"

He sighed and ran his fingers through his long, dark locks. "Although I receive many invitations, I am not often in London. I am much occupied by other affairs. My estate, for one."

The hurt and the pain came back into his eyes. How she longed to banish that look.

"I am glad you did go to the theater last night, Giles."

"And were you glad of my note to you?"

"I would not be here if I were not."

His arms had been crossed over his chest as he leaned on the tree, but now he reached forward, almost lunging at her, and pulled her to him and bent his head down and found her mouth with his.

Her first kiss.

His hard, muscled body against hers, his arms crushing her into him. The feel of his lips. So warm as the kiss grew more possessive, more demanding. She felt his tongue probing at her mouth.

She did not know what to do. So many sensations, one of

them fear that she would do something wrong and he would laugh at her. Or walk away.

She knew so little.

His tongue grew more insistent. She gasped as he pulled her head back with his large hand on her golden Grecian knot, his fingers laced into her hair. As she gasped, her lips parted, and his tongue entered her mouth. Such intimacy, such closeness. Warm and wet and powerful. He lapped at the inside of her mouth, and she wondered what his mouth might do to other parts of her body.

Like her neck.

She could feel something hard pressing into her abdomen as he backed her against a tree. It was his phallus, she knew. Her sister Mary had explained that part to her, and her own mother had sat her down for a talk a year ago, but Arabella could not abide to listen to her mother discuss the details of such things.

Oh, why had she not paid more attention? Why had she not asked more questions?

One of his large hands held her breast, and then he pushed himself away.

"I must see you again, Arabella. Meet me here tomorrow at the same time. But now I must go."

He wiped his mouth with the back of his hand and walked away quickly with a strange stiff-legged gait, quite unlike the swagger with which he had approached her.

She searched the ground under the trees thoroughly, but she never found her other glove.

She went home and wanted only to be by herself, in her room, so she could think on her first kiss. It had happened. It was here. Love. And he was the picture-perfect hero for her. Big, dark, and brooding. And so passionate, so wanting. He would not stand on propriety and introductions. He saw her and wanted her and kissed her. That was how it should be.

The next day was quite different.

Again, she lied to her mother and found a way to leave the house alone and go to Hyde Park. How fortunate she had been so guileless with her mother in the past. No one would suspect Arabella of lying in order to go and meet a man.

Giles was already in the little grove of trees and had spread a blanket on the ground.

"I have prepared a picnic," he said and smiled.

He had prepared a picnic. For her.

Giles helped Arabella to sit on the blanket and then came to recline on his side next to her, up on his elbow. The picnic turned out to be some wine in a jug. Arabella drank a little to be polite—he had gone the trouble of bringing some glasses—but she did not usually drink wine in the middle of the day.

"You mentioned an estate, Mr. Fortescue," she said. "Where is it?"

"Giles," he said sternly.

"Giles," she said softly and ducked her head.

"When you do that, Arabella, when you whisper and look away from me, I long to kiss you."

He was going to kiss her again, she thought.

But he didn't.

"It's in Northumberland," he said and drank more wine.

"So far away."

"You see why I am not often in London."

"Yes, I see."

Giles sighed and brushed a dark lock of his hair behind his ear. "I have been through so many difficulties of late, I dreamed of escape. So I came to London, hoping to lose myself in the diversions of the city."

There it was again—the wounded look in his eyes that contrasted so strongly with his broad shoulders, his towering size, his strong jaw.

"And have you managed to lose yourself?" she asked.

His mouth smiled, but his eyes still looked like they were in pain. "Even better, Arabella. I have found you."

"What have been your difficulties, Giles? Can I help you?"

"You can only help me by giving me your company, your smile. I would never weigh you down with my burdens. You," he reached up and ran a knuckle across her cheek, "are so beautiful, and that beauty is a balm to my soul."

Surely, he would kiss her now. But he did not.

"Tell me of the amusements you pursue in London, Arabella. Which are your favorites?"

The minutes flew by as Arabella spoke of museums and balls and Bond Street, and then she found the hour was so late that she had to leave immediately so as not to raise suspicion. And except for that stroke of her cheek and handing her down to the picnic blanket, he had not touched her.

He bowed to her as she was about to leave the grove of trees.

"Tonight," he said. "Meet me outside your stepfather's house at half past ten o'clock."

Four

She went out the servants' entrance, the door locking behind her, and crept through the rear garden and out the gate and into the back lane. Then she walked down the lane and around to the front of the house on the square and waited.

She had put on her favorite dress, a delicate white silk gown with very puffed bishop's sleeves and a scooped neckline that showed off the top of her breasts to great advantage. With this dress, there would be no question. Tonight, he would kiss her again as he had before.

A carriage rattled down the street with a coat of arms on the door. She wasn't surprised. She had known he must be a lord of some kind with his dominating demeanor, his immediate possession of her hand, her lips, her mouth. And then Giles, her Giles, flung open the door and helped her into the carriage and onto the seat across from him.

The carriage rolled away.

"You look cold, little one," Giles said.

"I am." Arabella shivered. The dress she had chosen to tempt Giles to kiss her was very pretty, but it was a summer dress, the silk was thin, and the sleeves were only to her elbow.

"I go away tomorrow, Arabella."

Her heart sank deep into the pit of her stomach.

"Oh, no," she said and tried to control the tremble in her voice. "Must you leave London so soon? I had hoped…we might picnic again. I would bring a hamper with sandwiches."

"My duties call me home. It cannot be avoided," he said and sighed.

Arabella looked into Giles' dark eyes. She saw so much emotion there—passion, sadness, tenderness. He reached across the carriage and put his hand on her leg and kneaded her thigh through her delicate gown.

She could feel her own breath grow ragged and her heart race.

"Arabella," he whispered. Suddenly, he was on the seat next to her. His large, powerful arms pulled her to him, and his head was bent to hers, and his mouth was on hers. He ravished her mouth with his, tearing at her lips with his teeth. As he filled her mouth with his tongue, she felt her nipples stiffen, and she pressed her breasts against his hard chest.

As if he knew what she wanted, he caressed and then clutched at one of her breasts. He kept his other hand on the back of her head, her hair gathered in his fist as he pushed her head forward into every one of his savage kisses.

He groaned into her mouth, and that sound lit a fire in her belly. His hand on her breast pulled at her dress, and she could hear a rip and feel him pushing her stays down and tearing at her chemise. Then his hand was engulfing her bare breast, and he was pinching her nipple, and the most exquisite agony of pleasure was running through her body.

He took his mouth from hers to lower his head to her now-naked breast, and he suckled at it. His hand on her hair pulled her up so she was on her knees on the carriage seat. His mouth stayed on her nipple, but the hand that had been on her breast came down to cup her mound, the place between her legs that had grown damp when he had first kissed her. The place that ached for him.

Her whole body was aroused, and all she wanted was for him to continue to touch her, to kiss her, to lay her whole body bare.

Now she was the one groaning.

He took his hand from behind her head and grabbed her fingers and put them on the bulge at his groin. His large hand over her small one, moving her palm up and down as the bulge grew and lengthened. When he took his own hand away, she continued to rub the bulge, the phallus.

He raised his head from her breast, panting. "You are a temptress. Yes. A beautiful, bewitching temptress. Your body. This sweet rosebud of a breast…" He lowered his head again and worried her nipple with his lips, his tongue, his teeth, and rubbed at the top of her mound with his thumb.

"Giles," she moaned. "Giles."

He raised his face and put his mouth inches from hers but did not kiss her. His lips were hanging open, his breathing heavy. He was sweating.

"I need—" he said.

"Yes, Giles." She pushed her mound into his hand and against his thumb, her own hand around his member, rubbing him through his breeches. "Yes."

"I need you to lie down."

"Yes," she said, and he got off the carriage seat, and she lay down, her breast exposed, the bodice of her pretty white dress torn. And he was raising up the skirts of her dress and her petticoat and spreading her legs and his hand was in her cleft.

"Ohhhh," he said. "Arabella, you minx. You are wet for me. So very sweetly wet."

As he rubbed her cleft, his fingers went over that most

sensitive place, her bud, the secret spot that spread fire throughout her body. In that moment, she knew she would do anything for him. For her Giles. He of the strong, muscled arms, the square jaw, the haunted eyes.

He took his hand from her cleft and unbuttoned the fall of his breeches, leaning over her, supporting himself with one hand next to her head on the carriage seat, as he stroked himself with the other.

She looked at his member in his hand. She had only seen marble ones in the museum, never one of flesh. It seemed quite large. Like he was. But Mary had said it would go inside her.

"I have to have you, Arabella. Don't be frightened."

"Yes…I mean, I'm not."

And she *wasn't* frightened. This was her Giles. Who thrilled her. Who caressed her. Who kissed her. He wouldn't hurt her. She wanted him. She wanted what was next.

He leaned farther down and kissed her, and she felt him take his member and rub it up and down in her wet cleft, spreading her folds, brushing her bud, and then sliding down towards her entrance.

A sharp pain. A quick inhale of her breath and a cry out, but his mouth was quickly on hers, his tongue pushing into her mouth even as his member pushed into her.

"Oh, Arabella," he groaned. He pulled back from the kiss and looked down at his phallus going into her. "You're so beautiful."

He was pumping in and out of her and she hurt and there was pain and all she wanted was to be close to him as he filled her and hurt her, but he held his body above hers, looking down at his member thrusting in and out of her, faster and faster.

He straightened up and was on his knees, and he was out

of her, stroking himself, his body jerking as he grunted, and she felt spurts of warm wetness on her thighs.

Then she got what she wanted. He collapsed onto her, and she could wrap her arms around him and hold him and feel him close. Her Giles. She kissed his shoulder, still covered by his velvet coat, and turned her head to kiss his ear.

"Kiss me, Giles," she whispered, and he turned his head towards her and kissed her. Sweet kisses. Short kisses. His lips were relaxed now, devoid of the hunger and the fierceness with which he had kissed her before. His eyes were closed.

"Look at me, Giles," she said, and he opened his eyes, and the melancholy in his dark eyes was gone. She was so happy. She had done that for him.

Despite the pain she felt down below, she also still felt a throbbing ache, an unmet need there. So she moved now, rocking her hips, trying to rub herself against him.

He smiled. "It's too late for that, love. I have spent."

She would have told him she herself had not spent, she still needed something from him, except he had called her *love*.

Love.

Her heart was full, and it mattered not a whit that her lower body still ached for his touch.

He had called her *love*.

The carriage stopped moving. He pushed himself off her and was back on his knees and buttoning his fall.

"There's some blood, but not much," he said.

She sat up. The right half of her bodice hung down. She saw some stickiness on her thighs and circles of blood on the back side of her white dress, just under her cleft.

She looked at him.

"There's almost always blood the first time. There won't be the next time for you," he said. "And I spilled my seed outside of you, so you don't have to worry. We are back at your house now. You should go inside."

Now? Leave him, leave the carriage?

"But how will I get into the house?" she asked.

He finished buttoning his fall and moved over to sit in the seat facing her. He ran one of his large hands through his hair.

"How do you usually sneak back into the house?"

For the first time, she felt exposed and pulled her skirts down over her legs and her chemise and her stays back up and put her breasts back into the cups of the stays.

"I don't," she said and tried to arrange the torn fabric of her bodice so it covered her.

"Don't worry," he said in his deep, comforting voice, and she looked up at him.

"I won't." She smiled. She didn't want him to worry. She didn't want to add to his unnamed burdens.

He was digging in the pocket of his waistcoat and pulled out a sovereign. He put it in her hand.

"Give that to your butler and tell him to keep his mouth shut. He'll let you in and find a way to get you upstairs."

"But…but Chelsom would see me. Like this."

"You look beautiful," he said.

She could feel herself blush but still blundered on. "I have known Chelsom all my life. He's known me since I was a baby. He's not going to *not* tell my mother."

He smiled. "You'd be surprised how much silence a sovereign can buy."

Her unquenched excitement, the late hour, his not understanding her dilemma—suddenly her eyes were brimming with tears.

"Now, Arabella, Arabella," he said and leaned forward. "You're a woman. You're not a little girl. There's no need for tears."

The coachman outside shouted "My lord!" in warning, and the carriage door was flung open, and now there was a very great need for tears.

A Fury had opened the carriage door. Her mother, the Duchess of Middlewich. Lips white. Shaking. Her mother said not a word but lifted her skirts and heaved herself into the carriage and reached and grabbed Arabella's arm and dragged her out of the carriage and onto the pavement, all in one continuous motion. And as Arabella fell from the carriage, the horses started moving, and by the time Arabella had her feet under her, the carriage was halfway down the street and she could see Giles' arm reach out and pull the flapping carriage door shut.

FIVE

Catherine held Arabella's arm, and her gaze swept over her baby. She saw her precious child, lips swollen from kissing, hair mussed, dress torn. She turned Arabella halfway around and saw the blood on the back of her dress.

"Please tell me it is the time for your monthly courses and that is the reason for the blood on your dress."

Arabella wrenched free of her mother's grasp and put her shoulders back. "It isn't. Time."

"Oh. Oh, Arabella."

A hack pulled up, and Catherine's stomach roiled. Three men spilled out. Her husband, James Cavendish, the young Duke of Middlewich, was the first man out of the hack, followed by her two sons-in-law, David Vaughan, the blond Viscount Tregaron, and Thomas Drake, the dark-haired Earl Drake.

Catherine swore. There could not be three worse people to witness this scene.

They had been at their club, drinking and playing cards, no doubt, and had likely come to the Middlewich town house for one last taste of James' excellent and illegal Scottish whisky before David headed to his town house where her pregnant stepdaughter Mary was probably asleep and Thomas went to the former Lovelock family town house where her other step-daughter Harry was almost certainly wide awake, either poring over mathematical texts or rocking six-month-old baby Hypatia back to sleep with a lullaby consisting solely of six-digit prime numbers.

Catherine could tell that the three men were not drunk, but they were not entirely sober, either. She stood in front of Arabella and started pushing her towards the steps to the front door of the town house. But she was not quick enough.

James, smiling, came up to her swiftly and kissed the side of her head and said, "Kate, my darling." He caught sight of her daughter and said, "Arabella." Then his face changed, and Catherine knew he had also seen the torn dress, the blood.

Catherine finished pushing Arabella up the front steps, still trying to block the other two men from seeing her. "Don't say a word, Jamie. Please."

She got Arabella into the house and took her upstairs and into her bedchamber. Arabella's lady's maid Green was there.

"That will be all, Green," Catherine said. "I will speak to you tomorrow."

Green, white-faced, scampered from the room.

"Green knows nothing of this, Mama," Arabella said.

"If that's true and she keeps her mouth shut, she won't lose her position."

In the lamplight of the room, Catherine looked at Arabella. So lovely despite the torn and bloody dress, the disar-rayed hair. She had her shoulders back, her chin up, and she was facing her mother bravely. With pluck.

Catherine went to the basin and dipped her hand into the pitcher.

"The water is still warm. Do you want to wash before we talk?"

Arabella's shoulders sagged momentarily before she rallied. "Yes, Mama."

"Do you want my help?"

"No."

Catherine left the room and stood outside her daughter's bedchamber door and wondered what she would say to her when she went back into the room.

She heard a soft voice. "You can come back in, Mama."

Arabella was in her nightdress, in her bed, her hair brushed. There was no sign of the torn dress.

Catherine sat on the bed. She had a difficult time remembering Arabella was eighteen. Even though Arabella was a full inch taller than she was, Arabella was still her baby girl.

Yes, yes, yes, Arabella had begged, and so Catherine had allowed Arabella to have her first Season just as she turned sixteen, but Catherine thought Arabella wanted the pretty dresses and the dancing and the late nights that went with the balls. She had not thought Arabella wanted a husband, a lover. Yet. There was plenty of time for that, wasn't there?

She should have remembered she had always thought Arabella was so very like herself. And Catherine had left home at age sixteen to become an actress and by age nineteen was the mistress of a dangerous man, ten years older than herself. Catherine should have known. She should have been on guard. Watchful. But she had been so caught up in the last two years with her own love story, marrying James, having baby Sebastian. She had neglected Arabella.

"The most important question is," Catherine cleared her throat, "were you a willing participant in what happened tonight?"

Arabella met her mother's eyes. "Yes."

"Good," Catherine said and bit her lip. She would not

have wanted it otherwise, but how could have Arabella been so foolish? "Did the man in question use a French Letter, a sheath?"

"No," Arabella said. "He spilled outside of me, at the end."

"Are you in pain?"

Arabella took a shaky breath in. "Not now."

"Is there anything you want to tell me or ask me?"

Arabella shook her head.

"In a bit, I am going to go downstairs. I don't know if your brothers-in-law saw anything, but I know Jamie will have some questions. And one of those questions will be the name of the man who coupled with you. He will ask me. And tomorrow, he will ask you. I am going to lie to my husband tonight and tell him I do not know, I did not see the coat of arms on the door of the carriage. And I beg of you, no matter what, do not tell him the man's name, either."

Arabella started to protest, but Catherine took her hands and shushed her.

"Has this man asked you to marry him?"

"No," Arabella said and lifted her chin. "But he will."

"If this man comes to you or me or Jamie tomorrow and states his intention of marrying you, then, of course, it is an entirely different matter. But if he does not, I never want my husband to know his name. Is that clear? And David and Thomas, they must never know his name either."

"But he loves me, Mama. He wants to marry me, I know."

"Yes, of course, he does. You are so bright and beautiful, so loving—of course, he does. But all the same, wait. Do not speak his name until he asks for your hand."

"But why?'

"Because if he does not, Jamie or Thomas or David will challenge him to a duel. And someone will die. Or be wounded. Or be prosecuted for murder. Do you understand?"

"Yes, but he *will* marry me. There will be no need for duels."

"I understand," Catherine said patiently while she screamed inside her own head. "But, still, you will not give his name to the men in this family until he asks for your hand. Are we in agreement on this point?"

Arabella tossed her head. "It's silly and unnecessary, but, yes, I agree."

"Good." Catherine smiled a smile she did not feel, but she was sure would appear genuine. She had not been an actress for thirteen years for nothing.

She went downstairs to James' study. All three men were standing, talking to each other in low voices, but they stopped speaking when she came in and turned and looked at her.

The mood among the men was dark. Angry. Dangerous.

"Who was the man?" James said.

Catherine folded her arms in front of her chest. "I don't know."

"Then I am going to get Arabella down here—" James started towards the door but Catherine caught his arm.

"Jamie." She looked at the other two men. "David. Thomas. Of the four of us in this study tonight, I will wager there is not one of us who hadn't done what Arabella did tonight by the time we were eighteen."

James stiffened. David and Thomas both looked sullen.

"I know it is expected of men. But I am not a man, and I cannot and will not cast the first stone at my daughter for doing something I myself did. I thought I had taught her the error of my ways, but I was wrong. It is entirely my doing."

The men were silent. They were still angry, she could tell.

"We treat her like a child because we want her to be one, but she is not. She says he loves her and will marry her. Let us hope he is a good man and he will be a good husband."

Thomas snarled. "A good man? A good man would—"

"Rut with whores before he would copulate with my unmarried daughter? It is hard for me to say this, but Arabella wanted this…intimacy. You three are all married to Lovelock women. Are you so surprised to find that the fourth Lovelock woman has a hard time reining in her passions?"

There. That had done it. She could feel the violence in the room dissipate as each man thought of his wife and what his wife had done with him and to him and for him in each one's respective bed.

She gave them a moment before she clapped her hands together and startled them out of their collective libidinous reverie. "So," she said. "I must know. Whom had you settled on as the one to challenge the unknown gentlemen?"

Thomas and James looked at David. David shrugged. "I am the best shot."

"Well, then," Catherine smiled, "I am sure your wife Mary will be very happy to hear we have all decided there will be no duels, no challenges. We will hope for a wedding."

Thomas and David drank their fingers of whisky and left shortly after that.

James turned to Catherine and held his hands up. "I didn't say anything to them. They saw."

"I know, Jamie." Catherine went to him and put her arms around his waist and turned her face up for a kiss. He kissed her a trifle absently. And she thought she knew why.

"I'm sorry I had to remind you of my past," Catherine said.

He leaned down again and kissed her more deeply. "I'm not. You were very wise to remind us all of our own appetites."

"Oh, I see." She laughed as she put her arms up around his neck and buried her fingers in his hair. "You were thinking of your old conquests just then."

"No," he said seriously. "I was thinking of you, and I was thinking I wished I had drunk a little less whisky tonight."

"The good news is that I will arrange to be next to you in the morning when you wake up and the whisky has worn off."

"Promise?"

"Promise."

She sent him up to bed, saying she would be upstairs soon but she had laid down her book and she wanted to find it.

She went to a shelf and scanned the volumes there. Yes, *Debrett's Correct Peerage*. 1820. This year. She took the first volume out and put it on the table.

She began to look at the coats of arms depicted, searching for the symbols she had seen on the door of the carriage. There it was. A dragon and a griffin flanking a shield with three chevrons, topped with a hawk. Morpeth.

She went to the front index and found Morpeth. Family name Fortescue. Baron. She flipped to the correct page and read. And blanched.

She had seen the man in the carriage. He looked about thirty. That matched the age of the Baron Morpeth, born Giles Fortescue.

According to *Debrett's*, Lord Morpeth was already married.

Six

Catherine went into Arabella's room in the late morning. She carried the *Debrett's*.

Arabella screamed. It was not possible. Catherine opened the *Debrett's*, and Arabella read it through her tears. Shaking. And then screaming again.

Catherine sent James and their son Sebastian out of the house, to the former Lovelock town house, now owned by her stepdaughter Harry and her husband Thomas Drake. She sent as many servants as she could to both the Lovelock and the Tregaron town houses. Harry and Mary came to stay at the Middlewich town house to help Catherine and the remaining staff of only the most-trusted and longest-serving retainers.

Mary and Catherine were experienced in dealing with unmanageable emotions—after all, hadn't they raised Harry together?—but Arabella was inconsolable. The only time she quieted was when Harry sat on her bed and held both her hands tightly while looking at the ceiling. Arabella's tears might stop then, and she would sleep. But only for an hour or two before she would wake and the tears and howls would begin again.

Catherine worried Harry's baby would miss her mother, but Harry assured her that Thomas did more for Hypatia than she did.

"It is not fair to call him a doting father," Harry said. "In truth, he is a mother without the breasts. Between him and the nursemaids, I scarcely get to hold her. They think I will drop her. Arabella needs me. And I am in no danger of dropping *her*."

After three days of Arabella's wretchedness, Catherine came into her room with a tray of breakfast. She would spell Mary and try to force Arabella to eat.

Mary was asleep in a chair, and Arabella was awake, staring at nothing. Catherine woke Mary and sent her to her own bedchamber.

"Good morning," Catherine said when the door closed behind the yawning Mary.

"It is not a good one, but I presume it is morning since you say so," Arabella said. Her voice was hoarse from screaming and crying and moaning for so many hours, for so many days.

"Will you eat?"

"Yes, Mama." Arabella took a spoon and had a bite of porridge. She laid the spoon down. "I am sorry to have been so foolish and false and caused so much trouble for so many people."

"You have been hurt and betrayed, dearest, and you know all of us would do anything for you."

"I woke up and saw Mary in the chair. She should not be sleeping in a chair, not with her pregnancy that she has wanted for so long! It made me feel dreadful."

"She has only been in the chair for two hours. We have been trying to make sure we each have a chance to lie down. But you're right that it would be better for her to sleep the night through in her own bed."

"Yes." Then, "No one need stay with me any longer. I won't do myself an injury. And I don't think I will cry anymore."

And she didn't.

The men in the family continued to mutter amongst themselves that they should know the name of the man in question. He was clearly a blackguard since there had been no marriage proposal.

But Catherine and Arabella kept their mouths shut and would not tell. Mary and Harry did not ask.

Catherine breathed a sigh of relief when Arabella's monthly flow arrived. Now her daughter could rise above this horrible experience and begin to heal. In time, Arabella would find real love.

Seven

How foolish she had been. How gullible, how rash, how exceedingly stupid. She had behaved as a child when she had longed to be a woman.

Arabella passed her days sitting in a chair in her bedchamber, her embroidery in her lap, but she never threaded a needle.

Yes, how foolish to mistake desire for love. To think the throb of her flower meant she had met her soul-mate. To believe the novels and poetry that said her heart and her desire would align and guide her, unerringly, to her true love.

Why should lust and love be so entangled that she could have mistaken one for the other? Surely, it was a rarity that the two actually went together.

Her mother and Middlewich, her sisters and their husbands—how fortunate they all had been, Arabella saw now. How exceptionally fortunate that their hearts and minds and loins had all agreed on a mate.

But she had not shared their good fortune. Twice now, she had imagined she had been in love. One man had not reciprocated. The other had not reciprocated, either, but she had thought he had. Because of what he had done to her body. Her wetness, her thrill, her licking flames of desire—she had thought these things meant Giles was her destiny when, in truth, these things were merely mechanical.

Simply friction and pressure.

Meaningless.

Except in a world where female desire made you a whore and male desire was indiscriminate.

Rumors began to circulate. At his club, James heard stories about a coterie of gentlemen. They called themselves the Pluckers.

David, the Viscount Tregaron, was confused. "What does the name mean?"

James exchanged looks with Thomas. David was older than they were and had never been part of a circle of young rakes who roamed from gaming hell to brothel to private club and back again. David's brother Rhys was the wild one in the Vaughan family. In fact, David prided himself on the fact that he had been *just this side of priggish*, as he put it, before Mary took him in hand.

Six years ago, an idea for a group similar to the Pluckers had been mooted about among James and Thomas' band of rakes. Thomas had clouted the man who had mentioned it to him.

"It's not my idea, I just heard the other fellows talking, Drake!" the man had whined, holding his ear. The loathsome proposal had withered on the vine. Or so James had thought, at the time.

But now, like the Hydra, it had reared its head again.

"It's to do with virgins," James explained to David. "Plucking, you know? Deflowering?"

"Oh."

"The villains rape virgins," Thomas said, scowling. "Or seduce them. They collect tokens of their despoiling. The winner is whoever despoils the most prominent or most virtuous or most noble virgin."

"Repugnant," David said.

Thomas grunted in agreement. As far as James knew, Thomas' only sexual scruple before he married his wife was that he would not bed a virgin. Thomas had strong feelings about virgins.

James cleared his throat. "It is rumored that the tokens of the Pluckers are to be pinned to the wall of our club on Guy Fawkes Day. The wall with the dartboards. The former virgin's initials are to be carved into the wall next to the token."

"Reprehensible," David said.

A growl from Thomas. "I'm of a mind to sit there all day and batter anyone who attempts it."

"I understand they are going to use a factotum of some kind to do the pinning and carving, Tom. You won't get much satisfaction from beating him." James put his hand on Thomas' shoulder.

"Revolting," David said.

The three shook their heads at the decadence of their fellow men.

A gentle wind blew on Guy Fawkes Day. There was a cloudless blue sky from dawn to dusk. The weather heralded no impending catastrophe.

A message came to James at the Middlewich town house at half past eight that evening. His face became grave, and he got up from his chair in the drawing room, kissed Catherine, put on his greatcoat, and left.

There were not many bonfires in Mayfair that night, but

there were plenty elsewhere in London. The air was full of the smell of smoke.

James arrived at his club and nodded at Chester, the barman who had sent him the note with the news that the manservant of the Marquess of Painswick had come into the club an hour earlier and pinned up the tokens and then carved initials into the paneling.

James walked up to the dartboard wall where several men were gathered. When they saw the Duke of Middlewich, they moved away hastily, some murmuring, some red-faced, some chortling and sneering.

There was an array of love letters, pieces of jewelry, a few dried flowers, and even a stocking held with small nails to the wall. But the place of pride was held by a small kid glove and a scrap of white silk, obviously torn from a gown, and the initials *AL* carved into the paneling.

James tore down all the tokens and threw them into the blaze in the fireplace. He took the poker from the hearth and methodically destroyed the paneling of the wall.

By the next day, it was all over the *ton*.

Catherine told James she thought Arabella had taken it remarkably well.

Maybe she was in shock, he suggested.

But, no, she wasn't.

"The greatest blow to me was that I gave my heart to a man who was so unworthy," Arabella said to James and her mother, dry-eyed. "The loss of my innocence was just a part of that. And I can't bring myself to be upset other people know. He should be ashamed, not me."

No one stepped forward to be the winner of the Pluckers' prize, which was unsurprising since David, trembling with rage, stood in the middle of the club with his dueling pistols at hand and demanded satisfaction from the villain who had done this.

The manservant of the Marquess of Painswick, the fellow who had pinned the tokens and carved the initials in the paneling of the club, disappeared and could not be found.

When James and Thomas interrupted Painswick in the bed of his favorite whore at Madame Flora's, the naked marquess said he had no idea who had gathered which token.

"So how were you going to give the damn prize out? Answer me that!" Thomas roared.

The marquess shrugged. "It was all on honor, like the genuineness of the tokens themselves."

"It is a foolish proposal," James said, "to trust in the honor of those with none."

The marquess laughed. "At this point, I would think it an honor for any of the young ladies in question to have any proposals, at all."

James removed Thomas from Madame Flora's before he committed an act that would result in the charge of manslaughter.

Arabella was now considered spoiled. Ruined. Publicly.

And that was the rub, Catherine thought.

Her beautiful, thoughtful, generous, playful daughter—her daughter who had been made for love, for caring for a husband and a brood of children, for being cherished and adored—that daughter would now never have any of that. There would be no marriage. No more Seasons and balls and calls from suitors and the hope of a good match.

Her stepdaughters—Mary so strong, Harry so eccentric—would have survived this blow. Would Arabella?

Arabella answered the question herself. She made some arrangements with one of the men at her deceased father's bank. She packed two trunks. She left London.

She was headed north. To Scotland.

EIGHT

January, 1823.

Over two years and two months passed.

The urgent letter from Edinburgh came at one of the worst possible times of the year for a country doctor. Dr. Joseph Murray, the man who had taken Alasdair Andrews off the streets at the age of ten years and arranged for him to undertake the study of medicine at age fourteen, was dying, and Alasdair desperately wished to be at his side. But it was January, a month when cold and damp laced the air and people were crowded together indoors, when pneumonia and influenza ran rampant. Alasdair couldn't possibly leave the environs of Sommerleigh to go to Edinburgh.

As luck would have it, he heard of a physician who had arrived in nearby Tavishbourn to join the well-established practice of an older physician. But the older doctor had decided, much to the chagrin of his wife, that he was still far too capable to stop practicing, and the younger doctor, anxious to make his name and earn some fees, was left at a loose end.

Alasdair immediately paid a call on the young man and found his medicine sound, his mind good, his way pleasant.

An agreement was quickly reached. Dr. Jasper would take over Dr. Andrews' surgery and his patients until Dr. Andrews could return from Edinburgh.

Alasdair went through his list of patients with the young doctor.

"Naturally, in my surgery, ye will find my own notes, but there are some particularly frail patients I must tell ye about." Alasdair described the various elderly folk and those children who seemed to always take sick in January.

"And then there is the Lady Drake. This is her third pregnancy. The other two have gone well enough, but this one has been a trial for her. She has had trouble eating and isnae gaining in size as she should. Ye must talk to the countess exactly as ye would another physician. Use exact, scientific language. Her husband, the earl, ye will treat just like any other overly protective and anxious husband. But the lady, she disnae tolerate euphemism and generalities. And she willnae look in yer eyes, but she will remember everything ye say. To a word. For years. That is her way."

Alasdair paused. "Tonight, I will tell Lord Drake I am leaving and ye will be taking my place. I am nae looking forward to that conversation. But I expect I will be back before the countess is in much danger of delivering."

The young Dr. Jasper looked aghast. "You deliver babies, Andrews?"

"I always have an experienced midwife with me, but, aye, I have delivered well-nigh onto three hundred babies. Have ye ne'er thought before that a physician should be present at the delivery of a child? 'Tis the time of greatest danger to women, the time when they are most likely to die. Physicians should be trained in childbirth, should attend on deliveries."

Dr. Jasper shook his head. "I will attend the deliveries of your patients since that is your wish, but I am glad of the midwife. I know little of this."

Alasdair clapped the young doctor on the back. "Mrs. Finch will take charge. She is a good midwife. Just remember, *primum non nocere.*"

First, do no harm.

The earl's words to Alasdair were sympathetic and reasonable. Certainly, Alasdair must go see his mentor, the man who had made it possible for him to be a doctor. But Alasdair could see the worry on Thomas' face.

"If I may, I will see Lady Drake before I go, my lord."

"She's been in her aerie all day. She sent me away this afternoon, saying she had to work when she could."

"Well, if she is working, I widnae want to disturb her. But 'tis a good sign, I would think, that she has turned her mind to Fermat's conjecture even when she has been ill."

"Yes," Thomas grumbled, "but if you leave without seeing Harry, she'll have my head." A thought seemed to strike him, and he rubbed his mouth to cover a grin. "We'll go see her together."

They climbed the main stairs and then a much smaller staircase, Thomas ahead of Alasdair, taking two steps at a time. They reached a door, and Thomas knocked, and, after a moment or two, Harry opened it.

Alasdair thought Harry looked better than she had on his last visit. She had some color in her cheeks. A few children's toys—a little horse on wheels with a string, a doll, some blocks—were scattered on the floor, evidence that young Hypatia and Richard spent time in the room that Lady Drake called her aerie, the place where she undertook her mathematical thinking and writing. Besides the toys, the room contained a desk, a chair, innumerable books, and piles of paper. And, oddly, a bed.

Harry lay down atop the counterpane of the bed, and

Alasdair took her pulse and felt her distended abdomen for movement—aye, a good kick there—and observed the bones in her face. He was glad to see, despite her poor appetite, she was still not as thin as she had been when she first came to Sommerleigh.

"I am feeling better, Alasdair." She sat up with the assistance of her husband's hand. "There is a clear broth Mrs. Haversham makes from our chickens that I am able to drink. And this peculiar and very dry cracker with almost no taste. And the whites of eggs."

"I am glad Mrs. Haversham has found some things for ye to eat. But I have come to tell ye I am going to Edinburgh tomorrow."

"Tomorrow?" Harry said abstractedly, her mind somewhere else already, her eyes on the ceiling. "I hope you travel safely."

"Thank ye, my lady. I hope to be gone only a fortnight or two—"

Harry clutched Alasdair's arm.

"Wait. Edinburgh. In Scotland."

"Aye, my lady—"

Harry rose and went to her desk.

"Tell me the place where you will be, Alasdair. I may wish to write to you."

Bewildered, Alasdair gave her the name of Dr. Murray's house in Edinburgh. He considered Harry a good friend, but he could not imagine what she might need to write to him about, not when he expected to be away only two weeks, a month, at the most.

Thomas came up behind his wife as she stood at the desk writing and put his arms around her and began stroking her rounded front, high up, close to her breasts, kissing her neck, and murmuring something to her.

"Tommy," she said, and her voice caught.

"I will go now. My lord, my lady." Alasdair bowed and closed the door on the couple.

So that was what the bed in the room was for. The earl had to come to where his wife lived.

Alasdair felt a bit wretched on his way back to his house in the village. He had known Thomas for seven years and Harry for almost five years, ever since she had married the earl and come to Sommerleigh. They had become his closest friends, the people he would seek out if ever he needed solace or help.

But, sometimes, the Drakes had a way of making him feel very lonely, indeed.

Even when they did not touch—or even when the earl did not touch his wife since Harry seemed to have an entirely different mode of affection—Alasdair could sense the tenderness and heat between them. The air was fraught with something palpable. Love, he supposed.

Nearly four years ago, he had had a glimpse of what it might be like to have a love like that. It had been during a fleeting exchange between Harry's half sister Arabella and himself.

Arabella. She had all of Harry's intelligence but none of her awkwardness. She had drawn him out and put him at ease despite his immediate attraction to her. She had a beguiling girlishness that made him feel—well, more a man of the world than he really was.

Add, shockingly, she had seemed interested in him.

She was exquisite. Masses of golden hair, big, blue eyes, such a small nose, such pink, plump lips—but no, he could not think on those lips. She was of short stature but with a ripe, womanly figure. Those curves were even more dangerous to think on. He groaned.

But after that meeting, nothing. She had been to Sommerleigh the Christmas before he met her, but he had stayed away at that time, occupied with illnesses around the county and not wanting to bring contagion to the house and its guests. If he had known Arabella was the woman she was, if he had anticipated his feelings towards her, he might have selfishly spent Christmas with the Drake and Lovelock families. But he did not know or anticipate, and so he did not come. And she had never visited Sommerleigh again.

He did not see how he could manage a meeting with her in London or in Middlewich. She was the stepdaughter of a duke and one of the wealthiest heiresses in England. Her brothers-in-law were an earl and a viscount.

True, the earl was his friend. But, he told himself, then and now, Alasdair Andrews was just a working man from the county of Caithness. A nothing who had landed on his feet despite his deficiencies.

A jewel of womanhood like Arabella Lovelock would have no use for him.

He had argued and struggled with himself for eighteen months after meeting her, alternatively urging himself to have courage and then chiding himself for presuming he could dare to bother her with his affections.

He had been on the verge of writing to her mother to ask permission to write to Arabella when he received word that all the Lovelock women and their families would be at Sommer-leigh for Christmastide. Christmas of the year eighteen hundred and twenty, just over two years ago. Thomas had written to Alasdair from London, to tell of the Drakes' impending return to Sommerleigh and to invite him to all of the festivities at the house.

This was his chance.

Then he heard that the Viscount and Viscountess Trega-ron, both of whom he had never met, would not come to Sommerleigh, after all. Mary, the eldest of the Lovelock daughters, was to have twins—the two heartbeats had been heard clearly by a London physician—and the couple would travel straight from London to their home in Wales. Better and better. An even more intimate party. It would be just Thomas and Harry and daughter Hypatia along with the Duke and Duchess of Middlewich and their young son Sebastian and, most importantly, Arabella.

He was fitted for new clothes. He had a waistcoat made up in a fine green wool that the tailor told him was a good match for his eyes. He had already read all the extant works of Mr. Walter Scott, Arabella's favorite author, but now he stayed up late, reading them again. So many of them were concerned with Scotland. That was a good sign, surely. Scott's most recent novel, the three volume *Ivanhoe,* was not set in Scotland, but Alasdair thought this aberration was unlikely to be among Arabella's favorites. Still, he reread it along with the others in case she would like to discuss that work with him.

His first invitation was for a dinner three days before Christmas Day. He dressed and shaved with care. He was nervous but hopeful.

Arabella was not there.

He asked. He was compelled to. Driven to. Was Miss Lovelock well? Her mother, the duchess, said yes. Would she not be coming for Christmas? No? She was away? Visiting? Where? The answers he got were vague and unsatisfactory. In fact, the duchess looked distressed, and the duke and Thomas looked ominous.

On Christmas Day, he cornered Harry. The others were playing with Hypatia and Sebastian and their new Christmas toys in the nursery. He invented a rather stupid question about logarithms and took Harry into the library to have her answer it on paper.

As Harry's quill raced across the paper, she said offhandedly, "I will have another confinement this year, Alasdair. In

June, I believe. I would like you to be present just as you were with Hypatia."

"Certainly." That accounted for Thomas putting his hand on Harry's still-flat abdomen several times today. "I am glad for ye and Lord Drake. Perhaps an heir apparent?"

"Perhaps. You will be the first to know, of course." She finished writing and sprinkled pounce on the paper and blew on it before handing it to him. He did not even pretend to glance at the equations she offered him.

"Harry, where is Arabella? I mean, Miss Lovelock." He betrayed himself with every word.

Harry averted her eyes. "I'm not supposed to talk about it," she muttered.

Alasdair waited.

She looked at him and narrowed her eyes. She seemed to make a decision and looked away again.

"She was seduced by a man two months ago. He is married, my stepmother says. The seduction was made known to the public, and Arabella left London. She has written she is safe, but she has been clever, and we don't know where she is, exactly."

Emotions warred within Alasdair. Fury at the immoral monster who had seduced Arabella. Selfish disappointment that Arabella had given herself to another. But primarily, a very strong and almost suffocating anxiety about the safety of Arabella.

Anxiety. He, who had the reputation as the calmest of men. The most steady-handed of surgeons when he was in the navy and amputated five limbs in the matter of an hour on a rolling ship under cannon fire from the French, with himself and his saw covered in blood, his boots slipping on the deck, not able to find purchase in the gore.

But now he was flooded with fear.

Harry peered at his face again.

"Sit down. Now. I'll get you a whisky."

He obeyed her. Harry poured him a finger from one of her husband's decanters and brought it to him. He drank.

She said nothing more but sat opposite him, slumped in a chair, her fingers steepled, studying him.

"Where was her letter from?" Alasdair choked out.

"Glasgow. That was where she left the duke's coach and told it to go back to London."

"Glasgow?"

"Yes."

"Does she have any acquaintance in Glasgow?"

"No. But she is not there now," Harry said with the same surety she had when she discussed the natural numbers. "It is a misdirection. As I said, she is clever. She has gone on to some other place. She did promise to write again, but I think she doesn't want to be found."

"Is there to be a child?"

"My stepmother doesn't think so."

Alasdair eventually came out of the library with Harry and made an excuse to Thomas and went home to have Christmas night in his very lonely house and his very lonely bed.

The pain was deep. Not just the pain of loss but also the pain of responsibility.

If he had had more courage, if he had felt himself more worthy, might he have been able to engage Arabella's affections and prevent this unhappiness for her? He did not know. He only knew he had not. He had been weak and shy, and she had been damaged by evil.

Better he had risked his heart and approached her. But he had waited. And what he thought might be his one chance of joy had now slipped through his fingers.

He deserved his pain. She did not deserve hers. How natural it would be for a spirited and affectionate young woman like her to abandon propriety in search of love. Oh, poor Arabella.

In the months and years that followed, he had not liked to ask Harry for further news of Arabella. However, Harry let him know she wrote to and received letters from her sister every month. But Harry did not say where the letters came from or their content. And he did not feel he had the right to ask.

He wondered if Arabella had taken a ship from Glasgow to America. Or, more likely, a ship from Glasgow to Liverpool and then on to America or Canada. He did not know why, but he imagined the dauntless Arabella in the New World.

NINE

Alasdair spent four very hard days and nights in the mail coach hurtling towards Edinburgh and the home of Dr. Murray. This was the home where Alasdair had first been allowed to eat all he wanted, where he had been encouraged to string more than two or three words together, and where he had sat up late at night, poring over his books, and, at one point, learning the calculus that had so endeared him to Harry in her first months at Sommerleigh.

"Dr. Murray," he said to the old man whose breath was laboring, who could not speak. He dropped his doctor's bag and pushed past the nurse and pulled the man upright by his arms so he was sitting perfectly straight.

"Pillows," he said peremptorily, holding Dr. Murray up with one arm and snapping his fingers. He was handed two pillows. "More!' he roared, and the nurse went to get more.

After a half dozen pillows had been stuffed behind Dr. Murray's back and he was able to sit precisely perpendicular to the bed and yet still be supported, the aged man's breath slowed.

Alasdair looked at his mentor's swollen, weeping legs.

Dropsy. He did not need to press on the limbs to know his finger would leave a lasting impression in the edema. He laid his ear on Dr. Murray's chest and heard sopping-wet crackles in the upper lung fields and no sound whatsoever at the bases of the lungs. The heart had a high-pitched murmur, easily heard over Dr. Murray's noisy breathing. The second heart sound could not be heard. And the carotid pulse was weak. And delayed.

He knew that if Dr. Murray were to die in this moment and have a post-mortem examination, his lungs would be found to be filled with a clear fluid, close to water, and the left lower chamber of the heart would be thick with muscle, leaving scant room for blood to collect in order to be pumped out. And the valve that lay between that chamber and the rest of the body would be small and narrow.

"Diagnosis, Dr. Andrews?" Dr. Murray gasped out.

"Diagnosis: once a teacher, always a teacher."

"I have," Dr. Murray wheezed, "been taking digitalis," wheeze, "but the efficacy," wheeze, "isnae what it once was."

"I might, with yer permission, drain the fluid from yer lungs."

"Nae," the man gasped.

"He has refused drainage from the finest physicians in Edinburgh, Doctor," the nurse said.

"If I were to have it done," wheeze, "I would have ye do it," wheeze, "but the fluid will only reaccumulate."

"Aye," said Alasdair. "But it will give ye some time. Some easier breathing. Ye willnae tire so soon."

"I am ready," wheeze, "to see my wife." Here, Dr. Murray pointed a finger up at the ceiling. His wife had died fifteen years earlier when Alasdair was still in school, and Dr. Murray had often said since then how much he looked forward to joining his wife in heaven.

"I was only waiting for ye," wheeze, "dear boy."

"Well, I am here." Alasdair worked very hard to keep his voice steady. His grief would not ease Dr. Murray's passage. "Would ye like some laudanum?"

"Nae." Gasp, wheeze.

"Please give me some sign when ye want some. And I have plain morphia as well."

"Aye." Wheeze. "Have ye married?"

Alasdair shook his head.

Dr. Murray pushed himself up even straighter with his arms. "Ye must!"

"Calm yerself, Dr. Murray. I will."

"When?" Dr. Murray beetled his eyebrows and tried to look fierce despite his panting.

"When I meet the right woman."

Dr. Murray labored for a minute and then said, "Ye have already met her."

How did he know? "Perhaps."

Gasp. "P'raps be damned!"

"I met a woman, once, years ago. But I hesitated. I didnae pursue her, and she ran away."

"Then ye must find her."

Alasdair had been awake for three days when Dr. Murray died. The man had not wanted any drugs for sedation or pain until the very end. He was ready to die, but he had not wanted to be unconscious until it was inevitable.

Eased by morphia, Dr. Murray's rattling and gasping at last went silent.

Alasdair walked through a door and into Dr. Murray's wife's former bedchamber, took off his boots and laid down on a chaise in his shirt, waistcoat, trousers and went unconscious for twenty-two hours.

He only woke because of a knock.

"Dr. Andrews?"

It was Dr. Murray's butler, the one who had let him in four days ago and directed him to Dr. Murray's bedside.

"There is a letter for ye."

Alasdair sat up and took the letter.

"Shall I bring ye some tea?"

Alasdair peered at the front of the letter. "Aye, please."

It was addressed to him in Harry's poor handwriting. The letter was quite fat. He broke the seal and another letter, a smaller one, folded and sealed, fell out of the now-loose pages. The loose pages were addressed to him and dated just three days ago. This letter must have come by some kind of exceedingly rapid express rider. He must make sure Dr. Murray's butler was not out money for the letter's delivery.

Dear Alasdair, the letter ran. *I hope this letter finds you* et cetera. *Tommy tells me your mentor is ill. Well, if anyone can make him well, it would be you. I am hoping when your teacher recovers, I could trouble you to deliver a letter to my sister for me.*

Upon reading the words *my sister*, a cold sweat covered his skin. He picked up the sealed letter, which had fallen out of the loose pages.

Miss Arabella Lovelock.

And *The School for Girls* was written underneath.

And then *Dunburn.*

She was not in the New World. She was in Dunburn. And he knew Dunburn. Dunburn was not six or seven miles from Bailebrae, where his uncle's farm had been. Where he had grown up until his aunt and uncle had died of typhus within a week of each other.

He had told Arabella—he knew he had—that he had grown up in Bailebrae. Had she remembered and gone there?

No, that was madness.

The miracle that she was here in Scotland must be enough for him. And her own sister had addressed a letter to her as

Miss Lovelock. She was not married. And he had a reason to seek her out. Harry had given him a reason. To deliver a letter.

He went back to his own letter from Harry.

Given my impending confinement and the difficulty of my pregnancy, I very much want both my own physician and my own sister with me. You must deliver the letter yourself and place it in her hand. And you must make her feel the import of my situation and my request. She will not say no to you, I assure you.

You will also impress upon her that she must not make any important decisions, any binding decisions, before leaving Scotland. She should abandon everything immediately and come south with you. Please engage a private carriage and driver at Tommy's expense. However, once you begin your journey with my sister, there is no reason to hurry, and I hope you will stop and see some sights before making your way to Sommerleigh.

Alasdair thought this was beyond the normal limits of Harry's eccentricity. First, she wanted Arabella to rush away and then for her to take a leisurely pleasure trip through Scotland and England with him. With *him*. The whole plan was madness. And highly improper.

Highly. Improper.

Was that why his mouth was so dry? No, surely that was from sleeping with his mouth open. And why was his heart racing? And why did he have the feeling in his clenching stomach that he might regurgitate even though he had not eaten in two days? And damn his nuisance of an engorgement at the thought of seeing Arabella.

He had plans to make.

The butler came in with tea. Alasdair, clutching his precious letters, jumped up from the chaise.

"I need to hire a coach. A coach to go into the Highlands. To Caithness."

The butler looked askance at him.

"Now!" Alasdair barked, and the butler jumped and spilled the tea.

Ten

There had been no snowfall yet this winter.

In the darkness, Arabella wrapped her woolen shawl around her shoulders tightly and walked the few yards between her small cottage and the slightly larger cottage that housed the school. She would light the turf fire in the large undivided schoolroom so it might be warm if any of the girls braved the cold and dark. Then she would return to her own cottage for her breakfast. This far north, this early in the year, the sun would not rise until after half past eight.

Maggie Gunn, her only servant, often told her that she, Miss Lovelock, should not be doing lighting the fire in the schoolhouse. Maggie would tend to it.

"Your job, Maggie, is the cottage and me. My job is the school and my pupils. I have learned how to set and light the fire, and I will do just that."

Maggie, a stout thirty-year-old widow whose husband had died in the Napoleonic Wars as part of the 79th Regiment of the Foot, went back to stirring her pot of groats, shaking her head.

Arabella had been in the village of Dunburn for two years.

When she had fled London, she had first gone to Edinburgh and then Glasgow, where she decided to send the Middlewich carriage back to London. The coachman had begged her to tell him her plans.

"Your father will have my head," he said.

"He's not my father. Tell the duke I will write to my sisters."

She laid some intentional misdirection for anyone who might follow her to Glasgow. A ticket bought in a conspicuous manner for a ship going to Liverpool, a main point of departure for ships going to America and Canada. Then she had taken an overcrowded mail coach from Glasgow to Inverness. She had been very lucky to have escaped with no insult to her person or her property. Finally, a privately hired coach farther north, up into the county of Caithness. The Highlands. Where Bailebrae lay.

She told herself it was a coincidence. That she was trying to go as far north as she could. To get as far away from London as she could. That she had gotten out of the coach with her two trunks because she had liked the look of the place and she was tired of traveling.

She had chosen to settle—no, not in Bailebrae, the home village of a certain red-haired doctor—but in the larger village of Dunburn, nestled by the mouth of the river. But Bailebrae was not far away.

She visited Bailebrae during her first weeks in the area. She asked a few questions of some older residents of the village, hoping she did not betray the intensity of her interest.

Aye, there had been a quiet redheaded boy Alasdair Andrews from these parts, twenty years back, raised by his aunt and uncle, both long dead now. Nae, Alasdair had still been a boy when he had gone off to some city after the aunt and uncle had died—was it Edinburgh?—and had nae been back since.

That settled it. He had not been back in twenty years. This place had no hold on him. She would never see him here.

The little flame of longing she had kept burning for a year and a half was snuffed out. Completely. She put all thoughts of Alasdair Andrews aside.

Except she saw and heard him everywhere. In the red-haired girls who came to her school. In the green eyes. In the burrs. In the height of the men of the village, Highlanders all. He was all around her, and, maddeningly, he was not there at all.

And now she had not seen him in over three and a half years, and she could not really remember what he looked like. Not even a little bit, she told herself.

Her money was her own. That had been part of her father's will. As long as she did not marry, she could use it as she wished. And she had wished to use a part of it to make her school. The building of the school already existed; it was the twin of the sandstone cottage she lived in. She bought both cottages and the land they sat on, just outside Dunburn on the main road. She had the downstairs of one cottage fitted out as a school room. For the last year, it had been a school for girls.

Such a thing had never been heard of. Not in this part of the world.

Arabella found a surprising ally in Boyd Cormack, the minister of the church in Dunburn. He stood up to the elders of the church, saying girls had as much need to read the word of God as boys.

"In fact, more," he said. "Are there nae more women than men in the kirk on Sundays? Let the women read the texts themselves, and they will bring His word into their own cottages. We will be the better for it."

Arabella did not tell Mr. Cormack her purpose was not to teach the girls to read the Bible. She wanted something more for them. But she didn't know what it was.

At first, she imagined the school as a place where she would teach the girls what she herself had learned from her governesses—reading, yes, but also reciting, writing in a pretty hand, French, geography and history, arithmetic, drawing, singing. There was no pianoforte to be had, but it didn't matter. Arabella had never had her sister Mary's skill and would find it difficult now to play even a simple piece. And how would one teach a schoolroom of girls on one instrument?

But then Arabella had been faced with the question of what might the girls do with such knowledge. Geography and drawing were near to useless unless they became governesses themselves. But who would hire Highland girls as governesses?

All her students spoke Gaelic, and most spoke some English. Since her Gaelic was rudimentary and she taught in English, very quickly all the girls became proficient in English. Yes, there was work on letters and numbers in the schoolroom. Some singing and drawing. Some attempt to bring a larger world to this small place, including stories from myths and history. But, in truth, Arabella spent much of her teaching time on cleanliness and manners.

Because the girls were young, achingly young, with none older than ten years and most under seven. She wondered out loud to Maggie where the older girls might be, and Maggie told her they needed to be of use in the cottages and farms.

Sometimes Arabella would see older girls passing on the road on market days, and she thought she saw some longing in their faces when they looked at the school.

One blustery spring afternoon, Mr. Cormack stopped in her cottage and caught her with her needlework in front of the fire.

She rarely embroidered these days, but this had been an afternoon when she had longed to sit and take up the small needle and thread and let her mind wander while she sewed something sweet and delicate.

"Ye should teach the girls this," he said in his blunt way, tracing the fine white-on-white pattern with his clean finger. "They might be able to make some money and keep the wolf from the door. The girls could work on it of an evening."

So she had.

At first, the girls' pieces were filled with coarse stitches and mistakes and bits of grime. She bought some of the earliest work done and now had a trunk full of these beginners' pieces. But she taught the girls to wash their hands before taking up the muslin. She showed them not to use knots to fasten their threads but instead to catch the ends under stitches so the pattern would lay flat and be almost as smooth and pretty on one side as it was on the other. She was patient, and, in time, they became patient with themselves and the thread and the needle and the patterns. And, after some months, the pieces—napkins, christening gowns, tablecloths—were good enough to send to Inverness and then to Glasgow and Edinburgh, and some money flowed from these cities up north to the families of her girls.

Because, of course, the money went to their families, to their fathers. She had wondered if there might be some way she could do for the girls what her father had done for her, give them some degree of liberty by having their own money. But she came up against law and tradition. She only hoped their fathers were using the money to benefit the whole family, including the girls.

She wrote once a month to Mary and to Harry. She did not tell her sisters where she was but told them to write to her in care of a bookseller in Inverness. And although she did not write to her mother, her mother wrote to her, surely having gotten the name of the bookseller from one of Arabella's sisters.

Tell me where you are, dearest. I long to see you, Catherine wrote. *Someday, you will have your own daughter or son, and you will know how cruel it is to keep a mother from a child, no matter how old that child is.*

Her mother was wrong. Arabella would never have a child. Never. She was apart from that now. She would never marry. No one would want her. And she had nothing to give a child. Nothing but her own bad blood, the same blood her mother had given her.

She knew she had ruined herself. It was a mistake to think someone else had done it to her. Giles had lied and used her cruelly, yes. But she had been stupid and swayed by the throb between her legs. Her sisters would not have done what she had. It was her fault.

But even as she told herself that she needed to shoulder all the blame, she knew she did not write to Catherine because she also blamed her mother.

It was her mother who had made her so reckless. So easily tempted and led by her desire. Arabella had inherited Catherine's strong passions, her wanton behavior, her *lust.* And then Catherine had sheltered Arabella, treated her as a child for far too long.

Her mother had done everything wrong.

Arabella should have been taught she would need to restrain herself. But no. She had been allowed to think her desire was infallible and that she would want the right man.

Her mother had failed her. And, therefore, she should be punished.

Arabella was aided in hiding from her family by a freckled thirteen-year-old boy from Dunburn who could not seem to settle to anything. Ewen MacEwen's stepmother and his two younger half sisters took in washing. His father was dead. For a fee, Ewen would carry a parcel of the students' embroidery and

Arabella's letters down to Inverness and came back with money and letters addressed to her.

Ewen MacEwen never asked why she did not trust her letters to the mail coach. He had a wry intelligence, but he also had a conspicuous lack of curiosity about Arabella. In that way, he reminded her of her sister Harry.

Ewen was interested in Arabella's books, however, and told her he would do her errands if he could only borrow her books. Nonsense, she said. He could borrow her books, one at a time, but she would pay him for his three days away from home. And she would arrange for him to have a book of his own from the bookseller's shop when he went down to Inverness.

The minister Boyd Cormack did not like this arrangement. "Ye will put him above his station, Miss Lovelock, encouraging Ewen's laziness this way. He should be an apprentice or working on a farm or on a boat. Nae off to Inverness, nae with his nose in a book."

"I am a teacher, Mr. Cormack. It is my job to put people above their stations. But if you like, I'll speak to Ewen about his prospects and his plans."

She tried, but Ewen laughed and said, "Miss Lovelock, people like me dinnae have prospects. We *make* prospects. Dinnae worry about me. Now, can I borrow the second volume of the book about the Roman Empire?"

Arabella had shaken her head and handed the boy the Gibbons. And she had reported to Mr. Cormack that Ewen MacEwen had a mind of his own and something great was sure to come of it, but she didn't know what.

And now Mr. Cormack had asked her to marry him.

It had been more than a month since his proposal. The second day of Christmastide, she had invited Mr. Cormack to dine at her cottage after hearing that his housekeeper was away and he would be eating cold food. After all, she had Maggie and a warm cottage and a roast chicken and neeps and tatties. He should come and eat. Maggie would be there throughout, so there would be no loss of propriety.

After dinner, when Maggie had shooed both of them out the kitchen and he and she had been sitting in front of the fire, he made his proposal.

"Would ye be my wife, Miss Lovelock?"

She was startled. She looked at him for the first time as a man. He had red hair, as many did in these parts, but his was light, almost blond. Not auburn. His skin was pale now, but in the summer, he was often sunburnt. She supposed he was not as tall as most Highlanders, but, of course, he was much taller than she. He had a handsome face and was kind, if somewhat humorless.

And he had beautiful hands. Hands that made her think of another redheaded man.

She told the truth. "I had not thought to marry."

He turned his head on its side and examined her. "I cannae think why ye widnae."

She evaded the implied question. "I did not know *you* wished to marry, Mr. Cormack."

"All men do." He paused. "I should nae say that. I dinnae ken what all men wish. And, indeed, before ye came to Dunburn, I didnae wish for marriage myself."

She still did not know what to say, so she fell back on the rote answer she had given half a dozen suitors when she still lived in London. Before Giles. Before her disgrace and self-imposed exile.

"I am very flattered. You must allow me some time to consider your proposal."

Boyd laughed briefly. She had never heard him laugh before. It was a quiet laugh, but it was pleasant, like a gentle tickle. Perhaps he was not as humorless as she had thought.

"Ye say that very well. I see I have surprised ye. I didnae ken how to make my interest apparent to ye. Of course, ye are very bonny. But many lasses are bonny."

"Yes," she said. "That is true."

This was unlike any other proposal she had ever had.

"And a minister should nae marry a bonny woman. So that is a mark against ye. That it pleases me so much to look on ye."

She did not know what to say to that, either.

"And ye are English. An oddity. Some say the enemy. But ye have settled very well here."

"I hope so."

He looked away from her and at the fire. "And I admire what ye have done here. I ken ye must have been raised as a fine lady, for such were yer clothes when ye first came here. But ye work like ye came from a farm. Sun up to sun down. With purpose."

"My mother came from farm people."

"Well, a minister is in need of such a wife."

"I see."

The fire crackled.

"Mr. Cormack," she said. "I meant what I said. I will consider your proposal."

And she did. Just after Hogmanay, she asked him to join her in the churchyard, ostensibly to talk to him about some plantings she hoped to make, months from now, when the ground was not frozen.

"I needed to speak to you privately, Mr. Cormack, and wanted to make sure there would be no impropriety in our meeting. So we are out of doors in the cold wind, I'm afraid."

She smiled nervously, shivering.

There was disappointment in his eyes. "Ye want nae impropriety because ye have decided to refuse me."

"No," she said quickly. "No, I have not decided. But there is something I feel you should know. It may change what you want from me, and you may wish to withdraw your offer. I am not…unspoiled. Before I came here, I gave myself to a man. A man I cared for. Or thought I cared for. Who was married. I did not know, at the time. But still. There was no child. No one here knows of it. But it is well-known in London. I was publicly shamed, and it is why I left England and came here."

"I see."

She could not read his expression.

"Now I must be the one to ask for time to consider." He turned and walked away.

She looked after him as he went into the church. She felt no relief from telling him, only a horrible churning feeling in her stomach. What did she hope for now? She didn't know.

Three days later, he fell into step beside her as she walked to buy some flour for Maggie to make a cake.

"I have searched my heart. I hold to my proposal. I would still like ye to be my wife."

She felt he was waiting for her to thank him or to make some other expression of gratitude. Perhaps he thought she would fall into his arms and accept him at this moment.

She bit her lip. The angry part of her, the part that felt she had unfairly been made to suffer for her desire, bubbled up. She had to push her temper down and control her voice to answer him.

"Then I will turn my mind again to your proposal and find an answer for you."

That had been three weeks ago. She must make a decision. Mr. Cormack deserved that. But she was waiting for guidance. She had impulsively written letters to her sisters, explaining her situation, the school, Boyd Cormack's proposal of marriage. She had tried to be as evenhanded as possible, letting them know the facts on both sides of the issue. Perhaps, without meaning to, she had hinted at her feelings. Or lack of them.

But her sisters—they who had love and desire and companionship all met together in their husbands—might not understand Arabella's predicament. It was too soon to expect return letters from them, but she would still send Ewen Mac-Ewen to Inverness in five days to retrieve any impossibly swift letters of reply.

She would see if there were any answers to be had from England.

Eleven

There was some inevitable delay in Edinburgh. Alasdair was the beneficiary of Dr. Murray's will, and the solicitor expected to meet with him. Suddenly, Alasdair had gone from being an ordinary country doctor, often paid in chickens and apples and baby boys named Alasdair or Andrew, to being rather well-off and the owner of a beautiful house in Edinburgh, to boot.

There was to be a funeral service at St. Cuthbert's. He must stay for that. However, Alasdair thought if Dr. Murray were still alive, the man would curse the notion of respect for the dead at the expense of the desires of the living. Dr. Murray would have shouted *Funeral be damned!* and shoved Alasdair out of Edinburgh, immediately, and on his way north.

At the funeral, Alasdair saw many of his schoolmates and a few of his old professors. Some of his schoolmates had also joined the navy or the army after their training and been surgeons on ships and battlefields. Some had not survived. Another reminder of the transitory nature of life. As if he were not already laden with awareness of it.

And, yet, despite his knowledge of his own evanescence,

he had postponed and delayed in the past, hadn't he? And missed what might have been. And was he not procrastinating again?

A year from now, he resolved, he would not be cursing his cowardice. He would be brave as he had been in the navy. He would live as he practiced medicine—with confidence, wisdom, and haste when necessary.

He engaged a coach, horses, and a large, taciturn driver named Paterson who was willing to take him north to Dunburn and then back south to England and Sommerleigh. It would take two days to get to Dunburn. Perhaps if they left very early in the morning and drove very late, he might be there by midday of the second day.

He collected some medical books and periodicals from Dr. Murray's quite up-to-date library to distract himself in the coach. Otherwise, he might go mad with the anticipation of seeing Arabella again.

The first person he saw in Dunburn was his second cousin. His mother's mother's sister's grandson. Alasdair had just gotten out of the carriage and into a cold wind and was about to go into the public house to get rooms for himself and the coachman Paterson. He also meant to enquire in the public house about the School for Girls. It must be a new institution because it had not existed when he had been a boy.

And there was Boyd, in the street. He was unmistakable. The same look about him as when he was twelve. The pale-red hair. The stolid gaze. The rigid way he held his neck.

"Boyd Cormack," Alasdair called out. "'Tis Alasdair. Andrews."

They met in the middle of the street and shook hands.

"Alasdair. I have nae seen ye in twenty years."

"One and twenty."

"Ye speak now."

"Aye." Alasdair grinned.

"I heard tell ye became a physician."

"Aye."

"And ye were in the British navy?"

"Aye."

Boyd nodded at the public house. "I see ye are going in. Let us get out of the cold and have some ale, and ye can tell me of yer life and adventures."

But Alasdair, mindful of his new resolve, did not want to engage in more delay. He ran his fingers through his hair and pushed back the one lock that persisted in falling in front of his left eye.

"I am looking for the School for Girls. Can ye direct me to it?"

Boyd examined him carefully. "What purpose do ye have there?"

"I have a letter to deliver to Miss Arabella Lovelock."

Boyd's face changed slightly. Hardened, perhaps. "Miss Lovelock?"

"Aye, I am acquainted with her sister. She entrusted me with a letter for Miss Lovelock."

"I am a friend to Miss Lovelock. I will take it to her," Boyd said and thrust his hand out.

Involuntarily, Alasdair took a step back. "Nae," he said. "Nae, I must…I must deliver it to her myself. Her sister asked me to."

Boyd's face became stone. "I will take ye to her then. Her teaching for the day is over."

"She's a teacher?"

"Aye."

Alasdair stopped to tell Paterson to stable the horses and arrange for rooms in the public house. Then he walked up the street with Boyd, away from the sea and the mouth of the river and out of the village. The way was uphill, but it was a gentle slope.

"I am the minister of the kirk here," Boyd said.

"I see," Alasdair said.

"Miss Lovelock is the teacher at the school. She is the founder, too."

"Well, she is…her whole family is quite remarkable."

"I have asked her to be my wife."

Alasdair kept walking although his legs suddenly felt like lead as did his heart, which plummeted deep into his gut.

She was to be Boyd's wife. His second cousin's wife. He was too late. Again.

In just a few minutes, they came upon two sandstone cottages. Alasdair briefly considered passing the cottages and continuing to walk up the rolling hill and over the prow and on until he crossed Caithness and reached the mountains in Sutherland where he might find a cave and live the rest of his days alone, a miserable hermit.

Boyd walked up to the door of the smaller of the two cottages and waited for him.

Alasdair would face Arabella. He would deliver his letter. He was a servant to duty, above all else. And he longed to lay eyes on her again, one more time.

He followed Boyd and stood behind him as he knocked on the door.

TWELVE

Arabella was deep in thought at the small desk in her bedchamber, the desk she used for correspondence. But today she wrote no letters. Instead, she pondered the future. How her school and Boyd's church might work together to make Dunburn a model village, a place where ordinary people might thrive. Ordinary girls, especially. Perhaps together they could do more than she could do alone, no matter her money. And that was what she wanted, wasn't it? To do some good for others instead of pursuing her own comfort, her own ends.

And Mr. Cormack had chosen her despite her looks rather than because of them. Surely, that was a mark in his favor. There had been no rapturous *ye are the most beautiful girl in the world*. Similarly, there had been no lightning strike in her belly, lying to her heart, telling her he was her one true love.

He knew nothing of the extent of her money, her dowry. He was not a fortune-hunter.

And he was willing to have her despite her past.

She might have children with Boyd. Redheaded children. But could she bear that? When she had hoped for so long to have red-haired children with another man. But she must not think on that. Or on him.

She heard a knock on the door. Her bedchamber was at the back of the cottage, so she could not look out the small window and see who was there. And Maggie was out for the afternoon, visiting her mam and da. Arabella went to the main room, where the peat fire was burning in the hearth, and opened the door.

Boyd Cormack and another person. At first, she saw just Boyd and an auburn head of hair behind him. Then Boyd moved slightly to the side.

There was no room for air in her lungs. Her heart had suddenly grown too large and was taking up all the space in her chest.

Her eyes were stuck on his.

It could not be.

It was.

The man who had just come into her mind seconds ago and whom she had pushed away as a painful impossibility. He had manifested on her doorstep.

"Dr. Andrews," she breathed.

"Aye," Boyd said. "I met my cousin outside the public house, and he told me he had a letter for ye."

"Miss Lovelock." Alasdair bowed but did not let his eyes waver from hers.

What a fool she had been.

Even if Alasdair did not want her, could not want her after her ruination, she would never marry another.

Never.

She was seventeen again, and he was standing in front of her, unchanged.

Arabella could not move or speak or think. Boyd had to clear his throat. Loudly. Twice. She came to herself then and looked at Boyd. "Please come in."

She pulled the door more fully open and stood by it, and Boyd entered. Alasdair followed, and, as he passed within inches of her, she reached up and put her hand on his chest.

Her palm flat and pressing on his woolen greatcoat. He was here. He was real.

She inhaled. He smelled of cold air and soap and leather.

He halted, stopping just inside the door, her hand resting on his chest.

She had no control now and moved her hand to the lapel of the coat and grabbed it. She would not let him leave. He would not vanish. She would not let go of his coat. She would keep him here.

She looked up into his worried green eyes, and a lock of hair fell down in front of his left eye. The same dark-red lock she had found so bewitching almost four years ago. She longed to move it out of the way, but she did not dare take her hand from his coat.

Boyd's voice went on, apparently not noticing the two of them had halted at the door. "It has been some twenty years, and then I saw him in the street, and he was asking about ye. Quite providential, I thought. For him to ask after my betrothed—"

She spoke. Quickly. Sharply. There was no time to spare anyone's feelings.

"I am not his betrothed." She was looking at Alasdair's right eye, the unobscured one. It was important he understand immediately and without constraint. "Mr. Cormack has asked me, Dr. Andrews. I have not answered."

There was silence except for the whistle of the wind and the peat burning in the hearth.

She was looking at Alasdair, and he was looking back at her. His right eye did not look worried anymore. The cold air blew in the open door, but she felt nothing but the current of heat between them. She kept his lapel in her grasp. Still, she imagined he could not leave if she kept her hand on his coat.

"I expect," Boyd's bitter voice filtered into her consciousness, "I ken what yer answer be."

He walked between the two of them, breaking her grip on Alasdair's coat, and went out the door, closing it behind him.

"I have a letter for ye," Alasdair said and pulled it from his coat pocket and handed it to Arabella, even as he used his other hand to push back the hair in front of his left eye. He was surprised his voice was so steady.

She took it from him.

There was a silence, and then they both spoke at once.

"I did not expect—"

"Forgive my intrusion—"

They both broke off.

"Ye are taller," Alasdair said. "From when I saw ye last."

She smiled. "But still too short. I was seventeen then. I am almost one and twenty now."

"Aye. Nae, I mean. Ye are nae too short. Yer height then, as now, suits ye. Perfectly."

She turned pink. A lovely shade of pink. And looked down.

"I'm sorry to disturb ye. I should leave ye now," Alasdair said with a great deal of difficulty. "To let ye read yer letter."

"No!" Her voice was high, loud, tinged with something akin to panic. She raised her hand as if to grab his lapel again but put her hand down before she touched him and licked her lips.

She said in a lower voice, "No, please, Dr. Andrews. I have not seen you in almost four years. I have seen no one of my acquaintance from England, no member of my family, in over two years. Please do not leave. Sit by the fire. I will bring you some tea. Please sit, Doctor, while I read my letter. Please."

It was his most heartfelt desire to stay, to sit. To be in her presence. But he had seen no evidence that anyone else was in the cottage.

To be alone with Arabella Lovelock. His knees trembled.

"I dinnae wish to compromise—"

"Hush." She stepped towards him and put her finger on his lips. "I live a simple life here. I am not encumbered by a household of servants. Nor by a family. There is nothing amiss in my asking a traveler from a long distance, an old friend of my family, to sit by my fire and drink tea. I implore you—" and here he thought her voice might have quavered for just an instant "—do not leave."

He wanted to speak, but he did not want her to remove her finger from his lips. Her finger lay there, warm. It was a physical contact of great intimacy. The greatest he had ever experienced.

She swallowed and took her finger away.

"I'm sorry for upsetting ye," he cleared his throat, "and I would be exceedingly happy to stay and sit by the fire while ye read the letter."

No, but first she must fetch him tea.

"I assure ye, I dinnae require tea. Please read the letter."

She sat on a stool by the hearth and patted the rocking chair next to her. "Please."

He sat and unwound his scarf from around his neck and looked at her. Her golden hair glinted in the light of the fire as she broke the seal on her letter and began to read. He saw now that she was more womanly, and it was not just her height. Her breasts had grown fuller in the last three and a half years. But he should not be looking at her breasts. He would look— where, where would he look?

He was loath to look anywhere but at her. He had not

known how starved he was for the sight of her. But where was safe to look? He looked at her hands holding her letter and only imagined them entwined with his hands, pressing on his chest, stroking his—no. He looked at her mouth and only imagined his own mouth on it. Again, no. He looked down at where her boots peeked out from under her wool dress and petticoat and imagined lifting her skirts to see her ankles and then her calves and then higher still—argh. Agony.

She finished reading and looked up at him.

"Dr. Andrews, my sister writes she needs me to be with her."

"Aye."

"Is she in danger, Dr. Andrews? Will Harry die?" Her eyes brimmed with tears.

Damn. What had Harry written in her letter to Arabella? He would not lie.

"When I left her, she was nae perilously ill. In fact, she seemed improved."

Arabella sighed, a noise of relief.

"She was working on the conjecture."

Arabella laughed.

What a glorious thing. The sound of her laugh, her head thrown back, the view of her white throat. He wanted to kiss that milky skin. He could not help himself. He was drunk on her now.

"Yes," she said, chortling. "That sounds like Harry. Always the Fermat's conjecture and the x's and the y's and the exponents."

"Aye, ye ken her well."

"As do you." She frowned. "But this letter. She is asking for me. She has…yes, she has never asked anything of me. Never. Harry doesn't ask. She demands, or she takes, or she does without."

Alasdair hesitated and then plunged. "She asked me to escort ye back to Sommerleigh."

"Yes, she says the same in my letter. It is as if she doesn't realize…"

That Arabella could hardly cross the length of Britain alone in a carriage with a man to whom she was not married.

Arabella folded the letter. "But I have Maggie. Mrs. Gunn. She can come with us. She will be back to the cottage soon, and I will ask her."

Alasdair's feelings were mixed upon hearing news of Mrs. Gunn. The danger of being alone with Arabella for days on end in a closed carriage had teased him wildly since getting Harry's letter.

But, yes, a chaperone was advisable. If a time came when he might court Miss Arabella Lovelock and ask for her hand, he would want to know propriety had been observed and she had chosen him freely and not because of a compromising situation.

Wouldn't he want that? Suddenly, he wasn't so sure he didn't want a compromising situation. It would accelerate everything. And, yes, take things out of his hands.

All this, of course, assuming she refused Boyd. And that she had any interest in him, Alasdair. As a husband. As a man.

He looked around the room. It was snug with a low, white plastered ceiling crossed by beams. Crisp, pink curtains on small windows. He had never seen pink curtains before. Many piles of books scattered about. A sewing basket with a piece of white frippery poking out of it. And he could smell something savory roasting. A meat pie, maybe.

He would like to sit in this room with pink curtains. With her. Forever.

But it was not to be.

"I must take my leave," he said and stood. "Would it suit ye to depart tomorrow?"

"Yes," she said and stood as well. "I will close the school for now. Until Harry is out of danger."

They faced each other. Three feet apart. He looked at her. She looked down at his right and then his left hand.

And then she raised her head and stepped forward onto tiptoes, putting her arms around his neck and pulling Alasdair's head down to hers. He had a moment—of fear or excitement?—when he thought Arabella would kiss him. But she did not. She pressed her pink cheek to his. He could feel his poorly shaved jaw scratching her soft skin. Her breath skimmed by his ear. She whispered something. He could not make it out.

Was it possible she said *at last*?

She released him, and he avoided her eyes, murmured his farewell, and left the cottage quickly.

Boyd was waiting for him in the public house with three large tumblers of whisky sitting in front of him. One was almost empty.

"Cousin," Boyd said. "Sit. One of these is for ye."

Alasdair sat. He held up his glass to clink against Boyd's, but Boyd did not hold his glass out. He just studied Alasdair.

Alasdair took a sip. The whisky was harsh, not the smooth, smuggled elixir he had drunk over the years with the earl at Sommerleigh.

"Ye told me ye ken her sister. Ye didnae tell me ye ken her." Boyd's voice was thick with whisky already.

"Our acquaintance was years ago and very brief."

Boyd stared into his glass. "Her feelings are strong for ye, I can see." His tone was bitter.

"I…"

Boyd drained his glass and wiped his mouth. "She's told me, ye see. About ye. And her. What ye did." The bitterness was edging into something stronger, something dangerous.

Something violent. Boyd seized his second glass and took a gulp.

Alasdair strove to keep his own voice calm. "Pardon?"

"Ye should be begging *her* pardon. I dinnae ken how these things are rectified down in England, but up here ye might remember that scoundrels like ye answer for yer actions."

Alasdair was lost. What was Boyd on about?

Boyd pushed back his chair and stood. The chair clattered to the floor. Voices stilled in the room.

"I willnae kill ye, cousin. I am a man of God. But I will beat ye until ye bleed."

Alasdair pushed his own chair back from the table but stayed seated and raised both his empty hands.

"I dinnae believe I have done anything intentionally injurious."

Boyd spat and wiped his mouth. "Injurious? To be married and to ruin… To take…"

Finally, Alasdair understood.

He stood up quickly, his chair now also falling onto the floor. Boyd was seconds away from coming over the table at him.

"'Twas nae me, cousin. I am unmarried. I didnae take anything."

Boyd became very still.

Alasdair went on, "We shouldnae discuss this here. Let us go outside. Let us go down to the shore, where the sand will soak up the blood from my beating. But I will tell ye now that I am nae the villain ye think I am."

They went down to the shore. The sea was gray and frothy. Boyd had calmed, and his fists were deep in the pockets of his coat. Alasdair kept his chin down, buried into the collar of his own coat. The brown knitted scarf he had been wearing was gone, lost on the street or in the public house.

"What has she told ye?" Alasdair asked.

"I willnae break her confidence."

Alasdair said carefully, "I will tell ye my end of it."

Boyd looked out at the horizon.

"Before today, I have ne'er touched Miss Lovelock except to take her gloved hand and bow over it. When I met her for the first and only time in St. Paul's Cathedral. In the presence of her mother. And the bishop. I havenae done anything untoward."

"Ye have met her only once before?"

"Aye."

"Ye didnae despoil her?"

"Nae. As I said, before today—"

"And today? What have ye done today?"

In truth, Alasdair thought, he still had done nothing. *She* had touched his chest, grabbed his coat, put her finger on his lips, pulled his head down, put her cheek to his. He had stayed in his mind, in his imagination, and *received*. He was either a coward or a genteel man. Given both the detail and the intensity of his thoughts about Arabella and her body over the years, he knew the scales came down on the side of coward.

"What are ye here for?" Boyd pressed.

"I'm here to take her to her sister."

Boyd's lip curled. He snorted and kept his gaze fixed on the line where the sky met the ocean.

"She'll nae be back," Boyd said. "When folk leave here, they dinnae come back. Like ye."

"I cannae say, cousin." But it was his dearest wish that Boyd was right in his prediction.

That evening in his bedchamber at the public house, Alasdair took from his bag the medical periodicals he had studied on his trip north from Edinburgh. And then he replaced them in the bag, knowing he couldn't possibly read tonight. He was far too occupied by other thoughts. Thoughts of Arabella.

What a miracle she was. She was entirely unchanged.

Oh, yes, there was the inch of height and the inch of bosom she had acquired in the intervening years. But, in essence, she was the same. Bright. Full of feeling. Thriving. She had not been spoiled or ruined. What idiocy it was that people should use those terms when talking about a woman who was no longer a virgin. As if that were the only thing a woman had to offer the world. As if all of her other gifts and qualities were naught.

He threw himself on his bed, thinking of how close she had been to him just before he had left her cottage. And the strong emotion and equally strong arousal he had felt, provoked by the soft skin of her face touching his.

He should find a way to sharpen his razor. In case, just in case, there was the slightest chance she might ever put her cheek to his again, he did not want to scratch her. He must have a smooth jaw for her.

And then he realized he was about to spend seven or more days in a carriage with Arabella Lovelock.

He must think of something to say to her.

He sat up.

Perhaps he should make some notes.

THIRTEEN

Wearing Alasdair's scarf around her neck, Arabella folded clothes and put them in her trunk. It was too bad she didn't have any really pretty dresses anymore. Just practical things. But Alasdair almost certainly did not care about dresses. And she would be in her coat in the carriage anyway, she told herself.

Maggie arrived back to the cottage and put her head in the door of Arabella's bedchamber.

"Miss Lovelock, what are ye doing?"

"Maggie." She could feel her face growing hot with the excitement of telling someone. "Maggie, what do you think? We are to leave Dunburn tomorrow to travel to England. To see my sister. You will come with me, won't you?"

"Come with ye? I've nae been to England."

"We won't stay long. A month or two. My sister's confinement approaches, and she asked for me."

"I didnae ken ye had a sister, Miss Lovelock."

"Yes, two. You will come, won't you?"

"'Tis warmer there?"

"In February? A little, perhaps. And I am sure the winds are not so fierce at Sommerleigh as they are here."

"How will we go?"

"By hired carriage. We will go with the man who brought me the letter from my sister. Dr. Andrews." She touched the scarf at her neck and felt her face become a trifle hotter.

"The lovely man who is staying at the public house? Mr. Cormack's second cousin? The one whom Mr. Cormack threatened to beat?"

Arabella could not find her breath. "What?" She started for the door of the bedchamber.

Maggie stopped her. "Dinnae be troubled, Miss Lovelock. They left the public house before there was a fight, and when they came back after half an hour, Mr. Cormack had sobered and they both seemed unhurt and ate a pie together."

Arabella stared. "You seem to know all about it."

Maggie shrugged as she turned to leave the room. "Ye ken villages, Miss Lovelock. There are nae secrets here."

Except Arabella *had* kept her secrets here. With great success. And she had become a different person, entirely.

Oh, what did Alasdair think of her now?

She buried her nose in his scarf. It smelled of him. She would not give the scarf back, not for anything.

The next morning, a carriage stood outside Arabella's cottage, and the coachman Paterson and Alasdair wrestled her and Maggie's trunks onto the top of the carriage.

Ewen MacEwen, he of the freckled face, approached. He looked almost fat, stuffed into his coat, like a bird who had fluffed the feathers of its breast.

"I hear ye are going south," he said to Arabella, who was standing outside the carriage, watching her trunk being tied in place.

"Yes, I will be away for a month or two." She reached into her reticule. "I will still pay you to go to Inverness and get my letters, if you like, Ewen, and a book."

"Nae," he said. "But I would like to go to England with ye."

"We are leaving within the hour."

"I am ready."

"But your stepmother, your sisters?"

He shrugged. "I have already said goodbye."

"And your clothes?"

"I am wearing all of them, all at once." That explained his stuffed appearance.

"And your books?"

"I ken them by heart, miss."

Arabella sighed. "All right, Ewen."

Ewen swung up onto the driver's seat. "I will ride on the outside. I want to see everything."

Boyd Cormack suddenly appeared, having walked up from the village. He helped Alasdair and Paterson finish lashing the trunks in place.

"Thank ye, cousin." Alasdair shook Boyd's hand and went into the cottage, saying he would try to hurry Mrs. Gunn along. Paterson went to the front of the carriage to investigate the boy who wanted to share his seat.

"Mr. Cormack," Arabella started. But Boyd shook his head.

"Miss Lovelock, ye dinnae need to say anything. I ken ye willnae be my wife. But I hope we will still be related, in some way."

Arabella felt herself color.

"He didnae speak much when he was a boy. Almost a mute. So be patient with him if he is slow to speak his mind now."

"I—I—" Arabella stammered. "I will endeavor to be. Patient."

"Goodbye, Miss Lovelock."

Then he did something she had never seen anyone in the village do. Boyd Cormack took her hand and bowed over it. And he was gone down the road, his pale-red hair glinting in the morning sun.

Maggie came out of the cottage, fussing, with Alasdair at her heels. As Maggie locked the door and walked around the cottages twice to check the windows, Alasdair came up to Arabella. His eyes went to her neck wrapped with his brown scarf.

"You left your scarf in the cottage yesterday," she said.

"Aye."

"I have another for you." She went into the reticule she meant to take into the carriage with her and brought out a piece of bright-green woolen tartan with fine red-and-black stripes. "I hemmed it last night."

"I'm sorry to have put ye to any trouble."

"Nonsense. I am the reason you have no scarf. Lean down, Dr. Andrews."

He did, and she wrapped it around his neck and crossed it over and tucked it into his coat.

"It's the Ross hunting tartan," she said.

He straightened up and looked at her with no sign of recognition.

"The Andrews wear the Ross tartan," she explained. "I bought a length in Inverness to make a dress." She realized then she was giving away perhaps too much of her secret life, so she finished in a rush, "But I thought it would also make a scarf for you. There is still plenty left."

She looked into his eyes. She had been right. Her memory from almost four years ago had not been faulty. The green of the tartan was the same as the green of his eyes.

Fourteen

Alasdair did not know what to make of his new scarf. He had no notion of the Andrews family wearing the Ross tartan. That had not been part of his childhood. His father had died when he was but one year of age. His aunt who had raised him from age four had been his mother's sister. He had never known any members of his father's family.

Arabella had bought the tartan, knowing it was for his father's clan. And she planned to make a dress from it. To wear herself, he presumed.

But perhaps she just liked this shade of green.

Alasdair sat backwards in the carriage, facing Arabella and Maggie. He did not have to make much conversation with Arabella on this first day as they headed south on the road towards Inverness because Mrs. Maggie Gunn was full of questions for him. Where were his people from? Really? She did not remember any Andrews in Bailebrae. And surely he and she were of an age? Oh, his mother's sister and her husband? The uncle was a Mowat? Yes, maybe she did remember some farmer by that name up by Bailebrae. But it had been long ago.

And his schooling and training? Edinburgh? And why had he not come back to the Highlands?

"We are in as much need of a good doctor as the people of England, sir," Maggie said.

Arabella interjected, "Maggie, you must leave Dr. Andrews alone. If he had never left Scotland, he would not have saved my sister's life."

Alasdair could feel the heat on his face. "I didnae save her life. Her husband and Sommerleigh and she herself did that. But as to why I didnae return…Bailebrae was just a place of deprivation. For me. Perhaps I was nae brave enough, and for that, I am sorry."

"Brave enough!" Arabella leaned forward. "You were in the navy, were you not?"

"Aye."

"On a ship that came under fire from the French many times?"

"Aye." He wondered at her knowing his history.

Arabella sat back and looked at Maggie. "I should think that brave enough for anyone. There is no reason for the doctor to apologize."

"Perhaps traveling to a place ye have ne'er been before, where ye have nae friends, and making a life for yerself," Alasdair said, "perhaps that is brave, too."

Arabella looked down at her gloved hands in her lap.

"Well, she has friends now," Maggie huffed.

"Aye," Alasdair said.

Arabella looked up and fixed her eyes on Alasdair's. "I count Dr. Andrews as among my friends. I hope I am not wrong in that, Doctor?"

He choked. "Aye, I mean, nae, Miss Lovelock. Ye are nae wrong."

Near the end of the day, the two women slept, their arms linked together, Maggie slumping onto the much-smaller Arabella's shoulder. Arabella's head was down, her chin on her chest, her face hidden by her woolen bonnet. Alasdair could see the stout Mrs. Gunn's head and arm were helping keep Arabella in place as the carriage bumped along the roads rutted by winter mud.

If he were sitting next to Arabella and, for some reason, he might be allowed to do what he wished, he would put his arms around her entirely and lock her in his clasp so she could not lurch off the seat. He would keep her from flying off.

He shifted in his own seat. Foolishness. He would never have license to do what he wished. Not with her.

He attempted to read a letter in a medical periodical about a bladder stone surgery. He leaned forward, his forearms on his thighs, head down, trying to make sense of the words.

The air in the carriage suddenly felt alive and prickling, as it might be before a thunderstorm. His skin tingled.

He looked up.

Arabella's eyes were open, and she was looking at him.

A smile curved her lips.

Suddenly, the world seemed a very good place to Alasdair. She was as wonderful and lovely as ever. She was unmarried. He was brave. She was with him. Happiness was within reach.

Then some worry in her face, the smile was gone, and she closed her eyes.

The world again became a place of uncertainty, of death and disease. Of endings. It became the world Alasdair had always known.

Arabella had been jolted awake by a rut in the road. She opened her eyes and saw Alasdair reading, leaning forward, his hat off, the top of his head just a few feet from her. Those waves of shiny auburn hair. She wanted to put her hands in that hair, lace her fingers into it, pull his head up and look at his eyes, his mouth, his dimples, his face. That face she had seen so briefly and imagined for so long.

What would it be like to be sitting on the other side of the carriage with him? To feel his leg next to hers, his arm next to hers. She would let him read, she would not disturb him, but perhaps she would put her arm under his elbow and rest her forearm on his and her fingers would touch the skin of his wrist. The wrist that led to one of his devastating hands. And then she might slide her hand off his wrist and to the inside of his leg and she would feel the muscle of his leg under his trousers. Then she could slide her hand upwards and make him moan as she touched his length.

He looked up just then and held her gaze. He smiled, and she saw his dimples, so she smiled back and could feel the slickness and the throb and the ache under her skirts.

Then she remembered he didn't want her.

Even before she had been a wanton and a scandal, he had not wanted her. He had done nothing to seek her out or find her. Even now, he was only here at the behest of her sister.

And, besides, she was not fit for the love of a man like him.

After her hard work of the last two years, how disheartening to discover she was the same foolish, needing creature, wet between the legs, aching for him.

She shut her eyes and shut him out.

At the coaching inn that night, she was quiet and pushed her stew around in her bowl.

"Miss Lovelock," Alasdair said. "Ye didnae eat. Are ye ill?"

"This mutton in the stew has too much fat left on it," Maggie grumbled. "'Tis nae wonder ye didnae like it, miss. Shall I ask for some broth for ye? Do ye want my bread?"

"No," Arabella said and attempted a smile. "I am merely

tired. I am sure my appetite will be better in the morning. Neither of you are to worry."

She brought a spoonful of the stew to her lips, but when Alasdair and Maggie looked away, she traded bowls with Ewen MacEwen so he could have her full one and she could have his empty one. Ewen was untroubled by this and started eating her stew without a word.

She could not fathom eating when her heart hurt so badly.

She wondered at herself being so happy just yesterday when Alasdair had come to her cottage. Yesterday, it had been enough that he had been there in the same room with her and he had let her put her cheek to his. And that she could wrap his scarf around her face and put her nose and her mouth on it and breathe him in. And that Harry had mentioned in her letter how Dr. Andrews remained unmarried.

But now she wanted more.

She wanted him to want her.

She was becoming a child all over again. Sick to her stomach with desire. Resentful when thwarted. Greedy and clinging.

This had been a mistake. She should have stayed in Dunburn, where she had learned restraint and put her energies to good purpose. Where she had become someone as far from her mother as possible.

In the middle of her sleepless night, the most painful of realizations wracked her mind.

She was such a dolt. A numpty.

Everything she had done in the last two years was for *him*. Well, no, not for him, but for some idea of him.

She had refashioned herself into a woman she thought he might like. He had not wanted her when she was a novel-reading stylish young lady of the *ton*. So she had become a hard-working schoolmistress in the Highlands.

It had not been scheming or deliberate. Hadn't she tried to shut away her thoughts of him as much as she could?

But he had been at the back of her mind, all along. Even as she had considered marrying Boyd and the good she might do as his wife, she had thought, *And Alasdair would like it if we kept the privies from draining into the river.*

She had done this—made her life in Dunburn—all for him.

And he still had not shown any special interest in her. And she still had nothing for herself.

The next day in the carriage, Arabella made sure she was bright and cheerful. She engaged Maggie in a discussion of the scenery outside the window of the coach and told her about Sommerleigh. She asked Alasdair about his medical reading and about Harry and Thomas and her niece Hypatia. And her nephew Richard, whom she had never met. And what of her half brother Sebastian, Marquess of Daventry, the Middlewich heir? He was three and a half now. He probably did not remember his sister. And any news of Mary and her family? Of course, she knew of Mary's twin sons and her daughter because of letters. But any more recent news?

She kept her pain at bay with a stream of chatter.

Maggie grumbled about how Arabella should have told her they were going to the house of an earl. And her sisters were a countess and a viscountess? And her brother would someday be a duke? Aye, she could see why Arabella did not make this widely known in the village, but why had she not told Maggie so she could have packed her best bombazine?

North of the Firth of Forth and Edinburgh, they stopped at the village of Strathlochirn at the request of Maggie. Her sister lived here with a husband and children. The coaching inn, Maggie said, was said to be a good one. The rest of the party settled in their rooms, and Maggie walked to her sister's cottage.

But as Arabella was sitting down to dinner in the chair Alasdair had pulled out for her, Maggie came rushing into the public house, her face wet with tears, her breath coming in big gasps. Arabella stood and seized Maggie's hands.

"Maggie, what is the matter? You're distressed. Is your sister not well?"

"Oh, Miss Lovelock," Maggie said and broke into a sob.

Arabella whisked her upstairs to her room. Maggie sat on the edge of the bed, and Arabella knelt in front of her and held her hands as she cried.

Eventually, Maggie was able to choke out that her sister's husband had abandoned her and their four children just a week earlier. Her sister had no idea where the gowk had gone, but he had told her he was leaving and she would never hear from him again.

"Oh, dear," Arabella said. She sat down next to Maggie on the bed and put an arm around her shoulders. "Oh, dear."

Maggie took a handkerchief from her reticule and blew her nose. "She is so desperate, Miss Lovelock. So scared."

"You must stay with her, Maggie. You can help her, and I will pay your wages ahead. I have plenty of money with me for the journey, and I will give you enough so you and she need not worry."

"Oh, nae, Miss Lovelock." Maggie was aghast. "I cannae do that. Ye need me."

"Your sister needs you more."

"But widnae be proper for ye…for ye…"

"For me to travel with two men and a boy? And one of the men, a family friend? I traveled alone with just a coachman when I came north two years ago."

"'Twas nae proper, neither."

Arabella stood. Her hands went into fists at her sides. Her face got hot, and she knew it had flushed red.

"You know what isn't proper, Maggie? A husband abandoning his wife and his children!"

"Aye," Maggie whispered, looking shocked by Arabella's vehemence. Arabella had never spoken this way in front of her. Maggie had never seen Arabella angry because Arabella had worked very hard to control her temper over the last two years. To model mildness and modesty for her students. And for the absent Alasdair.

But, now, knowing how pointless her own program of reform had been, Arabella was liberated. All that restraint and to what end? The doctor had not shown up at her doorstep because of Arabella's virtue, but because her sister had sent him.

She might as well voice her fury. She truly had nothing to lose.

"If folk spent more time worrying about things that really mattered instead of appearances, everyone's lives would be a great deal better. What's important is that your sister is frightened and alone. She needs to feed four children. She needs turf for the fire. She needs you."

"Aye."

Arabella took a deep breath. Her next words were quieter. "I hope you know I am not vexed at you, Maggie. I am angry at your sister's husband and your sister's situation. I am sorry I spoke in such a harsh manner. But," she sat down next to Maggie again, "my reputation cannot be any more ruined than it already is. Have no worries on that score. And I will be safe with the doctor."

As Maggie wiped her nose and thanked her, Arabella asked herself the unanswerable question.

But will the doctor be safe with me?

FIFTEEN

At breakfast, Ewen MacEwen asked Arabella if they might take the new steamboat from Dysart to Newhaven. He had been reading about steam as a propulsive force, and he thought he might be able to persuade someone on board to let him get a look at the workings of such a ship.

Paterson grunted, and Alasdair translated. They would be better off crossing the Firth of Forth at the old Queensferry crossing since they intended to skirt Edinburgh.

"Next time, Ewen," Arabella said. "On the way back."

"I dinnae think so," he said. "I'm nae sure I'm coming back."

"I will be," Arabella said and raised her chin. There was nothing for her in England. Alasdair being persuaded by Harry to act as her escort to Sommerleigh did not change that.

The carriage left the village of Strathlochirn with just Arabella and Alasdair inside of it. Both Arabella and Alasdair had tried to persuade Ewen MacEwen to come into the carriage with them, but he refused.

"I have nae been this far south before. Sitting inside would defeat the purpose of traveling," he said and climbed up next to Paterson.

"Besides," Paterson grumbled, picking up the reins, "the boy tells good stories. I have ne'er been entertained so well. And today he has promised to finish the story of Sir Gawain and the Green Knight."

It was the longest speech Arabella had heard from Paterson in their two-day acquaintance.

Alasdair handed Arabella into the carriage, and they sat opposite each other as they had when Maggie had been with them.

Arabella did not know if this arrangement was best. Yes, she had had wicked thoughts about what she might do if she were seated next to him, but, now, in this position, facing him, unchaperoned, even looking at him had become tinged with danger.

She stole a glance. The bit of sunburn on his nose—where had he gotten that? His mouth. His green eyes, the left one hidden by that lock of his hair. She looked down and saw his long legs, his gloved hands with those long fingers holding one of his medical journals. She turned her eyes to the window, suddenly shy.

They exchanged fewer than two-dozen words in the first hour of their journey that day until Arabella abruptly stood and turned around and sat next to Alasdair.

"I just needed a change," she said.

And their new positions relative to each other, seated side by side so they did not have to look into the face of the other, did seem to free both of them to talk.

He commented on Maggie's sister's situation.

"'Tis good she has Mrs. Gunn with her."

"Yes, Maggie will sort it out, what can be sorted out. But it's horrid for that man to leave them with no money, no word of where he is. He has condemned those children to poverty."

"But 'tis good the children have their mother. To have one parent who loves ye, 'tis important."

Arabella remembered then that Alasdair had been orphaned at a young age and raised by an aunt and uncle until they died, too.

"As ye had yer mother," he went on. "When yer father died."

She shifted on the seat. She did not wish to speak of her mother. "When you were a boy, where did you go when you left Bailebrae?"

"I went to Edinburgh. I dinnae ken why. I was ten or so. I must have heard something about the city to make me pass Inverness by and keep going. I walked. It took well over a fortnight."

"Only ten years of age? To make your way so far." In her mind's eye, Arabella saw a small, redheaded boy walking on this very road. Alone. She had to blink rapidly.

"I was lucky. 'Twas a very dry and warm September. But I remember dreaming of food."

And the solitary boy had been hungry, too. She made her gloved hands into fists and willed herself to betray no emotion in her voice since, after all, he could not see her face as they sat side by side. "What did you find to eat?"

"I cannae remember what I ate while walking. But I do remember the first thing I ate in Edinburgh. A carrot. Dr. Murray's wife saw me climb the wall to steal some carrots from their garden. She came out of the house, and I was frightened and started climbing the wall to get away, and she said, *Let me wash those for ye.* Meaning the carrots I had in my hand."

"Dr. Murray is the teacher Harry mentioned in her letter to me?"

"Aye. He and his wife took me in. And he helped me gain entrance to study with the Edinburgh Medical Faculty."

"Harry said he was ill."

"Aye. He died just before I came to ye."

"I am very sorry." She thought how important this man must be to him. "A very great loss. Were you with him when he died?"

"Aye."

"I am glad of that, for his sake. And his wife?"

"Mrs. Murray died when I was still in training."

"You are quite alone, then."

"Well, I had forgotten about the Cormacks. Until I saw Boyd. Then it came back to me that I did still have family."

"Mr. Cormack told me you did not speak much when you were young."

"Aye. I found I had nothing to say. I liked to listen."

She laughed a little. "I, on the other hand, have plenty to say and can't bear to listen, Alasd—Dr. Andrews."

"I am," a hesitation here, "very interested in what ye have to say."

Suddenly, she had nothing to say.

The carriage went over a rut, and they bounced a bit on the seat, and Arabella jostled into Alasdair.

"My apologies, Miss Lovelock," he murmured and pulled away.

The words burst out of her. "Mr. Cormack understands I have refused him."

She bit her lip. He said nothing.

Her body touching his for just a moment. And it had not escaped his notice that she had almost called him Alasdair.

But he did not say anything when she told him she had refused Boyd. And, surely, that would have been the right time for him to have said something to her of his intentions. To hint, at least. To have said something like, "Perhaps ye might accept someone else?"

But if she had rebuffed him, then to sit in this carriage with her for another five or six or seven days? It would have been torture. How could he have borne it? He would never be able to recover from that injury to his uncalloused heart.

And she would be witness to his pain.

He was still a coward.

She broke the awkward silence, rescuing him. Dauntless Arabella.

"What do you do for amusement, Dr. Andrews?"

He cleared his throat. "Chiefly, I read. But yer sister and her husband are kind enough to have me for dinner from time to time."

"And what do you read? Your medical books and papers?" She gestured at the forgotten periodical in his hand.

"Aye," he said slowly. "And the works of Sir Walter Scott." He looked at her out of the corner of his eye, thinking he might see some spark, some recognition, and she would seize on this topic, and he would finally be able to impress her with his interest in her own pastime.

But she was looking out the window at the backward-rolling scenery. He returned his eyes to the seat straight ahead of him.

"I don't seem to have much time for reading novels anymore," she said, absently. "But perhaps once at Sommerleigh, I might."

"Yer sister will be happy to see ye."

"And I, her. The best thing about Harry is that there will be no recriminations. She will accept me as I am." She shook her head. "No grudges, no what-ifs, no mourning. No living in the past. No being haunted by mistakes."

"Is that," Alasdair hesitated and then plunged ahead, "is

that why ye have nae asked yet about yer mother? Or even mentioned her? Ye fear how she will treat ye?"

He could feel Arabella stiffen next to him.

"Yes, but…Dr. Andrews, I don't know what you know about why I left London."

His mind raced. What should he tell her? As always, he felt the truth was the best course.

"Lady Drake told me something of it when I asked about yer absence."

"Harry?" Arabella leaned forward in her seat and kept her face resolutely turned towards the window.

"Aye. So, of course, I ken it may nae be exactly how others see it."

"What did Harry say?"

To have to tell this to her. It tore at his heart. But he repeated what Harry had told him on Christmas Day, years ago. That Arabella had been seduced by a married man and it had come to be known by many. He worked hard to control his voice. Whatever he felt could be nothing in comparison to what the event had meant to her since it had led to her separation from her family.

"No. Harry was accurate," Arabella said to the carriage window.

"But I am sure yer mother feels nothing but love for ye. Ye should nae be worried about seeing her."

"She will want to talk about things, and I don't want that. I want to leave that time behind. I know she feels shame over…what happened. Which she should not."

"And neither should ye." Alasdair could not believe his boldness.

The silence stretched.

"Thank you," Arabella said quietly. He felt a brief pressure on his gloved hand.

Cowardice be damned.

He grabbed at what he presumed was her hand, clamping it.

"I must tell ye," he said, not turning his head, still staring at the opposite seat. "I must tell ye the greatest regret of my life has been that I didnae ask yer mother if I could write to ye. In that time before ye left yer family. To say I am sorry disnae begin to express my remorse."

"You are very kind." Her voice was choked, as if by tears.

He moved to the seat opposite her, still holding her hand, leaning forward, looking at her blue eyes brimming with tears.

"Nae, I am nae kind," he said. "I am nae kind, at all. I am a fool."

"I won't have you talk that way about my personal physician," she said, smiling through her tears, clearly trying to make a joke.

Oh. Oh, no. His heart sank.

She did not want this intimacy from him. She did not want to hear he had wanted to write to her.

He thought her hand on his coat when he had come through her door in Dunburn might mean something. Her eyes meeting his. Then, the press of her cheek and her whisper when he left, the gift of the tartan scarf the next day—but no, he had been wrong. She had just been happy to see someone associated with her family. She was just expressive and affectionate in a way he had never been.

And what she had said just now. Her calling him her *personal physician*. She was pushing him away, reminding him he was a servant, a man who served others. He would never have any intercourse with her, outside of that between a doctor and patient. She was, like her sisters, destined for a life as a lady, the wife of a lord, no matter what had happened two years ago. He was beneath her and always would be.

He let go of the hand he had been clutching so tightly. He

sat back, crossed his arms over his chest, and ducked his head, avoiding her eyes.

"I am sorry. I ask yer forgiveness, Miss Lovelock. I forgot myself."

"I wish we could," she said abruptly, too loudly.

That made him raise his head and look at her. He had not heard this tone from her before. Her voice was harsh. She had gone from tearful to angry in a flash.

"If only we *could* forget ourselves, Dr. Andrews. That is what I wish for. I cannot again be the girl in the bishop's study, meeting the man of my dreams for the first time. That girl is gone. And I am glad of it. Because that girl could only be hurt and damaged. I want to be free of her. I want to be a woman whose expectations of the world are appropriate. What do you want to be, Dr. Andrews?"

It took every ounce of Alasdair's brain to pay attention to anything Arabella said after *man of my dreams*. He had thought— He had hoped— He had wished for so long that the feelings he had for her were in some small way reciprocated.

And, now, to hear her say those words.

He had been a very great fool, indeed.

But she was asking him something.

"I want to be a woman whose expectations of the world are appropriate. What do you want to be, Dr. Andrews?"

What did he want to be?

There could only be one answer to that.

"I want to be the man who exceeds yer expectations." He was startled by how strong his voice was.

He willed himself to get up and was equally surprised to find his will had overcome his writhing intestines, and he was, in fact, moving across the short distance between them.

"And I dinnae. "

He sat beside her.

"Want."

He took both her hands.

"To be appropriate."

He leaned down and put his lips to hers.

He had never kissed anyone. Long ago, he had practiced kissing by putting his lips to a mirror. He had been eighteen, about to finish his training as a physician, and he thought his medical degree meant he might look for a wife. But he joined the navy and never courted anyone. He had no opportunity. And he had no interest—French Letters or no—in seeking paid female companionship. He had spent his adolescence treating the ravages of syphilis and the clap in the whores of Edinburgh and the men who went to whores and the wives of men who went to whores. He knew enough to avoid that.

He was completely without experience. And kissing a looking glass had no relation to kissing Arabella.

Her mouth was so soft, so warm.

He had not expected to kiss her today—well, not ever, in truth—so he was glad he had shaved carefully this morning, thinking of her cheek against his. Yes, he was glad there were none of his ginger whiskers to abrade those delicate pink lips, that cupid's bow.

He took off a glove and cupped one of her cheeks.

He kissed her again.

She was allowing it. No, more than that. She gazed up at him and angled her mouth towards his. Her lips were slightly parted.

He felt such a rising excitement in himself. Yes, naturally, his member was engorged—how could it not be?—but it was more than that.

Could the kissing mean to her what it meant to him? That she was to be with him, now and forever? Should he say this to her?

No. Let him continue to kiss her. She seemed to like it. He

knew he liked it. If she did not want to look into the past, let him not look too far into the future.

For now, there was kissing. And it was glorious.

It was the lightest of brushes, a tender and brief pressure. So different from the other kisses she had had. The only other kisses she had ever had. Those from Giles. Those grasping, greedy kisses.

But this was different. The first kiss and the kisses that followed were a giving, not a taking. They were offers. They seemed to ask nothing of her. Even the hand on her cheek was a gift—his tenderness, his warmth suffusing her cheek already flushed by her outburst of temper.

She had not expected this from him. First, because she thought he did not share her feelings. In the past and now. Second, because he was a man bound by propriety. He had not wanted to sit in her cottage with her alone until she begged him to stay. For him to do this meant—

He pulled away.

She looked at him, and her surprise at his kisses turned into longing at the sight of his mouth, his gentle green right eye and the mischievous lock of auburn hair that tumbled over the left.

"You kissed me," she whispered.

"Aye."

"That," she swallowed, "exceeded my expectations."

He took off his other glove and put both hands on her face. Such gentle hands with those careful long fingers. They smelled of soap. She stared at his mouth. Those generous lips. She could not wait to hear what he would say next.

But he did not speak again. He cupped her face and kissed her once more. A longer kiss this time, his lips slightly less gentle on hers. And then again. And again.

And each time, between each kiss, he would pull back and look at her with his green eyes as if he were performing a test and assessing her reaction to it. She hoped her reactions were encouraging to him. Perhaps she should voice her appreciation of his efforts.

"Dr. Andrews," she said as softly as she could. "My expectations continue to be exceeded."

There were stirrings down below, a wetness between her legs, a piercing in her breasts. But she told herself to ignore those. Just, for now, let there be kisses. There could never be enough kisses for her. From him.

Alasdair noted their breathing grew more ragged as their kisses grew longer and longer. Arabella's gloves were removed, and she had her hands in his hair. Their exhalations mingled, and the windows of the carriage became steamed. Just before the carriage began to slow for a stop, Arabella let her mouth open a little wider, and he felt the moistness of her mouth and the brush of her tongue. It was unbearable, delicious, tantalizing. He had to push away thoughts of other lips and other penetrations, of what she might permit him with marriage and time.

The carriage halted completely, and they pulled apart.

After they had walked a bit around the ferry landing and eaten something and performed necessary but unspeakable functions and spoken to Paterson and Ewen MacEwen about the plan for the afternoon and where they might stop at nightfall, they got back into the carriage.

He handed her in and when he climbed in himself, he hesitated. Beside her? Across from her?

"It's growing colder," she said, taking off her gloves, her actions not matching her words. She patted the seat next to her. "Sit next to me, Dr. Andrews."

Yes, it was getting colder, and he was glad of it as it gave him reason to sit as close to her as possible. And as he sat beside her, she moved so her body was touching his from knee to hip, and she leaned forward, and he quite naturally put his arm around her and drew her upper body against his.

She put her hand on his leg, on the inside of his thigh, just above his knee. Her warm hand sat there as the carriage loaded onto the ferry, along with a few other carriages and some wagons. He suffered through that and the crossing. And then the unloading and, finally, the carriage was moving at a good clip, and no one could possibly be looking in.

She turned her head. He turned his. Again, their mouths met.

Dozens of kisses later, he felt that wetness and a brush of her small tongue again. He opened his lips wider, and she licked his tongue. He then did the same to her, and her taste was so sweet, the inside of her mouth even softer than her lips.

And warmer and wetter.

He felt a surge of lust, his cock was like a cricket bat in his trousers, and he wanted to press into her, to ravish her with his tongue, to take her mouth, to fill it and conquer it and make it his.

To mark it. To own it. Like a savage might. *This is my woman, my woman's mouth. No one else can have it. Mine.*

He very nearly growled.

But as he both pulled her even closer to him and pushed her down so she was forced against the seat, he felt Arabella tremble and swallow.

He took his mouth from hers and pulled his body away, taking his arm from her shoulder so she was free to move away from him. But she did not. She sat up with him. So he kept his face close and kissed her cheek with closed lips. Now her other cheek. Her forehead. Her trembling stopped, and he kept his hands by his sides and looked into her blue eyes.

"Forgive me," he said. "I grew too frenzied."

"I did, as well."

"Shall I sit across from ye now?"

"No! But perhaps we should not kiss anymore."

It was over.

He had offended her, had shown her she was at his mercy and he was a beast not to be trusted with her. After three and a half years of executing perfect, and perfectly craven, propriety in relation to her, he had lost control. In a matter of two hours, he had gone from having no expectations to having every expectation to once again being shut off from the physical closeness and affection he craved with every ounce of his lonely being.

He screamed inside.

As Alasdair ravished her mouth with his wilder and wilder kisses and leaned into her, she heard him groan, and the ache between her legs that she had felt all day, ever since that first very tentative kiss, that ache became overwhelming until she felt she was on the brink of pulling up her skirts and begging for him to touch her wetness with his hand, his phallus.

Anything.

She would do anything for that.

She trembled, remembering she had felt the same, years ago, also in a carriage. She would do anything.

And then he stopped. Not abruptly, but gently. He kissed her face with great tenderness and their bodies were apart, but the tension between them still hummed.

She did not want him to leave her side, but surely she was headed in the very same direction that had caused her such anguish before. She thought her ardor should be quieted for a moment. Banked, like a fire.

But when she suggested they stop kissing, she could feel his body stiffen.

"Just for now," she said.

His look of anguish was transformed into such a grin of relief that his dimples had dimples.

She reached up to put the tip of her pinky in one of his dimples. It fit perfectly. Then she did the same on the other cheek.

"I have not seen your dimples in a few days. I have missed them."

He took her hands and kissed the back of each one.

"The dimples will always appear on yer command. Ye need only say *Open, Sesame*."

A startled and shamed look in his eyes. He put her hands down.

"I apologize, Miss Lovelock. Ye asked for nae more kissing, and I kissed yer hands quite without meaning to."

His politeness was so sweet. But would he beg forgiveness for everything? Surely, he knew she wanted him to take liberties with her. She wanted his attentions. He did not need to apologize for that.

"I think," she said, smiling, hoping to encourage him, "hand kissing is allowed."

He picked up her hands again and began to pepper her palms and her fingers and her knuckles with tiny, dry kisses.

"Within reason." She laughed.

"Ah," he said and paused for a moment, but did not move her hands from his lips, "that is the problem. I have nae reason when it comes to ye."

If Alasdair only knew how little reason she had, as well.

"Then you will have to sit across from me!" But as he obediently went to move, she clasped his arm and kept him in his seat. "I will be too cold, Dr. Andrews."

"I suppose I had better stay here."

He put his arm around her again, and she *couried* or nestled into him, keeping her head bent down so she would not be tempted to reach up with her lips and kiss him again. And although the insulated contact with his body, he in his thick wool coat and she in hers, did not arouse her as his kisses had, it was wonderfully comforting.

She felt safe.

She had not felt that way for a long time. Even before she had left England, she had felt unsafe to herself. Wild. First, wanting him and his love beyond all reason. Then foolishly wanting anything that had to do with love. But, now, in his arms, knowing he was here and he wanted her, she felt nothing but peace.

She had not known how badly she wanted this feeling. She cried a little in his arms and hoped he wouldn't know.

The kissing was not over. The kissing would return, and, for now, that was enough. And he could sit next to her and hold her down in the carriage seat so she did not jounce—a privilege that two days ago had seemed fantastical and out of reach and now seemed perfectly natural.

She fit into his side as if she had been made for it.

He certainly felt like he had been made for holding her. Dauntless Arabella, in his arms. And the removal of the excitement of kissing let his mind wander to that which he had been pushing away since their first kiss. When should he let her know his intentions? That he wanted to hold her like this forever?

Not yet, he decided. Tomorrow. If she only wanted kissing and nothing else, if she wanted no part of his heart, let him have this one day of happiness.

He was delaying again. But only a day, he told himself. Did he not deserve a day of joy?

He held her and bathed in that joy.

Hours later, Alasdair held his breath as Arabella looked at

his watch. She then looked out the window, checking the position of the sun, he supposed. It had grown colder still, and the sky was still clouded. It was about an hour before they would stop for the evening.

She turned to Alasdair.

"A half an hour," she said. "A half an hour only for kissing and then a half an hour of no kissing for us to calm ourselves. I do not want to get out of the carriage in front of Ewen Mac-Ewen with my lips swollen again."

"Half an hour," he repeated solemnly and then reached out and drew her to him with a calm that belied his inner excitement.

He used his lips, his tongue, his hands. Her face, her wrists, her hands he lavished with attention. But then she thought she heard a noise outside the carriage and she turned her head and her white throat was exposed to him and he kissed her there and was rewarded by a breathy high-pitched noise that hardened his cock to stone. He thought he had never heard a more beautiful sound than the sound of her arousal.

But as he kissed her throat, he did not know what to do with his hands. He could not hold her hands, her arms were around his neck, buried in the hair at the back of his head. When he had been kissing her face, he had used his hands to hold her head, but that was awkward now while he was kissing her throat.

He thought for a very long time about touching her breasts through her coat. Her breaths were coming quickly now, and her chest was heaving up to him. But he remembered how his feverish use of his tongue in her mouth, his pushing her down, had made her tremble.

Let him advance cautiously, gradually. Let him explore his new territory thoroughly before sending out another vanguard.

Her throat, for example. This was his new dominion. And it was fertile, lush territory, at that. Her neck was beautiful, the skin luxuriously soft and warm and fragrant, and he could feel her pulse quicken under his tongue. And, even more importantly, as he had already discovered, the front of her throat was extremely sensitive and she made all kinds of sounds when he was not covering her mouth with his.

The half an hour turned into three quarters of an hour and then into just a minute before the carriage wheels came to a complete stop, and Arabella's and his own lips were quite swollen, their faces flushed, when they climbed out of the carriage to go into the coaching inn.

They were extremely decorous throughout dinner, and he walked her to the door of her bedchamber after dinner.

She did not kiss him in the passageway of the inn, but she held out her hand and he took it and was surprised to have her shake it, just as if they were two men who had greeted each other or made a bargain.

"I will see you on the morrow, Doctor." She lowered her eyes and looked up at him through her lashes. "In the carriage."

"Yes," he said, knowing the expectation of a kiss outside or inside her bedchamber was greedy. He did not mean to frown or look disappointed, but he feared he did.

She went into the room, and, as she was closing the door, she peeked around it with an impish look on her face and said, "Open, Sesame."

He grinned and showed her his dimples. After the door closed, he went off to his own bedchamber, heartened by the prospect of more kissing tomorrow. He would allow himself a full day with her in his arms. He would not press his suit until tomorrow evening. Then he would find out if she wanted any more from him. And if she didn't…he would not think on that now.

Sixteen

The sky was still cloudy the next morning. There was an even colder wind than before. They stood outside the coaching inn, Arabella shivering, and Alasdair longed to put his arm around her, there in the yard.

"We'll be in England in two hours," Paterson told them.

"What of these clouds?" Arabella asked, looking up.

Paterson shrugged. "We're close enough to England to have English weather. I only ken Scottish weather."

Alasdair also shrugged. "We may have some snow, a few flakes." He had no care for the weather. He was anxious to get into the carriage, to be closeted with Arabella, to have his arms around her, to kiss her.

"Ewen," Arabella said. "It's too cold for you to be outside with Paterson."

Alasdair's heart sank at this. He had spent much of the night in anticipation of the hours ahead, what she might allow, what he might dare. He did not want Ewen MacEwen in the carriage with them.

He was elated by the boy's response.

"We're going south, 'tis bound to get warmer as we go,"

Ewen said. He winked in Alasdair's direction before he turned to climb up on the driver's seat.

Then they were together in the carriage, and Arabella was the one kissing Alasdair, up on her knees on the seat next to him so he did not have to bend his head to hers. She held his face and kissed him, pressing into him, making sounds of impatient arousal. She was fevered, rushed, sloppy with her kisses.

Oh, the throbbing and the frenzy she was causing in him. The unbelievably sweet thrill of doing this with her. And the wonderful agony of pushing back against his overwhelming desire to lift her up and put her astride him and have her sex against his with only his trousers between them.

She took her hands from his face and unbuttoned his coat and then hers and took the hand he had on her waist and put it on her dress-covered breast.

He held his hand still as she continued to kiss him. Then he squeezed ever so slightly. She moaned. He squeezed with more force. How wonderful, so firm and yet soft, such a perfect handful of flesh. Oh, how he longed to see it.

Now he wanted to see her naked breast. Could he never be satisfied?

She broke her mouth from his, panting.

"We don't have much time today," she said. "Either the snow will come and we will have to break off our journey or it will get so cold Ewen will have to come inside the carriage."

"Ye are in a hurry, then," he said.

"Yes."

"But we must be careful." He felt he should say this. Be the voice of caution to this tiny but unbelievably powerful force of nature who had the capacity to induce an ache in his heart that matched the one in his groin. "There is so much hurt that can come from impulsive acts."

She knit her brows together. She got off her knees and sat

next to him. His hand slid from her breast as she moved, and his fingers ached, missing the roundness and the softness already.

"Is it impulsive though? It has been more than three and a half years," she said. "In the eyes of the world, I am already ruined because I was headlong and foolish. But the foolishness was in the man I used as a substitute for you. And there need be no danger of a child, Dr. Andrews." She ran her hand over the front of his fall.

He groaned. "Miss Lovelock, I am sorry, I dinnae…I mean, I do want…"

He felt her hand move, and he looked down as she unbuttoned his fall and his engorged shaft sprang free and she grasped it.

For the first time in his life, he felt a hand other than his own on his member. He shuddered as she wrapped her fingers around it. Her small hand. The world fell away and all he could feel was the most intense pleasure centered on his cock. He was unable to resist but felt he should make her aware of his limitations.

"I…Miss Lovelock. I willnae ken…"

"I will show you, Dr. Andrews. And you must know the feminine anatomy in question."

She moved her hand.

That one swift rub on his shaft, from the base up to the head, combined with his imagining of her own most private place, undid him. A dizzyingly swift climb to the heights of pleasure. And then, to his enormous shame, he spent himself.

He was only glad he did not get it on her coat or on her dress. Otherwise, he had no place in his heart or head for anything but mortification.

He could not find the words to express himself. His speech had fled. But what was there to say? There could have been no worse outcome for this moment.

He could not look at her. He turned from her, knowing his face was the same color as his hair. He fumbled with his trousers, to button himself up, and to get away. From her.

The woman he craved with every bit of himself.

She would not want him now.

He felt her get up from beside him and move around him so she was on the seat on his other side and he could not escape her. His eyes were down, but she put her face close, and he felt the softest brush of her lips on his. A hand on his hand, staying it so the fall of his trousers was left open.

"Have you coupled with a woman before, Doctor?"

Here it was. How he wished now he had taken up offers from other women in the past so he could have been better prepared for her touch. So he would have made his mistakes with those others instead of the woman he hoped to make his wife.

But she had bravely faced her past with him yesterday.

"Nae."

"But you like women?"

He raised his face to her. "Aye!" He did not want her to be in any doubt of that.

She made a strange noise—half gasp, half whistle—and spoke almost as if to herself. "I knew you were the not-stupid man."

He allowed himself a bitter smile. "In this moment, I very much feel I am the stupid man."

"Do you desire me?"

He looked at her face, her intelligent eyes, her sweet mouth. There was no place for equivocation here. His cock had not equivocated.

"Aye," he said.

"Then your eagerness is a compliment to me." She studied him.

"But for me...so quickly...like a boy."

"You are a man. The man of my dreams."

His head spun. She had said that yesterday before he kissed her, but he had not believed her.

She was speaking again. "You have denied your appetites for so long, is it any wonder you are like a boy in this singular way?"

"I regret—I widnae have myself be that way with ye."

She touched his lower lip with her thumb and brushed it slowly. "I would rather have you spend quickly with me than know you had used other women and had become inured to this kind of pleasure."

"I could ne'er become inured to ye." And indeed, he could feel his tumescence beginning to return just from her thumb on his lip. But then she took her thumb from his mouth and moved her hand away from his face and rested it on his waistcoat, on his chest, over his heart.

She left her hand there a long time. He remembered it was the same place she had first touched him, in her cottage.

Aye, 'tis my heart. Ye have it. Be careful, dauntless Arabella. Please be more careful with it than ye were with my cock. I can only spill my heart once.

"I would be quite willing," she said, "to undertake a program of exercises to build your stamina." She trailed her hand down his waistcoat to his member and took it in her hand again, and he felt how hard he already was.

He gasped, afraid he might spill abruptly once more, but he did not.

"Miss Lovelock," he said carefully. "I'm sorry, but I wonder if ye might remove yer—"

"Clothes?" One eyebrow of hers quirked, and her mouth was in a mischievous pout. "I think that will have to wait until we are in a warm room with a closed door."

And again he feared he would spill, this time from only her grip and her suggestion that he might see her body bared.

That ripe, surely perfect body he had imagined so many times over the last three years as he had lain in his own bed, alone, at night.

But he did not know what to make of this saucy Arabella who took his shaft in her hand and pouted and hinted at future nakedness. It aroused him. Unquestionably. But, for the first time, he wondered if she might have changed. Maybe she was no longer the Arabella whom he had worshipped in his mind for so long.

He struggled to speak clearly. "I was going to say *remove yer hand*."

"Yes, Alasdair."

She released him. He had a momentary pang of want and need, but his name in her mouth. For the first time. Oh, blazes. He wanted that even more—for her to call him Alasdair—than her hand on his cock.

"'Tis nae what I imagined," he said, his hands at his waistband. He had some difficulty, but he was finally able to button his fall over his engorgement. "Forgive me, but 'tis nae romantic."

She was no longer turned towards him but instead faced the opposite carriage seat.

"No," she said flatly, her eyes ahead. "It is not. Most decidedly, it is not. I was fooled by romance, and I will not be fooled again. I want only harsh light and cold air and your desire and mine."

So. She *had* changed. Had hardened. How was he to steer their course now?

"Miss Lovelock—" he started.

"You have spent in front of me, you can call me Arabella."

Last night, she had nearly thrown open the bedchamber door at the inn and invited him into her bed when she saw his smile and his dimples. How she had wanted him on top of her, holding her, having her. But she did not want to scare him. She knew how lucky she was that he knew her past and still wanted to kiss her. So she had restrained herself and did not invite him into her bedchamber.

But in the carriage today, she had forgotten her resolve.

She was restive. She yearned for him. She could feel the slick of her own wetness, the ache of her bud, the stiffening of her nipples. She did not mind that he had spent precipitously. She wanted the same for herself. With him.

But when she told him he could call her Arabella because he had spent with her hand on him, he drew himself back and colored deeply again.

Why had she said that? And in that way. She might have said it coyly, and it would have been seductive. Instead, she had been cutting. She had cast something up to him that was shameful to him. She had injured him. She had been cruel. She had not known she could be that. How terrible lust was.

But he was exasperating. Did he want her or didn't he?

"I would like nothing more than to have the privilege of calling ye by yer given name," he said, "but I willnae. I will continue to call ye Miss Lovelock. I have nae earned *Arabella*, yet." He visibly gulped when he said her name. "My lack of control disnae mean we are true intimates. And I dinnae have yer aversion to the romantic."

Her resentment spilled over. "I am spoiled, Dr. Andrews, or have you not heard? There is no romance left for me."

He answered her in a different voice. A voice she had never heard from him. A strong and sure voice. An assertive and commanding voice that brooked no opposition. This must be how he spoke as a physician. How he might speak when he ordered a headstrong patient to stay in bed.

"Ye are nae spoiled or ruined or damaged or blemished or marred or any of the other idiotic euphemisms that are bandied about in regards to a woman's virginity. Ye are perfectly ye, still."

Her own hurt dissipated as he spoke. He was not rejecting her, just her headlong foolishness and her impatience.

And the desire that had been washing over her body was gone, replaced by something else. Some deeper want. One that had been with her ever since she could remember, even as a small child. Some want that could only be assuaged by her mother or her father or her sisters.

The want to be both understood and loved, together, at the same time.

He went on, "And ye are nae the only party here. I am one and thirty. I have waited thirty-one years to have a woman in my arms. I want that woman to be ye and have wanted that for almost four years. But can I be blamed for wanting romance, as well?" His tone became bitter. "'Twould be the only thing that would warrant the wait. The possibility of love. Otherwise, I could have been with a lonely widow or a tuppenny whore, long ago."

The possibility of love.

She buttoned her coat. She turned and put her hands out towards him, and there was a moment when she thought he would flinch away from her, but he did not. She buttoned his coat and let her hand rest for a moment on his lapel—the lapel she had clung to when he first walked into her cottage in Dunburn. When she thought she could keep him with her just by holding on to his coat. Then she moved to the seat opposite him and put on her gloves.

The possibility of love.

Yes, here he was. The not-stupid man.

She was the one who should be ashamed. He was a man who had cherished an ideal for a long time. But he was wise enough to have no care what others thought of his ideal.

He wanted her. He had shown that. He had said that. What was her hurry, after all?

"You are quite right, Dr. Andrews. You deserve romance."

"Ye do, too, Miss Lovelock."

Her voice trembled, and she hated herself for it. "I don't deserve you, Dr. Andrews."

"That is," he took a deep breath, "the single most erroneous statement I have ever heard."

They sat in silence, looking at each other.

"You exaggerate, Dr. Andrews."

"I dinnae, Miss Lovelock." He was very serious.

"Open, Sesame," she whispered.

He smiled.

Her heart melted. Perhaps she had not made an irrevocable mess of everything.

The light inside the carriage changed. It grew dark.

She looked out the window at swirling snow. It clearly had been falling for some time as it lay thickly on the side of the road. And it was falling very heavily now. The wind was gusting. It was hard to see more than ten feet out the carriage window. Alasdair slid over and joined her in looking out the window.

He made a low whistle and said, "Stay on this side of the carriage." He moved back across the seat and opened the opposite carriage door. He stood so half his body was outside in the falling snow.

She could hear him shouting to Paterson, but she could not hear what he said or Paterson's answer.

He pulled himself back inside the carriage and closed the door.

She was shivering now. Alasdair sat next to her and put both arms around her and rested his chin on top of her head.

"Ye were right. The carriage will likely have to stop soon."

Her teeth chattered. "Dr. Andrews. You do not have to hold me."

"On the contrary," he said and unbuttoned his coat and pulled her onto his lap and into his chest and wrapped his coat around her. "Because of yer small size, ye have a greater surface area-to-volume ratio than I do, therefore ye shed heat more quickly and are more likely to get chilled. Our bodies together will effectively decrease our surface area-to-volume ratios and thus conserve our heat."

She could not get close enough to him, and she felt like she wanted to burrow into his waistcoat. "Now you sound like Harry."

"And besides," he said and hesitated.

"Besides what?" she asked, her voice muffled by his chest.

"Caught in a snowstorm? Romantic, maybe?"

"Definitely." The shivers were abating. "Unless you are cold."

"Shall I kiss ye then to warm ye?"

She stopped shivering.

He still wanted to kiss her.

"Yes," she said and turned up her face.

He kissed her lips. And in his kiss, there was none of the fervor of the previous day or the previous hour. It was all tenderness.

But the want and the need and the ache that had consumed her in the carriage today returned at the touch of his lips. She almost took her arms from around his body and out of the warm cocoon he had made for her and put them up to his neck to pull his mouth and tongue down to hers.

But she refrained from doing so.

She realized she had already done to him, in a way, what Giles Fortescue had done to her. She had used his affection for her and her own greater experience—slight though it was, it was still greater than his—to push him too quickly into new intimacy. She had only paid attention to her own clutching need. And that had led to his embarrassment and their first—could she call it this?—disagreement.

There would be a time, she hoped, when she might be able to show him her desire, but this was not that time.

She would be patient. As Boyd Cormack had advised her to be. Of course, it had not been in this area that he had anticipated she would need her patience with Alasdair.

That thought amused her, and her mouth curled into a smile under his kiss.

He must have felt some change in her lips because he pulled his head back to look at her face.

"Ye are smiling," he said with a touch of relief.

"Yes," she said. "I am happy."

The carriage came to a stop.

Alasdair and Arabella extricated themselves from each other, and Alasdair buttoned up his coat, put on his hat and gloves, rewrapped his tartan scarf, and got out of the carriage.

Within minutes, he had come back in, the cold and the wind and the snow coming with him.

"We are going to have to abandon the carriage. The snow is too high, and the horses cannae pull the weight of the carriage through the snow."

"But the horses—"

"Paterson and Ewen are taking the harnesses off now. We will have to lead the horses. Paterson had already turned the carriage down a drive and thinks it leads to a house. We will hope that we'll find someplace warm soon. We will have to leave all the luggage, but ye may bring yer little reticule."

"Yes," she said.

Arabella already felt very cold within the confines of the carriage. Alasdair must have sensed that because he reached out and took from her neck the brown scarf and rewrapped it around her so it covered her entire lower face and went up over her bonnet. He made a snug knot.

"Hold fast to my hand," he said. "'Tis hard to see."

He opened the carriage door and went out and turned and handed her down. She stepped out into the wind and snow.

She stood in a drift that came up over her knees. Her hand in his, they picked their way to the front of the carriage. Paterson and Ewen had almost finished unharnessing the four horses.

Alasdair spoke to Paterson, and once the horses were unharnessed, they started moving forward.

She had not known walking could be so difficult. The snow clung to her dress so even as she lifted each leg as high as she could to make forward progress, she was pulled down. Only half a dozen steps and she was tired.

And so very cold. The wind was cutting and fierce.

But she was not wet. The insulation provided by her thick woolen stockings kept the snow that clung there from melting with her body heat. The wetness would come afterwards, when they got somewhere warm.

It was hard to believe there might be somewhere in the world that was warm.

Everything was very white. The air seemed solid at times, there was so much snow in it. She could not see where they were going, but that did not bother her as much as it should have. She only had the strength to pay attention to each individual step. She held her reticule in one hand and kept her other hand in Alasdair's. His other hand was on the bridle of one of the horses. She knew Paterson and Ewen—each holding a horse's bridle with one hand and sharing the bridle of the lead horse between them—were ahead of them because sometimes she managed to step into Ewen's leg holes in the snow and that helped her.

Alasdair turned to her every third step or so. She assumed

he was checking on her, making sure she was all right. At first, she tried to smile at him, to reassure him, but then she realized he couldn't see her smile through the scarf. So she just tried to keep up with him and not tug at his arm.

Her legs were very, very tired.

Alasdair cursed his stupidity.

Why had he not thought of this earlier? He stopped walking forward and took a step towards Arabella and let go of her hand. Still holding the reins attached to the bridle, he wrapped his arms around her waist and picked her up. He put his mouth to the side of her head, where he thought her ear might be, under the scarf and the bonnet.

"I'm going to put ye on the horse!" he shouted.

She nodded.

He lifted, and she reached her arms up, and he boosted, and she was astride, the top half of her body lying flat on the horse's back, her free arm clutching the horse's flanks.

The horse did not seem bothered.

Alasdair put his hand on her stockinged calf. With no saddle, with her so exhausted already, he must make sure she did not fall from the horse.

And was it so very wrong of him to take note of the fact that his hold on her leg constituted new territory?

He stepped forward, and the horse stepped forward with him.

After what seemed to be hours but might have only been minutes, he saw a light ahead. And he could see Ewen MacEwen and Paterson—or at least he assumed it was they —and the three horses. He came up behind them and recognized they were at a lodge or a gatehouse of some kind, and there was another man with a lantern, taking the bridle of one of the horses and leading Paterson and the other two horses away. Ewen, relieved of his horse, pushed his way to Alasdair.

"Ye are to take Miss Lovelock into the lodge, Doctor! We will get the horses to the stable!"

"Where are we?"

"'Tis the house of a lord!"

Ewen put his hand out, and Alasdair nodded and handed him the reins of the horse he had been leading. He turned to the horse's flank and put his hands under Arabella's arms and slid her off. Her eyes were open above the scarf and looking at him, and she linked her arms around his neck, and he was able to get one arm under her knees and the other under her back. He began trudging through the snow towards the lit windows in front of them.

Her arms were strong around his neck. She was holding herself up. Those were good signs.

Pushing against a wooden door, he saw a small room with a stone floor and a large room beyond. There was light and warmth. They were inside the lodge.

He put Arabella down on a low stool by the door and was glad to see she sat up straight and looked at him with her blue eyes. He closed the door and knelt down at her feet, taking off his hat and pushing the tartan scarf from his face.

"Are ye all right?"

She nodded, and he unwound the brown scarf from around her head and face, noticing for the first time that his fingers were numb and clumsy in his gloves.

The bottom half of her face appeared, and although she was pale, she was not blue. She smiled, and when he leaned forward to kiss her lips, they were not as cold as he had feared they would be.

"Ewen and Paterson have gone with the lodgekeeper to stable the horses."

"Good," she said. And he was so happy to hear her voice, he kissed her again. And again.

He was kneeling in water. He looked down at the stone floor, and there was a puddle there that had not been there before.

She cleared her throat. "We are melting."

"Aye." He grinned and got off his knees and into a crouch.

"I want," she said and lifted her dress, and his breath hitched for a moment. She went on, "I want to get the snow off my stockings before it melts more, and they get too wet."

He helped her, using his gloved hands to pick off the pieces of snow that clung to her stockings and her skirt and her petticoat. And if at times his hand lingered on her stocking-covered calf or ankle, she did not say anything.

"Where are we, Dr. Andrews?"

"I assume we are in England, in Northumberland. Shall we take off our boots and find the fire?" he asked. "I dinnae think the lodgekeeper will mind if we avail ourselves of that before he returns."

He took off his gloves and had to laugh at how he fumbled at her bootlaces. He blew on his fingers.

"Give them here," she said, and, after unbuttoning her own coat, she took his hands and placed them by the sides of her breasts, under her own arms and held them there, pressed between her upper arms and her trunk.

At first, he only had the perception of returning sensation. Then warmth. Then an acute awareness of the swell of her flesh next to his palms.

Only this morning, she had put his hand on her breast for the first time. Now both of his hands were almost on her breasts.

Very slowly, he slid his hands towards the front of her body, his palms following the delicious curve of the sides of her bosom. Now it could be said her breasts were actually being cupped by his hands. These lovely, miraculous, generous bits of flesh. Even encased in what he knew must be at least three layers —dress, stays, chemise—he could feel the heat and the softness. And very gently, he now dared to apply a bit of pressure.

Her body twitched slightly, but she did not pull away from his hands. He had been looking at his own hands and their placement, but now he looked up at her face, to gauge her reaction to his boldness. Her mouth hung open a bit, and her gaze was far away. Then her eyes settled on him.

"I suspect your hands have been adequately warmed."

He could not read her. Had he ventured too far? Almost certainly, yes. Feeling chastened and the rising heat of a blush on his face, he withdrew his hands and applied himself to the laces of her boots. "I'm sorry, Miss Lovelock."

She spoke over his bent head. "No, you are very good, Dr. Andrews, to warm my bosom as well."

He kept his head down, working on her wet laces, hiding his grin from her.

In just a few minutes, he had her in front of a good blaze in a cozy room, both of them on a bench close to the hearth, feeling the heat on their faces, putting their stockinged feet close to the fire. She took her bonnet off and her hair glinted gold in the firelight.

"When the lodgekeeper comes back, we will find out what kind of accommodations there are to be had for ye, Miss Love-lock."

"I'm not worried," she said and folded her hand into his. "I was never worried."

Seventeen

The lodgekeeper was a bachelor with a shiny, bald head and a stout middle. After he found places to hang their wet coats and hats and gloves and scarves, he put a kettle on the hob.

Arabella was glad to see neither Ewen MacEwen nor Paterson looked any the worse for wear. Particularly Ewen.

"I am a Highlander, miss," Ewen said, rubbing his hands in front of the fire. "We are descendants of the Vikings. Ice and snow are in our blood."

"We've never had a storm of snow like this in Northumberland," the lodgekeeper said. "Not in my life. So much and it is still coming down. I think we'll be digging out for days."

"You are very good to take us in," Arabella said. She still sat next to Alasdair on the bench, but, at her request, he had moved it farther from the fire. She was surprised how quickly she had come to feel the fire's heat. In the snow, it had been impossible to think of being too hot.

Of course, part of the warmth she was feeling might be due to the man at her side. To be sitting next to him, thinking of what had passed between them, how he had told her she was not ruined. And how he had kissed her so tenderly, even when she had been so wanton with him and hurt his feelings.

He was good. There was no other word for it. Good. Much too good for her, foolish and hasty and cruel as she was. But he was at her side now, and she was not going to let him go.

She continued to hold his hand, not caring what Paterson or Ewen McEwen or the lodgekeeper thought. *I will use his behavior as a guide. He does not object to our hands being linked. He does not pull away. Therefore, my hand can stay here.*

"I told one of the grooms to go up to the main house and let them know we had some visitors," the lodgekeeper said. "Once we get you warm, I'll be taking you up there to see the master. There is a house party here now, but it's a very fine manor, so there will be room for two more. I'll get the lad and your coachman settled with the grooms."

"And who is yer master so I may thank him for the hospitality when I meet him?" Alasdair asked.

"Lord Morpeth, Doctor. This is his barony. And now for something hot. I'll get the teapot ready. A cup will do a wonder, I should think." The lodgekeeper left the room.

Arabella thought she might cast up her accounts. She dropped Alasdair's hand and clutched his sleeve. She stood from the bench.

"We must go," she said.

Alasdair looked at Arabella's pale face.

"We cannae do that, I fear," he said. "What has happened?"

"I-I..." she faltered. She sat down again heavily. Her eyes moved rapidly over his face, and she chewed at her bottom lip with such vehemence that he worried she would cut it open.

Suddenly, she turned her head and looked at Ewen Mac-Ewen and Paterson. She spoke in a hushed but urgent voice.

"What did you tell the lodgekeeper, what did you tell him about us? About me and Dr. Andrews?"

Ewen shrugged. "I said nothing."

"I said there was a doctor and a young lady with us," Paterson said, scratching his head, "and the young lady likely needed to get inside sooner rather than later."

"Did you mention my name? Did you use my name? Did you say Miss Lovelock?"

"Nae." Paterson shook his head.

"And we," she looked at Alasdair, "did not give him our names yet."

"Nae, we didnae." Alasdair wanted to know why she was so agitated, where this was leading.

"Quickly, we must all agree that the doctor and I are married. Ewen. Paterson. I am Mrs. Andrews. I am not Miss Lovelock. I am his wife." She looked at Alasdair. "I am your wife."

"But—"

She quieted him with a finger to his lips as she had done before in her cottage in Dunburn. He remembered that moment so vividly. How she had urged him to stay with her despite there being no chaperone present.

"Please, Alasdair," she breathed.

Again, his first name in her mouth. And the suggestion they might be man and wife. Which was, of course, his most hoped-for wish for the future. His mind briefly touched on all that being man and wife might entail. He could not help himself and had to shift on the bench. She took her finger from his lips.

"Why, Miss Lovelock?" he asked.

"No," she said. "That is my old name. Now I am Arabella Andrews, your wife. Mrs. Andrews."

Her eyes pleaded with him. Did she not know he would do anything for her? True, he thought honesty a virtue, but for Arabella, he would lie a million times over.

"Ye are Mrs. Andrews," he said. He turned to Ewen and Paterson. "She is Mrs. Andrews."

Ewen grinned and shrugged. "Mrs. Andrews."

Paterson narrowed his eyes and grunted. "Aye."

Arabella laced her fingers with Alasdair's. "Thank you."

The lodgekeeper came back into the room with a tray laden with a teapot and cups and saucers and set it down on a table. He went to the hob and took down the kettle and filled the teapot with steaming water.

"I'll make sandwiches. And, after this has steeped, will you do me the honor of pouring, miss?"

"Missus," Alasdair said, his voice suddenly deeper at finding himself a married man. "Mrs. Andrews. And I am Dr. Andrews."

The lodgekeeper looked at him for a moment and then turned back to Arabella. "I am Farley, and I beg your pardon, Mrs. Andrews, but will you pour? I'm afraid the spout does drip a bit. And I'll go find some sugar."

"Yes," Arabella said and went to the table.

How graceful she is, my wife.

"My husband does like sugar in his tea," she called after Farley, who had disappeared through a door. She gave Alasdair a small smile. A wistful smile, not a mischievous one, and he longed to go to her and kiss her and comfort her and know the source of her distress so he could banish it.

When she brought Alasdair his cup of tea, he could see she was shaking, and he could hear a fine rattle of the cup in the saucer.

"Ye must tell me why ye are so altered, so upset," he said in the quietest voice he could manage. "Why ye want this pretense."

She looked around them, and so he did, too. The lodge-keeper Farley was out of the room, in the place that must be the kitchen or pantry. Ewen was sitting a good distance away, gulping his tea, and Paterson was looking out the far window at the gusting snow, holding his teacup to his lips and blowing on it.

"You must never tell my stepfather or your friend Thomas or my other brother-in-law, the viscount. Or anyone else," she said, looking down.

He nodded.

"Lord Morpeth is the man…the reason I left London, two years ago."

Her eyes met his.

Many seconds went by as Alasdair digested the meaning of what she had just said. Then he pulled her down next to him on the bench and held her wrist tightly. Another minute passed as he grappled with himself and her words.

For the last two years, he had told himself the incident was only important because it was the thing that had driven her away from her family. And because she had been hurt by it. And in the carriage, he had meant it when he told her she was not ruined. She wasn't. In a way, wasn't she even more magnificent than ever? To go and start a school in Dunburn. She would have never conceived of such a thing if she had stayed in London. And, of course, if she had stayed in London, she would likely be married to a duke of her own by now and would have been forever out of his reach.

But, now, suddenly, the incident seemed to have a great deal to do with him. With his self-respect. His place in the world. His merit. Because she was *his*. Well, if not quite *his*, certainly well on her way to becoming *his*.

He remembered Boyd's words in the public house in Dunburn.

Aye. He agreed with Boyd.

Alasdair was going to beat this fellow bloody. Not for Arabella. But for himself, selfishly. And for Boyd. For all the men in the world who loved sweet women who had been hurt by other men.

She seemed to read his mind.

"You must do nothing to him." Her mouth was on his ear. "Do not let Lord Morpeth provoke you. We will stay until the road is clear, and then we will go. That is all I want. That we leave this place, together."

He gripped her wrist more tightly. He was still wordless.

"You're hurting me, Alasdair."

He came to himself and released his hold on her. He looked down and saw her wrist was red and showed the marks of his fingers. He swallowed.

"Forgive me, please."

"If you promise no violence."

He breathed. In. Out. In. Out.

Could he promise her this? Of course, he could. He had taken that vow long ago. *Primum non nocere*. First, do no harm.

"Aye."

She kissed his cheek.

After tea, Farley and Paterson became worried it would get dark soon, so they all bundled up again and went out into the snow to walk to the stables and the grooms' cottage where Ewen and Paterson would stay and then onwards to the manor house. The wind was dying down.

Despite the fact they had been inside the lodge for over an hour, the drifts were not as high here as they had been on the drive. But Alasdair took no chances and picked up Arabella and carried her in his arms as soon as she stepped out the door of the lodge.

"I can walk," she said, frowning.

"I ken ye can, Mrs. Andrews." He must be careful not to

wear out her new name, but it gave him such pleasure to say it. "I have seen ye do it. But ye are short. The snow is high. I widnae want to lose ye in a drift and not be able to find ye until it thaws."

She fell silent and said nothing until they reached the stables, and then she reached her arm out to Ewen.

"Come and find me, Ewen, if you need anything."

"Aye, Mrs. Andrews," the boy said and winked.

A few minutes later, they were at the front door of the large house, and Alasdair set Arabella down on her own feet. He felt her tremble as his arm left her waist, so he put a hand on her shoulder, and when he did, she suddenly stood up straighter, thrust out her chin, and flashed him a smile that cut his heart in half.

The door opened, and Farley said something to someone, and then Farley turned and walked away, and Arabella walked through the door, and he followed.

"Bother," Arabella said, as she took off her brown scarf. "We are bringing in the snow."

"Do not worry, miss." The tall, middle-aged butler with silver hair held out his hand to take the scarf.

"Oh, no, I will put my scarf in my reticule here."

"'Tis madam," Alasdair corrected the butler.

"Madam," said the butler and bowed and took their gloves and coats and her bonnet and Alasdair's hat.

"Nae, I'll keep my scarf, too," Alasdair said, snatching back the bit of bright-green tartan.

"And your names for when I speak to Lord Morpeth?" the butler intoned.

"Dr. and Mrs. Andrews," Alasdair said, folding his scarf carefully and putting it between his waistcoat and his shirt where it would not fall out. *So it is against my heart. My armor.*

"You may tell him he is already friends with Mrs.

Andrews," Arabella said and giggled, "from when she had another name."

As they stood together in the grand hall and pretended to look at the pictures hanging there, she said under her breath to him, "I am doing what I must to keep my pride, Dr. Andrews. I am acting like a woman who thinks what happened was unimportant and of no consequence. Which I am sure is exactly how Lord Morpeth feels."

She turned away from the paintings and rose up on her toes and threw her arms around his neck. "And, of course, I am madly in love with my husband," she said and pressed herself to him and gave him a long kiss.

He was caught off guard by this. The word *love* from her. It was like a dagger, piercing his soul. At first, it was sweet, but then he thought, *She is not speaking of me but of some facsimile husband she will use to score a point against this Baron Morpeth.* The sweetness became a wrenching pain.

But still his arms went around her with no thought, gathering her closer as if he could not get enough of her. And indeed, he couldn't—her fragrance, her warm mouth, the swell of her breasts. He was very much aware this was his first time feeling her soft curves against his whole body. A mere ninety-degree turn to make them horizontal, and it would be like they were in a bed together. Like a real husband and wife.

Surely, she could feel his length lengthening.

She broke the kiss—too soon, he thought—and came off her tiptoes and released his neck but did not step away. She looked down and then back up at his face. "I think you may like having a wife more than you let on, Dr. Andrews."

And that made him smile, and she said, "I did not even have to say *Open Sesame* this time."

Eighteen

Arabella knew she would not be able to carry on her brave act without Alasdair at her side, helping her tell the lie that he was her husband and she was cherished despite what had gone before. He made it possible for her to pretend she was the woman she might have been if Alasdair had declared himself years ago.

Unafraid. A bit mischievous. Satisfied. Well-loved.

She wanted Giles to know someone *had* wanted her the way she should be wanted—as a wife. She wanted him to know she had not shriveled up and died from the pain and humiliation he had caused her. She had survived, and now she was here with the love of her life, her husband. Even if the doctor had not yet made that promise to her. But there was still hope for that, wasn't there? Alasdair had forgiven so many of her flaws already.

A laugh rang through the hall, a laugh she remembered. She did not hide her cringe from Alasdair.

"I wondered who among my former acquaintance this might be, but I would have never guessed Arabella Lovelock!"

Giles was walking towards her with swaggering, long

strides. Just as light on his feet. Just as big and towering. Same dark hair, dark eyes. She should not be surprised he looked the same. It had only been a little over two years.

She curtsied. "Lord Morpeth." She could feel Alasdair bow next to her. She put her arm through his and clasped her own hands, forming a link. She felt Alasdair's other hand settle on top of her forearm.

"This is my husband, Dr. Andrews. Darling, this is Lord Morpeth." She looked up at Alasdair, willing him to behave.

"Thank ye for yer hospitality in this snowstorm, Lord Morpeth," Alasdair said stiffly. "I am obliged to ye."

Oh, good, he was trying to be civil.

Giles' eyes swept over Alasdair with a degree of curiosity, but his gaze quickly returned to Arabella, and, as he bowed, he let his eyes continue to rest on her.

"I had not heard you had married, Miss Love—I mean, Mrs. Andrews."

She smiled coquettishly even as the bile rose in her throat. "And I had not heard you were married, either, when last we met, my lord."

Shock came to his eyes because she had brought their history forward openly and without shame. Oh, yes, she had startled him, she could tell. Here, in his own house, she had put him on his back foot. She felt a great deal of pride in that.

"Oh, but I forgive you for your deceit, Lord Morpeth." She wished she had a fan or a lorgnette so she could tap him with it. "How young and foolish I was. Not to read my *Debrett's* and find this out. I look forward to meeting Lady Morpeth."

"Yes," he said, and his eyes took on the hurt and pained look she remembered. "She is not well."

"Oh, I am sorry." And she was. She almost made a move towards him to show her sympathy, but Alasdair held her tightly by his side, and she remembered that the man with the wounded eyes was not a good man. The man with his arm laced through hers was. She looked up at Alasdair, hoping to catch his eye, to show him how much she cared for him and how little for the man across from her, but Alasdair was looking at Giles.

"My husband is a physician," she said. "Perhaps he could attend on your wife."

Giles hesitated. "Yes." He seemed to make a decision. "Come and meet the house party. We are all drinking rum punch and making wagers on how long we will be buried in snow."

Their host led the way down the hall to the open door of a large, light-filled room beyond. As they walked, Alasdair removed his hand from where it had rested atop her arm, but she kept her hands clasped, her arms linked around his, staying close, deliberately bumping his arm with her breast and his leg with her hip as they walked.

He did not seem to notice.

Then they were in the drawing room, and Arabella was surprised in the most marvelous of ways.

"Rebecca! Juliana!"

It was the Dalrymple girls, those dear, sweet girls whom she had not seen since she had left London. She broke away from Alasdair's arm, and there was such hugging and kissing and squealing and giggling.

But she was mistaken. It wasn't the Dalrymple girls, plural, anymore. Rebecca was still a Dalrymple, but Juliana had married Sir Timothy and was now Lady Colborne.

Arabella curtsied to Sir Timothy, who seemed the same vaguely irritated and fatigued man he had always been.

"And Rebecca, Juliana, you must meet my husband." In her excitement, she found it easy to think he was her husband, and she longed to show him off. "Dr. Alasdair Andrews. Alasdair, these are my friends, my very dear friends." She was unexpectedly emotional. "Lady Colborne and Lady Rebecca Dalrymple."

With a serious face, Alasdair bowed and said, "I widnae have guessed ye three were friends." But then he raised his eyebrows, and Arabella knew he was teasing her, just like a real husband might. How kind, how good he was. She felt such a warmth that she longed to put her arms around his neck again.

Rebecca clutched Arabella's arm.

Juliana gasped.

"Dr. Alasdair Andrews," breathed Rebecca.

"He of the auburn hair," Juliana said.

"Green eyes!" Rebecca squeaked.

"Scottish burr." Juliana smiled.

Arabella knew there was one more thing to show her friends.

"Alasdair." She tugged on his arm, and, when he leaned down with a bewildered look on his face, she whispered in his ear, "Open Sesame."

He grinned.

"Dimples!" Juliana and Rebecca shrieked simultaneously. Arabella gave Alasdair an impulsive kiss on the ear.

Alasdair shot a questioning glance at Arabella. He must think the three of them were Bedlamites.

"I'll tell you later." Arabella formed the words silently with her lips, and Alasdair nodded in acknowledgement. She sighed happily as she moved away from him to sit on a sofa with Juliana and Rebecca.

Arabella cared not one whit she was in Giles' house in her plain gray woolen traveling dress or that she had pinned her own hair this morning and had not looked at it since then. Juliana and Rebecca were here, Juliana sitting on her right side and Rebecca on her left.

And Alasdair, her Alasdair, was in the room with her.

"You must tell us, Arabella, when did you get married?"

"We have not heard one word of this! Does your mother know?"

Arabella now started to feel uncomfortable. What if Alasdair had no intention of marrying her, ever? She would be caught in the lie if ever she returned to her life in England. But if Alasdair didn't want her, she would never have a life in England. Never.

"It is very recent," she temporized.

"Is that why you don't have a ring?" Juliana asked.

A ring. She didn't have a ring. She had not thought of that.

"Perhaps you eloped," Rebecca said.

"Y-yes," Arabella faltered.

"So not a big wedding," Juliana said.

Rebecca clutched at Arabella's hand. "Oh, how romantic. And he is Scottish just as you said. Did you elope to Scotland?"

"We were in Scotland," Arabella said slowly.

She felt something cold and metal in her left hand. She kept it in her palm but pressed it with her fingers to see what it was.

A ring.

She looked at Rebecca, who smiled at her. She looked at Rebecca's right hand and saw a red line around her pinky. A red line where a ring had sat until just a moment ago.

"Your fingers are so small compared to mine. I think it will fit your ring finger," Rebecca whispered in Arabella's ear as Juliana talked about the elopement of Miss Sarah Lymington to a lieutenant in—now, which regiment was it?—and how they gotten lost on the way to Gretna Green.

And, indeed, the ring did fit.

. . .

As Arabella settled herself with her friends, Alasdair met the Marquess and Marchioness of Painswick. He didn't much like the look of the marquess, who seemed a vain and preening man. And the dark-haired and bejeweled marchioness was clearly taking very high doses of some opiate, likely laudanum, as her pupils were approximately a sixteenth of an inch in diameter and she seemed confused as to where she was.

Lord Morpeth introduced Mr. and Mrs. Swinton.

"But," Alasdair said. "I have surely made yer acquaintance before, Mr. Swinton, Mrs. Swinton."

The Swintons—he silver-haired and perhaps fifty, she buxom and red-haired and Alasdair's age—shrugged.

"We travel a great deal for pleasure," Mr. Swinton said. "It would not surprise me if we had crossed paths at an inn somewhere."

"Have ye ever been to Sommerleigh?" Alasdair asked.

They looked at each other and again shrugged.

"I don't recall, Dr. Andrews," Mrs. Swinton said.

Lady Lyndmouth was introduced next. Petite, blonde, supercilious. About Alasdair's age as well. Wearing lavender, the color of half mourning. A fairly recent widow, then. Sometime in the last year. She was constantly reaching out to touch Morpeth, to brush his arm or his shoulder. And if she was not touching him, she was looking at him, following him with her eyes.

Alasdair next bowed to Morpeth's brother-in-law Sir Timothy Colborne, brother to the unseen Lady Morpeth and also the husband of one of Arabella's friends on the sofa. Sir Timothy yawned in the middle of the introduction.

Alasdair turned to look at the three women on the sofa, and he could hear Arabella's laugh and was happy for her. Then he turned his head and observed Morpeth downing a glass of rum punch, also staring at Arabella.

I still want to beat him to a bloody pulp.

A half an hour later, Alasdair could tell Arabella was exhausted, despite the giggles and whispers on the sofa with her friends. She had had that long walk in the snow before he had thought to put her on the horse. And, since breakfast, all she had taken was a small cup of tea, having refused the sandwiches in the lodge. Perhaps she felt she could not eat after hearing she would be soon facing Lord Morpeth. But how well she had done in the front hall with Morpeth, how brave she had been. Dauntless, as always.

But now she needed someone to arrange her rest and nourishment.

With a start, he realized that someone was Alasdair Andrews.

"Mrs. Andrews should retire. My lord," he turned to Morpeth, "would it be possible for someone to take us to our rooms? And perhaps for some food on a tray to be brought for Mrs. Andrews? I dinnae think she will be able to stay upright for dinner."

"Certainly," Morpeth said smoothly. "In my experience, Mrs. Andrews has a great deal of trouble staying upright, no matter the circumstances."

Daggers of light flashed in Alasdair's vision. He would have thought he was about to have a seizure except the moment passed and he could feel his nails digging into his palms. He willed himself to recall the promises he had made as a young doctor during his training and the promise he had made to Arabella in the lodge.

He then also remembered the piece of tartan sitting between his waistcoat and his shirt. His armor, yes, but also a favor from a lady. He could still parry.

"The privilege of being a husband," he said through his teeth, "is that I ensure Mrs. Andrews has nae trouble, at all. With anything. Ever. Anywhere. From anyone."

Morpeth inclined his head. "Indeed, Dr. Andrews." He

turned to his butler, who had been serving the rum punch, and told him to take the doctor and his wife to their rooms.

Oh, to have the privilege of a husband, really and truly. For Arabella to be Mrs. Andrews in law as she already was in his heart.

When they were away from this evil man and his house, Alasdair would lay his soul bare to her.

Nineteen

Arabella yawned as she went up the stairs on Alasdair's arm. She hadn't minded Alasdair interrupting her talk with Juliana and Rebecca since she had been about to doze off in the warm room after drinking a glass of rum punch on an empty stomach. And she would see her friends tomorrow. It was wonderful.

"I understand your luggage is with your abandoned carriage, of course," the butler said as he led them up the stairs. "If the snow stops tomorrow, we will send someone out to recover it. Until that time, we will endeavor to supply whatever you need."

At the top of the stairs, the butler took a right turn and went to a door and opened it. The chamber behind the door was a lovely boudoir with a big bed that looked like a piece of soft heaven to Arabella right now.

"Lady Rebecca Dalrymple says she wants her lady's maid to attend on you tonight, Mrs. Andrews."

"Goodness." Arabella laughed. "I don't need a lady's maid. I just need a nightdress and some warm water. And a hairbrush for the morning."

The butler bowed. "I will send the lady's maid along with those items." He stepped outside the room and waited.

Alasdair hesitated by the door. "Goodnight, Mrs. Andrews."

She turned. How handsome and kind and not-stupid he was, and how glad she was that he was with her. How she wished they really were married.

"Goodnight, Alasdair. And thank you."

He closed the door.

The butler had walked a dozen yards down the hall before Alasdair caught up with him.

"Excuse me," Alasdair said. "I dinnae ken yer name, forgive me."

The butler stopped and turned to him. "It is Andrews."

"Oh, I see. Aye. A good name. Are ye a Scot?"

"My great-grandfather was, Doctor."

"Will ye show me to my room?"

"Down this way, in the other wing."

Alasdair considered.

"Nae, thank ye." He turned and started walking back. "I'll sleep with my wife tonight."

He rapped on her door and heard her say, "Come in."

He opened the door to see she was sitting on the edge of the bed. It looked like she might have fallen asleep sitting up and had only come back awake at his knock.

"What is it, Alasdair?" she said with her eyelids half-mast, her head nodding.

He closed the door behind him. "I'm sorry, but I'm going to sleep here tonight, Miss Lovelock. I dinnae feel comfortable leaving ye alone in this house owned by that man."

"You're going to sleep here?" she said, suddenly looking very wide awake.

"Dinnae be alarmed," he said. "I will sleep on the floor or in a chair."

"You will not."

"Aye, I will."

"You most certainly will not!"

A knock came, and it was Lady Rebecca Dalrymple's lady's maid with hot water and a nightdress and a hair brush.

Alasdair excused himself and waited in the hallway, hovering until the maid left. Then he knocked and re-entered. He must make it clear he only wished to protect her. She was safe with him.

Arabella was standing in the middle of the room in bare feet and a white nightdress that was much too big for her, with her golden hair twisted into a thick plait. Her face was flushed and shiny, and he knew she must have just washed it.

She stamped one foot. "You will not sleep on the floor or in a chair when there is a perfectly good bed to be had."

She pointed at the bed. Her bed.

Oh. Oh. She did not distrust him. She had not objected to him sleeping in the room with her. She had been concerned only for his comfort.

Well, she should distrust him. In so many ways, she was still an innocent. Did she not understand men? And she was his responsibility.

"A perfectly good bed that ye should be in right now. 'Tis far too cold for ye to be out of bed in just," he swallowed, "a nightdress."

"Is that a doctor's order?"

"I—pardon me?"

"I said," she smiled, "is that a doctor's order or is that a husband's order, Dr. Andrews?"

"I suppose 'tis nae one or the other."

She lost her smile and looked almost sad. She used both hands to lift up her long nightdress and walked to the bed and climbed in using the bed stairs, still having to hop a bit at the end. She stayed sitting up but pulled the covers over her legs.

"I thought you might flirt with me a little, Alasdair."

"I am sorry. I dinnae ken how to."

Her smile came back. "I will teach you. I am very good at it. Or, at least, I used to be."

There were brief daggers of light in his field of vision again as he thought of the hypothetical other men with whom she might have flirted. And the very real one downstairs with whom she almost certainly had. He took a breath and attempted to calm himself.

"So if I were to flirt with ye, what would be the right answer to yer question?"

A knock again and it was a footman and two chambermaids. The footman carried a large tray with several covered dishes. He put it down on a table by the fire and bowed and left. The two chambermaids were giggling quite a bit, clearly amused by a husband in his wife's room, and they carried more hot water and towels and a nightshirt and a banyan for Alasdair.

"Whose are these?" he said suspiciously. He did not want to wear Morpeth's clothes and not just because they would have reminded him how big the man was.

Both chambermaids giggled, and one said, "They belong to Andrews, I mean our Andrews, the butler Andrews, that is to say, Dr. Andrews." After curtsying, the maids beat a hasty retreat.

Alasdair put the nightshirt and the banyan down on a chair and went to the table. He started lifting covers from dishes.

"What would ye like to eat? Cake and two different tarts. A cream soup of some kind, codfish, I think. And roast pheasant with potatoes. And some beef. And some pickles. What would ye like, Miss Lovelock?"

There was no answer.

He looked over. Arabella had fallen asleep, sitting up against the pillows in the bed.

He covered the dishes. He went to the bed and, through the covers, he tugged on her legs so she now lay flat with her head on a pillow. He pulled the counterpane up to her chin. She did not move.

He went over to the fire and looked at it for a long time. Eventually, he took off his tailcoat, and, as he went to unbutton his waistcoat, he felt a bit of wool there. The bright-green tartan scarf Arabella had made for him. He took it out and held it to his face. It was soft against his jaw, his nose, his mouth. There was no scent of her on it; there never had been. But the fact that she had made it for him and its softness—he couldn't help thinking how all parts of his face had touched all parts of her face in the carriage.

And the piece of wool itself. She had chosen it some time ago, knowing it was meant for someone of his name.

He still did not know what to make of that. He was afraid of construing something hopeful and romantic from something that might be merely coincidence. Or fondness for a color.

He laid the scarf down and finished taking off his waistcoat and his shirt, then his boots and stockings. He went to the basin and poured the warm water into it and washed his face, his upper half, and, finally, his feet. He toweled himself dry quickly and went and put the scarf around his neck and donned the nightshirt and the banyan and sat down in a wing chair by the fire. He would leave his trousers on. In fact, he might have to put his thick stockings back on. It was cold.

"Cake, please."

He jumped. He turned his head, and Arabella was lying in the bed, in the same position he had put her in, only with her eyes open.

"Only cake?" He wondered how long she had been awake and was glad he had never completely undressed.

"Well, that's all I remember you saying." She sat up, and dozens of tendrils of her hair had escaped the plait and surrounded her head like a golden nimbus. "Why don't you bring it all over here, and we'll have a picnic?"

He brought the large tray over carefully and put it down on the center of the bed.

Arabella patted the mattress next to her.

He chose instead to sit at the foot of the bed, on the other side from her. He took all the covers off the dishes.

"What appeals to ye, Miss Lovelock?"

She scooted down and over a little bit so she was only partly sitting up.

"Oh, it all looks lovely. I'll have some of everything."

But then she made no move to pick up a fork or a plate.

"I am so tired," she said and yawned.

"Ye have to eat something."

"Yes," she said and laid her head back on the pillows and looked at him through her half-mast lashes.

A slow dawning.

"Is this flirtation?" he said.

Arabella sighed. "Not yet. I am flirting with you, but it only becomes flirtation when you flirt back."

"And I would flirt back by...?"

"Perhaps by offering to feed me."

"Feed ye?"

"Yes, because I am so tired, you would feed me. Like I'm a baby bird in a nest."

"Have ye ever had other men feed ye?"

"Alasdair!" She sat bolt upright. "I would never!" He could tell she was furious.

"But," he said weakly, "ye said ye were good at flirting. How did ye become good at it if ye didnae practice it?"

She tossed her head. "Some things come to some people naturally."

"I see." He could not think of a single thing that came to him naturally. Hadn't he put his head down and worked hard at everything his whole life?

"Like kissing. You are a natural kisser, Alasdair. Even your first kiss yesterday…oh, it was wonderful."

He colored. "I, uh, I think ye are only saying that because I am now yer husband."

She smiled. "That's it. Very good. That's flirtation."

"I see," he said. But he didn't really. Had she been sincere about his kissing? "Shall I feed ye now?"

"Yes, please. You'll see. It will be fun."

It was fun. It made him laugh. It made her laugh. He and Arabella on a bed. His spooning up bites for her to eat and having a reason to stare at her pink lips. Her insistence he take a bite for every bite she took.

They had eaten the soup, the cake, the beef, one of the tarts, and he was tearing bites of pheasant off the carcass for her to eat from his fingers.

"So what was the right answer?" he said. "Ye ne'er told me. For flirtation. Doctor's orders or husband's orders?"

She smiled. "Do you really not know?"

"Nae, I dinnae." He tore off a small piece of pheasant and put it in her mouth and thrilled to the sensation of her taking his hand in her two small ones and carefully licking the juices from his fingers.

"The right answer," she licked his thumb, "is," she licked his index finger, "either one," and she licked his middle finger.

He could hear his own breath becoming heavy, feel his blood rushing places where it shouldn't.

She released his hand. "If you had said husband's orders, then we could have had a delightful exchange about how you weren't really my husband, but maybe," she gave him a sidelong look, "you wanted to be, and what you might do to me if you were. And if you had said doctor's orders, then we could have had you examine me. Maybe. Under the nightdress."

He throbbed.

She paused for a moment and laughed. "Do you know, Alasdair, four years ago, just after we met, that was my fondest wish. That I would become ill or pretend to be ill and you would come and examine me."

"Ye must ne'er wish to be ill."

"No, of course not, it was just foolishness, I didn't really wish to be ill, I just wished…for you."

He lunged forward and kissed her. He was still holding the plate of pheasant, so it was awkward, but she put her hands in his hair and held him there.

When the kiss was over, he returned to his seated position at the far end of the bed. He had pressed his body against hers during the kiss and had felt her softness, her curves, her warmth under the nightdress. The temptation to keep kissing her, to lie down beside her, to run his hands all over her body was very strong. To give her a version of the examination she had once longed for.

"Is flirtation," he said and then cleared his throat. "Is flirtation the same thing as romance?"

"No," she said. "And you prove that."

"How is that?"

"You are terrible at flirtation, but I suspect you have a gift for romance."

"I see."

"And that," she said, "is far preferable to the opposite case."

An hour later, they had eaten all the food off the tray. Arabella was lying back and groaning and saying she was exceedingly full and why had she thought eating the second tart a good idea? Alasdair understood this was a rhetorical question and did not answer. He removed the tray to the table and lowered the wicks on the lamps and went and sat in the wing chair and put on his stockings. Then he took his tailcoat and draped it over himself.

The room was dark except for the glowing embers of the grate.

"You're very far away, Dr. Andrews."

"Aye. I saw ye have a ring on yer left hand now."

"Yes, Rebecca noticed I had no ring and gave me one. I don't think she will share our secret with anyone else."

"She is a good and true friend, then?"

"Yes." A silence. "Are you really going to sleep in that chair?"

"Aye."

"Is there anything I could say that might convince you to come into the bed?"

"Nae."

"But I have thought of something. A text in support of my cause. *If two lie together, then they have heat: but how can one be warm alone?* Ecclesiastes."

He couldn't help himself. "Did my cousin— Did Boyd Cormack say that to ye?"

"Dr. Andrews, you must not always be so suspicious of me."

"I'm sorry. 'Tis nae ye I'm suspicious of."

"I forgive you. A little jealousy can add to the excitement of flirtation. But only a little. It's like whisky for me. A little goes a long way. Too much is tiresome."

He noticed she had not answered his question. He mustered his memory.

"*God will nae suffer ye to be tempted beyond what ye are able.* Corinthians. Good night, Miss Lovelock."

"Good night, Alasdair." And the sound of a body shifting on a bed.

It was cold. He should have looked earlier for an extra blanket or rug to cover himself. But he didn't want to get up now and disturb her with his movement. Then a much more urgent thought occurred to him, and he got up from the chair and locked the door.

TWENTY

Despite having a good deal of practice sleeping in a chair, Alasdair slept fitfully. Finally, he heard some stirrings in the house. In the darkened room, Arabella continued to breathe deeply, evenly. He crossed to the windows and twitched the curtains aside. The sun was up, but the morning was a gray one. Snow still fell. He crossed back to his chair and dressed himself in the dark. Then he sat and waited.

Just as he was about to drop off into a doze again, he heard Arabella stir.

"Alasdair?"

"Aye?"

"Is it morning?"

"Aye."

"Would you light a lamp or open the curtains so I can see you?"

He crossed back to the window and opened the curtains. The weak light filtered in. He turned back to her.

She was sitting up in the bed, her hair a wild, golden mass around her head. "Is it still snowing?"

"Aye," he said and smiled at the sight of her. She was heart-breakingly beautiful.

"Come sit next to me." She patted the mattress. He saw she had his brown scarf next to her.

He crossed to the bed and hovered for a moment before sitting down next to her.

There was a warm, sweet scent around the bed. It was the smell he had come to think of as Arabella's.

The bedcovers were at her waist. The nightdress was the only thing shielding her breasts from his eyes, and he thought he could see a shadow of her areolas and her nipples under the thin fabric. But he wasn't sure.

"Am I so frightening, Alasdair?" She reached out and straightened the tartan scarf at his neck.

"Nae," he said and forced himself to look at her face. "But ye do have the mane of a lion this morning."

"Yes," she said but made no move to arrange her hair. "I always have in the morning. My lady's maids have always despaired of me and my hair."

He permitted himself to touch her hair as a reward for not spending the night in her bed, for not touching her breasts now. He stroked a tendril, pulling on it gently so it straightened and then releasing it so it curled back again.

"Yer hair is like an alive thing." He brushed another tendril near her temple with his fingers.

"Yes, you will see it is quite untamable," she said and turned her face into his hand and kissed his palm.

Her lips on that sensitive place. Warm. A small lick of a soft tongue. His cock throbbed, and he thought of ripping off the covers and her nightdress, baring her entirely to his eyes, his hands, his body.

After a moment, he withdrew his hand and got up from the bed.

A fortuitous knock and a rattle of the knob of the locked door.

"'Twill be yer friend's lady's maid," he said. "I will leave ye."

Her eyes looked hurt, so he added, "I look forward to breakfasting with ye, Miss Lovelock. Do ye think it will cause a scandal if I feed ye at the table?"

"Certainly," she said and laughed. "But I hope you will do it anyway."

At the breakfast table, Alasdair made a very good breakfast of ham, toast, smoked haddock, black pudding, porridge, tea. There were no eggs, he was informed by the butler Andrews.

"The chickens do not seem to like the snow, Doctor."

"Thank ye, by the way," Alasdair said under his breath, "for the nightshirt and banyan."

"You are welcome, sir. I thought we might be of a size." He bowed and went to refill the marquess' teacup.

Alasdair was afraid to look at Arabella eating porridge, worried the sight of her lips sliding over a spoon would elicit in him the same savage and possessive desire that her kiss on his palm had.

Instead, he looked at Morpeth throughout the meal.

The baron was a big, tall man. Alasdair was just over six feet, but Lord Morpeth must be at least three inches taller. And he possessed a massive chest and shoulders. Alasdair flashed on Ewen saying Highlanders had Viking blood. Morpeth had the body of a Viking—a conqueror, a pillager, a rapist.

But Lord Morpeth was no Viking in his coloring. His overly long hair was near-black, and his eyes were just as dark. There was mat of thick hair on the backs of his large hands, and his jaw last night had been shadowed, a sure sign his valet's razor could not keep up with his beard.

Alasdair hated his red hair more than ever.

And Lord Morpeth was…what was the word? Oh, yes, brooding. Probably couldn't tell a joke to save his life. Definitely couldn't save a life. Probably modeled himself after that other baron—what was his name? The mad poet? Byron, that was it. Lord Byron. Morpeth was a Visigoth Lord Byron.

No wonder women couldn't resist him.

It was a tedious morning. There were cards, books, idle chat. Alasdair partook in none. The sight of the Swintons playing whist was so familiar to him, but he still could not place where or when he might have met them before.

He paced the halls, climbed the stairs up and down, but did not like to get too far away from Arabella. She was his sun, and he was a comet in a highly eccentric orbit around her. She sat in the drawing room and talked for hours with her friends.

He did not know what there could be to talk about. It had only been two years or so since Arabella had last seen her friends. He had had thirteen years separation from his schoolmates, but, at Dr. Murray's funeral, he had found five minutes was more than adequate to discuss the events of the intervening years.

He noticed Lady Lyndmouth hovered around Lord Morpeth in much the same way he circled Arabella. Not directly engaging the baron's attention but not moving too far away from him either. Always in the periphery.

The snow continued to fall, but the wind did not blow.

Maybe tomorrow he and Paterson would be able to get to the carriage and retrieve Arabella's trunk. Having her dresses was likely important to her. The borrowed nightdress had been fine—he sucked in his breath at thinking of her in the nightdress, how he had pressed briefly against her body last night when he had kissed her in the bed and how he had wanted to rip it away this morning—but she was too small to borrow the dresses of her friends.

But he could remedy that for her. He longed to do something. For her.

Arabella did not enjoy her breakfast. Alasdair did not feed her as he had teased he might. He sat several seats away from her. He conversed politely with Sir Timothy and Mr. Swinton. He did not even look at her.

There had never been such a long morning. Alasdair barely paid her any attention. He was preoccupied, fretting, constantly walking. He probably had never had a day of idleness like this in his life, and he had no idea what to do with himself. His medical journals were all in the carriage.

In one morning, she had caught up on an entire two years of gossip. She still loved Juliana and Rebecca, but to talk to them for so long was wearing when what she really longed to do was to shut herself away with Alasdair, run her fingers through his hair, and continue the kissing from the carriage. Being in a warm house with fewer thick garments might make certain things possible that had not been before.

At one point, she and Juliana got up and linked their arms and walked the halls and the stairs of the house to get some exercise. Rebecca stayed in the drawing room, looking at an illustrated book with Lady Lyndmouth.

"I wish you so much happiness, Juliana. You married Sir Timothy, after all, just as you said you would."

"Yes, and I had a dozen new dresses for all the parties before and after the wedding, and once I was married, so many new jewels. And you, Arabella?"

"Me?"

Juliana hugged her arm closely. "We are married women now, so you can tell me. Is your Scottish doctor all that you thought he would be?"

"He is," Arabella said slowly, afraid Juliana might ask questions she could not answer. "He is and more."

"Well, he is spying on us."

Arabella turned and could see Alasdair, down the hall, staring intently at a painting.

"He doesn't let you get too far away from him," said Juliana and led Arabella up the stairs. "He is quite attentive."

"Yes."

"And deliciously handsome. I know, of course, what happened to you two years ago and why you disappeared," Juliana said. "Sir Timothy told me. Rebecca does not know. It has been hard to keep it from her and the rest of my sisters. They all wanted to know why you had left London. But Mama and Papa said, of course, none of them could know. It wouldn't be right for them to hear that kind of salacious gossip when they were not yet married. Mama and Papa now think it was a mistake they ever let us girls be friends with you. Since your mother was an actress before. They said bad blood will out."

They were at the top of the stairs. Arabella dropped Juliana's arm and opened her mouth to defend her mother, herself, her blood. But she could not. After all, Juliana was just echoing Arabella's own most private thoughts on the matter.

Juliana continued down the upstairs hall. "But I think the doctor gives you an excellent sort of excuse."

Arabella was forced to follow. "What do you mean by that?"

"Well, one would not expect a physician's wife to move in society. Your marriage explains your absence. But I must know," she lowered her voice, "was he the one who ruined you?"

Arabella's mind churned. She had long tried not to think about her scandal and what details might be known. Because of the Pluckers and her initials and the tokens pinned to the wall in her stepfather's club. But she was glad Juliana did not know who had lain with her.

But she would not let anyone think ill of Alasdair. Better she be thought promiscuous than Alasdair be falsely accused of doing what Giles had done.

"No, it wasn't him."

"And yet he married you. You are so lucky, Arabella."

"I don't feel lucky."

Juliana's retort was bitter. "You should. It is inordinately unfair that your used-up old mother wound up with a catch like the Duke of Middlewich—almost two decades younger than she!—and you should have a handsome, doting doctor, and neither of you obeyed the rules."

Arabella looked at Juliana and saw her pain. "Are you unhappy?"

"Of course not. I am to have a completely new set of dresses for spring from Madame Dupont. Everyone says she is the next Madame Beauchamp. And I am thinking of taking a lover."

Arabella gasped.

"You gasp, Arabella? You dare to be shocked at me?" Juliana did not veil her anger. "You defied propriety. Why shouldn't I? Sir Timothy is so dreary. Now that I know what it is all about and have an inkling of what it could be, I must have some thrill in the bedchamber before it's too late. The marquess, Lord Painswick, has been giving me that look, you know? But I would much prefer Lord Morpeth, I think."

Arabella swallowed. "I want you to be happy, Juliana, but I don't think either of those men will make you happy."

"Well, then, shall I set my sights on Dr. Alasdair Andrews?" Juliana nodded down the hall, and Arabella turned her head and saw Alasdair, poised on the top step of the stairs, pretending to look at his watch. "I think, however, given his devotion to you, I would be quite out of my depth."

"Juliana, please don't do anything hasty."

"Why not? I am already married. I have all the time in the world to repent in leisure."

The bell for luncheon rang, and Arabella was glad to separate from Juliana and sit next to Rebecca at the table and talk of pleasant things such as the books Rebecca had read recently. Strangely, Rebecca did not discuss the upcoming Season and her hopes for a proposal. Could she no longer have any interest in such things? Perhaps she had a secret love like the one Arabella had harbored for Alasdair. Arabella had always thought Rebecca was quite the prettiest of the Dalrymple daughters. It was surprising she was not yet engaged or married.

After eating, as everyone was standing to leave the table, Arabella yawned. Alasdair was at her side immediately. He did not say anything, but she looked up at him and could feel herself pinken. His hand brushed hers. She took his arm.

"Thank you, Dr. Andrews."

It was the first time he had touched her today besides playing with her hair. And that did not really count, did it? It wasn't the same as skin. After all, her hair could not feel.

She made her apologies to Rebecca, saying she was still tired from yesterday, and Alasdair led her to the stairs.

As soon as they got into her bedchamber and Alasdair closed the door behind them, Arabella had her arms up around his neck.

"Kiss me, Alasdair," she said. He put his arms around her and bent his head down and his warm lips pressed against hers. She trembled as the kiss went on, his mouth becoming hungrier as the seconds passed, his tongue dipping into her mouth, his lips roaming over her jaw and back to her lips.

She could feel his arousal growing, his member pressing

into her upper abdomen. She also had an ache between her legs, and she cursed her height. Oh, to be six or eight inches taller. Like her older sisters.

When he broke the kiss and they stood there, he leaning against the closed door and she leaning against him, her cheek on his lower chest, she told him what she had been thinking.

"I wish I were taller."

"Why is that, Miss Lovelock?" he said and brushed a kiss on the top of her head.

"So our necks didn't get cricks from looking up and looking down when we're kissing," she said. She had intended to tell him about her ache and how she wanted to put it against his phallus, but then she thought better of it.

"Do ye want me to pick ye up?" he whispered. She felt his arms clasp her more tightly and lift her in the air. Now they were face-to-face, and she pulled the skirt of her dress up a bit and put her legs around him so she could press her ache against his hardening length.

"Is that better?" he asked, and his voice was slightly strained.

"Yes," she said and did what she had been longing to do all morning. She buried both hands in his auburn hair and rocked her lower half against him.

He groaned.

She watched his face. Her breath hitched in her own chest. It seemed so very…right to be against him and to be rubbing her own throb against his body, his ridge of hardness.

"I thought ye wanted a…rest…when ye yawned." He was struggling.

She shook her head. No. She kept rocking against him.

"Ye are nae tired?"

She shook her head again.

"Ye brought me up here to…do this?"

She nodded. Was it so very terrible of her to do this? It felt so wonderful.

A loud knock on the door, just behind Alasdair's back, and he jumped and almost dropped her.

"Dr. Andrews?" The voice of the butler Andrews came through the door.

She put her mouth to his ear and whispered, "You've been rescued." She unwrapped her legs from around him and slid down his body. She stepped away and gave him a moment to pull the fall of his trousers away from himself.

"Are you ready?" she asked. He nodded.

She went to the door and opened it.

"Begging your pardon, Mrs. Andrews."

"Yes, Andrews?" she said. She could sense Alasdair had turned around and was standing behind her.

"Dr. Andrews, so sorry to disturb, but Lady Morpeth has heard there is a physician here and has requested you attend on her."

"Uh, aye, give me just a moment, Andrews."

Alasdair reached over her head and pushed the door closed. When she turned around, he had dropped to his knees in front of her.

"How is this, Mrs. Andrews?" he whispered.

"Now you're the one who is too short," she said and leaned down and kissed each of his dimples as he rested his hands on her waist. She ran her fingers through his hair one last time. "I had better let you go, I suppose."

"I'm sorry to leave ye."

He stood, and she had a thought. She put her hand on his arm and stopped him before he opened the door.

"Don't let yourself be alone in a room with Juliana," she said.

He looked confused.

"Lady Colborne. Just promise me you won't."

"I promise."

And then he was gone, the consummate professional physician, barring that one dark-red lock that still fell in front of his left eye.

It was, she thought, her first taste of what life as a doctor's wife might be like.

Twenty-One

A thin woman opened the bedchamber door. The butler Andrews murmured something and walked away.

"I am Nurse Gastrell," the woman said. Her eyes were pale, her brown hair flecked with gray.

"I am Dr. Alasdair Andrews. Yer mistress asked to see me."

Nurse Gastrell stepped aside from the door and allowed him to enter the room.

The windows were covered, but many candles and lamps burned so the room was almost blazing with light. The smell was not foul, as it was in many sick rooms. There was a fresh green smell, quite like rosemary. Alasdair took heart from that.

He followed the nurse farther into the room.

A small figure lay in the bed, so small that Alasdair's imagination almost led him to believe she was a child-bride until he drew close enough to see the lines in the woman's face. She might be the same age as Alasdair. She might be older.

The woman was blonde, but her hair was thin and patches of her scalp showed through. Her eyebrows were so fair as to be invisible. She opened her eyes as Alasdair approached the bed, and he could see her eyes were blue.

"My lady, I am Dr. Alasdair Andrews." He bowed.

"You are Scottish?"

"Aye."

"My butler told me there was a physician here in the house, and I decided I should consult you. But how do you come to be here? I heard from my nurse there is a snowstorm raging."

"I was on my way south with…uh, my wife when the snowstorm blew in. We asked for refuge, and yer husband was good enough to provide it."

"It is our luck then that you landed on our doorstep."

"'Twas lucky for us, I assure ye. There is a dangerous amount of snow."

The entire time they had been talking, he had been taking note of her skin, her breath, the look of her eyes.

"Tell me about yer illness, my lady."

"I am an invalid, Dr. Andrews." She sighed and looked at the ceiling. "I have been ever since my husband married me. I have consulted countless physicians. None of them know the cause of my illness. That, however, has not stopped them from subjecting me to many cures. Cures, I believe, that have worsened my condition, rather than improving it."

"What are yer symptoms?"

"Diarrhea, abdominal pain, headaches. Sometimes I am, apparently, delirious. Sometimes my vision changes."

"Fevers?"

"None." This was from Nurse Gastrell, who was standing in the corner, watching him.

"Can ye eat?"

"I could until recently. I have been vomiting, of late."

"Yer monthly courses? What are they like? When was the last one?"

Lady Morpeth looked at her nurse who shrugged.

"They are…scant, I believe, as compared to other women," Lady Morpeth said. "But I cannot remember the last time I bled, Doctor."

"May I examine ye further, my lady?"

"Yes."

Lady Morpeth's pulse was very slow but regular. Her lungs were clear. Upon palpation of her lower abdomen, her uterus was slightly enlarged but not tender.

"I wonder…" he said.

"Yes, Doctor?"

"I ken it disnae explain yer many years of illness, but is it possible ye are with child right now?"

Lady Morpeth grew agitated and tried to sit up on her elbows but did not have the strength and fell back. Her nurse came and helped her sit and put pillows behind her.

"I suppose…I suppose it is possible."

"She has been so ill," the nurse said. "It hardly seems likely she would have the strength."

"I have never been able to bear a child, Doctor."

"I dinnae ken what yer underlying illness is, but if ye usually have monthly courses and ye have nae blood within the next month, I believe ye may be pregnant."

"What will you do for me, Doctor. Will you bleed me?"

"Nae."

"No bleeding?"

"Nae. At this juncture, I dinnae ken it will help since I dinnae ken what disease ye have. And it will certainly nae help if ye are with child. However," he paused here, "I will speak to the cook. There may be some foods that will settle yer stomach. To eat might help ye to feel better."

The nurse spoke. "You are going to do nothing for her, Doctor?"

"I only do things when I think they will improve the

patient's health. So I will undertake to make sure my lady takes in some food without vomiting."

Lady Morpeth held her hand out to Alasdair.

"Thank you, Doctor."

He nodded, bowed over her hand, and went away.

He thought Lady Morpeth's appearance very odd. She was very small, blonde, blue eyes. So much like Lady Lyndmouth downstairs. And like Arabella. Lady Morpeth was some older, bedridden version of Arabella.

Lord Morpeth had a kind of woman, apparently.

Alasdair shuddered. How very glad he was that his Arabella was healthy.

He went down to the kitchens and found two scullery maids washing the dishes from luncheon. One of them went and roused the cook for him, and he sat with her at a well-scrubbed wooden table and explained the broth from chickens, the egg whites, the dry cracker. The cook scoffed at first, saying the baroness had never been a good eater. But the cook would endeavor to make the broth and a dry cracker tomorrow. And the whites of egg could go up right now.

"I have heard ye have very few hens' eggs right now," Alasdair said. "May I suggest ye reserve all egg whites for Lady Morpeth?"

At dinner, Morpeth confronted Alasdair.

"I heard you went to see my wife, Andrews. Without my permission."

Alasdair finished chewing his bite of meat, took a sip of his small beer, wiped his mouth.

"Aye." And then, reluctantly, "I apologize. I should have spoken to ye first." Another sip of small beer. "Although it would have made nae difference what ye said. I ne'er refuse the request of a patient to see me."

Morpeth sneered. "As long as they can pay your fee."

"No." That was Arabella. "Dr. Andrews sees any patient

in Sommerleigh, without asking a fee. It makes no difference to him who it is. It could be a tinker," Arabella must have heard that tragic story from Thomas or Harry, "or a countess like my sister."

"Well, Andrews," Morpeth said. "I wonder how you might feel if I paid a visit to your wife's bedchamber without telling you?"

There were a few gasps at the table.

Alasdair saw daggers in his vision again. Red ones. He felt a kick under the table. Arabella was glaring at him. He took a deep breath.

"I widnae like it, Lord Morpeth. Hence my apology to ye."

"Which I do not accept. Stay away from my wife."

"If she asks for me, I will go to her. But I will make sure ye are told, Lord Morpeth, so ye may also be present."

"That seems perfectly fair," the Marquess of Painswick interjected. "After all, the man has a duty. Be reasonable, Morpeth."

The baron laughed, said he was not known for his reason, and asked for more wine for himself and Lord Painswick. But Alasdair did not forget the very real menace that had crackled between them. And Lord Morpeth's threat to visit Arabella in her bedchamber.

Twenty-Two

Lady Colborne retired after dinner. "Not all of us were able to nap after luncheon," Juliana said with a sniff and a look at Arabella.

But Arabella did not care about Juliana's jab. After finishing his professional obligations, Alasdair had returned to Arabella's bedchamber, where she had waited for him. He had told her he was sorry for having been away so long. She had told him not to be silly—he was a physician and must go when called upon. She had tilted her face up to him, and he had kissed her then, most obligingly.

Mmm. She had to find a way to convince him to stop apologizing so much. She didn't want that kind of politeness. Not from him. Her Alasdair did not need keep asking forgiveness from her. It was just another way for him to put a distance between them, despite the kisses.

Fortunately, even though he was a trifle distracted, Alasdair had been persuaded by her to sit down in the wing chair where he had passed the previous night. Arabella had perched on his lap and kissed him. In this position, he was still taller than she, but to a much lesser degree. And she could satisfy her desire to touch his face and neck and hair while kissing. In a very short period of time, Alasdair had grown less distracted and more interested in the kissing and running his hands up and down Arabella's back, careful not to dip below the waist or come to her front, even though she longed for him to touch her breasts again as he had done before.

Oh, why had she not encouraged his hands to roam more when he had held her bosom in the lodge?

She knew why. Because she had been both frightened of the strength of her desire and keenly aware of the need to hide it from him.

And she felt she still must hide it from him. What she had done earlier, rubbing herself against him, had been unwise. She must let Alasdair have what he wanted. His romance. He must feel his desires—both of the carnal and the romantic variety—were guiding what passed between them. It was important to him.

And important for her, too. He must prove he was choosing her, prove that he was not here with her solely because of events out of his control. Because of her sister or her sister's health. Or because he had already been in Scotland for another reason. Or because of a snowstorm.

But even if he never proved he wanted her, she still wanted him.

She still craved him.

She had squirmed a little bit while sitting on his lap to give some pressure and friction to his tumescence, but she felt it was unfair to tease him too much in the middle of the afternoon. And her own ache was ever-present and unrelieved as she squeezed her thighs together tightly while they kissed. Despite the restraint exercised by both of them, they had been panting and flushed when Arabella got off Alasdair's lap before coming down to dinner.

The whole of the party, excepting Juliana and Lady Painswick, congregated in the drawing room after dinner, and Alasdair sat down to a chess game with Sir Timothy while Arabella joined Rebecca on a sofa, and the Swintons, Giles, and the Marquess of Painswick played whist. Lady Lyndmouth hovered near the card table. Her presence seemed to annoy the Swintons, who clutched their cards closely to their chests.

The butler Andrews entered the drawing room and bent over and said something in Alasdair's ear. Alasdair nodded and stood, saying something to Sir Timothy.

Giles halted his card play as Alasdair crossed the room. And when Alasdair passed the sofa, Arabella reached out and snagged the sleeve of his tailcoat.

"Where are you going, darling?" she asked in a loud voice.

"Ah." Alasdair looked at Sir Timothy.

"He is going upstairs to see Lady Colborne, at her request." Sir Timothy seemed exhausted by the mere idea of going upstairs. "The woman is always indisposed."

Arabella and Rebecca looked at each other. Juliana had always possessed perfect health.

"We'll come with you," Arabella said, and she and Rebecca stood.

Giles had gone back to his hand of cards after Sir Timothy had spoken but looked up when Alasdair addressed him from across the room.

"Lord Morpeth, after I attend on Lady Colborne, would I have yer permission to attend on yer wife?"

Giles grunted and waved his hand.

"Thank ye," Alasdair said through his teeth.

Arabella admired Alasdair's control when Giles had been so rude, so dismissive. As she climbed the stairs, she decided she must find a way to show him her appreciation. Perhaps tonight she would dare to take his hand and put it on her breast again. But surely, at some point, he would do it himself?

Maybe she should just tell him what she wanted and see if he was shocked or delighted.

But what if his shock made him turn away from her? As he had in the carriage after she had stroked his member and made him spend. She would wait, she decided. She would follow her current course of kissing him, letting him think he was leading, and waiting to see what he did next.

Lady Colborne's bedchamber was large and did not feel crowded, even when they all came into the room. Juliana was likely taken aback that it was a party of three, but she hid it well, Arabella thought.

Juliana sat in a chair, dressed as she had been at dinner, but her hair was down, and Arabella felt sure she was wearing rouge, which she had not been wearing at the table. There was a cloying scent of perfume in the room. Arabella looked around. Juliana's lady's maid was conspicuously absent.

"We're all here to make you feel better," Rebecca said. "Your sister, one of your oldest friends, and her husband."

"Aye," Alasdair said. "Please tell me what is wrong, my lady."

"I…" Juliana hesitated. "I'm sure it is nothing, Dr. Andrews. Just a feeling of being lightheaded at times. And fatigued."

"With yer permission?" Alasdair said, and when Juliana nodded, he stepped forward and picked up her wrist and felt her pulse.

Arabella thought suddenly of how much she loved Alasdair's hands. *But they will always touch other women.*

"Is the lightheadedness with standing?" Alasdair asked when he had released her wrist.

"Er, yes," Juliana said.

"Standing up quickly? May I touch ye under yer eye?" Juliana nodded, and Alasdair lightly pulled down one of her lower eyelids.

He bent at the waist and whispered in Juliana's ear.

Juliana colored. "Before Christmas."

"Are ye having any pain or difficulty breathing?"

"None, Doctor."

Alasdair leaned down again and said something more. Then he pulled back and looked in Juliana's eyes. Juliana looked…what? Apprehensive, Arabella decided. But Juliana nodded, as if to show she understood.

Alasdair straightened up and spoke at a normal volume. "Please have me brought to ye if anything worsens, Lady Colborne. I would avoid drinking an excess of wine. And rest when ye feel the need."

Arabella and Alasdair took their leave, but Rebecca stayed behind, and Arabella could hear Rebecca saying, "Now, what was that all about, Juliana?" as Alasdair closed the door.

Alasdair and Arabella stood in the corridor.

"Thank ye for protecting me, Miss Lovelock. 'Twas very thoughtful," he said as he lifted a wild tendril of golden hair off her forehead, "but I assure ye 'twas entirely unnecessary. I have avoided all manner of entanglements over the years. I am a skilled evader. Widows, spinsters, matrons, maidens. I have nae been trapped yet."

Arabella put her arms around his waist. "Are you sure about that?"

"I dinnae feel trapped, but if ye tell me I am, I will believe ye, and I willnae ask for rescue." He put his finger under her chin and kissed her pink lips. She tasted of the custard she had eaten for dessert—sweet, rich, with a hint of vanilla. And made entirely with egg yolks, Alasdair being sure the egg whites were being kept in reserve for Lady Morpeth.

"That was very good," she said when he was done kissing her.

He went to kiss her again.

"Get away with ye!" she said in his accent and playfully pushed at his chest before and pulling him back close to her again. "I'm not talking about the kissing. That is uniformly good, as I have told you before. You know that already. I meant the flirting."

"That was flirting?" It had been so easy.

"Yes, Alasdair."

"And 'twas good?" He started to feel a swell of pride.

She shook her head as if in despair and got up on her tiptoes and brushed his lips with hers. "Go see your other patient and then come to me."

"I dinnae want ye to worry about my going to see Lady Morpeth," he started. "She actually is ill, her nurse will be there, there will be nothing improper—"

She cut him off, shaking her head. "I'm not worried about that. I trust you. Or I must learn to, mustn't I? My honest Scottish doctor. I just don't trust Juliana. And I wasn't going to suggest I go with you to see Lady Morpeth. I would not want to cause the lady any pain in case…she knows about me. And her husband."

After the successful flirtation in the hallway just now, he had almost forgotten about the history of Arabella and Lord Morpeth. Well, not forgotten, but it had seemed a great deal less important.

"And I don't want you to worry about what I meant when I said you should come to me, Alasdair. I meant come to my bedchamber, and we will sleep. If you went to your own room, I would miss you terribly."

Alasdair felt three inches taller as he walked to Lady Morpeth's bedchamber.

Lady Morpeth was glad to report to him that she had eaten the egg whites and not cast them back up.

He was a long time with Lady Morpeth and Nurse Gastrell that evening and into the night. Asking more questions, taking a longer history. There was a mystery here. He might not know enough to solve it. He wished he had some of his medical books.

It was quite late when Alasdair eventually made his way to Arabella's room. He was glad to find a lamp had been left burning and Arabella was already in bed and asleep. He prepared himself as he had the night before. However, this time he did search for and find a blanket in a chest. Tonight would not be as bone-chilling as last night.

It was about one o'clock in the morning when Alasdair heard someone try to open the locked door.

No one must have told Lord Morpeth that Dr. Andrews was abed with Mrs. Andrews.

"Who's there?" Alasdair barked out in his deepest, most unfriendly voice.

Silence on the other side of the door. Then footsteps moving away.

A whisper. "Alasdair?"

He padded over to the bed. "'Tis all right. Someone mixed up about the rooms, I should think."

A small hand reached up and grasped his hand.

"I think you're lying so I won't be scared."

He sat down on the edge of the bed. "Are ye scared?"

"No, because you're here."

"Good."

"Your hand is cold." She brought it to her cheek. Her skin was warm and soft.

"Aye."

"Somebody once told me something about a ratio of surface area and volume." She yawned. "You should listen to your own advice. I think it would be lovely and warm to fall back asleep with you holding me. If you go back to that chair, I am going to feel very sorry for myself."

He didn't want her feeling sorry for herself. And, in the bed, he would be in an ideal position to protect Arabella.

"Move over, Miss Lovelock."

He would keep on the trousers and the banyan. He was no fool. He thought it would be best if he laid on his side and she was behind him and holding him. But she had specifically said she wanted *him* to hold *her*. And it didn't seem right to have her—such a little thing—on what he thought of as the outside of the arrangement. Facing her was out of the question. It would definitely lead to kissing. And perhaps breast touching and so on, despite the banyan and the trousers. The *so on* that he had imagined so many times.

Therefore, he had her roll on her side away from him, and he settled in behind her, putting his top arm around her waist and his bottom arm pillowing her head.

"*Courie* into me, Alasdair," she whispered.

Courie. Nestle. Snuggle.

He had not heard the word *courie* in over twenty-five years. It must have been his mother who had said it to him before she died, before he was sent to his aunt and uncle in Bailebrae. He could not imagine anyone else would have ever had occasion to use the word with him.

His throat tightened, and his eyes stung. He was glad the room was dark and Arabella would not have been able to see his face if she turned towards him.

And then his imagination was taken by the smallness and the softness of her waist under his own hand and what seemed a very thin and delicate and impractical nightdress. He wondered if he would be able to sleep at all, here in bed with her. But her own breath was calm. She put her hand on top of his and made a sighing noise that sounded suspiciously like contentment, and he surprised himself by falling almost immediately into a deep, warm sleep where he dreamed of standing in a bishop's study with Arabella.

TWENTY-THREE

Arabella woke in a delicious wash of warmth. She had woken several times during the night, and Alasdair was always there, holding her. She had toyed with the idea of turning and kissing him and undressing him and climbing on top of him. He might sleep on, like an enchanted prince, and she could have her wicked way with him. But she thought it might be a great deal more pleasurable if he would participate. And then his long, deep, even breaths would lull her back to sleep and to her dreams of what he might allow in the morning.

He was still holding her now, just as tightly as before.

She knew he was still asleep.

She lay very still. But in time, his breathing changed.

She dared to make a quarter turn on the bed and lay flat on her back so she could turn her head and see him, still lying on his side. She clutched his hand on her stomach so he could not withdraw it, but he made no move to do so.

And there he was, green eyes, waves of auburn hair, ginger whiskers. She put her other hand on his cheek to feel his stubble. Mmmm.

"Good morning," she whispered.

"Aye," he said and smiled and the dimples flashed for just a second before he winced.

"Alasdair, what's wrong?" She raised her head.

"Nae a thing," he said. "I just…" He slid his arm out from where it had cushioned her head all night. "My arm has gone numb." He shifted to lie flat and took his hand off her stomach and began to rub his arm. "A little compression of the radial nerve, that's all."

She sat up. "I'll do that. It's my fault, after all. My big head." She began to knead his upper arm through the banyan.

"Yer big head." He put his other hand on her leg. "Filled with so many—ow!—marvelous things." She had worked her way down to his elbow. "'Twas an honor to be its pillow for a night, Miss Lovelock."

"Have you noticed I call you Alasdair all the time now?" She rubbed his forearm.

"Aye."

"Do you think you might call me Arabella? You really cannot go on with *Miss Lovelock*. You will slip and call me that in front of the others."

"But shouldnae I call ye Mrs. Andrews then?"

She mashed his hand now in the most unforgiving manner.

"I suppose you should, even though it's a lie." *But how I wish it weren't.* "Whereas Arabella is not. So, perhaps in private, I could be Arabella? It seems silly that you kiss me and yet you don't call me Arabella."

He bit his lip as if he were thinking of something. "Ye may be right, Miss Lovelock."

"How is your arm now?"

"Better." He flexed his fingers.

She moved away from him to the other side of the bed and hopped off.

"I am ready for an enormous breakfast," she said and went to the window and peered through a crack in the curtains. "It's still snowing. And it's still cold."

Then, as if she were a girl of ten, she picked up her long nightdress and ran back to the bed and scrambled in and was under the covers in a flash and curled next to him.

"Let's stay in bed until the snow melts," she said and put her hand on the banyan, just as she had held his coat lapel in her cottage in Dunburn.

"I'm sure yer friend's lady's maid will be here soon," he said, "and I should be dressed."

With a groan, he got up and left the bed.

Arabella sat up. She wanted him to stay in bed with her, of course, but if he would not, she would wait for him to be ready. She had been, and, she told herself, she could continue to be patient.

And now she would see him undress and dress. Unfortunately, he had his trousers on already, so not all of his secrets would be revealed to her this morning. He took off the banyan and the nightshirt, and she could see his narrow waist, a smooth back where muscles flexed as he picked up his clothes, his straight shoulders.

But she was greedy.

"Alasdair?" she called out.

He turned and faced her as he tried to find the armholes in his shirt.

"Aye?"

She said nothing, but she sighed in appreciation as she lay back on the pillows. He was beautiful. Like one of the statues in the museum. Carved from marble, but with some soft, coppery fuzz across his chest and a little at his navel. Flat abdomen and a lovely swell of some muscle on the chest and in his shoulders and upper arms. And his skin was a little rosy, maybe from the heat of the bed he had shared with her.

"Miss Lovelock?" He had the shirt on and was tucking it into his trousers.

"I just wanted to see the front half of you."

The rosiness at the neck hole of his shirt now deepened to a dark flush that rose up his throat and spread across his face. Even to his ears. She wondered where the redness started and how far it spread. The next time she made him blush, she would make sure he had his shirt off. Or everything off.

"Is that flirtation?" he mumbled and sat down to put his stockings on.

"No," Arabella said. "It's just wanton lust."

"Women dinnae have that."

She thought he must be joking, so she sat up to see his expression. He had no dimples. He was serious.

"What?" she said.

"Well, nae lust." He got his boots on. "Nae like men. Women inspire lust, they dinnae feel it."

He was using his doctor's voice, the one he had used in the carriage when he had told her that she had not been ruined. But now his arrogant surety was not comforting or reassuring. It was infuriating. Arabella felt her temper flare. Immediately.

This was intolerable. How dare he dismiss her, her wants and needs—no, the wants and needs of half the human race!

"Your knowledge of women being so extensive," she said, clenching her fists by her sides.

He had walked over to a looking glass to tie his cravat. But now he paused, and his shoulders went back. He looked at her.

"I may nae have much practical experience in the matter, Miss Lovelock, but I am a physician. I have read hundreds of treatises and texts on physiology. I have treated hundreds of women as my patients. I assure ye women and men dinnae experience the same need."

She jumped out of the bed.

"Since I will never be a man," she said, struggling to keep

her voice low and losing the struggle, "and you will never be a woman, neither of us is in a position to say that. And who wrote those medical books and treatises you are speaking of?" She did not wait for his answer. "Men! Men, that's who. And why would a patient tell you what she feels, what she desires when she is ill or scared or in pain?"

His mouth hung open now.

She went on, recklessly, loudly. "You think Giles took me against my will? No! I wanted to be touched, to be kissed, to be taken. I wanted ecstasy. He was not the man to give it to me, and he was a liar, but my want was not a lie. The want was real! For days now, I have restrained my own desire for you in order to shield you, to allow you time, to make you feel you were leading. To let you be sure of me. Even though I have waited for you a very long time, Doctor, I made myself wait longer. I did not want to do to you what Giles did to me and force you to go too quickly. But I see now that was a mistake. I should have seduced you, I should have done what I wanted with you! So you would know—"

She was crying through her fury, and she wasn't sure when the tears had started.

He was aghast. First, he, who had exerted his will a thousand times in the past to stay awake all night to tend a patient in crisis, who had gone days in his boyhood without eating, who had spent his youth in Edinburgh hunched over books sixteen hours a day, had just carried out what he felt was the most self-denying act of his life. He had left the warm nest where Arabella lay. Where they had slept together. Where he had *couried* into her.

Where so much else could have happened, but he had restrained himself.

Then for her to contradict him so vehemently, to talk so

freely of having wanted to lose her innocence, to speak of seducing him, and now to be crying?

"Miss Lovelock." He stepped towards her.

"No!" she screamed. "You cannot even give me that, can you? My own name. Not even that intimacy. You must hold me at arm's length. You, with your damned stupid ideas about women!"

He had been cursed at by laboring mothers, sworn at by drunken men with bleeding heads, threatened by grief-crazed parents after the unavoidable death of a child, but he had never felt himself as reviled as he did now.

And he could not face that. He could not confront the fury of the tiny figure in the room with him now.

He left his cravat untied and collected his waistcoat and tailcoat and walked out the door of the bedchamber.

Alasdair had no idea where the other wing of rooms was located, and, even if he did, he had no idea which might be his chamber. He tied his cravat, noticing he had picked up the tartan scarf along with the rest of his clothes. He got his waistcoat on and the tailcoat over it and was walking down the corridor away from Arabella's room, trying to button the waistcoat, when he almost bumped into the Marquess of Painswick.

"Dr. Andrews, do watch where you're going," the marquess said.

Alasdair bowed. "My apologies, Lord Painswick."

"You are headed quite the wrong direction for breakfast, Dr. Andrews. Come with me. And after breakfast, I'll arrange to have my valet shave you."

"Thank ye, my lord."

They turned around and walked back down the corridor in the other direction, back towards Arabella's room, towards the main staircase. Alasdair held the tartan scarf in his hand.

The marquess raised his eyebrows as they passed Arabella's room.

"Just a few minutes ago, I thought I heard a raised voice from this end of the passage. Was it your wife?"

"Uh, perhaps." Alasdair pushed back the lock of hair that had fallen in front of his left eye.

"Wives are difficult creatures, aren't they?" the marquess said as he started down the stairs. "So needing, really. It's best to find something they like so they can be distracted. Then one can get some peace."

"I cannae say."

"Well, you're newly married, aren't you?" The marquess flashed a smile, one that seemed to show entirely too many teeth. He continued to go down the stairs. "The novelty of having an available, tight quim that is legally obliged to open up for you has not yet lost its charm, I see. In the long run, though, wives turn out to be much more expensive than whores. But for producing heirs, one really has no other choice."

Alasdair stopped in his tracks and balled his fists by his sides. He thought about using the scarf in his hand to strangle the marquess.

The marquess noticed Alasdair was not beside him and paused his descent and turned and looked back up the stairs at him.

"Dr. Andrews, do not take offense. I speak in generalities, of course. And you should never pay attention to anything anyone says before breakfast. Including your wife."

When Alasdair did not move and did not answer, the marquess sniffed, turned, and walked down the rest of the stairs. Alasdair stood for a long time, trying to decide whether to go down the stairs or back up to Arabella.

Ultimately, he decided the marquess was a degenerate arsehole, but he had one thing right. Breakfast might improve the situation, and it certainly wouldn't hurt. He folded the scarf, tucked it between the left side of his waistcoat and his shirt as he had yesterday, and walked down the stairs towards tea and breakfast.

He could not brave Arabella's rage, even with his tartan armor over his heart. He was a coward, and he knew it.

She flung herself onto the bed and kicked and punched and sobbed. He had seen her as she truly was. A screaming, lustful, undone chit. He would never bed her now, let alone marry her.

And although she felt it was fair to blame her lust on her mother, she could not make her mother culpable of her rage. She had never seen her mother lose her temper, except the one time. Those ten seconds when her mother had dragged her out of Giles' carriage. Even then, her mother had not shouted or yelled like Arabella had.

It had been Arabella who had screamed herself hoarse in grief and pain and, yes, fury at her betrayal by Giles.

By the time Rebecca's lady's maid entered the room along with a chambermaid bearing a breakfast tray, Arabella had dressed herself in her one dress, arranged her hair, made the bed, and was staring out the window at the swirling snow.

"Is there anything else you need, Mrs. Andrews?" the lady's maid asked after she had poured hot water into the basin.

Arabella stayed facing the window. Her lashes were still wet, and she knew her face was red and swollen.

"No, thank you."

"My mistress wanted me to tell you she will be very glad to see you today."

"And I, her."

"Yes, Mrs. Andrews." A silence. "Shall I go now?"

"Yes, please."

So much snow. She put her hand on the window. So cold.

When the snow stopped, she would go south to her sister. She did not know how she would do it, but she was determined she would go alone.

She had seen his face when she had screamed and cursed. His expression had been blank. As if she were a patient in an asylum and he was studying her and her madness.

She knew she had lost him.

And this time it was all her fault.

Twenty-Four

Alasdair joined an almost full breakfast table. The entire party was present save Arabella and, of course, the marchioness. Lady Painswick, the marquess declared, was still asleep.

Rebecca was seated next to Alasdair and turned to him. "And Mrs. Andrews?"

"I think she might break her fast in her room?" Alasdair said.

Everyone else had already started eating.

Perhaps, he thought, he had voiced an opinion in too confident a manner. After breakfast, when Arabella was calmer, he would apologize. His regret was real even if he did not understand her rage. Where was the offense in saying women were less susceptible than men?

"There's no sign of the snow letting up," Lord Morpeth said and wiped his mouth and threw down his napkin after only a few bites of his breakfast. "We are stuck inside for another day."

Stuck inside with the villain Morpeth who had tried to open the bedchamber door last night and get to Alasdair's

Arabella. At least, Alasdair *had* thought she was his Arabella. He was not so sure now.

And smarting under Arabella's rebuke, he loathed this man even more. This man whom Arabella had said she wanted years ago when Alasdair had been yearning for her, far away at Sommerleigh.

"It's a good thing you have such a fine cellar laid by, Morpeth," the marquess said. "Otherwise, we should all go mad, and you would have yourself a little Bedlam here."

Rebecca Dalrymple spoke. "Do you think Arabella will be down later, Dr. Andrews?"

"I am sure of it, my lady," Alasdair said, not feeling sure at all.

"I am so glad to meet you," Rebecca said. "Arabella told us all about you—oh, it must have been three and a half years ago. She described you perfectly, and she was in despair at that time because she could not think how to meet you again. But I told her you would find each other. I didn't tell her this then, but I'll tell you now, if you like. I secretly knew you two would someday be wed. And, you see, I was right."

"Aye."

"My sister," Juliana said from across the table, "is prone to knowing things but not announcing she knew them until they manifest as reality."

"I foretold we'd have snow, didn't I?" Rebecca said.

"You didn't predict we'd have this much, though. And that would have been the useful prediction, sister!"

Juliana turned to the Swintons to discuss the possibility of a game of whist later.

"I hope I didn't disturb you very much last night," Rebecca said in a very low voice. "I couldn't sleep, and in the old days, when Arabella came to stay with us, I would sneak into her room when I couldn't sleep, and she would tell me a story. Last night, I thought…well, I had forgotten that sometimes husbands and wives sleep together. Please do give her my apologies."

It had not been Lord Morpeth trying to get into the bedchamber in the middle of the night. It had been Arabella's friend.

Alasdair looked at the head of the table again and noted the large size of Morpeth's hands. The man was still despicable.

After breakfast, Alasdair spoke to Morpeth. The baron was irritable and terse. He gave his permission in a very surly manner, and Alasdair went and knocked on the door of Lady Morpeth's room. However, Nurse Gastrell opened the door and told him her lady was asleep.

"Would ye have someone tell me when she is awake and would permit a visit?"

Nurse Gastrell nodded and closed the door.

Arabella did eventually come downstairs and sit with Juliana and Rebecca on a sofa in the drawing room. She made a small curtsy to Alasdair when she came into the room, but she did not speak to him or smile. She did not join the others at cards and neither did Rebecca. When Juliana got up from the sofa to play, Alasdair made sure to slide into her vacant seat in order to prevent anyone else—like, say, Lord Morpeth—from doing so. Arabella kept herself turned towards Rebecca, but Rebecca leaned forward occasionally and tried to include Alasdair in the conversation.

After a time, Rebecca left the room to fetch a book she wanted Arabella to read. Alasdair was now alone on the sofa with Arabella.

"I am nae certain what to say to ye," Alasdair started, thinking out his apology.

"I think it best you say nothing at all, then, Dr. Andrews." Arabella stood and straightened her dress and walked to the sideboard across the room.

She had not looked at him. Her tone had been polite but without warmth. This was not the Arabella he knew. Even when she had been angry with him in the carriage because he was trying to apologize for not writing to her and she had declared she wanted to forget herself and her past, she had been fiery. And he loved that fire. Yes, it cowed him a little, but he already knew that rising to meet that fire would make him a better man. Had it not been her fire that had led him to kiss her? And all the wonders that had followed from that kiss.

And now she was cold to him.

He had not known how much he would miss flirtation until it was gone. And he was still lost as to how he had upset her so grievously. Hadn't he made it clear women were more noble, less base than men? She should have been flattered, not angered.

There were decanters on the sideboard, but Arabella made no move to pour herself wine. Instead, she went up on her toes, leaning forward, trying to examine some engravings hanging on the wall there.

He saw Morpeth approach the sideboard and pour himself a glass of claret. Viewed from behind, it was hard to believe Arabella and Lord Morpeth were part of the same species. He so large, so hulking. She so small, so delicate. It was obscene that they had coupled. It was impossible Arabella had been a willing party to that. He could not believe it of her.

Alasdair stood, having suddenly developed a fierce thirst that required a glass of claret from the sideboard.

Morpeth walked around Arabella, his hand trailing over her bottom, the bottom that Alasdair himself had never touched, had restrained himself from touching even though he thought it might be the next territory to explore.

Morpeth settled himself on the wall right next to Arabella, facing her, and leaned down as if to kiss her.

• • •

Arabella wasn't ready to speak with Alasdair. Yes, she was still angry at him and what he had said about women and lust. But, in truth, she was far angrier at herself for losing her temper, for shouting at him. Couldn't she have reasoned with him? And now she didn't know how she could withstand hearing an admonishment from him when, so far, he had only been loving to her. She couldn't hear he didn't want her anymore. She couldn't know she had ruined everything between them. She wouldn't be able to bear it.

She had to delay this pain, somehow. So she crossed the room and pretended interest in some engravings.

She felt Giles' presence next to her at the sideboard before he spoke.

"You have been in my thoughts constantly these last years, Arabella," he said.

"Mrs. Andrews," she corrected him and rocked back onto her heels.

"Mrs. Andrews, yes."

"That is so strange, Lord Morpeth, because I have not thought of you at all. But these are some handsome engravings you have hanging here."

"Yes." Giles took a decanter and poured himself some wine. "I value beautiful things. I collect all kinds of lovely trinkets and rare curios."

"Such as gloves, Lord Morpeth?" Arabella couldn't help herself. Today, she was in a rage against all men. "Gloves and scraps of silk. And flowers, I seem to recall."

Giles walked around her, briefly stroking her bottom with one of his large hands, and then turned himself so he was leaning on the wall, just next to her.

"I am not averse," he whispered, stooping down and leaning forward, his lips just inches from hers, "to revisiting flowers I may have already collected."

Arabella was taking a step backwards and preparing a

cutting retort—something along the lines of the lie that she was irrevocably in Alasdair's permanent collection or the truth that Giles might find her a very poisonous bloom indeed these days—when she became aware of a sound that was halfway between a growl and a cry of pain.

A glimpse of movement and Giles' shoulders were back against the wall with Alasdair pressing him there. Alasdair raised his fist, but then his face changed, and he hesitated and lowered his arm. Giles sneered and ducked out of Alasdair's grasp, moving very quickly for a man of his size, grabbing Alasdair's arm and twisting it behind him.

"Alasdair!" Arabella tried to get to him, but she was shoved out of the way by Lord Painswick who had gotten between the sideboard and the two men.

"Don't spill the claret, Morpeth," said the marquess.

Arabella darted around the marquess and could see Alasdair was not resisting or struggling against Giles' hold on him. His face was white, and he held still as Giles twisted his right arm up.

"Let go of him!" Arabella screamed.

"My shoulder joint is out of place," Alasdair said quietly. "I assure ye I am nae danger to ye."

Giles laughed. "I was never worried you were a danger to me." He grimaced and let go of Alasdair, who stumbled forward a step.

Arabella was by Alasdair's side and put her hand on his uninjured left arm. "Come with me, Doctor."

Alasdair pulled out of her grip, and Arabella was forced almost to run to stay near him as he strode out of the room. His right arm dangled oddly. But when he got out of the room, he clutched his right arm with his left hand and bent his head and gagged.

"Alasdair," Arabella whispered in horror.

His eyes darted around the hall as if he didn't know where to go or what to do. Arabella could see his legs were trembling.

"I broke my word to ye. I didnae control myself. I was going to strike him."

"You're hurt. We'll go to my bedchamber. You'll tell me how to help you. Can you make it there?"

His face was even more white than before, and the pallor made his eyes very green.

"There's nae a thing wrong with my legs," he said.

But he walked very slowly and completely cradled his right arm in his left. He winced with each jar of his body as he took the stairs.

The butler Andrews suddenly appeared behind Alasdair and Arabella on the stairs.

"What can I do, Mrs. Andrews?"

Arabella turned to Alasdair questioningly.

Alasdair said through his teeth, "Ice or snow. Two strong men. And a bedsheet or a rope."

"Please send for Paterson," Arabella said. "Our coachman staying with the grooms. And is there another man who can assist him?"

"Yes, Mrs. Andrews. I am capable of helping."

"Of course you are, Andrews. Thank you."

The butler bowed, and Alasdair continued his slow upward climb, Arabella next to him until they reached the top of the stairs and then she ran ahead to open the door to her bedchamber for him.

In Arabella's bedchamber, Alasdair very gingerly sat on the edge of the seat of the wing chair as Arabella, under his instructions, held the tails of his coat out so he did not sit on them.

"The tailcoat will be the most difficult article of clothing to remove," he said. "But we cannae cut it. 'Tis my only one here."

With Arabella holding the end of the left sleeve and Alasdair resting the right arm on his lap, he was able to extract his left arm. Then Arabella moved the coat around his back, and, very slowly, trying to jostle Alasdair as little as possible, she drew the right sleeve and the entire coat over his right arm.

"That was very gentle, very good," Alasdair said, but he had grimaced several times, and his face was still very white.

The tartan scarf fell to the floor when she unbuttoned his waistcoat. She sucked in a breath. What hope she had held in her heart when she had hemmed that length of wool for him back in Dunburn. And now that hope was all gone. Ruined by her temper.

When she picked up the scarf and put it on top of his folded tailcoat, she looked at his face, but it was unchanged. She was sure his mind was wholly concentrated on controlling his own pain.

In comparison to the tailcoat, the waistcoat was easier to remove—no sleeves. The shirt was next. Alasdair pulled his left arm out of the sleeve by bending his own elbow towards his trunk as she held the cuff. Shirt gathered towards his neck, Alasdair's chest exposed. She was close to him, her breasts almost brushing his face as she lifted the shirt over his head.

Maybe she *was* an aberration, and Alasdair was right. Maybe women as a rule did not feel lust. Only she did. She and Catherine, her shameful mother.

Because, even now, when Arabella was angry, when she was sure they had no future together, when he was hurt and she was worried, the appearance of his bare chest aroused her. She wanted to press her hands to it and feel him, his muscle, his ribs, the beat of his heart. And the smell of him made her want to bury her face in the copper hair of his chest and breathe deeply.

She bit her lip. She was wanton like her mother. She was

bad like her mother. No wonder she had been seduced so easily two years ago.

But maybe her thinking was wrong. What of Mary, her half sister? Mary had walked with Arabella on the shingle in Cornwall and spoken of many things regarding the mysteries between men and women. Mary felt desire, too—strong desire from what she had said. If Arabella were an aberration, Mary was one, too. And Mary had none of Catherine's blood in her.

Alasdair's head was down, and he was purposefully not looking at her bosom even though it was right in front of him. Oh, if only he would lift his head and look at her and she could kiss him.

But it would do nothing for his pain. And it would only remind him she could never be a good wife for him since she could control neither her lust nor her temper.

She very carefully brought the shirt down over his right arm and removed it and stepped back.

Standing in front of him, Arabella could see how the right shoulder was too squared off, too bony in comparison to the smooth roundness of the muscle of the left shoulder.

"Is it broken?"

"Nae, I dinnae think." He finally raised his head and looked at her. "The shoulder is a joint where a ball sits into a socket. The ball has come out of the socket. It must be put back in. The more quickly, the better."

"Will," she faltered, "will you be able to use the arm again?"

Her blonde brows were knit together, and there was a small crease just over the bridge of her little nose. Her voice trembled when she asked about his arm. She was worried. For him.

Her worry gave him some hope they would get beyond this horrible time. When he was out of pain, he would fix this mess between them. He would apologize for any and all wrongs, and she would be his Arabella again.

He wished she would step back where she had been just a moment before. When her perfect, high, round breasts had been where he would most want them to be—inches from his mouth. They had been both so beautiful and so close that he had had to look away. But now he wanted them back. He wanted her close. He wanted to reach his left arm out and draw her to him, but when he began to release his grip on his right arm, the pain surged, and he kept his left hand where it was.

"Aye." He tried to smile. "Aye, I mean I willnae be able to use it for a few days, but it will all come right as a trivet. Ye will see."

The butler Andrews knocked and came in. He carried a basin of snow, some folded sheets, a bottle of amber liquid, a drinking glass.

"I have sent for your coachman. I do understand your wanting your own people around you, but I assure you that I and all the footmen are more than willing to do whatever you require of us, Dr. Andrews."

"Thank ye, Andrews," Alasdair said and winced. "The snow should go on the shoulder until Paterson gets here."

"And I have some whisky here, Doctor, for your pain."

"Nae, thank ye."

Arabella took the basin of snow from the butler Andrews and scooped up a handful and pressed it against the front of Alasdair's shoulder.

"Yer hand will get too cold, Mrs. Andrews," he said.

"It's just until Paterson gets here, as you said, Dr. Andrews."

And he was very glad to have her close to him, her tending to him, her pressing the snow into his shoulder.

It was not long before Paterson was brought to the room

by a footman. Ewen MacEwen had also decided to come along. In those minutes waiting for Paterson, Arabella had to gather more snow into her hand twice, and Alasdair saw her hand had turned red from the cold. Oh, how he wanted to warm that hand in some way.

"The snow has helped the pain," Alasdair said, looking at her.

Her brows relaxed a bit when he said that. He carefully rose from the wing chair and walked to the bed where he had *couried* into her.

"I thank ye."

As Alasdair sat on the edge of the bed and gave instructions to Paterson and Andrews, Ewen investigated the room.

"'Tis the size of a whole cottage, miss," Ewen explained. He seemed to like the curtains, particularly. "'Tis like the fur of an animal." He stroked the velvet with his hand.

Arabella shushed him. She wanted to hear what Alasdair was saying.

"Paterson, ye will put the sheet around my chest and kneel on the bed behind me and pull the ends of the sheets back towards ye with all yer might."

"Like reins," Paterson said.

"Exactly. And, Andrews, ye will take my right arm and extend it straight out and pull as hard as ye can. The two of ye will be pulling in opposite directions, and the shoulder should pop back into place."

The butler Andrews nodded. Paterson looked at the ruffled counterpane and said, "Begging yer pardon, miss," and took off his boots before he got onto the bed. He knelt behind Alasdair and looped the sheet in front of his chest and gripped the two ends tightly.

Alasdair took a deep breath.

The butler Andrews took hold of his arm, and Arabella could see Alasdair was close to screaming.

"On three, pull," he said through his teeth. "One, two, three–"

He did scream then. And though the men pulled with all their might, when the butler Andrews finally relaxed his pull on Alasdair's arm and Paterson relaxed his reins made of a bedsheet, the right shoulder was still bony, still squared off.

Through his tears, Alasdair said, "I am sorry, Arabella, I should have sent ye out of the room."

He had called her Arabella. Finally. Maybe he didn't hate her.

"Nonsense," she said. "I wouldn't have listened." She stepped up to him and touched his left shoulder gently. "Why didn't it work?"

"I'm too tense in the shoulder girdle. The pain keeps the muscle from relaxing."

"Perhaps the whisky, Dr. Andrews," the butler Andrews said and went to get the bottle he had set down on the table.

"I'd rather keep my wits about me," Alasdair said, trembling.

"I'd rather get your arm back in its socket," Arabella said. She moved her hand on his left shoulder towards his neck and the triangle of muscle that lay between the neck and his shoulder. Then she felt the same muscle on the right. It felt very hard on both sides. Surely, these muscles were not always this rigid. "Give the doctor a very large whisky, Andrews."

The butler Andrews poured four fingers, and Alasdair took the offered glass into his left hand and drank it. Three long gulps. Arabella took the glass from him as he shook his head and exhaled through his teeth.

"All right," he rasped. "Let's try again."

"Let the whisky work, Dr. Andrews." She did not know

how he would be able to bear having his arm pulled like that again.

"Miss," Ewen said. He was standing by the window. "Miss."

"Not now, Ewen. We must fix Dr. Andrews' shoulder."

"'Tis about Dr. Andrews' shoulder, miss."

"Yes, Ewen?" Arabella knew she sounded very irritable when she wanted to be calm and accommodating.

"I need to tell ye alone, miss."

Arabella was vexed. The boy was not helping, and now he was distracting her, and Alasdair was hurting. And Alasdair had said the sooner the shoulder was put back in place, the better. She walked over to the window.

"What is it, Ewen?"

Ewen leaned and spoke in her ear.

The whisky was beginning take hold of Alasdair. Despite the terrible pain of his shoulder, warmth spread from his chest up to his head.

Where was Arabella?

Aye, she was at his side now.

"Ye shouldnae be here. Ye have to leave."

"I won't leave. You know I won't."

"Husband's orders," he said and hiccoughed, which jolted his right shoulder and made him wince in pain. "Or doctor's orders. Either one."

"Yes, either one. That's right." She put a hand under his chin and peered into his eyes. "Are you ready, Doctor?"

She had her hand on his face. She was standing very close to him. He could feel Paterson pick up the sheet and pull it up to chest level.

"I'll count," Ewen said from somewhere behind him.

Andrews picked up Alasdair's right arm, and the pain was agonizing even though the pulling had not even started.

"One, two," Alasdair could hear Ewen counting.

And then a sweet smell and Arabella held his face in both of her hands and she crowded her body into him and put her mouth on his. And she was kissing him. In a totally unconstrained manner. She was kissing him the way she had in the carriage before he had warned against impulsive acts. Before she had handled his cock and made him spend and they had disagreed about romance. She was fierce with her tongue and teeth, and he was worried she was going to stop, this wild female sweetness who was giving him all her attention, so he curled his left arm around her and pulled her to him tightly, and his right arm hurt like the devil, but he was also hard as Aberdeen granite in his trousers, and then he heard and felt a pop and his right shoulder stopped hurting. Not completely, but the pain went from excruciating to bearable in the blink of an eye.

"Stop!" he yelled into Arabella's mouth.

Arabella took her mouth from his.

"Nae ye, darling, please," he said, looking up at her. "Them."

The butler Andrews gently put Alasdair's right arm at his side. Alasdair felt the sheet relax on his chest.

Arabella pulled away from Alasdair and stood in front of him. The right shoulder now looked the same as the left, with the same delicious rounding of muscle at the top.

"What do we do now?" she asked.

"Ye come back here next to me, darling."

"You are drunk, Dr. Andrews. What do we do with your arm? Oh, dear," she turned to Andrews, "we should have asked him before we had him drink the whisky."

"I'm nae incapacitated. We make" Alasdair hiccoughed, "a sling and a swathe to keep the arm still."

Paterson had gotten off the bed. "I ken how to do that, miss. May I use this sheet?" He looked at the butler Andrews, who nodded.

In very short order, Paterson had ripped the sheet in thirds, and Alasdair was in a sling and swathe.

"Thank you," Arabella said to Paterson. "And thank you, Ewen." She turned to the butler. "And, of course, thank you, Andrews."

"Yer welcome," Alasdair said with his eyes closed. He lay back on the bed.

Ewen grinned and said, "Aye, yer welcome, miss. Can I borrow a book?"

"The books in this house are Lord Morpeth's, Ewen, and right now," Arabella cast a glance at Alasdair, "I don't care to ask the baron for anything. But wait." She had a thought. "My friend was to loan me a book."

Arabella went down the hall and knocked on Rebecca's bedchamber door. Rebecca answered the door herself and drew Arabella inside the room.

"Oh, Arabella, is the doctor well? I couldn't find the first volume of *Kenilworth* for the longest time, and when I finally got downstairs, I was told…And then I heard some screams. Is he all right?"

"I thought he was not stupid, but it turns out he is a fool, like many men. However, I am hoping his arm will be fine," Arabella said. "May I borrow the *Kenilworth* and let the lad who has been traveling with us read it? I assure you he quite worships books and will be as careful as can be with it and will return it tomorrow and likely ask for the second volume."

"Certainly," Rebecca said and picked up the book and gave it to Arabella. "You can ask anything of me, as you know."

Arabella met Ewen and Paterson in the hallway and gave Ewen the book.

She had promised herself she wouldn't blush. "Thank you again, Ewen. For your…er, idea. And thank you, Paterson, for pulling so well."

The butler Andrews was still in her bedchamber. He had taken off Alasdair's boots, and Alasdair still lay crosswise on the bed, his knees bent and legs hanging off the edge, his eyes closed.

"I am glad Dr. Andrews' shoulder is in place," the butler Andrews said as he gathered the whisky, the glass, the basin. "I worried we would not be successful."

"As did I. Thank you again for your help. And for bringing the whisky."

"That was clever of the boy to think of having you distract the doctor. I do not think the whisky alone would have been enough."

Arabella looked down and felt her face grow hot.

"But you should tell the coachman and the boy to stop calling you *miss*. Someone might misunderstand, *Mrs. Andrews*."

Arabella looked quickly at the butler Andrews, who had his usual grave expression on his face.

"I—"

"And I am glad to see you found your wedding ring sometime between entering the house two nights ago and yesterday's breakfast."

"Yes," she said.

"Please let me know if you or your husband require anything else, Mrs. Andrews." He laid the barest trace of an emphasis on the word *husband*, and she was not sure whether or not she had imagined it. But, clearly, he knew they were not married.

Arabella nodded, and the butler bowed and closed the

door behind him softly. She walked over to the not-stupid fool who was lying on her bed.

His eyes fluttered open as she approached, and he reached towards her with his left arm.

"Come lie with me, darling."

"This is very dangerous," she said and sat on the edge of the bed on his right side, a few feet from him, out of his reach.

"Dangerous? Nae. Ye are the one who keeps wanting *me* to get in bed with *ye*."

"I quite like you when you're drunk."

"I'm nae drunk." He raised his head. "Why do ye say that?" He laid his head back. "Ye are awfully far away."

"You're acting drunk, and you had four fingers of whisky in one go."

"I'm a Scot. I'm a man." He rapped on his chest with his left arm. "I can handle my whisky. I am, perhaps, tipsy. I meant, why do ye like me?"

"Why do I like you when you're tipsy?"

"Aye." He patted the mattress next to him on his left side. "At least come to this side of me, my good side, my good arm."

She did not move. "Do you really want to know?"

"Aye."

"I'll tell you, and then I want you to go to sleep."

"Aye." And he yawned as if to show he meant it.

"Because you're affectionate when you're drunk."

"Tipsy." He closed his eyes.

"When you're tipsy."

"I'm always affectionate. With ye. Arabella."

"Go to sleep."

He fell silent.

It was true, he told himself. He wasn't drunk. But the alcohol and the pain and then the merciful liberation from the pain, along with her wildness, had released some shackle within him. He wanted her close, as close as possible. What he would do with that closeness, he did not know. But he had no care for the future. He only knew he wanted her with him. Now.

Suddenly, it seemed stupid not to call her Arabella. She wanted it from him, so why would he not give it to her? And, of course, to have her kiss him like that. What man would reject that?

I would, he realized. *I did. She would have given me everything in the carriage that morning before the snow.*

He thought about sitting up, but it seemed impossible to do so.

Damn me. Damn that man I was two days ago. Damn the man I was just an hour ago.

Oh, now he felt drunk.

He might have dreamt it, but at one point he thought Arabella bent low over his chest and put her nose and mouth against his chest and inhaled.

But when he woke, the room was empty.

TWENTY-FIVE

rabella knocked on Rebecca's door again.

"May I sit in your bedchamber with you?"

Rebecca drew her into the room immediately, her forehead creased with concern.

"Of course. But why?"

"The doctor and I have become estranged. I do not want to be with all the other guests, and yet I don't want to be alone."

Arabella was glad to sit down by the fire with her friend. The brown scarf was in her hands, and she busied herself, folding and unfolding it.

Rebecca said, "You and the doctor? That makes me very unhappy."

"You may have guessed, but we are not married."

"I thought perhaps you just did not have a ring, yet."

"No."

"So you are his mistress? He is already married?"

"No! No. You should not think anything ill of him. He is not married, and he would never take a mistress. He would be the most faithful of husbands." Arabella's throat closed up, and her last words were choked.

"I hear you defending him but not yourself."

Arabella got up and walked around her friend's bedchamber.

"In truth, I cannot defend myself. If I had had my way, the doctor and I would have…I would not care. Married or unmarried, I would be his mistress a thousand times over."

"I don't understand. If he has no wife, why are you two not married? He adores you. I can see it, Arabella. It's no good denying it."

Arabella stopped pacing. "He has not asked me yet. And now I feel sure he won't. We have only just met again. And I have found that the doctor…I don't know how to explain this. The doctor does not believe in female desire."

Rebecca laughed. "So you will teach him."

"You don't understand."

Rebecca was silent for a minute.

"You think because I am unmarried, Arabella, that I don't understand desire?"

"No, of course not, I just…no."

"Of course not, because you are unmarried yourself."

"Yes."

"You have just fallen into the habit of thinking of me as a younger sister. You should not."

"No."

"So here we are. Two unmarried women who understand desire."

A very long pause, one that was weighty and filled with import. Arabella felt a prickle of unease. She looked at Rebecca, who was still seated, looking at her, waiting. Measuring her reaction, somehow.

Rebecca bit her lip and looked away. "I don't know what Juliana told you yesterday. But I do know some of why you left London. And I know Lord Morpeth was the one. I heard the Marquess of Painswick whisper it to Mr. Swinton."

Rebecca brought her eyes back to Arabella's. Arabella could see sympathy there, and she was so grateful to her friend. But there was something else there, too, wasn't there?

"You know then that I am not an innocent and have not been one for years," Arabella said.

"Yes."

"And your parents regret your family's connection to me."

"Well, I don't!" Rebecca was very loud. "I only regret I did nothing to help you afterwards."

"You are very kind."

"No, I'm not." Rebecca's tone was mutinous.

This was the second time in the last three days Arabella had thanked someone for being kind, and that person had refused the compliment. The other person had been Alasdair, just before he kissed her for the first time in the carriage.

She gazed at Rebecca. How strange she felt almost the same tension coming from her friend. Some bubbling, dangerous mixture of worry and dread and hope and courage.

"But you *are* kind, Rebecca, and I am most grateful to you." She didn't know why, but it seemed best to stay away from Rebecca, stay on the other side of the room.

Suddenly, the tension vanished, and there was her friend of old. Indeed, tender-hearted Rebecca's eyes were filling with tears.

"You are safe with me, Arabella."

Arabella crossed to her and held her hands.

"Of course, I am."

Rebecca smiled through her tears. "And when the snow stops, I will do everything in my power to help you get to Sommerleigh. To your real sister. But please, I beg of you, reconsider."

"Reconsider what?"

"The doctor. Punish him only briefly. Unlike most men, he is educable, I believe."

Alasdair sat on the edge of the bed in the room he had shared with Arabella for two nights now. He waited. He delayed putting on his shirt, remembering his dream of Arabella pressing her face to his chest in his sleep. And, this morning, before she had lost her temper, how she had sighed when he had faced her bare-chested. And how she had said lust had driven her to ask him to turn around.

The swathe covered part of his chest, but not all. Perhaps enough of his chest still showed to draw her closer to him. And she might kiss him again in that wild—and wildly generous—manner, just as she had before his shoulder had gone back into place.

She must have overestimated the time he would sleep. He hoped she would return to the room shortly. Because he wanted to tempt her. He thought he could.

So, he must, in some deep way, believe in her desire. Of course, he did. Were all the kisses and touches for him and him alone? And, if that were true, how selfish he was. No, he believed she felt something, it was just hard to believe it could be in any way as profound and desperate as what he felt.

Because if women felt as men did, every female who went to her wedding bed a virgin had practiced the same self-restraint that Alasdair had.

He shook his head. He could not sort this out right now, when he was alone and had so much turmoil inside of him. He must find Arabella and talk to her. He managed to get on his shirt by putting his head through the neck hole and his left arm through the sleeve. His right arm stayed in the sling and swathe, hugged to his body under the shirt.

He put his head out the door and waited. After ten minutes, a chambermaid walked by, carrying a stack of sheets.

"Pardon, but would ye ask Andrews, the butler, to come and speak to me?"

The butler Andrews told Alasdair he believed Mrs. Andrews had closeted herself with Lady Rebecca Dalrymple. Alasdair asked if the butler could inquire if Mrs. Andrews would come and speak to him.

Andrews' face was grave when he returned to Alasdair, hovering in the doorway of the bedchamber.

"She will not."

"Pardon?"

"She asked me to tell you she was not disposed to speak to you at this time.'"

"Oh."

"She seemed quite determined."

"Did she seem upset?"

The butler shrugged. "I could hear laughter before I knocked on the door."

Alasdair looked around the room.

"I cannae really be seen downstairs in just my shirt, can I? And the waistcoat and tailcoat are out of the question for now. I suppose ye had better show me to my own room, finally."

"Yes, Doctor."

After the butler Andrews had helped Alasdair into his boots and shown him to his much more modest room in the other wing, the butler lingered for a moment.

"You should not give up so easily, Doctor," Andrews said before he left.

It was not a matter of giving up easily. It was a matter of his inability to dress correctly. It was a matter of her refusing to come to him. It was a matter of his letting everything slip through his fingers. Once again.

Twenty-Six

Arabella went down to dinner, arm in arm with Rebecca. But Alasdair was not at the table. Should she have gone to him when he sent for her? She still had not been ready to face him once he was sober. She feared the end of her happiness with him. And some vain, childish part of her felt *he* should come after *her*, rather than her going to him. Despite her resolve, time and time again, she had been the aggressive one, even kissing him so passionately when his shoulder joint was out of place. In truth, she had kissed him that way because she thought it was likely the last time she ever would kiss him and she wanted, she wanted…she could not admit what she wanted just now. Even to herself. It hurt too much.

Perhaps he was still too drunk to come to dinner. Or was he in pain? Did he need her help? She was suddenly rent by anxiety and thought of excusing herself to go to him.

She had not noticed Giles was not at the table, either, until Lord Painswick spoke.

"Why have we no host, Andrews?" the marquess demanded of the butler.

Arabella conjured a picture of two men out in the snow, dueling. Giles with pistols and her Alasdair in a sling and swathe, with just a lancet in his left hand, and some bright-red blood staining the white drifts.

"I believe Lord Morpeth is not feeling well," the butler said.

Lady Lyndmouth got up from table immediately, without offering an excuse, and left the room.

Arabella was washed by relief. The butler Andrews leaned over while holding the serving platter of carved goose for her.

"The doctor did not feel he could be seen outside his own bedchamber with just his shirt over his sling."

"I see. He will get something to eat, won't he?"

"Of course, Mrs. Andrews." The butler almost bristled.

"And he has gone to a different room?" Arabella suddenly felt the piece of goose she was putting on her plate weighed a thousand pounds.

"I will show you to his bedchamber after dinner, Mrs. Andrews."

"That's not necessary." She returned the serving forks to the platter.

"Mrs. Andrews?"

"Yes?"

"In case you change your mind, he is in the third room on the left in the other wing."

"I won't change my mind."

The dinner was dull. The guests felt the absence of their host, the lack of exercise, the sense of being trapped. But the snow had mercifully stopped falling.

Alasdair had been glad to eat alone. He took the shirt off again when he realized how messy the job of eating with just one hand would be. He could cut nothing. He sat on the floor, cross legged, naked from the waist up except for the sling and swathe and leaned over and forked up the meat from the plate and tore off pieces with his teeth.

He was quite wild with not seeing Arabella for half a day, and eating in this primitive way matched his mood.

A knock. He got up quickly, thinking it might be Arabella. He looked down to make sure there was no gravy on his chest or the swathe. No. Good.

He opened the door.

Arabella averted her eyes when she saw him and how he was dressed. Or not dressed. His heart sank. Down deep, into his abdomen.

"Will you put on your shirt before I come into the room?"

"Aye." Alasdair retreated, found his shirt, and managed to get it over his head and then the left arm through the sleeve. He came back to the door, which he had left ajar. She met his eyes. She had such a serious expression. He did not think that boded well, and his heart sank to about the level of his knees.

Arabella came in the room and sat in a chair. He sat in another one and faced her.

He ached for her. His shoulder had an ache too, but it was a tolerable ache. He wished he could have a nip of whisky before having this conversation, but he had none at hand. And he knew it would be a mistake. It would be a weakness.

"I want to speak to you about what happened this morning in the drawing room."

"Aye." He was surprised. He had anticipated she would want to discuss what he had said to her about lust in her bedchamber. He was ready to admit he was wrong and, of course, women felt desire. He even hoped she might be willing to kiss him with that same raw passion again and demonstrate her desire to him. Because if her desire matched her fiery temper and it was for him, what a fortunate man he would be. The most fortunate man in the world.

But she wanted to discuss his own temper.

"Why did you attempt to strike Giles, Dr. Andrews?"

She used Lord Morpeth's first name while addressing him as *Dr. Andrews*. He felt the sour taste of bile rising in his throat.

"He touched ye."

"Yes, and he should not have. And I would have made it clear to him he should not have. And since you are my friend, you could have done the same."

Her friend. Five days ago, she had said she counted him among her friends, and he had been filled with such joy he could barely stammer out a reply. But, now, with two days experience as her husband, he wanted so much more.

Arabella went on, "But with words. We were in a room, filled with people. What could he have done in that room, *against my will*," she laid heavy emphasis on this last phrase, "that would have merited violence? With all those ladies and gentlemen present?"

"I didnae like the way he looked at ye."

"I would have thought you might be more concerned with how I looked at him."

"How *ye* looked at *him*?"

Arabella's gaze went down to her hands in her lap, and she spread her fingers wide apart.

"Why does his desire matter?" she asked.

Because Lord Morpeth is a man used to getting what he wants. And, finally, there's a chance I might get what I want. And I willnae let him ruin it. Even if I am nae a lord, dinnae I have a right to stake my own demesne? Am I nae a man, too, with a man's instinct to lay claim, to possess?

"We are back to our discussion from this morning. If you," Arabella swallowed, "are truly interested in a romance with me, you should be concerned with my desire. And mine alone."

"What is yer desire, Miss Lovelock?"

She gritted her teeth and looked away. "It is not for him."

"So why did ye tell me?" Alasdair spoke loudly. He could hear the anger in his voice, but he had no interest in softening it. "Why did ye tell me Lord Morpeth was the man who had enjoyed ye?"

Suddenly, she shrank, withdrawing even as he felt his own fury growing.

"I…don't know why. In the lodge, you asked why I was upset. I didn't want to lie to you."

"Why did ye tell me but then tell me nae to tell yer brothers-in-law, yer stepfather?"

"My mother told me never to tell them." She looked at the table. "She was afraid they would challenge him to a duel."

"But ye dinnae fear that from me? Ye felt ye could tell me. Safely."

She met his eyes. "Yes. I did."

"Why?"

"Because—"

"Because I am weaker, more craven than the duke, the earl, the viscount? That my sense of honor isnae as developed as theirs since I am nae a peer of the realm?"

"Because—"

"Because ye dinnae fear losing me in a duel the way yer mother did for the duke?"

"Because I trusted you! I trusted you would not do something foolish and leave me alone and unprotected. I trusted you to be a man of reason. I thought you were the not-stupid man. And I did not want Giles to have something to lord over you—I could not have borne that, to have him know something about me that you did not."

"Well, ye are two years too late for that."

Even as he said it, he knew it was the worst possible thing he could have said and she would never forgive him.

. . .

Oh.

He had told her in the carriage she had not been ruined. Exactly what she had longed to hear.

But it was not true. He did not really feel that way. And here was the evidence. He had cast it up to her, her loss of her innocence.

He would only ever see her as something that had been used. He would never absolve her for having let Giles know her first.

She took a deep breath.

"I will remind you that you were late, too, Dr. Andrews." Her voice trembled, and she hated that. "I did something that was hurtful to my family, and I will always regret it. Perhaps I should have been like you and done nothing. After all, that is what you and this world want from me. To do nothing. To sit by the fire with my embroidery and to wait."

"I dinnae want that, Miss Lovelock." His voice was still angry.

"Well, everyone else does. And I have been punished most thoroughly for my impatience. I threw everything away in my haste and poor judgment. The chance of real love, of a husband, of children. All gone. Do you think I need you to remind me in this hurtful way? To hear it from you, whom I had hoped—but, no. Let me just say that is the unkindest cut of all." She was about to cry in front of him again, so she stood. "And this idea that somehow someone could repair my honor by hurting the man who hurt me—it makes me ill."

There was a knock on the door, and she went to it, turned the knob, and walked out, pushing past the butler Andrews standing in the hallway.

She must give up now.

She must surrender to her fate, just as she had two years ago.

How foolish she had been to hold hope for a different outcome. How cruel life was to give her a glimpse of what she might have had and then take it away again.

She got down the hallway and to the other wing and into her own bedchamber. Somehow. She did not remember the steps she took. She closed the door behind her and sank to the carpet and lay there.

She had made her own bed in that cold London carriage over two years ago. She could see the years of lying in that lonely bed stretching out in front of her. And when she rose from that lonely bed in her cottage in Dunburn, there would be an endless parade of red-haired and green-eyed girls she would teach but who would never *courie* in her lap as they might if they were daughters.

A life of usefulness but one devoid of that which she had been seeking from the beginning. Love. Received and given. By someone who understood her. And whom she understood.

She had hoped he was strong enough to see her. All of her. He had made her think he was.

But either he was too weak or she was too much of a whore. Or both.

TWENTY-SEVEN

She was gone.

She had come to him, and he had only made the situation worse by revealing his frailty, his jealousy, his acquisitive nature. He had lost control, just as he had in the drawing room when he had almost struck Morpeth. And, worst of all, he had made her feel ashamed of her past when he should have been the one healing that wound, not the one ripping it open again.

He had been the stupid man. Again.

The butler Andrews was standing in the door Arabella had left open. He coughed to get Alasdair's attention.

"Lord Morpeth is ill, Dr. Andrews. Will you come?"

Alasdair felt himself about to cry or vomit. Still, he had never refused a request for his skills as a doctor, no matter his own anguish. No matter how ill he had been himself when a terrible fever had swept over his ship, far out in the Atlantic. No matter how weak his own bowels had been when he was on duty during his training and dysentery had crippled the hospital in Edinburgh.

And he needed to get away from his wretched self. Work

had always been his best escape. It was much better to be consumed by someone else's pain than to be dwelling in his own.

He followed the butler down the hallway to the central part of the house, to the bedchamber next to Lady Morpeth's.

The baron was in only a shirt and trousers, lying supine on the bed. When the butler and Alasdair came into the room, he tried to get up but winced and had to lie back.

"I did not ask for a physician," he growled.

"I did." A sharp voice. Alasdair then saw Lady Lyndmouth was in the room.

She went on, "Lord Morpeth has been having some pain in his belly for some hours now. Perhaps since luncheon?" She turned to Morpeth, who said nothing.

Alasdair waited.

"You must help him, Doctor," Lady Lyndmouth said.

"Yes." Morpeth grinned, a few beads of sweat on his forehead in the cold room. "Yes, we will see, won't we, if you really do treat everyone the same. Even those you may have a grievance against."

"I can only help if Lord Morpeth wants my help," Alasdair said.

"Giles," Lady Lyndmouth pleaded, all sharpness from her voice gone. "Giles."

Again, Morpeth tried to sit up, his face contorting in pain, and had to fall back.

"Fine. The bloodletter can examine me."

Alasdair approached the bed.

"I apologize for my appearance, Lord Morpeth." Alasdair meant he was wearing what Morpeth was—just trousers and an untucked shirt.

"We are dressed the same, Doctor. Illness is a great equalizer." Morpeth grimaced.

"Aye." Alasdair was surprised to hear one of his own deeply-held beliefs from the baron.

"What did ye eat for luncheon?" he asked.

"He did not eat," Lady Lyndmouth said.

"Why didnae ye eat, Lord Morpeth?"

"I was not hungry."

"Perhaps the pain had started before luncheon then?"

"Perhaps."

"Perhaps even yesterday?"

"Yes. But very little then."

"Have ye seen any blood in yer urine? Or in yer stool?"

"No."

"And the pain is where?"

Morpeth pointed to the center of his abdomen.

"And obviously the pain is worse when ye move."

"For the last two hours, the only thing that eases it at all is holding perfectly still, Doctor. Even then, it is still present."

Alasdair looked in Morpeth's eyes and could see fear. Big men like Lord Morpeth were not used to physical limitations. And to be a big man *and* a lord—Alasdair could see how one might feel omnipotent, might have the arrogance to think the world existed only for one's pleasure. How one might reach out and destroy a young woman's life with as little care as one might have in picking a daisy.

Alasdair wondered what kind of man he might be if he had been born into Lord Morpeth's position and had never starved or struggled or endured bone-aching weariness.

He would never know, and he was glad. He was more than glad. An unexpected surge of joy ran through him.

He suddenly felt free.

For the first time in years, he could not imagine envying any other man. He was not jealous of any lord, positioned high above him in the strata of society. Not Lord Morpeth. Not even his friend, the earl, Thomas Drake.

Alasdair Andrews had kissed Arabella Lovelock. He had held Arabella Lovelock. He had slept next to Arabella Lovelock. And now every effort in his life must be bent towards making sure those things happened again. And again. And again. And so on, for the rest of his life.

At one time, she had thought he was the not-stupid man. He must be that for her. And the first step was continuing his life's work. Being the best physician he could be, even if it was for this man in front of him.

Arabella had defended Alasdair, his practice. He must be worthy of that defense.

"May I touch ye, Lord Morpeth?"

Morpeth started to laugh and then stopped.

"The tensing of the abdominal muscles hurts, my lord?"

"Yes. I wondered how you were going to examine me with one arm, and I felt the irony of it, Doctor."

"I only need one arm and hand to examine ye."

Morpeth bit his lip. "I heard you scream some hours ago. I hope you have less pain now."

It was not an apology, but Alasdair wondered if this was the first time Lord Morpeth had experienced sympathy, so close on the heels of Alasdair's severe pain had his own followed.

"The pain is considerably improved now that the dislocation is reduced, thank ye, Lord Morpeth." Alasdair took Morpeth's wrist in his hand and felt his pulse. It was rapid, and the skin was hot. He noted a chamber pot by the bed, filled with clear gastric juices. "Ye have vomited, I see."

"When I move and the pain is bad, I vomit."

"I would like to raise yer shirt and unbutton the fall of yer trousers."

"Yes, Doctor," Morpeth said.

Alasdair looked at Lady Lyndmouth.

"I am not leaving," she said. "I have seen everything, I assure you." She did not blush.

Alasdair raised the baron's shirt but found he could not unbutton the fall of the trousers with only one hand.

Lady Lyndmouth pushed him aside. "Let me." She unbuttoned Morpeth's fall but left it in place and stepped back.

Alasdair observed the skin of the abdomen with its pelt of dark hair. It appeared normal. He leaned down and put his ear to all four quadrants of the abdomen and heard bowel sounds. Perhaps decreased, but present. He straightened and observed again how still Lord Morpeth was. Alasdair took his left hand and pushed on the umbilicus.

"Unh."

The abdomen was slightly rigid under Alasdair's pressing hand. He now moved to the left upper quadrant, right upper quadrant. The same pain reaction from Morpeth, the same degree of rigidity. Now, he pressed in the left lower quadrant.

"When," Morpeth gasped, "when you pressed me there, I felt it on the other side."

Alasdair now pressed on the right lower quadrant.

Rock hard.

Morpeth came up off the bed in a spasm and grabbed Alasdair's left arm in a pincer grip of iron.

"Don't," he said through his teeth, "touch me," he fell back but did not release Alasdair's arm, "there."

"Let go of the Doctor, Giles, before you break his one good arm." Lady Lyndmouth's voice continued to be cool.

Morpeth released Alasdair's arm.

"Now I must examine yer scrotum." Alasdair folded down the unbuttoned fall. Both sides of the scrotum looked normal. Morpeth appeared to have no increase in his pain when Alasdair palpated the testicles, both of which had a normal lie. Alasdair allowed himself an unprofessional moment of satisfaction in seeing that Lord Morpeth's flaccid phallus did not seem much larger than his own when in the same state.

He put the fall back in place. "That didnae hurt, Lord Morpeth, did it? When I felt yer testicles?"

"No." And then Morpeth grinned. "I was worried for a moment you might twist one and exact a little revenge for your shoulder."

"Forgive me," Alasdair said and put his left hand under Morpeth's right knee and lifted his leg.

Again, Morpeth came off the bed, and this time a scream escaped his lips. Alasdair put the leg back down gently. Lady Lyndmouth was sitting on the bed, her hands on Lord Morpeth's face, and she was attempting to soothe him.

"We will get you something for your pain, Giles." She looked at Alasdair. "Won't we?"

"Aye. We will have to ask the Marchioness of Painswick for some of her laudanum."

But Morpeth shook his head and said through his teeth, "No, I don't want it."

Lady Lyndmouth stroked his face. "Just a little, Giles. So you can rest."

"No."

The butler Andrews, who had been silent throughout, spoke. "Is there anything you need, Dr. Andrews?"

Alasdair went to the window, pulled back a curtain, and looked out. It was pitch dark.

"The snow stopped earlier. When the dawn comes, if the snow continues to hold off, some men might go to the carriage and recover my medical bag. I will describe it for ye." He crossed to the butler Andrews and said in an undertone, "Please ask Mrs. Andrews which of her trunks she would like, as well. She would appreciate another dress to wear, I am sure. And endeavor to ask the marquess about his wife's laudanum. If he resists, tell me, and I will ask him myself."

His voice had clearly not been low enough. Lady Lynd-mouth stood. "I will go to Lord Painswick now. I will have him take me to the marchioness' room, and I will bring the laudanum."

"I will not take it," Morpeth said.

Alasdair stepped to the bed again. "We will only have it ready, my lord, in case ye change yer mind. Perhaps the pain will pass."

"What is it, Doctor?" Morpeth asked. Alasdair could hear him try to mask his fear with gruffness. "What is the cause of the pain?"

Alasdair kept his face impassive. "I am hoping 'tis a small ureteral stone, my lord." But he knew it was not. The man had florid peritonitis. But it was not a lie to say what he hoped. The alternative was so much worse. "A small stone, much smaller than a bladder stone, moving from the kidney to the bladder. They cause excruciating pain. Like giving birth. But when the stone passes, the pain goes away."

A frowning Morpeth searched his face. "You know it's not a stone."

"We will wait and see. I will attend on ye and see if yer condition improves or worsens."

"Andrews," Morpeth said peremptorily.

"Yes?" "Aye?" Alasdair and the butler answered simultaneously.

Morpeth turned his head to the butler. "Go get the doctor some kind of cloak so he can stay warm. He is not burning with fever like I am. And I would prefer my physician not to succumb to the cold while he is tending to me."

"Yes, my lord," the butler Andrews said, and after Lady Lyndmouth kissed Morpeth once on the lips, she rose and left the room with the butler.

The two men, patient and physician, were alone.

"I would," Alasdair cleared his throat, "like to inform yer wife of yer condition."

"No."

"My lord—"

"Dr. Andrews, it does not inspire confidence that you want to tell her anything. You must think this is more serious than you let on. But I will not have my wife worried until she must be."

"Aye, my lord."

Alasdair sat in a chair and prepared, as he had so many times before, to wait through the night.

The butler Andrews quickly returned with a cloak and then left again, saying he would arrange for men to go to the carriage at first light and Dr. Andrews should ring if he thought of anything he needed. Lady Lyndmouth was back in half an hour, clutching two bottles of laudanum.

"We must hope," she said, smiling thinly at Alasdair, "the marchioness still has enough for her own use so you don't have another patient on your hands, Doctor. Because I am not giving these bottles back."

At midnight, Morpeth consented to his first dose of laudanum.

Two hours before dawn, Lady Morpeth came into the room through a door in the wall that lay behind the head of Lord Morpeth's bed. Nurse Gastrell supported her with one arm.

"Doctor," Morpeth gasped as Lady Morpeth drew near. He looked accusingly at Alasdair.

"I could hear, Giles," Lady Morpeth said as she approached the bed. "I could hear you in pain, the doctor's voice, Lady Lyndmouth's voice." She fixed Lady Lyndmouth now in her gaze. "My bed is just there, on the other side of the wall. I can always hear what passes in this room."

Lady Lyndmouth's perfect composure was shaken. "My lady—"

Lady Morpeth raised her hand. "No. Not now." She turned to Alasdair. "I am glad you are here, Dr. Andrews."

He bowed. "Yer butler Andrews has said some men are going soon to fetch my bag from the carriage. Once the morphia in my bag thaws, we can give some to yer husband. 'Tis more potent than the laudanum."

Morpeth raised his head. "No!"

Lady Lyndmouth instinctively lunged forward to touch his face and then stopped and withdrew her hand.

"Please, Lady Lyndmouth," Lady Morpeth said and stepped away from the bed. She murmured to her nurse, and Nurse Gastrell guided her to a chair, and Lady Morpeth sat down heavily. "Please give him comfort. I would not deprive him of that since I cannot give it to him myself. Like so many other things a wife should provide."

As he had so many other times in his career, Alasdair marveled at the resilience and infinite courage of the human female.

Lord Morpeth lay in his bed, rigid, covered in sweat, whimpering in pain.

The bedchamber continued to have three women in it. A weak Lady Morpeth, sitting in a chair, determined not to leave her husband's room. Nurse Gastrell with her, of course. And Lady Lyndmouth was also there, clutching Lord Morpeth's hand, changing the wet cloths on his forehead, murmuring to him.

Alasdair had never treated a patient where the mistress and the wife were both present at the same time. There was no etiquette governing this. He would have to make it up as he went.

He re-examined Morpeth before turning so he faced both Lady Lyndmouth and Lady Morpeth.

"I fear 'tis typhlitis," he said.

There was a sound behind him. He turned. It was the butler Andrews, much the worse for wear like all of them in the room. He was clearing his throat and coming in the door with the basin of snow Alasdair had requested ten minutes earlier. He looked at Alasdair apologetically.

Arabella was behind him. "What is typhlitis?"

She had slept fitfully, weeping and then dreaming and then weeping some more. She did not want to get out of bed, to begin the first day of the lonely future she had conjured for herself in such detail last night, but she forced herself to rise and dress. She started downstairs for breakfast but saw the butler Andrews in the hallway with a basin of snow. She worried it was for Alasdair's shoulder, but Andrews told her that her husband's shoulder was fine. Her trunks had been recovered from the abandoned carriage and would be brought to her room shortly so she might have fresh clothes.

She stayed the butler with her hand on his arm.

"But my husband is well?"

"Yes, Mrs. Andrews, but I must deliver this snow to him before it melts."

She wondered what need Alasdair had of snow if his shoulder was fine. She followed the butler Andrews to this room.

Alasdair, she noted, did not look tired. He was in his element. But he stiffened when he heard her question and saw her.

"Miss L— Mrs. Andrews, ye should nae be here."

"Is it contagion?"

"Nae," Alasdair said abruptly.

"Then why should I not be here? I can be of use." *To you,* she added in her head.

"'Tis nae seemly."

Arabella looked at Lady Lyndmouth. She was holding Giles' hand, staring at him intently, her lips moving, perhaps in prayer. She looked at Lady Morpeth and the nurse.

She got very close to Alasdair and said, "Along with two of the other ladies here, I already have knowledge of Lord Morpeth's body. You know I have no care for what is seemly, Dr. Andrews."

Alasdair's face went white. A muscle at his jaw flexed. He held himself very still. Oh, why had she reminded him of that? She had no right to hurt him, no matter how he had hurt her.

"Typhlitis is an inflammation of the bowel," he said. "There is an outpouching of the intestine, here," he pointed to his own right lower abdomen with his good left hand, "and 'tis called the vermiform appendix. It can become inflamed— sometimes because 'tis filled with stones—and it can rupture. Parkinson and Wegeler have described it."

"Then what happens?" Arabella asked.

He took her arm and drew her aside, away from the sick bed and Lady Lyndmouth and Lady Morpeth.

"Some die. Some get better."

"How many get better?"

"Many. But I dinnae ken how many get well when they are as ill as Lord Morpeth is." Alasdair kept his voice and face calm, but Arabella could sense the situation was grave.

"What is the treatment?"

"Morphia and laudanum. We keep his fever down with cold compresses made with snow and ice."

Lady Lyndmouth spoke with urgency, "There must be something that can be done!"

Alasdair turned to her. "We will give more morphia."

"I do not mean easing his pain. I mean curing him."

"There have been…but 'tis dangerous."

"Tell us," Lady Lyndmouth begged.

"There have been attempts to remove the appendix with surgery."

"Where has this been done?" asked Lady Morpeth.

"In London, but the appendix had herniated into the scrotum. A much easier surgery. In France, but the patient died."

"Giles is a man who thrives on risk. He will not turn away from risk now, I believe. Not when the stakes are his life on either side," Lady Morpeth said.

"I am nae the man for it," Alasdair said. Arabella admired his mild voice, his stoic expression.

"We will send for another doctor," said Lady Lyndmouth, her own voice tinged with panic.

The butler Andrews spoke up, "The roads are still impassable."

"I dinnae ken there are many doctors who are familiar with the history of the surgery and disease," Alasdair said. "I am because I had a patient die this way five years ago."

"Did you operate on him, Doctor?"

"I did. The surgery was a failure. And I caused him a great deal of pain before he died. I should have let him alone."

"*Primum non nocere,*" Arabella said without thinking.

Alasdair glanced at her, and she wanted to tell him how much she admired his courage. How bravely he faced death every day in his profession.

"I do not understand," said Lady Lyndmouth angrily. "He is going to die."

Lady Morpeth stood, clutching her nurse's arm. "I must talk to my husband, and we will see what he wants you to do." She approached the bed. She leaned forward and spoke in Giles' ear. No one else could hear what she said.

Giles' eyes opened and sought out his wife's face hovering above him.

"Dr. Andrews said that?" he asked, and there was a smile even as he gasped in pain.

"The doctor said maybe. From…that time three months ago. Maybe."

Giles' hands fumbled at Lady Morpeth's and grabbed them and held them to his lips and kissed them. Arabella was strangely moved by this. The man who was the villain in her own life, so tender with his wife.

"Giles, you must listen now," Lady Morpeth said gently. "Dr. Andrews says you have a diseased bowel. There is a surgery to cut away the bad part. Very few people have had the surgery. Even fewer have survived."

"None," Alasdair's voice cut through. "Nae of the type of surgery that Lord Morpeth requires."

"What do you want?" Lady Morpeth asked, but the man had closed his eyes. "Giles!"

He opened his eyes. "As in everything else, I leave it to you, my wife."

Lady Morpeth straightened and looked at Alasdair, her gaze steely even as her stance wavered and Nurse Gastrell rushed to her side to steady her.

"For now, I will defer to the physician in the room."

Over the next hour, Alasdair continued to try to persuade Arabella to leave the bedchamber, but she refused. She would not leave Alasdair's side. She hoped he knew it was for him that she stayed and not for Giles, but how was she to let him know?

"Let Mrs. Andrews stay, if she wishes to," Lady Morpeth said. "She has a power over you, Dr. Andrews, that the rest of us do not. She may convince you to do what the rest of us cannot."

"Cut me, Doctor," Giles now moaned from the bed. "I do not want to die."

"Ye may still recover, Lord Morpeth," Alasdair said.

Giles raised his head an inch or two. "But, if I worsen, you will perform the surgery?"

"I…"

Giles' head fell back to the mattress. "Promise me."

"I cannae."

"Why?"

"'Tis nae how medicine should be done."

Giles groaned.

"And…" Alasdair hesitated.

"What, Doctor?" Lady Lyndmouth seemed frantic.

"I would need to take my arm out of the sling, and I fear there is still enough residual pain in my right shoulder that my skills would be limited."

"I will help."

Everyone in the room, save Giles whimpering on the bed, turned to look at Arabella.

Arabella did not know why she had said that. She only knew it was her instinct to help Alasdair. And she had always had a strong stomach and no fear of her father's sickbed, even when she was only ten years of age.

"Dr. Andrews will tell me what to do. I will do what he cannot with his right arm."

"Ye have nae training," Alasdair sputtered.

"That is true. But you have the training. And I am very good with fine work."

"Fine needlework!"

"Yes." Arabella straightened her shoulders. "That is what I have been allowed to do. But my fingers are nimble, and my eyes are sharp. And, as you said, you will only attempt the surgery if there seems no other way for Lord Morpeth to survive. And I will only become involved if your arm should hamper you."

"There will be blood."

"Do not women face their own blood every month without fear? Is fresh blood from a man so different?"

"Ye could kill him."

"Yes. It will be a terrible responsibility. The same one you would shoulder."

"I forbid it."

"Well, as you said, I have no training. I can do nothing without your help." She pulled him down and whispered in his ear, "But if you are forbidding me as my husband, I will remind you that you do not have that power over me."

He flushed and said nothing.

Lord Morpeth continued to worsen. He was delirious. He gave off a foul heat that filled the room. His pulse grew thready.

Alasdair knew the crisis was imminent.

Lady Lyndmouth begged. Lady Morpeth looked grim.

Alasdair, Arabella, and the butler Andrews gathered in Lord Morpeth's dressing room. With Arabella's help, Alasdair took off his shirt and the swathe and sling. He tried moving his shoulder. He winced.

"Can you use the arm?" Arabella asked.

She stood close to him. Even with his increasing fatigue, he longed for her, wanted to touch her cheek, feel her hand on his chest.

"To a certain degree. 'Tis more that the pain restricts movements I would normally do with ease."

The butler helped him put his shirt back on, now allowing the right arm to be inside the right sleeve, and left the dressing room.

"You will be able to do the surgery?" Arabella asked.

"'Tis nae advisable."

Arabella said quietly, "So you will do nothing."

"Usually, 'tis the best course." Alasdair returned his right arm to the sling, leaving off the swathe. Arabella helped position the sling in place, and, for a moment, her hand lingered on his forearm.

"But not always," she said.

"Aye. Only most of the time."

"So we will wait until he dies."

"I willnae kill him."

"Are you worried you will be accused of that?"

"Nae. I am worried I actually will kill him."

"But you may also kill him from inaction. Sometimes, Alasdair, isn't great harm caused by doing nothing in the attempt to avoid harm?"

He did not know if she was talking about the surgery or about his own failure in regards to her. Years ago, he had done nothing when every part of him had yearned for her. He had let fear of rejection keep him from pursuing her. He had not risked failure.

To protect himself, he had chosen to cherish her only in his heart rather than to cherish her in his arms.

And that had been a mistake. If he could take her at her word, she had yearned for him and would have welcomed his affections. And, in time, she would have likely consented to be his wife.

So much hurt would have been avoided if he had been brave. If he had risked himself.

Now, alone with her in the dressing room, he thought of making a bargain with her. *I will perform the surgery, Arabella, if ye consent to be my wife.* It was a bittersweet fancy he quickly put away.

"Aye, Arabella." He put his left hand to her cheek briefly and strode out of the dressing room.

"Every man with strong arms and a strong stomach will need to help. We must have the best light possible. And I will go now to the kitchen and look at the boning knives."

Twenty-Eight

The room was blazing with light, as bright as Lady Morpeth's room the day Alasdair had first examined her. The curtains were open to allow the sunlight to pour in and join the lamplight. He only hoped the sunshine, the first he had seen in days, was a good omen.

Lady Morpeth and Lady Lyndmouth had been escorted from the room, told there was nothing they could do, they must go and rest in their own rooms.

"Because he will need yer strength afterwards," Alasdair said with a confidence he did not feel.

Every footman and groom had been called upon. Lord Morpeth was a large man and would need a great deal of strength to hold him down, even with straps tying him to the bed and despite the dangerously large dose of morphia Alasdair intended to give him.

Paterson assisted the head groom with using the leather straps from the stable to secure the delirious Morpeth to the bed.

"I was a surgeon's assistant for a time. In the Royal Navy,

as ye were. The blood willnae bother me. I can help hold Lord Morpeth."

Alasdair looked at him hopefully. "So ye might be able to help if my right arm fails me with the most delicate work?" Arabella could leave the room and be spared this horror.

"Nae." Paterson shook his head and held up his right hand. Alasdair cursed silently. He had never noticed Paterson had no right thumb. Paterson grunted and went on, "Cannon. One of ours, misfiring."

"Ye have done very well without it," Alasdair said and clapped him on the shoulder. "And I will appreciate yer help in holding."

"The lad Ewen wanted to come, too, but I locked him in with the cows to keep him away. I must remember to let him out when this is done."

"Aye."

Alasdair allowed himself to glance over at Arabella. Like him, she had shrouded her clothes in an apron from the kitchen. For the moment, she was sitting in a chair and drinking tea the butler had brought her.

Dauntless Arabella.

He thought briefly of taking her back into Lord Morpeth's dressing room and kissing her. Because he longed for her. And because she would never permit it afterwards, not when she no longer needed him to save Lord Morpeth. And certainly not when Morpeth died and Alasdair had allowed her to be part of this desperate endeavor.

But kissing would not help sharpen his mind. Or hers.

It was time.

Alasdair took off his sling and gave a large draft of morphia to Morpeth, his head held up and immobile by the largest footman and Paterson. Morpeth swallowed and did not choke. Alasdair only hoped the dose was not so large that it would stop Morpeth's breath.

His shoulder ached without the sling. He turned to Arabella. He did not know how to address her, so he said what was in his heart.

"Arabella, my love." She looked up at him, astonishment in her eyes, the same astonishment that had been there when he had first kissed her. Did she know him so little?

"Let us wash our hands."

"Yes, Alasdair."

"I dinnae ken why, but washing hands before surgery seems to improve the chances of recovery."

She watched how he scrubbed his hands with the bar of soap that had been brought from Lady Morpeth's boudoir by Nurse Gastrell earlier. He rinsed his hands carefully, and she followed him.

"'Tis unnecessary for ye to see this part. I will tell ye if I come to need ye."

Her face was a bit pale, but she stood taller. "I have to see what you do with your hands in case I must manage something myself."

They walked together to the bed. Half a dozen men held Lord Morpeth, and half a dozen men held lamps aloft. There was a space for two people on the right side of Morpeth's abdomen.

Alasdair took a deep breath. He selected a small boning knife. Using his left hand, he created a tension in the skin over the man's right lower abdomen.

"Hold him, men."

He cut. The men did very well, and, although Lord Morpeth moaned, his trunk moved very little under Alasdair's knife. Alasdair knew the morphia helped, but he also thought Morpeth's strength was near its end.

Alasdair made a large incision, much larger than the organ he hoped to remove. He might need a large surgical field to see well. And, in truth, he had only ever seen one vermiform appendix and did not know if he would be able to find it today.

In addition to the knife, he used some instruments from his bag, tweezers and small forceps, to assist in dissecting through the skin, the scant subcutaneous fat, the fascia, and, finally, the muscle. It took him quite a long time and despite the coldness of the room, he felt himself covered in sweat.

Throughout it all, he was aware of Arabella at his elbow. He had feared she would be a distraction, but she was not. He felt almost as if she were a replacement for Dr. Murray—observing, urging him on silently, supporting his efforts with her own intense absorption in the problem. A few times he almost turned to ask her opinion before remembering she would have never seen something like this before.

He cut through only a few small vessels, and he was able to cauterize them quickly with his metal tweezers heated in a candle flame so there was some blood, but not much.

Finally, he was through the peritoneum. His shoulder ached. He put the knife and tweezers down and flexed his fingers.

He looked at Morpeth's face. The man still breathed. Alasdair could see his rapid pulse in his neck. Good.

He looked at Arabella. Her eyes were on him, not on Morpeth, not on the gaping abdomen in front of them. She was not pale. She did not look as if she were about to vomit.

"How is your arm, Dr. Andrews?"

He smiled. "'Tis fine," he lied.

"You must tell me how and when I can help you," she said.

"Aye."

The butler Andrews was at his side, averting his eyes from the surgical site as most of the rest of the men were. He offered Alasdair some water from a cup, and Alasdair drank thirstily.

Alasdair had bent some long-handled metal spoons into hooks, and he put those now into his opening and had men with long arms reaching over and pulling on them to keep his incision open. He asked for more light.

He knew it was likely only minutes, but it felt like he was hours poking in the peritoneal cavity, going over miles of intestine, before he found what he was looking for.

There. A swollen finger of a thing, a worm oozing pus, firm and full of stones, apparently partially perforated. The vermiform appendix. Yes, here is where it attached to the rest of the bowel. He must remove it. Then close the stump, the hole in the bowel he would create by cutting off the appendix. Wash the pus from the area. And then the slow surgical withdrawal from the peritoneal cavity. Closing the layers of fascia, skin.

Alasdair managed to get a firm grasp on the proximal end of the appendix with his forceps.

"Please hold these, Arabella. Dinnae let them go." Her small hand came into his field of view and took the forceps from him. He seized the distal end of the appendix with his tweezers in his left hand and took the boning knife in his right and cut the appendix free.

Relief.

But just as he did that, his right arm was shaken by a spasm, and he nearly dropped the boning knife.

"Alasdair," Arabella said, her voice hushed.

He brought the appendix out of the cavity with the tweezers still in his left hand and put the grotesque specimen on a cloth on the mattress next to Lord Morpeth. He also put the tweezers there and used his left hand to take the boning knife from his right hand.

He allowed himself a look at Arabella. "Hold those forceps tightly now. Dinnae let them go. Cutting is done. Now 'tis all sewing."

"Yes, you had better let me do that, hadn't you?"

He looked down, and his right hand was trembling uncontrollably.

"I can sew, Alasdair."

He put the boning knife down. "I'll have ye thread the needle to start." He used his left hand to take the forceps from her.

A man holding a lamp on the other side of the bed turned his head to the side and vomited onto the floor.

Arabella found one of the lengths of gut Alasdair had taken from his bag and threaded it onto one of his needles.

"This looks like one of my embroidery needles." She pulled the gut through the tiny eye, sticking out her tongue and biting on it as she did so.

"Aye, I buy all my needles at ordinary shops. I get odd looks from the shopkeepers."

"Shall I double the thread?"

"Aye, and knot the two ends together. I dinnae want to risk the gut coming out of the needle before I finish."

Arabella made a neat knot and looked at him expectantly.

"Ye take the forceps again and give me the needle."

"Yes." She took the forceps from his left hand and put the needle flat on his left palm.

But when he attempted to transfer the needle to his right hand, his right hand shook, and he could not get his fingers to close properly around the needle.

He looked at Arabella. Her blue eyes, so trusting, were fixed on his.

She longed to push the dark-red lock away from his left eye. But she did not. She stared at his right eye and waited for him. For his direction.

I am here, Alasdair. Tell me what to do. I can be your hands.

"I think," he said slowly. "I think ye had better do the sewing. I will tell ye what to do. Ye will do nothing unless I tell ye to do it."

"Aye," she said without even thinking about her choice of word.

He smiled briefly. "Dinnae worry. There are plenty of good surgeons who dinnae hail from Scotland."

But none who are women.

"I must be here, at yer back," he said and stepped behind her. She moved into his place, still holding the forceps tightly. She felt his breath on her left ear, his left arm coming down and taking the forceps from her. On her other side, his right arm came around her, and he held out his shaking right palm with the threaded needle on it.

She took the needle.

"First," he said, "do ye see where the forceps are, where I made my cut?"

"Yes."

"This is the most important part of the sewing, Arabella. We must close this stump so the contents of the gut dinnae leak out into the cavity. That has already started because the appendix was perforated, and 'tis what has made Lord Morpeth so ill. If we fail in this, the surgery will be for naught."

She liked that he said *we*.

"Do ye ken how to make a stitch like the top of a purse? That we can draw together, and it will be tight?

"Yes, Alasdair."

"Ye might need the tweezers to move the tissue as ye sew. I try nae to touch the bowel too much. I will stop ye if I see anything amiss."

"You will tell me if I do something wrong?" She was able to keep her voice from quavering, and, for that, she was glad.

"Since nae a one has ever done this before, in precisely this way, 'twould be a difficult task for me to correct ye."

Arabella stuck her chin out. He had said that before, but she had not taken it in. She was among the first. Maybe she *was* the first. She would do this.

She leaned closer and asked for more light. Obliging grooms and footmen raised their lamps to help. She sank the needle into the small tube of flesh, not drawing the thread taut, but leaving a sizable tail. She waited.

"Good. Go on," Alasdair said.

"How many stitches do you think there should be around the edge, Alasdair?"

He considered. "Five to seven."

She made six careful circumferential stitches around the stump. She waited.

"Good. Now ye will gently pull on the purse string so it cinches the stump closed."

She did so.

"Tighter," and then, "Tighter still," and then, "Stop and knot it off without losing the tightness of the cinch." She did so. He came around her, bent over and was able to get the tweezers into his right hand to poke and prod at the stitch.

"Very good. It looks fast. The tissue here is healthy. It should hold."

Arabella breathed a sigh of relief. He stepped behind her again.

"But this is exactly when new doctors and surgeons make their errors. When they think the most difficult part is done. Ye need to cut the tails of the knot. Ye must nae cut anything else. Nae flesh, nae bowel, nae the stitches ye have just made."

She picked up the boning knife, and, using the utmost care, she cut the tails of the gut free from the knot. She straightened her back.

"Can we," she cleared her throat, "send someone to Lady

Rebecca Dalrymple and ask for a loan of her smallest embroidery scissors?"

"Aye." She heard Alasdair dispatch one of the footmen. She started threading the needle with more gut. Alasdair poked at the stitch again and released the forceps.

"I will see if I can wash the pus from this area. Water and linen, please."

Arabella stepped away, and Alasdair poured water into the cavity and then soaked it up with linen. He did this several times, using clean linen each time. Then he inspected her stitch again.

"'Tis a good ligature, Arabella."

He looked up at Giles' face, and she followed his gaze. Giles was pale, and his breathing was shallow.

"I cannae give him more morphia. Ye men will have to continue to hold him fast as the wound is closed."

Under Alasdair's direction, Arabella used a running stitch to close the first layer of fascia. The footman came back with Rebecca's little gold scissors, and Arabella felt much more at ease cutting the tails of the knot off with the scissors as opposed to the sharp boning knife.

Giles did not move. He did not cry out.

She repeated her work with the next layer of fascia, her and Alasdair's left hands working to bring the fascia together as she stitched.

And then, finally, blessedly, the skin. Alasdair had moved away from her, trusting she could tie off the gut and clip it. He was at the head of the bed, feeling Giles' pulse at his neck.

Arabella had a sinking feeling. Had all this been for nothing?

"He is warm. He still has a pulse. He still breathes," Alasdair said.

A ragged cheer erupted from the men around the bed.

Arabella stepped away and quickly found a chair. She did

not want to faint. And Alasdair was at her side, kneeling, taking her pulse.

"I think I need some luncheon," she said.

He put his hands in her bloody ones.

"Ye are very brave," he said. "And ye have good hands. A strong stomach. A stout heart."

"Thank you for trusting me. What now?"

"A bath and luncheon for ye. And rest." He stood and released her hands.

"What now for Giles?"

"He sleeps. And I watch and wait."

Twenty-Nine

Alasdair managed to leave the sick room one time in the next eighteen hours. The butler Andrews had his trunk of clothes brought from the snowbound coach, and Alasdair luxuriated in a quick, hot bath and changed into a fresh shirt and hose and trousers. He was glad to get back into a waistcoat and a tailcoat and to note he no longer needed the sling although he would continue to rest his right arm as much as possible. He returned to the sick room and snatched short naps while sitting up in a chair, as every physician learns to do.

Lord Morpeth continued to be delirious and required being tied to the bed as well as strong men standing by so he would not thrash and tear his stitches loose. Lady Lyndmouth and Lady Morpeth returned to keep vigil, often together.

The next morning, Arabella came into the sick room.

Alasdair had his eyes closed, but he was hovering on the edge of sleep, still somewhat aware of what passed. He noted Arabella's sweet scent first. Then he heard her soft steps. Lady Lyndmouth's voice, very quiet, came to his ears.

"Mrs. Andrews, Lord Morpeth still lives. We are so grateful to you and your husband."

"It's all to do with Dr. Andrews, I assure you."

"He is a miracle. That he should be here just when he was most needed. And he has only left the bedside for twenty minutes altogether."

Feeling guilty for his inadvertent eavesdropping, Alasdair rubbed his eyes and yawned noisily.

She was by his side instantly.

"Dr. Andrews."

"Mrs. Andrews."

If only she were. He gazed at her, trying to drink in every detail of her face, her hair, her body. She had slept, he could tell. She looked rested and fed. She had a different dress on.

"Alasdair, you must go to your own bed and sleep, or you will become a patient as well."

He stood. "Nonsense."

"Tell me what to look for in Lord Morpeth's condition, and I will have someone fetch you if there is a crisis."

"Ye did admirably with the surgery. It widnae have been successful without ye. But this isnae yer task, this is mine."

Lady Lyndmouth called, "Doctor?"

She was at the head of the bed. Lord Morpeth's eyes were open and looking at Lady Lyndmouth.

Alasdair felt the man's forehead. "His fever is down." He felt the wrist. "The pulse disnae race, and 'tis strong."

"Water." This was from the baron. A very weak and cracked voice.

"Just a sip." Alasdair directed the footman and the groom who had been standing by to release Lord Morpeth from his straps. Morpeth clasped Lady Lyndmouth's hand, as Alasdair supported his head and brought a cup of water to his lips.

Morpeth took a sip and swallowed with no difficulty.

"More," he said.

"In time, Lord Morpeth." Alasdair turned to Lady Lyndmouth. "This cup of water should last an hour. Only a small sip every few minutes. If he vomits or chokes, ye must have someone come get me immediately. If he does well with the cup of water, he can have two cups the next hour, and so on."

"Yes, Doctor," Lady Lyndmouth said as she took the cup from him. "I will have Lady Morpeth come to the bedside, as well.

"Aye. Have someone fetch me if fever returns, if his pain worsens."

"Yes, Doctor."

Only then did Alasdair let Arabella take him from the room and into another. And only after she had led him to the bed and taken off his tailcoat and waistcoat and eased off his boots and made him recline did he realize he was in her bedchamber.

He drifted off, secure in the knowledge she was in the room with him. Dauntless Arabella, guarding the doctor's sleep.

THIRTY

He woke in a dark room, and she was there by his side, asleep. On her stomach, he thought. He could see only a dim outline of her form with the scant light coming from the embers of the fire.

She was not touching him except for one small hand over his left chest, grasping his shirt, exactly where she had pressed her hand when he had walked into her cottage in Dunburn.

He moved a little, and she woke immediately. She pulled herself to him, and her mouth sought his. Even as she kissed him, she was tugging at her nightdress. She broke the kiss and knelt at his side, pulling the nightdress all the way up, over her head.

She leaned over to kiss him again, and he knew what he felt grazing the shirt over his chest were her naked breasts. He put a hand up and touched her back. She stopped kissing him and held still, kneeling, as his fingers brushed against the warm, velvet skin overlying her shoulder blade. He allowed himself to stroke his hand down her back, and, as he did so, she exhaled slowly. And then the bone and muscle of her back ended, and he felt the fleshy roundness of her buttock under his hand. A new, beautiful, lush territory she was offering him.

"I don't want to die," she whispered.

"Nae," he said.

"I don't want to die without having you."

His hand, as if it had a mind of its own, was now moving from the cheek of her buttock to her hip bone and then following the curve of her waist upward, upward, seeking and not stopping until the hand was filled with the softness of her breast. Surely, a naked breast constituted new territory, as well.

"Yer nae going to die, Arabella," he murmured.

"Yes, I am, and so are you."

His thumb also seemed to be acting independently, and it swept over the front of her breast, brushing her nipple. She inhaled sharply even as the nipple drew to a hard point under his thumb.

"I'm going to undress you, Alasdair."

She pulled at his shirt, and he half sat up so she could raise the shirt over his head. Her face came against his chest, and she kissed him there, and her bare breasts were rubbing the skin of his abdomen. Small, skillful fingers were at his waist, and she tugged on his trousers, and he lifted his pelvis off the bed, and she slid the trousers all the way off him, down his legs. He could feel his member spring away from his body as soon as it was released from his clothing—hard, throbbing, aching for release already.

He was unable to move. Frozen.

She lay down on her back next to him, very near, but not touching him.

"You know," she said softly, "people have been coupling for a very long time."

"Aye."

"Since Adam and Eve."

"Aye."

"It should be entirely natural what happens next."

"Aye."

"I want you to be my Adam."

She must have lifted and spread her legs as she spoke because something nudged his cock. The side of her thigh, he thought.

Then, in the darkness, he did what he had imagined doing so many times.

He turned and got on top of her, finding her face with his hands so he could plunder her mouth with his tongue and lips. His knees landed on the mattress between her already-spread thighs, and he was pushing her into the bed with the weight of his upper body, even as his erect cock blindly stabbed between her legs. He felt her legs around his waist and one of her hands clutching his flank and the other hand on his shaft, and she was pulling him towards what must be her introitus. He could feel wetness and warmth on the head of his cock.

"Yes," she whispered.

He plunged in without a thought of anything but his pure, aching need to bury himself inside her.

He had conquered a whole kingdom with a single thrust.

It was a miracle he did not spend himself immediately. Her walls grabbed at his member, enclosing him in her heat. He thrust once, twice, three, four times. And, on his fifth thrust, he knew he was about to lose control and pulled out of her entirely and felt himself pulse with the most agonizing pleasure, spilling onto the bedsheet.

Her small arms were around him, pulling his body close to hers, and she was kissing his chest, the part of his body her mouth could reach.

He was panting and coated in sweat, even though he had been awake no more than two minutes.

His darling Arabella was dotting his chest with kisses. He

bent his head and kissed her face and tasted salt. She was crying.

"Did I hurt ye?"

"No," she said.

"I'm sor—"

She strained upwards under his weight and pulled his head down and managed to reach his mouth and cover it with hers so he could not apologize as he intended.

He wanted to say he was sorry for so much. Sorry for not knowing what to do. Sorry for being so quick. Sorry for not tending to her body and understanding her needs. Sorry for wanting to beat Morpeth. And, most of all, sorry for not coming to her long ago and making sure she knew he wanted her to be Mrs. Alasdair Andrews.

She kissed him as his heart rate slowed and returned to normal. He settled on his side next to her, and she pulled herself up so her head was even with his. He could feel her breath on his lips in the dark. One of her hands was resting on the hair on his chest, and the other hand was in the hair on his head. Both of his hands were on her waist, but he was thinking very seriously about moving them upwards to rest on her breasts.

"Thank you," she said.

"I'm sor—"

Again she stopped his mouth with hers.

When the kiss was over, he said, "Thank ye."

She fell back, supine on the mattress. "Now I can die."

He chased her body with his, pressing into her side, pulling her into him, putting one of his legs over hers.

"I'd rather ye didnae."

"Well, what is left for me?" One of her soft hands cupped his unshaven jaw. "I've had Alasdair Andrews."

"Well, maybe ye can have him again."

The room was very silent. Was she holding her breath in the dark?

A whisper from her. "Is that a promise?"

"In fact, if ye let me light a candle, I think ye could have me again very shortly."

"A candle?"

"So I can see ye."

He heard a sigh, and her body pulled away from his and lifted up off the mattress, and he could hear her touching something beside the bed. The unmistakable sound of a tinderbox and and a candle was lit and he could see her mane of hair in silhouette before she lay back.

Lying there in the candlelight, she looked like she was made of molten gold. Her beautiful breasts with their rosy areolas and nipples. Her perfectly smooth abdomen except for the divot of her umbilicus. Her triangle of golden maidenhair at the top of her thighs.

He took her in, almost feeling he could not dare to caress her as he had in the dark. And, as his eyes feasted, he could feel his tumescence returning as he had known it would once he saw her body.

"Touch me, Alasdair," she whispered.

"I'm sor—"

This time she lunged, cutting off the candlelight with the shadow of her body and her head as she kissed him. And, as she put her tongue in his mouth, she took one of his hands and put it on her breast.

When she broke the kiss and lay back again, he discovered the divine pleasure of using his mouth on her other breast. The skin so soft, the flesh so taut, the tip of the breast so responsive to his stimulation, tightening and becoming a nub as he lapped at it. And the groans that came from her as he suckled were aphrodisiacal, heating his simmering blood into a boil.

He didn't need the candle, he realized, to be ready again. All he needed was her arousal. Although now that the candle was lit, he did not want it snuffed. He wanted to see her.

She was moving on the mattress in an almost fretful way, her legs apart, her pelvis thrusting upwards. He took his hand from her breast and moved it down to her mound. He first felt her curling maidenhair. Then he dared to place a finger in her cleft. Warm, wet, so soft and silky. She groaned more loudly. But what would give her pleasure here? He suddenly felt he was rather a second-rate Adam. But his Eve would help him.

He released her nipple from his mouth.

"Arabella," he said. "I dinnae ken what to do."

"Do you want me to show you?" Her voice was graveled in a way he had not heard before.

"Aye."

"I get my fingers damp," she said. She put her hand down to her thatch of maidenhair, and he moved his own hand out of the way.

"Wait," he said. He leaned over her and got the candle and repositioned himself so he was below her on the bed and close to her beautiful sex. He could see and smell the evidence of her desire. The glistening of her wetness, the odor of her sweet musk.

She took her hand away and started to close her legs.

"Please dinnae stop," he said.

"I didn't expect you to be so near," she whispered but kept her legs open.

He smiled. "I *am* a doctor."

"Yes," she said and smiled.

"And yer flower is, like ye, beautiful."

"My flower," she breathed.

"Ye have petals," he said and reached out and very lightly touched her swollen labia.

She shuddered. "Yes, and this is my bud." She touched what he would have called her *glans clitoris.*

"Aye."

His eyes were on her hand as she dipped her middle finger into her introitus and withdrew it, coated in dew. "It is my bud that gives me pleasure." She touched it now with her middle finger. "There are other places where I can press and rub and it makes me wet, but if I am to spend," she increased the speed of her finger's movements, "this is the place where I must touch myself."

"Please dinnae stop."

"I…won't."

He wanted to touch her, but he also wanted to see what she did to make herself spend, so he gripped her tiny ankle and watched.

Her breathing became more and more ragged. He lifted his eyes from her flower to her face and found her eyes on him.

"Alasdair, when I tell you, will you look at my face?"

"I'll do whatever ye want."

So she gazed at him as he gazed at her flower, which had not been taken from her, that she would always have and that would always be part of her. He watched what she did, and he thought he would be able to replicate the movement of her finger. When she said, "Alasdair," he looked up and saw a concentration in her eyes, a furrowing of her brow. He thought it might be a signal of her impending release, and he was right. She shook, and her hand stilled. She shook some more and gasped.

The look on her face changed and became something so peaceful, he thought she might fall asleep in that moment.

He carefully put the candle back beside the bed and lay down next to her and held her. But he was wrong about her drowsiness. She reached out and grasped his hard member.

"Please," she said.

"Now?"

She did not answer but turned her face to him, looking at him with half-lidded eyes, and rubbed her hand up and down on his shaft. He found himself on his knees between her legs again. This time, she let go of his cock, and he guided himself into her, and she held on to his haunches and pulled him into her and raised her own hips up off the bed to meet him.

Having spent just minutes ago, he was able to thrust slowly, to enjoy the sweetness of her warmth, her wetness, her closeness, the pleasure of having her naked body rubbing against his.

And he could see her. Her hair spread out on the pillow. Her lips. Her breasts. Her eyes, hazed either by lust or by sleep.

Lust, he decided as she began to arch her body and clutch at his upper arms and his back. She was making the sounds she had made when he had suckled at her breast. Those wordless groans that came from such a deep place within her.

She raised her hips to him in a faster rhythm now, wordlessly urging him to stroke into her more and more quickly.

He plunged in again and withdrew.

"Uhhh," she said. "Alasdair."

He did it again.

"Nnngh." Her eyes were on him.

He did it again. He was perilously close.

She must have been closer still because she began to thrash, and he could feel her walls contract around his member. He stilled himself so he would not also spend. She had her hands on his face, and she was telling him she loved him, and, even without movement, he felt he would almost certainly release inside her in the next ten seconds. He came out of her and, with one stroke of his hand, spilled again into the bedsheet.

He blew out the candle and shifted them both onto the other side of the bed. He turned her and pulled her shoulder blades into his chest and the soft cheeks of her bottom into his groin. He held her there, one arm under and around her waist with a hand splayed over her mound, the other arm over her flank with a hand holding one of her sweet breasts.

Just before he fell asleep, he realized he was no longer a virgin.

And she loved him.

In the morning, he awoke alone and full of regret.

He was a physician. He knew what he had done with Arabella could lead to a child, despite spilling onto the sheets. As a novice, he should not have trusted he had the capacity to withdraw in time.

He turned his face into the pillow and smelled her sweet scent. Was it his imagination or was it also tinted with the intoxicating musk of her arousal?

He thought of her flower, her wetness, her release she had shown him. That had been a great intimacy shared with him, and he wished she were in the bed with him now. He longed to know if he could do for her what she had done for herself. He began to burn with the thought. Perhaps she would return shortly, and he would find out.

His initial feeling of remorse was washed away by longing.

He knew what the events of last night meant to him. It meant they should wed and have children. They should spend the rest of their lives together as companions and lovers.

But did she have the same feeling or thoughts about their coupling? She, who had experienced it in the past as an act that did not lead to marriage.

It was clear to him she had wanted to copulate because of what she had just witnessed—the harrowing illness and near death of a previously healthy and hale man. She had seen her father die after a long illness at age eleven. But had she ever seen someone young succumb? Perhaps not. Alasdair could see how that might lead someone to make an unwise decision. To throw caution to the winds in the pursuit of pleasure. *Carpe diem*. Seize the day.

But surely it had been more than pleasure? She had said she loved him when she had been in the throes of her own ecstasy. And before he had penetrated her, she had been very different than she had been in the carriage when she had made him spend, when she had alternated between being coy and cutting.

Last night, she had figuratively held his hand and led him to the threshold, where she had dropped his hand and waited. For him. What a very delicate tightrope she had walked, he realized. To make it absolutely clear what she wanted from him but still to allow him the very masculine privilege of taking her. To guide him to the precipice and to let him make his decision.

He almost laughed. She was still an innocent. Did she really think he would have been able to restrain himself from ravishing her once they were both naked in the bed?

Then he sobered. She was the reason they were both in the bed. He would never have presumed to seek that out. Indeed, he would not have allowed it if she had not days ago playfully made it easy for him to lie in the bed and *courie* into her. She was the reason they had both been naked; she had undressed both herself and him. She had assured him he would know what to do in order to couple with her. Adam and Eve. And, after she had helped him take her, she had very gently schooled him in her own pleasure.

She had also kept him from apologizing several times. She didn't like when he said he was sorry. He knew she hated regret. So he wouldn't offer apologies anymore. Even if he angered her.

Her anger. Yes. She had a temper. He would need to learn

to be brave and face it. Not shrivel from it. Admit he was wrong when he was but without apology.

But he wouldn't change her temper, even if he could. He couldn't imagine her without it. Wasn't it part of her passion, her energy, her courage? Wasn't her fire one of her great attractions? Dauntless Arabella.

And now he couldn't wait to see her. He would go and find her. And he would ask her, without fear or apologies or regret, to be his wife.

No, that was a lie. There would be a great deal of fear.

But not fear of her temper.

Only that she might say no.

Thirty-One

After Alasdair had pulled her to him and *couried* into her, Arabella had not slept. *I will not miss a moment of this night.* She stayed awake for the remaining hours of darkness—memorizing the sensation of his arms around her, the feel of his breath on her neck, the warmth of his body coiled around hers.

There had been two moments during their coupling that had been of great significance to her. She felt certain Alasdair would say the most important moment had been when they had first joined. That had been important to her, as well, but only because it had been important to him. She wanted him, yes, but she had also wanted this *for* him.

But for her, there were two entirely different times that would be engraved in her memory forever.

The first had happened after he had spent himself the first time. He had then said to her that she could have him again. She had stopped breathing, thinking the moment had come when he would promise her a future with him, an endless series of nights stretching into tomorrow and next week and next year and beyond.

But he had only meant he was capable of getting hard again right away.

Oh.

Her romantic Alasdair had become daringly wicked. And she had experienced an instant of mourning for what she had thought was going to be a proposal. But only an instant, as a wash of desire came over her, demanding he touch her.

The second important moment came when he had been inside her the second time, and, beyond the excitement of knowing his pleasure and the satisfying feeling of being filled, she had sensed a rising tide of her own need. He was going to make her spend. She had reached the heights of ecstasy and had her first climax from someone besides herself.

She should have told him at the time that he had been her first. After her discussions with him about her desire, he would surely see it was a far more significant event for her than her penetration years-ago by Giles.

If only he had spent inside her, though. Then, even if he never asked for her hand, she still might have something of his forever. A redheaded baby. She smiled. If that happened, she really would have to go to the New World and start over completely. As a make-believe widow, perhaps, living on some forested frontier with an auburn-haired daughter by her side.

She heard sounds in the house, knew it was morning despite the closed curtains, and managed to squirm from the lock of his arms. Her exhausted Alasdair slept on as she dressed and crept from the room. She took the brown scarf with her and held it to her nose as she descended the stairs. It no longer smelled of him, and she felt a pang of loss until she realized she, Arabella, smelled of him instead.

There was a sound of dripping from the eaves. The sun was out, the snow was melting, and Arabella could not bear to stay inside any longer.

She sought the butler out. "Please, Andrews, may I have my coat and bonnet and gloves? I must go for a walk."

"We'll be serving breakfast in half an hour, Mrs. Andrews."

"Just let me have a piece of toast or something. I long to get out."

That is how Arabella found herself tramping through three-foot drifts with a ham sandwich in her hand, feeling quite gloriously alive and very grateful to be so. She was getting out of breath from the exercise of walking in the deep snow, and that invigoration was exactly what she wanted.

She was halfway done with the sandwich when Alasdair got within shouting distance of her.

"Good morning," he called out.

She turned and waited for him to catch up with her. With his long legs, he had a much easier time wading through the snow than she did. And, of course, he was making use of her partially broken path.

"Good morning," he repeated when he drew even with her.

She smiled. "Good morning. Would you like some of my sandwich? It's not hot anymore, but it's still delicious."

"Uh, aye," he said and took the sandwich from her gloved hand and sank his teeth into it.

She watched him chew. He had no hat on, but he had the tartan scarf around his neck. From her point of view, it seemed like the blue sky and his red hair and the bright-green tartan were the only bits of color in the entire landscape.

"It's good, isn't it?" she asked, knowing he had his mouth full and couldn't answer.

He nodded.

She turned and started walking forwards again.

He followed but made his own path next to her. In a bit, he said, "Thank ye," and handed the sandwich back to her.

She took a bite and handed it back to him. He took another bite and handed it back to her.

She looked at what was left of the sandwich. There was one large bite left or two small bites. She took a small bite and handed it back to him, thinking they were done.

But then he said, "Arabella," and handed her half a small bite.

She laughed and put the piece up to her mouth and used her teeth to carve off a little bit of the morsel. She gave him the tiny crumb of sandwich that was left and stopped walking, waiting to see what he would do next.

He popped it in his mouth.

"You finished my sandwich!" she said in mock-anger.

"I was hungry." He put his hand into the pocket of his coat and drew out a napkin-wrapped shape that looked suspiciously like another ham sandwich. "But I'll give ye my whole sandwich to make up for it."

"Alasdair, your coat pocket!" The pocket, composed of a patch of matching tweed on top of the tweed of his great coat, was half-hanging down. "When we get back to the house, don't give your coat back to the butler Andrews, give it to me, and I'll fix your pocket for you in a jiffy."

"Aye," he said.

"But I'm not hungry anymore. I want you to eat your sandwich."

"Nae," he said and tucked the napkin-wrapped sandwich into his other pocket. "I'm nae hungry as I thought."

They took more steps forward in the snow. Six of Arabella's steps for perhaps three of Alasdair's.

He cleared his throat. She looked over at him. He was squinting with the reflection of the sun on the snow.

"Ye remember what ye said about my pocket?"

"That I would fix it for you?"

"Aye."

They trudged forward.

"What would ye say to the idea of having as much time as ye like to fix it?"

"But it won't really take that long, Alasdair."

He stopped walking and turned towards her, so she stopped walking, too. His eyes were fixed on the snow between them.

"Nae, I'm saying what do ye think about having the rest of yer life to fix my coat pocket?"

Oh.

Oh.

It was here.

She *thought* it was here.

But after her misunderstanding last night, perhaps she better make sure he didn't really mean to make her his eternal seamstress.

"What do you mean, Alasdair?"

He raised his eyes to hers.

"The evening Lord Morpeth became so ill. When we were in my room. Ye said…Ye said ye had thrown it all away. Being married, having children. That's nae true."

"No, I suppose it isn't. I could have married Boyd Cormack."

"Ye could marry me."

He had said it. Almost. Not quite. But, oh, so very, very close. If she wanted to, she could pretend to herself he had said it. But no. This was going to be her one and only proposal from Alasdair Andrews. She was going to make him say it. Actually, she was going to make him say both things.

She took a step towards him and stood on her tiptoes and reached up and brushed back the lock of hair that hung in front of his left eye.

"Could I?"

He grabbed her wrist.

"Would ye marry me?"

There was the first thing. She did not pull away from him and he gentled his grip and put her gloved hand on his coat over his left chest, over his heart, in the very place where she had put her palm when he had walked into her cottage in Dunburn.

"I love ye, Arabella Lovelock."

There was the second thing. He had done it.

"Ye are the woman of my dreams. Marry me."

She looked up at him.

"Aye," she said.

Thirty-Two

Despite the melting snow, Alasdair and Arabella—along with Paterson and Ewen McEwen—could not yet leave the Morpeth estate. Alasdair felt obliged to wait until another doctor arrived. The baron seemed largely out of danger, but Alasdair pointed out that the whole surgery had been a risky experiment with a fortunate outcome.

"It could so easily have gone wrong," he said. "It might still go wrong."

Lord Morpeth continued to have pain, but the fever did not return, and he was able to eat.

Even though Alasdair was the only one of their party with a professional obligation to stay, he was the one most anxious to leave. He had a wedding to get to and get through. He wanted to be husband and wife and to feel free to give Arabella the redheaded babies she longed for. And he thought he might very much like to spend inside her instead of on the sheets, which he had continued to do, despite knowing it was not ideal.

Because now that he had had the ecstasy of coupling with Arabella, he could not give it up. But he also wanted a baby that came nine or more months after a wedding.

Arabella said she didn't care and urged him to spend inside her.

"I'm ready, Alasdair."

Though the temptation was great and there were some very narrow margins in his timings, he found himself caring. After what Arabella had been through with her scandal, he wanted the calendar of their child's birth to be perfect. And he knew Arabella had resented that her mother's confinement had come only three months after wedding the Duke of Middlewich.

"Ye are marrying a poor boy from Bailebrae," Alasdair said, brushing his lips over her tiny pink ear. "I dinnae want people to say ye had to marry me, *mo leannan*, my beloved."

"But I do have to marry you," she said, purring. "Because I love you."

He kissed her then, deeply, slowly.

"When the roads are finally clear, let us get to Sommerleigh," Arabella said many minutes later, her arms around his neck, "and be married there. Once we are there, we need only purchase a license and wait seven days. Or we could have less expense with three weeks of banns."

He growled. "We are getting the seven-day license. I dinnae care about the cost."

And despite it being the morning and both of them having already dressed for the day and the breakfast waiting for them, he seized her and kissed her and discovered the pleasure of holding her and penetrating her in an upright position against the wall of the room in broad daylight where he could see every twitch of pleasure that danced across her face.

As he waited for the snow to clear, Alasdair found himself

retiring to bed earlier and earlier each night because Arabella joined him there. He also found his long fingers could afford her a great deal of pleasure. And the long winter nights meant he accumulated what he thought of as a great deal of experience very quickly. Very little time was spent in sleep when there were hours of lovemaking to be had.

"Now," Arabella said to him one night as she ran her fingers through the copper hair on his chest before moving on to the auburn hair on his head. "I know why my mother needed so many naps."

Arabella said she really must leave the bed and have several hours a day in public view.

"If only to make you hungry for me again," she said teasingly even though he assured her that his appetite for her would never be sated.

Arabella spent her time away from the bed with Rebecca, trudging through the slowly melting snow-covered gardens or sitting in the drawing room and giggling.

During those times, when the blood flow was finally directed away from his cock and towards his brain, Alasdair had some thoughts about Lady Morpeth's condition and what could be causing it. He now had the books and the periodicals he had brought on his trip from Dr. Murray's library, and he pored over them, looking for hints. However, they did not provide him with the information he sought. He needed to rely largely on his memory for the unusual cases he had read about during his training and his subsequent career.

Finally, the likely diagnosis came to him when he remembered Lady Morpeth said sometimes her vision had a yellow tint.

And he was struck with horror.

He asked the butler Andrews to make up an excuse to prevent anyone else coming into Lady Morpeth's bedchamber.

Alasdair went to the room, knocked, entered, found her alone, and asked her a question.

She looked confused but answered, "No, Dr. Andrews."

He smiled. "That is good news, Lady Morpeth."

He escorted Lady Morpeth into Lord Morpeth's room and asked the footman who was there to leave. The footman, having been ordered to play backgammon with Lord Morpeth so that he would be entertained sufficiently to stay in bed voluntarily, was happy to exit. Lord Morpeth was bad-tempered while being confined to bed whether he lost or won.

Lady Morpeth settled herself in the footman's chair by the bed and reached out and held Morpeth's hand.

"My lady," Alasdair began. "I believe ye have been suffering from foxglove or digitalis poisoning. That is the cause of yer long-term illness. I still think ye may be pregnant, but the interference in yer courses may be due to the foxglove. I cannae say with certainty."

Lady Morpeth gasped.

Morpeth's brows were drawn together, and he looked murderous.

"But how might I be poisoned?" Lady Morpeth asked. "I don't take digitalis. I have never taken it."

"Just minutes ago, I asked ye if yer symptoms ever improved when yer husband was weeks from home, and ye denied it. So, to my mind, that eliminates Lord Morpeth as the cause of yer illness. The most likely person at fault is Nurse Gastrell. She is the logical person to administer the poison. Through yer skin, perhaps. Is there some herbal ointment Nurse Gastrell uses for ye?

"Yes."

The strong, clean smell of rosemary in her room. Likely the dried foxglove had been mixed in with it.

"Why would she do this evil?" Morpeth rumbled.

"Sometimes," Alasdair spoke carefully, "people benefit

from keeping someone ill. If Lady Morpeth were to become well, Nurse Gastrell might lose her position. So perhaps she keeps Lady Morpeth ill. Alive, but ill. I dinnae ken if it can be proven. I do recommend she be confined to her own room until the magistrate can come to the house."

On Lord Morpeth's orders it was done, and it must be said Lady Morpeth's health improved as soon as she was no longer under the care of Nurse Gastrell.

The snow finally melted enough for both another physician and the magistrate to be sent for. Arabella was happy for Alasdair's sake. She knew, despite his excellent care of Giles, that he was uncomfortable taking hospitality from the baron. Arabella herself did not care; she only wanted to be where Alasdair was.

Paterson would continue to drive Arabella and Alasdair south to Sommerleigh. But Ewen MacEwen said he was going to stay at the estate. He had been offered a job as a stable boy by the head groom.

"But 'tis just for a short time. Horses and coaches are the past. I have a mind to get into railroads and steam locomotives. There's a man named Robert Stephenson in Newcastle. Once I earn a little money, I am going to go work for him."

Arabella had no doubt it was true.

On the morning of Arabella's and Alasdair's departure, Rebecca stood in the stable yard and hugged Arabella. "I am so happy for you."

Arabella slid the ring from her finger and handed it back to Rebecca. Then she held her friend's face in her hands.

"I can't wait for you to find your happiness, too, Rebecca. Please promise me you will come visit us in Sommerleigh. You can stay with me and the doctor once we are married."

Rebecca promised to come and quickly retreated into the

house, not looking back at the carriage that contained so much happiness.

Finally, they were moving, headed south.

Arabella looked around the snug confines of the carriage. "This is the place where you first kissed me."

"I'm of a mind to have Paterson sell us the carriage," Alasdair said.

"That's not necessary." She took off his gloves and began kissing his palms and his fingers. "If you must know, it was your hands that first attracted me."

"Nae my dimples?"

"I didn't see your dimples until the very end of our first meeting. Your dimples made me decide I must marry you. But I fell in lust with your hands. I remember you were not wearing gloves, and you took my hand and—oh, your fingers, so long and strong and gentle, and that very little bit of copper hair on the back of your wrists here." She rubbed her cheek on the back of his hand as if she were a cat.

Alasdair grunted, making a show of still not believing, she thought, so she might continue to play with his hands.

"There were many nights that year I touched myself in my bed, imagining my hands were your hands, Dr. Andrews."

He shook his head. "I cannae believe that."

"You must tell me if you hate that I wanted you because of the wanting or because it's you, Alasdair."

"I hate neither. I love both of those things. I hate that it could have been my hands all along but for my cowardice."

She smiled. He was learning not to say he was sorry. "And now it will always and only be your hands."

"Ye are the woman of my heart."

"You are a brave man to have me."

He kissed her. As always, under the pressure of his mouth, she melted. All the hunger, the care, the tenderness, and the unyielding tenacity of her Alasdair were present in his kiss., and she surrendered to it completely.

But after minutes of heat and softness and tongues and lips and the mingling of breath and wetness, she suddenly had a terrible thought. She stopped kissing him and pulled away. He opened his eyes.

"Alasdair." There was a clutching at her chest.

"Aye?"

She gulped. "I cannot believe I have been so foolish. I am not yet one and twenty. My birthday is still a month away. We will have to go to Middlewich or London and have my mother's consent to be married."

"Do ye think she will oppose us?"

"I…don't know," Arabella faltered. "I have treated her very badly. I am sure she likes you because of what you did for Harry. I am not so sure she likes me. Or trusts me."

"Of course, she does. Ye are her daughter."

"You must promise me." She clutched the lapel of his coat. She felt she might suffocate.

"What, my love?"

"You must promise still to marry me even if we have to wait."

He wrapped his arms around her. "Aye, nae a one can stop me."

"You mustn't leave me. We mustn't be separated."

"I will ne'er leave ye."

"When we get to Middlewich or London, whichever place she is, you will go to her to ask her, and I will stay away, hidden somewhere. If she gives her permission, we must be wed first so she cannot take me away from you before we are married."

"She widnae do that, Arabella. Ye have turned her into a witch in yer head. But I willnae have ye anxious on the matter."

Alasdair released her and rapped on the roof of the

carriage and the coach stopped. He buttoned his coat and got out.

Arabella buttoned up her own coat and strained her ears, but she could not hear what Alasdair said to Paterson. After a few minutes, Alasdair got back in the carriage and stooped down and picked her up and turned around and sat back down again so she was lying across his lap, her shoulders supported by one arm as he leaned over her and kissed her mouth while his other hand unbuttoned the coat she had just buttoned. He began touching her breasts through her dress.

"What did you say to Paterson? Did you tell him to go to Middlewich instead of Sommerleigh?" she asked when he paused for a breath.

"Do ye like what I am doing with my hand now, Arabella?" He was very delicately shifting the material of her dress over her nipple with the lightest of rubs.

Arabella shuddered and nodded. and he bent his head to hers again.

But he had not answered her, and she could feel the carriage swaying, turning.

She broke the kiss. "What are we doing?"

He grinned. Those dimples. He was teasing her. She cursed inwardly that she had taught him anything about flirtation. Where was her plain-speaking Scottish doctor when she needed him?

He must have seen something in her eyes because he relented. A bit.

"We are turning around."

Arabella sat up. "What?"

"I decided I couldnae wait to find out if yer mother would consent. And if she didnae, I couldnae wait a month. It would drive me mad."

"But why turn around?"

"We're going back to Scotland."

"Why?"

"Because in Scotland there isnae need for a license or banns or permission from yer mother. I am going to marry ye today, Mrs. Andrews, and then I am going to bed ye today, Mrs. Andrews, and give ye the beginning of a redheaded baby, and the issue will be decided."

Thirty-Three

They crossed the border back into Scotland at three in the afternoon and stopped at the first village with an inn. Alasdair insisted there must be an inn. He did not want to get back into the carriage with Arabella after marrying her. He wanted a bed.

The name of the village was Morebattle. Arabella told Alasdair she was surprised they were not in Gretna Green, but he explained it was actually the closest place in Scotland from where the carriage had turned around.

It was not a place well known for elopements and ceremonies conducted in a Toll House. There was no large trade built around a demand for hasty weddings. But the innkeeper was willing to perform the ceremony. Then Alasdair regretted Ewen MacEwen had been left behind in England. Paterson was only one witness, and they needed another.

Alasdair found an only slightly inebriated Mr. MacDonald who was willing to sign as a witness if Alasdair lanced an abscess on his scalp. Alasdair agreed, on the condition that the drainage of the abscess occur after the wedding. He rather thought Mr. MacDonald might forget his duties if the lancing happened before the ceremony. He also thought it would be better if his witness were not bleeding from a head wound when he told Arabella he would love and care for her forever.

The perfunctory but blessedly legal ceremony over, Alasdair lanced the abscess in the yard of the inn, where the late-afternoon light was best. He felt he did a rather neat job of it, considering his desire to finish as quickly as possible. His amorous, beautiful wife was waiting for him, after all.

But when Alasdair went back into the inn, he was told Arabella had been granted leave to use the only bathtub in the small coaching inn and she was still waiting for her hot water. Alasdair supposed he should not be selfish and deprive Arabella of her wedding toilette since there had been no church, no dress, no ring, no breakfast, and no family present to join in their celebration. She deserved a thousand hot baths.

While he was waiting for her in their bedchamber, he added more coals to the fire. He wanted the room warm for what would happen next. He washed his hands thoroughly and took off his tailcoat. He sat in a chair and removed his boots and his stockings. It didn't seem right to take off more than that without her there.

Suddenly, he felt quite shy. As well as impatient. Which made no sense. Hadn't he coupled with her many times over?

But now she was his wife.

She came into the room and closed the door and leaned against it, her hands behind her back. She was dressed, but her skin was flushed and her hair was down around her shoulders, the tendrils curling more tightly than ever from the humidity of her bath.

"I am yours, Alasdair," she said.

"Aye." He could scarce believe it. Arabella Lovelock was Mrs. Alasdair Andrews. He stood from the chair, aching for her.

Arabella took a step towards him and bent over to take off

her own little boots and stockings. Then she straightened and reached around behind her back and unfastened something. She crossed her arms in front of her breasts and raised her dress up.

"I have learned," she said with her head muffled in the dress, "only to have dresses I can remove myself. I had no lady's maid in Dunburn, so we will not have that expense going forward, Alasdair."

The dress was laid aside, and she untied her front lacing stays and loosened the laces and pulled the stays down over her hips and her petticoat, and stepped out of them.

"Stop," he said, his voice strangling. She stood there, in only her chemise and petticoat.

"Do you want me to stay dressed, Alasdair?" she whispered.

"Nae," he said. He closed the distance between them in two steps. "Nae, I want to undress the rest of ye."

He untied the drawstring of her petticoat and let it fall to the floor. He drew her chemise over her head.

He stepped back.

She was before him, naked. For him, she was everything feminine and nubile. Her round breasts. Her small waist that flared to her generous bottom and curved hips and soft thighs. Her cleft covered in golden maidenhair. Her round calves and tiny ankles.

He burned, he throbbed, he was consumed by a wave of passion so strong he was tempted to take her on the floor of the room.

"Arabella," he said. "Ye are beautiful."

"Hold me, Alasdair." Her voice was husky.

He reached for her even as she stepped up to him so their bodies collided with an unintended force, and his cock, already so hard from looking at her body, was pinned between them, and he knew she could feel how much he wanted her.

His hands quickly found the cheeks of her bottom and seized them, and his lips sought hers, and he ravished her mouth with his tongue even as he was desperate to be inside her in other ways.

She untucked his shirt from the back, undid his cravat, did anything she could to undress him while still keeping her body pressed against his.

"I must," he panted, moving his mouth off hers, "get ye on the bed."

But she was past listening and wilder than she had ever been with him before. She pushed herself away and undid his fall. She pulled his trousers down, brushing her breasts against his cock as she did so. He congratulated himself on his wisdom in taking off his boots before she had returned to the room. He kicked off the trousers around his ankles, and she undid his waistcoat, and he pulled off his shirt. Now they were touching skin against skin everywhere. She wrapped her hand around his cock and straddled his thigh, rubbing herself there, moaning, and he could feel her heat, her wetness.

He groaned and picked her up and finally got her on the bed where he wanted her.

She lay on top of the counterpane but sat up part of the way, resting on her elbows. "Come to me, Alasdair. I want you."

He stood by the bed and looked at her as her chest heaved with deep breaths. Her face was flushed, her breasts creamy white except for the small, pink peaks, her knees up and bent and slightly apart so he could see the glisten of her folds in amongst her golden maidenhair.

"Aye."

But he did not join her in the bed as she clearly expected.

"I want to pleasure ye," he said.

"You will." She lay back and held out her arms.

"Nae. I want to pleasure ye and only ye. Ye have

made me spend once in a carriage. Ye have made yerself spend once in front of me. I have spent in the sheets seventeen times after being inside ye. I have made ye climax with either my hand or with my cock seventeen times."

She laughed. "I didn't know you were counting!"

"It seems to me the points stand at nineteen to seventeen with ye leading, and 'tis my turn to make someone spend. And since I feel I have lived most of my life making myself spend, I would rather it be ye. I want to kiss ye."

"Then come and kiss me."

His cock twitched.

"Nae. I want to kiss ye where ye spend."

Arabella sat up.

"You do?"

"Aye."

"How do you know about this, Alasdair?"

"Remember how I told ye I wouldnae talk but would listen?"

"Yes."

"I may have been a virgin up until four days ago, but sailors are prone to boasting loudly about their experiences with their wives and...other women."

He could see she was thinking, and he suspected she was not completely opposed to the idea.

"Afterwards, can I kiss you where you spend, too?"

"We'll see," was all Alasdair would say, barely able to allow himself to think of Arabella's mouth on his member.

He pulled her to the edge of the mattress so her legs dangled down, and he leaned over her and suckled briefly at each one of her nipples. She sank her fingers into his hair as he trailed a line of kisses from her breasts down her abdomen to her navel and then her thatch of maidenhair. She released his head, and he knelt on the floor by the edge of the bed and put her small legs over his shoulders. He could feel her thighs quiver.

"You don't have to do this, Alasdair," she whispered towards the ceiling.

"Dinnae ye want me to? Because I want to, Arabella. I very much want to."

"I don't know."

"Ye must promise to tell me if ye don't like it. I might do it wrong. But I want to do this to ye, very much."

She lifted her head and looked at him. "I'm sure I'll like anything you do, Alasdair."

He turned his head and kissed one of her thighs.

She put her head back on the mattress.

He turned his head the other way and kissed the other inner thigh. Her skin here was so soft, so warm, so sweet. So delicate. And the smell of her arousal was getting stronger.

He slowly kissed up her legs, alternating between the right and the left thigh. There was no hurry. Had she not just promised to be in his bed forever?

But he had not counted on his wife. She was squirming, and were those mews he heard from her? She was eager.

With his kissing his way up her thighs, he had reached her flower. She was open, wet, aroused. He kissed her softly on her outer petals. The mews from Arabella now turned into full-throated groans. He used his tongue on her inner petals, lightly lapping at her dew, tasting her. He was not surprised to find she was sweet here, too, but there was also a tang, a saltiness, and a musk that made him want to bury his face in her, to coat his nose and cheeks and lips with her.

He made his tongue soft and felt all of her folds. He found her entrance and used his tongue to probe at it.

She made a sound that was close to a strangled scream.

He raised his head. "Did I hurt ye?" he said.

"Noooooo," she gasped, "I am just in such a state!"

"Should I keep going?"

"I should think so, *mo leannan*. Definitely." She reached down and laced the fingers of her right hand with his left.

He knew her most sensitive place was her *glans clitoris*. She had shown him that and called it her bud, and he had touched her there with his hand many times in the last few days. He went back to her flower, and using the most delicate of touches with his tongue, he found the hard bud near the top of the crease. He licked there and felt the bud enlarge and harden under his tongue, and her outer and inner lips began to swell, and she became very, very still.

Despite the swelling of her flower, he did not know if her quietness and stillness were good signs. So he licked again. In the same place.

"Yes," exhaled Arabella.

He thought he should try to copy with his tongue what she had done to herself with her finger in front of him and what he had learned to do with his own fingers. He licked the bud lightly at first—not knowing how much pressure he should give—but she raised her hips to him. So he licked more firmly and he let go of her hand to use both of his forearms to push her thighs down more firmly into his shoulders and her bottom into the bed so he could keep her in place.

He let himself range more freely over her flower now that he had pinned her. He wanted her aroused, he wanted her to spend, but he also selfishly wanted to know all of her. He moved his tongue off her bud and down her lips and then back up. He licked the edges of her introitus and made his tongue pointed and firm and put his tongue inside her. His cock twitched, wanting to be where his tongue was. Then he withdrew his tongue and used only his lips to mash against her labia, coming back to her bud.

He cast his gaze up towards her face, but all he could see was the heave of her round breasts. He wished for six hands so he could hold her breasts, pin her hips down, put his fingers inside her, all at the same time. Make that eight so he could also cup the smooth cheeks of her buttocks and raise her flower to his lips.

But he also longed to see her face. Next time, he would put a pillow under her head so he could see her eyes and mouth, so he could have some hints as to what she was experiencing. A pillow was more achievable than the extra hands.

But although he held her tightly at her hips, her upper body was arching away, the curve of her spine separating from the bed, her nipples pointing even more skyward.

He paused for a second and pulled his head back from her flower.

Her labia, pink when he had begun kissing her thighs, were now swollen and flushed red. He wondered briefly now at how little he had known of an aroused woman's anatomy, how secretive and hidden it all was compared to the hard cock that insistently throbbed below his waist.

Arabella's hands were groping across the bed.

"Alasdair, Alasdair, Alasdair. Please, please."

"'Tis good for ye, Arabella?"

But all she could do was groan and say his name and, "Please."

So he put his mouth on her again and put all his attention on her bud, licking at it savagely and adding his grunts to hers as she tensed under his hands. He briefly considered nipping at the little protuberance with his teeth and then thought better of it and instead gave her dozens of quick, fierce licks until she spasmed rhythmically, her thighs squeezing his shoulders, her flower contracting under his tongue, and a small gush of sweetness hit his lower lip.

He did not know what to do now—the sailors' stories did not say whether he should continue or stop. He thought of the sensitivity of his own cock right after his own climaxes and thought he should stop.

He put his tongue back in his mouth and waited.

Her legs went slack, and one almost slipped from his shoulder, but he caught it and held it. His lips were still on her labia, and he lightly kissed her, away from her bud but on her outer lips that were still engorged.

It was so quiet.

"Arabella?"

He took the other leg off his shoulder and stood so he could see her. Her hands were over her face.

"Arabella?"

Her soft, white abdomen heaved. He lay down next to her and gently took one of her hands from her face.

She was crying. Large tears coursing down her face, her nose running, her lashes darkened and clumping with tears.

"Oh, my darling, did I hurt ye?" He gathered her to his chest. What a fool he had been. She had likely not wanted to tell him he had been too rough with her, with his tongue. He was glad now he had not bitten her bud.

"Oh, oh, oh." She raised her face to his, her blue eyes brimming, "Oh, Alasdair, that was wonderful. Wonderfully wicked. You're a miracle. Can I really be so lucky as to be married to you?"

Her lips came to his, and her tongue replicated in his mouth what he had done to her introitus, and a grateful wash of relief mixed with lust came over him.

But he wanted to be sure. After a minute of Arabella ravishing his mouth with her tongue and lips, he pulled away.

"Ye liked it?" He could hear his own voice had become gruff.

"I loved it almost as much as I love you, Alasdair."

"I didnae stop too soon? I didnae want to hurt ye."

"I don't know. Next time, don't stop, and we'll see." She

suddenly had a worried look on her face. "There will be a next time, won't there? This isn't something people only do on their wedding night, is it?"

He grinned, and she squirmed delightedly, and he remembered he must make more of an effort to smile since his dimples gave her so much pleasure.

"I intend to kiss yer flower as often as ye let me, Mrs. Andrews."

She whispered, "Maybe even again tonight?"

He let go of her, intending to slide down the mattress and onto his knees again, but she clutched him and smiled shyly. "No, no, not yet."

"Yer wish is my command."

"I want to kiss *you* now."

He found her mouth with his and palmed one of her breasts, thinking this was now the time when he might slake his thirst for touching her ripeness, her nipples, the soft skin and firm flesh of her breasts as he kissed her.

But she laughed under his lips and tongue and when he broke the kiss, she said, "Yes, but no, Alasdair. I want to kiss your sex."

His cock, which had stiffened considerably with her passionate kiss, became now throbbingly, fully hard, poking into the crevice between her lower thighs.

"I can feel you like that idea." She put her hand on his cock and began to slither away from his face, down towards his groin, stopping briefly to lick one of his nipples and to inhale the scent of his chest.

"Uh, uh, uh," he said and grabbed her under her armpits, lifting her back up so her face was even with his again.

"May we have a moment of discussion, please?" His voice was a little stern.

Disappointed, she released her grip on his member—oh, his shaft was so hard, but the skin was so silky smooth, and she had already imagined that skin gliding under her tongue and over her lips.

"'Tis nae something wives do," he said.

"How do you know?"

"How do *ye*?"

She shook her head. "Are you asking me if I have done something like that before? Then ask me!"

"I would ne'er ask ye something like that!"

She rolled away from him. "Then you will never know the answer."

There was a pause. She had a strong sense this might be a crucial moment in their new marriage. She waited. But she did not know how long she would be able to wait.

She did not have to wait long. After all, her husband was the not-stupid man.

She felt him shift on the mattress, and his beautiful chest pressed against her shoulders, a long, strong arm came over her arm, his abdomen formed a mold around her buttocks, and she felt his hardness poke into the back of her thighs. And the most delicious, soft whisper in her ear.

"Have ye ever done something like that before, Mrs. Andrews?"

She pushed her bottom back against him. "Since you ask, Dr. Andrews, no."

"Then why do ye think ye should?"

"Because I want to," she said, still facing away from him but sliding down lower on the bed so the cheeks of her bottom rubbed against his shaft. She was rewarded with heavier breathing in her ear. "Because I think I would like being wicked like that, and I know," she reached behind her and found his stiffness and held it, "you would like it. This gentleman here certainly approves of the idea." She gave a little tug on his cock, and he groaned.

"A month before I first met you, Alasdair," she gave a squeeze and elicited another groan, "I was traveling with my sister Mary and her husband in Cornwall. You have never met them, have you?"

"Uh," he grunted.

She moved her hand down to the base of his shaft and felt his hair there tickling the side of her hand. As she spoke, she kept her hand loosely on his member and trailed her hand up and down his shaft, over and over again.

"We were at an inn near the shore for about a week, and, one day, I went into Mary's room. She had said she wanted to rest after luncheon, but I had forgotten and went into the room to fetch a book she said she had finished reading. As soon as I entered the room, I saw David, her husband, standing and facing away from me. He was fully dressed, so I almost said something, but then I saw my sister—also dressed—on her knees in front of him, her husband's hand resting on her head. There was a sound of some wetness, I suppose, and something like the smacking of lips, and David was whimpering. You will be astonished by this story when you meet the viscount, Alasdair. It's hard to imagine him discomposed, let alone whimpering. I fled and thought my sister had not seen me. But later that afternoon, she took me on a long walk along the shore, and we discussed many things. About what men and women do together. Mary is very sensible. I think you will like her."

He was panting. "I…ken…I will like…her, too."

She discovered something unexpected and stilled her hand.

"You are a little wet," she said.

"Aye."

Arabella realized she had never stroked him for so long. At this point, he was usually inside her.

"I'm sor—" Alasdair started.

She whipped around, transferring her hold on his cock from one hand to another, and blocked his apology with a kiss.

After the kiss, he said, "It means I am aroused. I cannae control that."

Good, no apology. Her training was working. Unless, of course, he learned to start saying he was sorry just to get her to kiss him. She would have to be alert to see if he ever became that canny. But for now, the kiss just seemed to remind him that she did not want his apologies.

"Oh, Alasdair." She kissed his nose. "When are you going to learn the things I love most about you are the things you can't control?"

Her angle was better now, and she could hold him both as loosely and as firmly as she liked. And she could look down and see the glistening at the tip of his member and rub the palm of her hand in the wetness and then drag it down the length of his member.

"Like…what?" Alasdair choked out.

"Your auburn hair, especially the lock that flops down and covers your left eye. Your dimples. Your hardness. And now this little bit of wetness that tells me even more that you want me."

He groaned and closed his eyes.

"Alasdair, what do you want?"

"I want…to be inside ye and to spend inside ye and make a baby."

"How wonderful," she cooed, "because I want that, too." She released him and lay flat on her back.

"Now?"

"As long as you promise this will be a long night in a lifetime of long nights and you will reconsider my desire to kiss you—everywhere."

He kissed her mouth and grinned. "I promise."

He fumbled a bit, getting on his knees between her legs, and she spent that time looking at him, taking him in, paying particular attention to the parts of him she could not see when he was dressed. His shoulders and his long arms that matched those long fingers. His pale skin, flushed over his shoulders and his chest. His chest with its soft copper hair. His flat abdomen that led to his other copper-colored hair and his engorged cock. As she breathed in, she shuddered. She was consumed by her need for him. She salivated and gulped. She felt her nether regions drip. He had just made her spend in the most wonderful way, and, so soon, she was ready again. She leaned forward and kissed him over his heart.

"Feel me with your fingers, Alasdair," Arabella whispered into his chest. "Feel how wet I am."

He would do anything she asked. He felt her, and she lay back on the bed and exhaled with a sound that was halfway between a sigh and a moan.

"Put a finger in me."

He did that, looking at her face, her breasts. His Arabella. His wife.

"What does it feel like, Alasdair?"

"It feels like heaven. Smooth and soft and wet and warm."

"Mmmm. And now," she said, her voice rough, "I want something bigger."

He withdrew his finger and grasped his own cock and put the head at her entrance.

"I want you," she said.

Alasdair felt certain he would have staying power. After all, he was a man of experience now. And he wanted their coupling to last as long as possible, so he went as slowly as he could. But far too soon, far too quickly, he was all the way inside her and withdrawing and plunging and withdrawing.

She said, "My husband," and lifted her hips to him and he was adrift in a sea of pleasure that had as much to do with his heart as it did his cock.

"Ahhh," she said.

A bead of sweat ran down his temple.

"Does it feel good, Arabella?"

"Yes." She flattened her palms on the sides of his ribcage. "Please."

He thrust.

"Uhhh," she said and raised her hips.

He did it again.

"Nnngh." She gave the sweetest of little grunts.

This spurred him, and he thrust again, feeling quite wild now, and once more and another time to boot and she was grabbing his buttocks, pulling him into her, and he was mindlessly bent on a single driving urgency and she was saying his name and he was saying he loved her and a spasm ripped through his body and he felt himself spend inside her glorious tightness.

He fell to the side of her, still inside her, and she immediately turned her head to look at him and put both her hands on both sides of his head.

"Alasdair," she said.

He could not speak.

"Alasdair, we are going to have such a good married life together. And dozens of redheaded babies."

His lips found hers, and he kissed his beautiful wife.

Later on, he did reconsider his position about her mouth on his member. The ability to correct oneself in the face of a compelling argument was one of the many gifts that came with being the not-stupid man.

. . .

In the morning, the total score stood at twenty-three to twenty-two, Arabella having kept her lead, narrowly. As per Alasdair's system, points went to the one who caused the climax, not the one who had it. They agreed coitus counted as a point to Arabella if only Alasdair climaxed and a point each if they both climaxed. Arabella felt quite accomplished in keeping her lead because Alasdair had a decided advantage since she recovered more quickly than he did.

But she kept her mouth shut. It was not nice to gloat that her physiology allowed her so much more pleasure than his did. But she honestly gave him all the points he earned and just worked that much harder to keep her lead.

When the sun rose, two naked, wrung-out specimens of the human race sprawled on the bed, Alasdair on his back, Arabella on her stomach with her upper body and her cheek on his chest. She was completely still. One of his hands was making lazy circles on her back.

She felt very sure they had made a baby sometime during the night.

She raised her head. "Alasdair?"

"Aye?"

"Would you like a draw?"

For a moment, he looked confused. And then he understood and smiled and carefully rolled over, flipping her onto her back.

"Which way would ye like me to earn my point, Arabella? I dinnae think I can be inside ye right now but maybe my hand or my mouth would do?"

"Your hand, Alasdair, your marvelous fingers so I can kiss your mouth and look at your face at the same time." After all, the baby had been made, and the poor man deserved some rest.

"And I can tell ye I love ye as ye shake," he murmured and

put his hand between her legs, and she felt those gentle fingers begin to explore her already wet folds.

"There are two conditions, however," she said.

He stilled his hand.

"Conditions?"

"First, we end the game in a draw and give up keeping score."

"Aye."

"And you admit you were wrong. Entirely. About women having lust."

His face and neck turned the most delicious, deep, dark red, and he was naked, so she could observe the blush did start at his neck and spread upwards, but sadly, from his chest down, he did not blush at all.

"I have been wrong about many things, Arabella, but I can admit I was more wrong about that than anything else, as ye have proven."

"Oh, Alasdair, I do love you," she said and threw her arms around his neck and kissed him with an ardor that matched the intensity of their first kiss in this room fourteen hours earlier.

He began to touch her in the way she liked and her breathing turned into panting as they kissed and she groaned into his mouth.

"You should know, Alasdair…nothing…uh…arouses a woman more than a man…yes…who can admit he is wrong."

"Then I will be sure to be as wrong as often as possible, Arabella, if only so I can admit it for yer pleasure."

"Oh, but Alasdair, I can feel it is for your pleasure, too."

And, sure enough, the feel of her on his fingers, her groans, her kisses had made him hard again, and his cock was poking into her thighs.

"I have nae seed left, Arabella. I am empty. And tired."

"I have an idea," she said.

She turned her back to him and nestled her bottom just above his member. She got up on her elbow and took one of his arms and put it under her and clamped his hand to her breast. Then she reached between her legs and stroked his cock several times and put it inside her wet entrance.

"I will push back on you. You don't have to do anything except what you were already doing with your hand before."

She climaxed more quickly than he did, but he got even harder when her walls clutched at him, and so although he had thought it was an impossibility, there was some seed left to spend.

"Ye ken what this means," he panted in her ear.

She smiled. "I'm still winning."

THIRTY-FOUR

Almost a week later, they arrived at Sommerleigh at two o'clock in the afternoon. As the carriage came down the drive, Alasdair checked his watch.

"Yer sister and the earl may be busy."

Arabella snorted. "Harry is always busy with the conjecture."

"They might be busy some other way."

"With the children?"

"Well, yer sister has had a bed put in her room where she does her mathematics."

"A bed?"

"So they might be busy the way we have recently been busy."

Arabella goggled. "Harry? In the daytime?"

Alasdair laughed. "Yer sister is about to have her third child. Ye surely are under nae illusions how that might happen, day or night."

"I know, but—yes. Well, good. We will play with the children until they are *not* busy."

The carriage stopped, and they could hear Paterson

speaking to a footman about where the stables were and how the luggage should be disposed of.

Indeed, the earl and the countess could not be easily accounted for by the household staff, so Arabella and Alasdair did go to the nursery. Almost three-year-old Hypatia and Richard at twenty months knew the doctor. However, they were both shy of Arabella.

Arabella knelt on the floor.

"Do you know who I am? I am your Aunt Arabella."

"Anchabella?" dark-haired Hypatia said, with a look of recognition. "Mama says you live far away and are very brave. You fight dragons."

"Mama!" said Richard, clapping.

"Papa got me a doll what looks like you." Hypatia whirled away and brought back to Arabella a wooden doll with painted blue eyes and golden hair.

"What is her name?" Arabella asked after admiring the doll.

Hypatia turned her head and squinted at her and Arabella could have sworn it was the same look Harry used to give her when she had very briefly taken over Arabella's very rudimentary mathematical training.

"Anchabella. Of course."

Arabella laughed.

"Aye," Alasdair said, squatting down and putting his arm around his Arabella's shoulders and kissing her on the side of the head. "She is very Harry-esque in her condescension to us mere mortals but nae sign of mathematical obsession just yet."

"Richard, do you have a toy to show your Aunt Arabella?" Arabella asked. But Richard was pulling at the crotch of his high-waisted trousers and didn't answer.

Alasdair murmured, "And Richard definitely takes after his father."

There was only about half an hour between the Andrews'

arrival and the appearance in the nursery of the very pregnant and flushed Harry and the slightly perspiring Thomas Drake. Harry's hair was falling down a bit, and Thomas' shirt wasn't quite tucked into his trousers all the way around.

Arabella went to Harry immediately and was about to ask permission to hug her sister and was surprised to have Harry throw her own arms around her neck. Arabella could feel the tears pricking her eyes.

Harry whispered to her, "I have been well recently, but I was tired of waiting for you to remember what you really wanted and deserved. And I was tired of Alasdair pining for you. Don't be angry at your *soror ex machina.*"

Arabella pulled back from her, astonished. She had never spoken to Harry of her secret feelings for Alasdair. And she would have never thought this sister might be the one to sense anything about Arabella's desires.

Harry shrugged and looked at the ceiling. "You're welcome." Then she spoke more loudly. "You can touch if you like. She's moving around a lot right now."

Arabella felt Harry's stomach, and the baby, which Harry insisted was a girl, was indeed kicking. Then Alasdair, as Harry's physician, had to feel, and so did Thomas. Even Hypatia reached up and felt the underside of her mother's belly for a moment before running away to pull her brother's hair.

"I hope you got married in Scotland before coming here," Harry said, gazing at her husband's waistcoat buttons. "Otherwise, there will be such a fuss over you two sharing a bed when Mama Katie gets here."

Arabella sputtered, "Harry!" and turned to her husband.

Alasdair was blushing and holding his hands up. "I didnae say anything. I have been with ye the whole time."

"I take it that congratulations are in order?" Thomas asked and shook Alasdair's and Arabella's hands with a large grin.

"Yes, your mother and Jamie have planned to come in a week. Though once we send word to Middlewich that you are here, I wouldn't be surprised if your mother comes as soon as she gets the message. And Mary and David are coming as well."

"Yes," said Harry. "So you all can distract Tommy while I work on the conjecture. I have a lot to do before the baby comes."

"Harry," Arabella said. "You are not going to work on the conjecture with your whole family here, are you?"

Thomas laughed. "When Richard was born, Harry was making notes between contractions. She says labor wonderfully concentrates the mind."

The Andrews spent that night at Sommerleigh, but the next day, after Paterson had left to start his long trip back to Edinburgh, Alasdair took Arabella to his house in the village. A few months ago, he would have been overwhelmed with anxiety to have her see where he lived. But he had been in her cottage in Dunburn and saw she knew how to live modestly. And she was bound to him now. Still, he wanted her to be happy.

She walked through the house, looking carefully at every room. His housekeeper had kept the place tidy and dusted while he was away. But what would Arabella think of it? He promised himself to make no apologies for anything she might find amiss. She turned to him and smiled.

"It's lovely, Alasdair. Let's spend tonight here."

"Do ye think we might have pink curtains on the windows in the drawing room?"

She laughed. "I'll sew some for the nursery."

He knew it was too early to know if she was with child, but her plans for a nursery made him very happy indeed.

That night, the lonely bed in the lonely house was no longer lonely.

The next morning, they were enjoying the sunshine while slowly walking to Sommerleigh, having promised to join the Drakes for luncheon. Alasdair was glad the road was empty because he was finding it extraordinarily difficult to keep his hands off his wife whilst in public.

It was fortuitous then that he was not stroking her heart-shaped bottom through her dress or brushing the back of his hand against her breast or leaning down to kiss her pink lips when a rather grand carriage with several footmen and a large team of white horses overtook them on the road and then a slowed a hundred yards or so ahead of them, coming to a rather abrupt stop.

A small figure spilled from the carriage while it was still moving, not waiting for a footman to open the door or assist with steps. It was a woman, and now she was running back towards them.

"Mama," Alasdair heard Arabella say, and his wife picked up her skirts and was also running down the road. The women fell into each other's arms, and Alasdair wisely slowed his stroll even further so he would not interrupt the reunion.

When he reached them after several minutes, the mother and daughter were no longer embracing but holding hands, faces wet with tears, and smiling.

"Yer Grace," he said and bowed.

"Thank you, Dr. Andrews," Catherine said. "I understand you brought Arabella home. You have rescued another of my daughters."

"Nae, she has rescued me."

Catherine looked at him and then looked at Arabella, and Alasdair realized Catherine must not know yet they were married. Arabella had not told her, still fearful of her reaction.

He steeled himself for what might happen next. "Yer Grace—" he began.

Arabella interrupted him. "I am Mrs. Alasdair Andrews,

Mama." She let go of her mother's hand and came to his side and put her arm around his waist, and suddenly his own arm was also around her, with his palm on her shoulder blade, his fingers curling into that delicious piece of flesh between her arm and her ribs, the place he considered the beginning of the breast. The place where she had warmed his hands in the lodge. The place where he put his hand when she would fall asleep on her stomach, as she had done last night in his bed.

No. In *their* bed.

"We are married," Alasdair said, and Arabella *couried* into his side, as much as one can *courie* while standing.

Alasdair remembered Catherine had been a noted actress, but he was still impressed there was nary a beat of hesitation between their shared announcement and Catherine's smiling reply.

"I am very happy for you. Both." Catherine embraced Arabella and shook Alasdair's hand and then went up on her tiptoes and pulled him down for a kiss on the cheek.

James, the Duke of Middlewich, carrying a tow-headed three-and-a-half-year-old boy on his shoulders, was coming up the road behind Catherine. He was grinning as he put his own hand on Catherine's shoulder. "I'm not used to seeing my wife kiss a man who's not me on a country road in the middle of the morning."

Alasdair felt himself start to blush. He was not used to being teased by a duke.

"Yer Grace." He bowed.

"Jamie." Catherine turned to him. "Arabella and Dr. Andrews are married."

Her voice was calm and sweet, but Alasdair noted the duke's hand came off her shoulder and grabbed her hand and squeezed it quickly.

"Wonderful! Congratulations to all. Let me kiss you now,

Arabella!" James put his son Sebastian down and leaned over and kissed Arabella's cheek.

"Thank you, Middlewich," she threw her arms around his neck, "and thank you for taking care of Mama." Now it was James' turn to blush.

As Alasdair shook hands with James, Arabella bent at the waist to speak to her half brother. "Sebastian, I am your sister Arabella. Can I pick you up?" He nodded and held up his arms. She picked him up and put him on her hip, and he touched one of her golden curls by her face.

"Oh." Catherine exhaled. "These days, he won't let anyone pick him up except Jamie and me and Nurse Davis."

Sebastian looked at his mother and then at Arabella and then back again at his mother.

"He thinks I'm like you, Mama." Arabella laughed.

"Yes," Catherine said and smiled.

There was a quiet moment, and James broke into it with the suggestion they all walk back up the road to the carriage and ride to Sommerleigh together.

This they did, and Sebastian sat comfortably on his sister Arabella's lap all the way there.

The Viscount and Viscountess Tregaron arrived the next day, and Alasdair agreed with Arabella that it was very hard to imagine David Vaughan whimpering. He also expressed to Arabella privately that he, Alasdair, felt immense gratitude towards the viscount. After all, he was the reason Alasdair had broadened his horizons about what wives did and did not do. Arabella said this was rather unfair, and she or Mary really deserved the credit. After all, they did all the work.

The two-year-old identical twin boys Morgan and Owen and the six-month old baby girl Gwenllian had traveled to Sommerleigh with Mary and David.

"My lord, which of the boys is the heir?" Alasdair asked. "Which is the eldest?"

"In private, I hope you will call me Tregaron, as Middle-wich and Drake do. Or David, as our wives do. I'll tell you the truth, Andrews," the viscount leaned forward, "I don't know."

It took a moment for Alasdair to recover from the warmth he felt in his chest when David had said *our wives*. He still wasn't used to that.

"Uh, aye, Tregaron, does yer wife ken which boy is the heir?"

David leaned back into his perfect posture and winked. "She does, but she's not telling."

Mary heard this last bit and stuck her tongue out at her husband and took her children upstairs to the nursery and asked Arabella to come with her.

That night, as Alasdair toyed with Arabella's hair while she lay on top of him in their bedchamber in their house in the village, her cheek on his chest, he asked her if Mary had told her which boy was the heir.

"No." Arabella raised her head to rest her chin on his sternum and look him in the eye. "We talked about truly important things."

"Like what?"

"Like you."

Alasdair could feel the heat in his face.

"I do wonder why you only blush from the neck up, Alasdair. I'll tell you what Mary said. I'm sure she wouldn't mind. First, she told me she had written a letter to Inverness in response to my letter to her, asking if I should marry Boyd. The letter said, without question, I should not marry without love. And then today, while she was nursing Gwenllian, she said she could tell I was in love with a good man."

Alasdair noted Arabella was blushing now as well, but her pink extended to her upper chest and perhaps even her bosom, but he couldn't see her lovely breasts at this moment as they were pressed into his upper abdomen.

Alasdair wanted to investigate the extent of her blush, so he held her to him and rolled over and placed her on her back and went up on his elbow next to her. Yes, the pink of her blush was fading, but it definitely tinted the tops of her breasts. He cupped one of those breasts now and teased a nipple with his thumb.

"And what did ye say back to her?" His voice was suddenly raspy.

"I told Mary she was wrong."

Alasdair stilled his thumb.

"I told her I was in love with the best man."

Alasdair felt his wife's arms around his neck, her lips on his, a leg wrapping his waist, and he thought it wise to prove to her, once again, that he really was the best not-stupid man.

The next afternoon, Catherine sought Alasdair out in the library at Sommerleigh. Arabella was with Mary in the nursery with the children. Harry was in her aerie. Thomas, James, and David had gone out to shoot some wild hare.

Alasdair had declined to join them and was feeling rather proud that he had not felt he *must* go. But he might go some other time. It might be interesting to go shooting with a set of lords, and Lord Tregaron was said to be a crack shot, and he, Alasdair, might learn something from the viscount. However, today he was tired as Arabella had woken him early and in quite a demanding way that had set his blood coursing and kept him from going back to sleep.

So he was drowsy. And he had not yet resumed his medical duties in the village, so he could indulge in an afternoon nap. This was part of his honeymoon, after all. He was sitting in a chair in the library and dozing when Catherine came in.

"Dr. Andrews."

He started awake and stood and bowed. "Yer Grace."

Catherine sat opposite his chair and gestured for him to resume his seat.

"I really think," she said, "we had better find something for you to call me besides *Your Grace*. I'd like you to call me Catherine."

He inclined his head in agreement.

She went on. "And may I call you Alasdair?"

"Aye, Yer—Catherine."

"I hear we have a great deal in common. We both grew up on farms. We both made our ways to big cities when we were young and alone and somehow survived and found our professions."

"Aye, that is true."

She spread her hands out on her lap and looked down at them. "I want you to know I am very happy that you and Arabella are married."

"Thank ye."

"I did not want you to think otherwise."

"Nae."

The case clock ticked in the otherwise silent room.

"And you are all that I would hope for her."

He looked at her carefully. She appeared sincere.

"I just— I just still have a hard time remembering she is a woman and not a girl. You will have a daughter, yourself, one day, Dr. Andrews, and you will understand."

"Alasdair."

"Pardon?"

He cleared his throat. "Ye said ye would call me Alasdair."

"Yes, I did, didn't I?" She smiled but only briefly before her face became serious again. "I wonder if you might tell me why Arabella never wrote to me."

"I cannae. But I will tell ye that yer daughter, whom we both love, disnae like to return to the past. She disnae like regret."

"Yes." Catherine bit her lip. "Yes. She wants to move forward."

"Nae, she *has* moved forward. In fact, she has moved all of us forward."

Catherine was silent again. Then she stood, and he stood, as well, and she took his hands.

"I am very sorry for disturbing you, Alasdair."

"Ye didnae disturb me, Catherine. I am always happy to talk about my favorite thing in all the world. Yer daughter."

"Yes." She squeezed both of his hands tightly and turned, her skirts whirling, to leave the library.

That night at dinner, he was happy to see Catherine smiled a great deal and laughed more easily than the night before, and there was no trace of tension or worry in the looks she gave Arabella, only affection.

After dinner, over port in the dining room with the other men, James first told Alasdair how he envied him his time in the navy and then leaned forwards and said to him in a confiding tone, "I don't know what you said to my wife this afternoon, but thank you, Andrews."

Alasdair mumbled something noncommittal, but Thomas had overheard what James had said. "Yes, Alasdair is the chief luller of wives. He invariably soothes Harry. It's the physician's touch. I can't think but that he will never have any problem with his own wife."

Alasdair shook his head, thinking of Arabella's temper. There would be disagreements in the future, how could there not be? But he trusted he and Arabella would be able to kiss these out.

And that night, in their house, even though there were no disagreements pending, Alasdair found Arabella entirely amenable to the idea of kissing.

Epilogue

The ever after.

Arabella published an advertisement in a London paper and quickly found a teacher—a wiry, brilliant spinster named Miss Finley—and sent her up to Dunburn to take over the school. Arabella told Alasdair she was not at all surprised a year later when Miss Finley accepted Mr. Cormack's offer of marriage. Arabella then promptly hired another teacher and sent her up to Dunburn. She wondered aloud if this teacher would be seduced by a Highlander, too. Really, she would not blame her if that happened.

Maggie Gunn returned to Dunburn to take care of Miss Finley and all the school teachers who came after her. Maggie's sister's husband was never heard from again, and Maggie reported via letter that her sister felt well shut of him and had moved back home to Dunburn with her children.

Ewen MacEwen never lost his freckles, but he did eventually hold fifteen patents, all related to steam locomotives. Paterson met a nice Lowlander girl in Edinburgh and stopped driving coaches long distances and took up driving a hack so as to stay close to his lass, who eventually became his wife.

Within the next year, the butler Andrews took a brief holiday from service to travel to Caithness County and found that his great-grandfather was brother to Alasdair's great-great-grandfather, which made Alasdair his third cousin, once removed. Alasdair was glad to have found more family.

Lady Rebecca Dalrymple did find happiness. That is a story for another book.

Lady Colborne found motherhood, with a son born six months after the snowstorm, but she never settled happily into her marriage. That is *not* a story for any book.

Nurse Gaskell was prosecuted for poisoning Lady Morpeth and sentenced to seven years in a prison. Alasdair had to travel back to Northumberland for the trial. His appraisal of Lady Morpeth in the courtroom showed her appearance and her health were much improved, despite being eight months pregnant.

Alasdair never had any knowledge of how the unusual situation between the recovered Lord Morpeth, Lady Morpeth, and Lady Lyndmouth played out, and he was glad of it. How wonderful it was to be bound to his Arabella, his one and only woman, now and forever.

Harry and Thomas' third child was born healthy and well the day before Arabella's twenty-first birthday. As Harry had predicted, the baby was a girl. She was named Jane after Thomas' beloved late sister.

Mary and David had three more children, including twin girls and one more son. The question of which of the twin boys—Morgan or Owen—was the heir to the Tregaron *isiarliaeth* was settled eventually. Yes, in yet another book.

Catherine and James had no more children, but Sebastian Cavendish, Marquess of Daventry, was a handful and kept them busy enough.

The young doctor who had taken over Alasdair's patients had settled in very well, so the two of them divided the practice between them, with Dr. Jasper doing the bulk of the work and taking the bulk of the fees. After all, Dr. Andrews did not need the income, not after Dr. Murray's estate was settled. And Arabella had spent a mere fraction of her fortune on the school she still endowed.

But Alasdair could not imagine *not* being a physician. "I must keep my hand in," he told Arabella. "'Tis how I was happy before ye, and I dinnae want to forget what I owe the profession and Dr. Murray."

Arabella said she was grateful the arrangement Alasdair made with the young doctor kept *her* young doctor in her bed more nights than not. And the arrangement allowed the couple some freedom to travel away from Sommerleigh. Alasdair and Arabella came to enjoy Augusts in Dunburn, where they built a third cottage near the sea, and September in Edinburgh at the Murray house.

And there were children, of course, who traveled with them. Arabella did not waste the nights she had Alasdair to herself.

The children were numbered eight, with the first one coming exactly nine months after the wedding, to the day. Margaret, like the brothers and sisters who followed, was delivered by her father, and so she was welcomed into the world with nothing but pure love and devotion. All eight children were red-haired, in shades ranging from the darkest of auburns to the most blond of strawberry blonds. Four were green-eyed and four were blue-eyed, but Alasdair held out hope that someday number nine might have one blue eye and one green eye. Alasdair called his children his *bunch of carrots* and underwent a complete change of his own opinion about red hair. After all, Arabella loved his, and he loved it on his children, who were the delight of his life.

Their wedding night was the last time Arabella was ever in the lead. Alasdair kept the points and made sure of that. He was very much aware he had made his Arabella wait for him, and because he could not apologize with words any longer, he would make it up to her in other ways. Wicked ways that permitted the Not-Stupid to bed and wed and continue to bed the Dauntless for the rest of their lives.

More

When Ardor Blooms, the free prequel novella to ***The Lovelocks of London*** series, is available exclusively to Felicity Niven's newsletter subscribers. ***When Ardor Blooms*** tells the love story of the oldest Lovelock daughter Mary and how she comes to meet and marry the arrogant Viscount Tregaron during her first Season. In addition to ***When Ardor Blooms***, subscribers to Felicity Niven's newsletter receive dispatches from the writing trenches, news about upcoming romance releases, and free stories.

Subscribe at www.felicityniven.com/lovelocks

There is a short excerpt from ***When Ardor Blooms*** in the pages ahead. And if you haven't read the other books in ***The Lovelocks of London*** series yet, be sure to check out ***Convergence of Desire*** (Harry's love story) and ***Clandestine Passion*** (Catherine's love story).

Author's Afterword

The fictional Dr. Alasdair Andrews is an atypical physician for the time period.

First, in the Georgian/Regency era, physicians had more training than surgeons but did not usually perform the duties of surgeons (who were addressed as Mr. rather than Dr.). However, Dr. Andrews had been a ship's surgeon in the navy, so he would have had no hesitations about using a knife or a bone saw.

Second, physicians did not attend births unless the labor had been ongoing for many days. Physicians often spread infection from one patient to another, and the laboring women were almost always better off with only a midwife attending on them. However, Dr. Andrews does deliver babies.

Third, he washes his hands. There was no *germ theory* at that time, but some doctors must have learned from their own experience that if they washed their hands before treatment or surgery, patients had better outcomes.

Digitalis was in use at the time as a therapeutic. Foxglove, the source for digitalis, is toxic and can be used as a poison and can be applied topically.

There had been no known successful open abdominal appendectomies for appendicitis in 1823 when this book takes place. The cases discussed by Dr. Andrews in the book are real.

And, yes, there was a massive snowstorm in early February, 1823 in the north of England, and people did have to dig their way out of their homes.

This book is dedicated to Dr. James Barry (c.1789–1865) who was born in Ireland as Margaret Anne Bulkley (only a year before the fictional Dr. Alasdair Andrews was born). The adult Barry lived as a man both publicly and privately and was a highly ranked military surgeon in the British Army. Like Dr. Alasdair Andrews, Dr. Barry obtained a medical degree from the University of Edinburgh. Only after death, during a post-mortem examination, was it discovered Barry had female genitalia.

Dr. Barry's life does not parallel any of the characters in *A Perilous Flirtation*, but the story of Barry reflects the only possible path for a person born as a biologic woman to become a physician or surgeon in this time period in Britain. Otherwise, in my mind, Arabella Lovelock Andrews would certainly have become a physician like her husband.

A Perilous Flirtation was partly inspired by Charlotte Brontë's *Jane Eyre*, a book with which I have had a long love-hate relationship. I love Jane but always found Mr. Rochester to be a troubling, self-centered, and immoral hero, especially when you consider the prevailing religious beliefs of the day. By lying to Jane and tricking her into a bigamous marriage, he is condemning the love of his life to burn in hell for a sin she would never knowingly commit. He's a bad, bad man who is only stopped by chance and good timing.

I loved being able to write a version of the story that channeled the advice I always wanted to scream at Jane: "Forget that rich, mysterious guy with a secret, sick wife. He's a selfish arse." I was filled with glee to have Arabella wind up with her sister's nice doctor friend.

When Ardor Blooms

When Ardor Blooms
*is currently only available to the subscribers
of Felicity Niven's newsletter.*

Even a pragmatist wants a prince.

Mary Lovelock begins her first Season, and every bachelor in London wants a dance with the rich beauty. But how can she know if a suitor is grasping or genuine?

David Vaughan, the extremely proper Viscount Tregaron, seeks a wife with blood so blue, it's indigo. How unforgivably disappointing that the most remarkable of the Season's young ladies is Miss Lovelock, a commoner.

When his rogue of a brother lays a despicable challenge before him—which one of them can bed Mary first—the viscount is compelled to act as Miss Lovelock's protector. But will he be willing to protect the bewitching heiress from himself?

What a stench. Perfume and wine and spoiled food and tobacco smoke. And yes, the unmistakable odor of arousal and human sweat.

David Vaughan, the Viscount Tregaron, raised a handkerchief to his nose and picked his way across the drawing room of the Vaughan town house in London. The usually elegant room was littered with bottles, glasses, and plates with half-smoked cigars stubbed out in half-eaten food.

"Hello!" he shouted.

There was no answer.

His brother Rhys was to have arrived a fortnight ago and made sure the town house had been staffed and properly prepared for David and their mother. After no butler or footman had answered his knock, David had told his mother to wait in the carriage while he went round the back of the house to use his walking stick to break a small window, lift a latch, and gain access by the servants' entrance.

The viscount made his way up the stairs. The secondary bedchambers, including his brother's room, were empty. He opened the door to his mother's chamber.

A naked Rhys sprawled across the bed, stomach down and rump up, head hanging off the edge of the mattress. David could see his brother was drawing deep, even breaths, so the scoundrel was merely asleep and not dead.

Not yet. But he might soon be.

David took six quick strides to the bed and laid a whack on his brother's rear with his walking stick.

"Owwwwww!" Rhys screamed and grabbed his backside.

Only then did David notice not one, but two women occupied the large bed with his brother. When Rhys cried out, the buxom redhead in the middle of the bed rolled over onto her back so both of her breasts were on full display. The smaller brunette on the far side of the bed stretched her arms above her head, yawned, and kicked off the sheet tangled around her legs.

The two women stared at David with frank curiosity. Neither made a move to cover herself.

Rhys was still holding his buttocks. He glared at David.

"Daff, that was uncalled for."

"Dear brother," David said through his teeth, "our mother is outside, waiting in the carriage as we speak. She is expecting to enter this house and find it staffed. She is expecting to find it unsoiled. She is not expecting to find her own bed occupied by her youngest son and two wenches."

A grinning Rhys crawled off the bed.

"One for me and one for you, Daff. I'm thoughtful that way."

"But not thoughtful enough to remember Mother and I were to arrive today."

Rhys sorted through a pile of clothing on the floor, found a pair of trousers, and started putting them on.

"I remembered. But you weren't supposed to be here until the evening. The staff is coming this afternoon, and I was going to be ready by five o'clock."

"And what do you propose we do with Mother in the meanwhile?"

Rhys pulled a shirt over his head. "I propose we send her off to Lady Huxley for an impromptu call, and you and I get back into bed with these two extremely naughty minxes."

The women tittered. David turned to them.

"Has my brother paid you yet?"

Now both women howled with laughter.

Rhys found a waistcoat and guffawed as he buttoned it up. "My dear Lord Tregaron, this is Lady Ludlow and her friend, Lady Letitia Bloomley."

With his face burning, David bowed and said stiffly, "Good day, ladies."

He turned on his heel and exited the room, chased by the laughter of the trio. He descended the staircase, his limp bothering him only slightly.

He had assumed the women were whores. To find out they were members of the peerage! Horrifying. And not just because of his *faux pas* but also because he still expected the nobility to be…noble.

But why did he still expect that?

Just look at his own brother. Rhys was a rake through and through and as profligate with his own seed as he was with his older brother's money. He had surely bedded half the women between the ages of fifteen and fifty in a ten-mile radius around Tregaron. At market day in the town, David hesitated to peer into a pretty mother's basket or bundle, afraid he would see his brother's eyes or wicked grin in the face of the baby looking back up at him.

But David still clung to the notion that high birth corresponded to the highest of principles. It had been one of the first lessons he learned at his father's knee. Bloodline was significant in forming one's character. The peers of England were only ranked above their fellow men because they were innately superior. Lords and ladies embodied all that was best in the British Empire—loyalty, courage, strength, self-denial, and restraint.

Clearly, Rhys had missed all those lessons. But one rogue cannot destroy over seven hundred years of destiny.

David waited just inside the front door, and, in a few minutes, his brother bounded down the stairs, tucking his shirt into his trousers. He pulled to a stop so David could push his hair off his forehead and straighten the lapels of his rumpled tailcoat. David blanched at the alcohol fumes and stink of tobacco on Rhys' breath.

"When you embrace Mother, don't exhale." David noticed the love bites on Rhys' throat. "And where's your cravat?" David took off his own cravat and started tying it around his brother's neck. "You can't let Mam see you this way."

"Thanks, Dafydd."

Rhys grinned and went out the door. David stayed where he was and heard his brother's shouted welcome.

"Mother, how good to see you. No, no, no, don't get out of the carriage. Yes, let me lean in and give you a squeeze. There's been a bit of a hiccough, so why don't you head to Lady Huxley's, and we'll send word when the staff have arrived, there's a good Mam."

David shook his head. As usual, there would be no problem for his mother's darling baby. The viscountess would go to Lady Huxley's, the staff would appear, and when Mother arrived back at the town house, everything would be in tolerable order.

And that is how the Viscount Tregaron came to spend the first afternoon of his 1814 Season collecting wine bottles, opening windows, stripping soiled sheets off his mother's bed—all with barely-contained umbrage and a wrinkled nose.

———

"You look lovely." Catherine Lovelock surveyed Mary with a critical eye. "This exact shade of rose-pink is perfect for you."

Mary looked down at her dress. "It's not too soon for me to appear in pink? I wouldn't want to do anything unseemly."

"Nonsense. You have already been deprived of two Seasons with your father's illness and then his death. You are twenty, almost one and twenty. You deserve a Season, a real Season."

"But you are still in mourning for Papa."

Her stepmother's answering smile held a bit of sadness as it always did when mention was made of Mary's father.

"I am in half mourning, and I can't imagine I will ever cast it off. But lavender suits me well. Just as pink suits you so well. Your pink cheeks, your dark-brown eyes."

Mary turned and looked at herself in the cheval glass. "My plain brown hair."

"Your curly, glossy, rich brown hair." Catherine shook her own golden-blonde head. "Believe me, you are a paragon of prettiness. And how envious I am of your height."

Mary sat down on an upholstered stool and removed her pink satin slippers. "Tell me again why I am having a Season with the *ton* and not with the people we know well. Our friends."

"Well," Catherine said, taking the shoes from Mary to give to her lady's maid Baker, "your father wanted the best for you, and there's always room in society for people with money. Your dowry has opened doors which would otherwise be closed. Many young lords are rich in land and titles but have empty coffers. They will be extremely eager to make your acquaintance tonight. After all, you are one of the most monied heiresses in England."

Mary blinked her eyes. "I don't think I would like a husband who married me only for my money."

"Naturally, you wouldn't. But with all your other attractions, the right man will love you for yourself. Your kind heart, your even temperament, your good sense."

"Yes. I am sure my good sense will exhibit itself in the ballroom tonight, and men will flock to me for it."

Catherine laughed, and Mary smiled, glad to have lifted her stepmother's spirits.

"Mama Katie, what will you do without me to make you laugh?"

Catherine pushed an errant curl off Mary's forehead. "Yes,

it's true you've been a blessing to me. Even when you were a little girl and I had just married your father, you were so helpful. With Harry. And then with Arabella. And, finally, with your father's illness—well, I don't know what I would have done without your strength." Catherine trembled a little as she took a step back and smoothed the front of her dress. "But now I *do* know what I shall do without you. I shall sit back and knit and wait for the grandbabies."

Mary loosed her own laugh at the idea of her stepmother doing such a thing. "You have never knitted a day in your life!"

"Well, I could learn. Someday." Catherine paused. "Darling, I sense your reluctance about tonight. I thought you would be thrilled to attend your first ball."

Emotion was rioting inside Mary's normally calm belly, but it smacked more of dread and fear than of excitement and happy anticipation.

"Everyone there will outrank and outshine me. I will feel my true insignificance."

Catherine cupped Mary's cheeks in her hands. "I can promise that you will not feel insignificant tonight."

———

Indeed, Mary did not feel insignificant at the Wadhurst ball. A hush accompanied her and her petite stepmother's entrance into the ballroom. This was followed by an excited buzz, and, shortly afterwards, a rather large group of gentlemen gathered around Lady Wadhurst, asking for introductions to Miss Lovelock. Within five minutes, Mary had met a dizzying array of barons, viscounts, earls, marquesses, and even a silver-haired duke.

She felt flustered and did not know exactly what she should do. She curtsied and looked each gentleman directly in the eyes. She smiled and nodded politely. But she wasn't really listening properly. Her stepmother had to prod her to say, "Thank you, I would be delighted," when a young redheaded baron asked to partner her for the first dance, a Scotch Reel.

Her second dance was with a dark-blond man with brown eyes, broad shoulders, and a roguish smile. Reece Vaughan. No, it must be Rhys, the Welsh spelling. Brother and presumptive heir to the Viscount Tregaron.

"Miss Lovelock," Rhys said as she passed under his arm during a figure, "I do hope you will receive me tomorrow or the next day. And I must have the dance after this one."

Mary knew it was impolite to refuse a dance with a gentleman to whom one had been introduced by the hostess, but surely one should not dance twice in a row with the same gentleman? Her stepmother could tell her what to do. Mary cast a look at the periphery of the ballroom, trying to spot a lavender dress. But she was not able to see Catherine, and even if she had been, she could not leave her partner in the middle of a dance to solicit Catherine's advice. Mary would have to be guided by her own compass.

On her quick survey of the ballroom, she saw a tall, fair man with excellent posture looking at her. He had one hand on the back of an empty chair, and his other hand was holding a glass of wine. The wine glass gave her an idea.

"I think," Mary said slowly, "you may call on me at a future date if you wish, but I will need some refreshment before I consider my partner for the next dance."

"Clever girl," Rhys said and flashed his dazzling grin. "You give me half of what I want, so I am left knowing I must work harder to get the whole of what I want."

"Not at all, Mr. Vaughan."

"Good," Rhys said and held her hand a little too tightly, "because I don't know how to work hard. I'm used to relying solely on charm."

"Hence, your charm is so practiced."

Rhys laughed loudly. Mary's eyes narrowed. She was not used to being laughed at by a man whom she had just met. Especially when she had not meant to be funny.

"I did not mean to say your charm was a result of study—"

"No, you meant my charm was perfect. As in, practice makes perfect?"

"Yes. That is, no. I meant only that one can see you are quite adept at being charming. That is all."

The dance was over. He bowed. She curtsied.

As Rhys took Mary's arm to lead her away from the center of the ballroom, he leaned quite close and whispered into her ear, "I am very adept at other things, too, Miss Lovelock."

She turned her head and gazed at him. At first, she supposed by *other things* he meant kissing. But no, with that swagger, those tight breeches, that knowing grin, he must mean...other things.

Her first flirtation. She had always thought it would be with someone she admired, someone who aroused her passion. How peculiar it should be with this silly rascal of a man.

"I am sure you are," she said with no trace of a blush and curtsied and went to find her stepmother.

David had come to London for one reason and one reason alone—to select and take a wife.

And not just any wife. A woman of the greatest refinement. A woman from one of the oldest noble families. A woman with the bluest of blood running through her veins, the same blood as the men who had fought with William the Conqueror at the Battle of Hastings. He sought the daughter of an earl or a marquess or even a duke. After all, that is what Father had done by marrying *his* Viscountess Tregaron, formerly Lady Margaret Wilsingham, daughter of the Duke of Shrewsbury.

And, luckily, the Duke of Middlewich had several daughters who were certain to be at this ball. Ah, yes, there was Lady Anne and Lady Grace Cavendish with their mother, the terrifying Duchess of Middlewich. However, no sign of the heir apparent and drunkard brother James Cavendish, Marquess of Daventry. That was good. Daventry would be sure to egg Rhys into some ill-advised and bawdy behavior.

David's searching gaze now located his brother on the far side of the large ballroom. Rhys had bathed and dressed quickly and still looked a hundred times better than David did, despite David's care. Damn Rhys and his insouciance. David would never be able to pull off that carefree, rakish affectation that seemed to make all the young ladies swoon.

Rhys was part of the cluster of young men—and some not-so-young men—gathered around someone. Someone David could not see, so thick were the lords around her. Oh, yes, a Miss Lovely, he had heard Lord Brodrick say as he had broken off his conversation with David in order to cross the ballroom floor to join the other hopefuls in meeting Miss Lovely. A plain *Miss* meant she was not the daughter of a duke, a marquess, or an earl. She was the daughter of a viscount or a baron or a baronet or a knight.

Or, shockingly, she could be a cit, buying her way into a Season. After all, many lords were willing to stoop to marrying a commoner if she came with a large dowry.

David procured a glass of wine and stood with one hand resting on the back of an empty chair. His mother had assured him over and over again that his limp was barely noticeable, but he liked the security of holding on to something since a walking stick had no place in a ballroom.

The music began, and the dilemma presented itself.

David didn't dance. He had broken his leg after falling off a horse when he was a boy, and the bone had never set properly. He probably could dance, if pressed, but he would never willingly get up in front of a group of people and demonstrate his weak leg. But how was he to woo a young lady when he did not dance?

And then he saw his future wife.

Elegant, almost regal. A long neck. A tilt of her chin. Dark brows over dark eyes. High cheekbones under fair skin that flushed to a pink which matched her dress. Beautiful, red lips. A serious mouth—not frowning, not smiling, but serious. Thoughtful. And she danced beautifully. She was a rose— flawless, exquisitely formed, and of the most genteel sort.

He cursed under his breath when he saw the bounder who took her hand for the next dance. His debauched brother had no business touching such perfection.

An hour later, during an interlude between dances, Rhys made his way to David and took the wine glass out of his hand and gulped down the contents.

"Thanks, Daff," he said and handed back the empty glass.

"I live to serve you, little brother," David said wryly,

"Have your eye on anybody yet? Seen anyone you fancy? Any top contenders vying to be viscountess?"

David straightened his back even further. For the last hour, he had only watched the rose, the young woman in pink, as she had danced with numerous partners.

"I have seen many lovely ladies but have not yet been intro- duced to any."

"You have to go to Lady Wadhurst, you know that, to get introductions. That's what I did. And did you see the tall chit in the pink dress? The one I partnered in the second dance? They say her fortune is over a hundred thousand pounds. Not that you would care, but as a younger brother, I can tell you, things like that matter."

"What was that young lady's name?" David asked, taking out his watch and looking at it, trying not to betray his true interest. "The one you partnered for the second dance?"

"Miss Lovelock. Her father was the banker Edward Lovelock. She's that rarest of things—a rich beauty. What could be more perfect?"

Nausea roiled David's stomach. The rose was a cit, not an aristocrat. The world was full of pretenders.

"And I tell you, Daff," Rhys clapped him on the back, "I'm going to get in between her legs if it's the last thing I do."

David was suddenly brimming with an inexplicable rage and immediately had to go in search of another glass of wine. Anything to get away from his brother.

Mary was sitting in a corner with her stepmother, sipping on some lemonade. Their hostess Lady Wadhurst stood a dozen feet away, surrounded by a group of guests, all laughing at jokes being made by a rather drunk marquess.

"Are you enjoying yourself? You have danced every dance so far. I told you that you would not feel insignificant." Catherine patted Mary's hand.

"I am enjoying myself, Mama Katie. But it's almost over-whelming."

"Who has been your favorite partner so far?

"Everyone has been quite convivial."

"But has someone been more convivial than everybody else?"

"Perhaps," Mary said and would say no more.

Catherine turned to the lady next to her and began to discuss when the supper might be served. The inebriated marquess was finally taken away by his friends, and Mary saw the tall, blond man with the excellent posture. She had first noticed him while she had been dancing with Rhys Vaughan. The man had been looking at her then, and later, too, when she had been partnered with other gentlemen.

He was not looking at her now but was crossing the ball-room floor to speak to Lady Wadhurst. Their hostess was hard of hearing, spoke loudly, and required others also to speak loudly, so Mary could hear everything that passed between the pair.

"Lord Tregaron, I am so pleased you came tonight. And you brought your brother."

Oh.

The blond man was the Viscount Tregaron, Rhys' brother. No wonder he had been looking towards Mary. He had been searching out Rhys. She felt a small pang of disappointment. She had not drawn his eye; his brother had.

The viscount was exceedingly handsome, in his own way. So different from Rhys who was all sly, warm mischief, while the viscount was carved of ice. Light-blond hair, the color of the best butter. Pale blue eyes. A good jaw. A very fine and straight nose. A well-formed mouth. Perfect posture. He reminded her of someone.

"You were most kind to invite us both," the viscount said.

Lady Wadhurst tapped his chest with her fan. "Now, I have often extended an invitation to you, but this is the first time you have come to one of my balls during the Season. Can one hope you are finally seeking a wife?"

"I think it is time, Lady Wadhurst. My mother certainly thinks it is past time."

A prince. That's what he looked like. Just how Mary had imagined the prince when she had read Perrault's *Sleeping Beauty*. Of course, not when the thorns slashed him on his way to Beauty's sleeping chamber. But afterwards, at the wedding.

Lady Wadhurst went on. "Your brother was quick to ask for an introduction to a delightful young woman who has come to her first ball tonight. Miss Lovelock. Would you also like an introduction, my lord?"

Both Lady Wadhurst and the prince—she meant, the viscount—were turned away from where Mary sat, but Mary could see him stiffen when her name was mentioned.

"No, thank you, Lady Wadhurst. I am looking for a wife whose rank matches or exceeds my own. A wife who will enrich my bloodline, not my purse."

"Oh, but Miss Lovelock is so fetching and such a lovely dancer. You really should have an introduction and ask for a dance."

"I will have to decline. I do not dance, and if I did, I would not dance with her."

"How will you ever get a wife if you do not dance?"

The viscount turned his head at that moment and saw Mary sitting within earshot.

Mary willed herself not to adjust her gaze. She looked at him serenely and without malice, she hoped, and raised her lemonade to her mouth and sipped.

The viscount colored and turned away.

Feeling she had won that skirmish, Mary shifted her position in her chair towards her stepmother and joined in the speculation about whether the supper would be at midnight or half-past.

She would not let a rude viscount, no matter how handsome, ruin her first ball of her first Season.

When the supper was finally served, she noted Lord Tregaron was far away from her, down at the other end of the table, talking to one of the Cavendish sisters. Rhys was sitting by Mary, having captured the last dance before supper, thus ensuring he had the right to escort her and fill her plate. She smiled several times at things Rhys said, but when Catherine asked her later what had been so amusing, she could not recall.

She could recall, however, that the viscount had laughed only one time in the course of the supper. She wondered what Lady Anne Cavendish had said to provoke that laugh. No doubt some piece of scathing patrician wit Mary couldn't hope to duplicate.

Read the rest of ***When Ardor Blooms***, the prequel novella to ***The Lovelocks of London*** series, to find out how Mary and David fall in love. ***When Ardor Blooms*** is not available for purchase at the time of this printing; only subscribers to the Felicity Niven newsletter can receive this free novella.

Acknowledgments

Thank you to Molly Gunn, Jace Anderson, Sharon Gunn. You have kept me going. You and coffee.

Thank you to the readers who have embraced the Lovelocks.

As always, enormous gratitude and affection to my family.

About the Author

Felicity Niven is a hopeful romantic. Writing Regency romance is her third career after two degrees from Harvard. And you know what they say about third things? Yep, it's a charm. She splits her time between the temperate South in the winter and the cool Great Lakes in the summer and thinks there can be no greater comforts than a pot of soup on the stove, a set of clean sheets on the bed, and a Jimmy Stewart film on a screen in the living room. She is the author of ***The Bed Me Books*** and ***The Lovelocks of London*** series.